FIRST FLEET

FIRST FLEET

A NOVEL OF THE PIONEERS OF AUSTRALIA

BY

M. HOWARD MORGAN

www.Penmoreprepress.com

First Fleet
Howard M Morgan
Copyright © 2023 Howard Morgan

This is a work of historical fiction. While based upon historical events, any similarity to any person, circumstance or event is purely coincidental and related to the efforts of the author to portray the characters in historically accurate representations.

ISBN-978-1-957851-18-1(Paperback)
ISBN 978-1-957851-17-4(e-book)

BISAC Subject Headings:
FIC014000FICTION / Historical
FIC032000FICTION / War & Military
FIC047000FICTION / Sea Stories

Editors: Chris Wozney. Lauren McElroy
Address all correspondence to:

Penmore Press,
920 N Javelina Pl,
Tucson, AZ 85737

PREFACE

During my first visit to Australia in 1980, I learned of the existence of a young marine from South Wales, who, together with his wife and only son, accompanied the First Fleet of convicts in 1787 to the land that became Australia. That young marine was a distant relative, and although very little is known of him before or subsequent to his joining Major Ross's detachment to New Holland, thankfully a good deal more is known of many of those marines, sailors and convicts who landed on 'The Fatal Shore' in January 1788.

That discovery triggered an interest in the history of early British settlement of New South Wales—the convicts, of course, but also the Marines who made up the garrison of guards for the wretched people whom Britain dispatched to the other side of the known world. I became determined to learn more, and consequently obtained copies of all the extant journals of the 'First Fleeters'. I spent years researching individual stories, and the many books and articles that have subsequently described and documented this extraordinary feat. Like a few others, I came to understand that Arthur Phillip is one of the forgotten men of history, who deserved more for his remarkable achievement.

Because I elected to retell the story through the life of a marine officer, rather than a convict or naval officer, I created, I very much hope, a new military hero in Jack Vizzard. Many of the incidents and scenes in which I have placed this character did indeed take place, though, sadly, history has not recorded the individuals most directly involved. Jack has therefore 'borrowed' those little-known footnotes and made them his. He will do so again, and I make no apology for that.

It is customary to acknowledge the contributions made to a novel by the many academics whose painstaking research brings the detail of history to the writer's keyboard. There are so many that I decline to name more than two: Robert Hughes, whose seminal work has done more than most to add to our knowledge; and John Moore, whose contribution to the knowledge base and reputation of the corps during those early years should be mandatory reading in every Australian and British school, in my humble opinion. I am greatly indebted to those officers of the Royal Navy and of the Marines who made the original First Fleet possible, and who recorded in exquisite detail their experiences. I single out for special mention the books by Captain Lieutenant Watkin Tench, *Narrative of the Expedition to Botany Bay* and *Complete Account of the Settlement at Port Jackson*. At least 12 people kept journals of their personal experiences. Arthur Bowes Smyth was a surgeon on board *Lady Penrhyn*. His *Journal* is notable for its detail of natural history and for being one of the most detailed eyewitness accounts. William Bradley was First Lieutenant on board HMS *Sirius*, sadly lost at Norfolk Island in 1788. The diaries of Lieutenant Ralph Clark, a marine officer, constitute a more personal record of a young man who was quite homesick for much of his time in the colony. That did not stop him marrying a convict girl, whom he later abandoned on his return to England. David Collins, another marine officer, was Judge Advocate for the colony. Vizzard becomes his assistant. I obtained and studied all these documents.

My deepest thanks go to those friends and family members who have, occasionally unwittingly, encouraged and supported this project. I owe a particular debt of gratitude to those friends and family who contributed insight into the writer's world and provided words of comfort and encouragement. My especial gratitude goes to my wonderful, supportive wife, to Lorri Proctor and Greta van der Rol, and I'll be flogged if I forget to mention Keith Penny Esq.

For the others, you know who you are.

MHM

Prologue

The Beginning

'Through the erudite language of your counsel, you have sought to evade responsibility for your heinous crime, you scoundrel.   The jury, to my approbation, have found you guilty of murder at common law. The plea for clemency presented to me has moved me to commute the sentence I should pass on your soul. You shall not hang, boy, but you shall serve fourteen years hard labour. Take him away.'

The boy groaned, his family, nearly crushed in the public gallery, cried out in anguish. Others in the gallery applauded.

Jack Vizzard, barrister-at-law of the Middle Temple, sat back on the bench, greatly saddened by the fate of his young client. This trial had been longer than the others, but the outcome as predictable as an English winter. The magistrate, faced with a stream of London's villains, convicted without compunction. The condemned were sent to the gallows for any of two hundred offenses. Some were more fortunate: sentenced to transportation 'across the seas.'

It was left to individual victims, such as shop-owners and merchants, to prosecute criminals. Such people knew little or nothing of the law nor what evidence could be presented and what could not be. Jack had appeared before many such magistrates, unpaid amateurs, prone to influence by wealthy merchants. Henry Fielding had founded the Bow Street Runners, who had become an effective police force, but the quality of the men on the bench was, in Jack's opinion, woeful. As Horace Walpole had written, 'the greatest criminals of this town are the officers of justice.'

Jack pushed his way out of the court in Southwark, hoping his clerk would have something of more substance for him, such as a case to try in the Crown court. A case where laws of evidence were given respect, where the judge was a seasoned, experienced, and knowledgeable lawyer. Where he had more difficult work to do than simply make pleas in mitigation, little more than begging for a life. A case where he could use analysis and logic to properly examine witnesses' evidence. He had been 'cutting his teeth' on these cases for nearly a year since being called to the bar. And he was bored.

Placing his wig and gown and the morning's briefs into his brief bag, he pushed through the press of families come to learn the fate of their loved ones, sensation seekers here to listen to the details of the crimes committed, and victims attending to plead their claims against perpetrators responsible for harm suffered, or damage or theft of goods.

He stepped out into the bustle of Borough High Street. There were other lawyers haggling over the hire of hackney cabs to return them to their respective chambers. On an impulse, he walked towards the river and turned east, eager to put distance between himself and the four gaols in Southwark. Past the burnt out ruin of the Clink prison, then on through the fields to Rotherhithe. Within an hour his feet had taken him to Deptford, the great shipyards where warships were built for the Royal Navy.

By now he was sweating in the afternoon sun. Stopping at an ale-house in Deptford Broadway, he found a seat by a window overlooking the street. He called out his order to the pot-man, who brought him a pewter tankard and a jug of ale. Jack drank half the tankard before his attention was drawn to noises in the street.

Two dozen or more men, in dirty, ragged clothes, shuffled along under the watchful eye of an overseer assisted by four soldiers, their scarlet coats a stark contrast to the grey attire of the prisoners, for so they were, dragging chained legs. The men were bound together in pairs, held by a length of chain between the iron shackles clamped to their ankles. It was a pitiful sight, one that Jack had not witnessed before.

He stepped outside with his tankard to watch the convicts, each one carrying either a pick or shovel. They had been ordered to halt their slow progress and given water from a water barrel carried behind them on a horse-drawn cart. There were two men directly in front of him staring at him, perhaps dreaming of being free men, able to enter establishments like the Dover Castle. The overseer approached and beat each man with a cane until it broke, then kicked the nearest man in the shin. 'You idle buggers!' he shouted. 'Stop day dreaming and get on with your work. Get thee in that ditch and start clearin' it out!'

The overseer stepped over to Jack and said, 'Best you get thee back inside, mate. No need for you to be distractin' them buggers, wavin' pots of ale in the ugly faces.'

Jack stared at the man, who was a good head taller than he, with a sun-stained, pockmarked face. A tall, battered black hat sat atop his long, lank hair and his bloodshot eyes looked hard at Jack. The man stepped back and spat sideways into the dirt, then stomped away, yelling at the convicts. Jack continued to watch as the convicts raised their shovels and labored to dig out the detritus accumulated in the ditches on both sides of the road.

He took the last mouthful of ale as one of the soldiers approached, clearly intent on entering the inn. 'They'm be a desperate gaggle of rogues, sir,' said the soldier, 'put a knife in your back as soon as you like or lift your purse wivout you feel a damn fing. But that overseer's a right bastard. Flogs the buggers shamefully, 'e does.'

'Where do the poor wretches live, Sergeant?' Jack asked. Over his shoulder he called inside, 'A couple of ales over here, if you please.'

'Well, gawd bless ya for a gentleman.' The sergeant moved into the shadow of the doorway, keeping an eye on the road. Of average height, he was stocky, with shoulders that filled his uniform coat. He had traces of powder burns around the right cheek. 'They be kept aboard the hulk down that aways. Just on the bend in the river.' He pointed with his musket. 'We gotta keeps 'em somewheres, now we can't ship 'em off to the Americas.' He took the pot of ale delivered by the scowling pot-man. 'So guvment be taking old ships outta the line and using 'em to hold the scum from the Rookeries, sir.'

'I see.' Jack pondered the matter. 'What regiment are you? I have some experience with the Gloucestershire Yeomanry.'

'Ah! Gotcha there, sir. I'm a sea soldier, a Marine. Sergeant Albert Connor, at your service.' He swallowed half the tankard in a series of noisy gulps.

'Would it be possible for me to see one of the prison ships? I have a professional interest in the criminal fraternity.' Jack had read 'The State of the Prisons' by the reformer, John Howard, while a student at Oxford, and it had made a deep impression on him. He had visited Oxford's new gaol the previous year.

The sergeant looked at Jack with a puzzled expression on his care-worn face. His brown eyes gazed into Jack's. 'I could ask the Master when we's march 'em back at the end of the day. Not sayin' he'll agree, and more likely he will think you have lost your senses, but I will ask 'im.

Jack pulled his watch from a pocket. 'You will find me here, Sergeant. I will await your call.' He strode back into the inn and spoke to the pot-man, ordering a meal and asking for a room, as he was not likely to be back in chambers that evening. Then returned to his table and watched the miserable men work with picks and shovels, the more alert of them darting glances at the people passing by.

The pot-man brought Jack a beef pie and some cheese. Jack was ravenous, but when he started to eat, he thought of the men in the road and suddenly lost his appetite. To pass the time, he studied the briefs of as yet untried cases. He wondered if any of the accused would end up sent to the prison ship.

A little over an hour later, as he pulled his pocket watch to check the time, the sergeant came back. 'If you be ready, sir, we'll be taking the prisoners back to the hulk now.' Jack pulled on his coat, followed the sergeant outside, and took his place at the end of the gang, making sure to keep his distance. The overseer shouted orders and the sergeant marched them off.

When he had first seen the work gang, Jack had noted that some of the men showed some spirit and wielded shovels with vigor. Now each man shuffled slowly. Each step was heavy and clumsy, made more awkward by being chained together in pairs. Heads were bowed and shoulders hunched. They reached the dockyard and, as in the biblical story of Noah and the Ark, slowly crossed into the dark wooden mass two by two.

Jack followed. The sergeant introduced him to the gaol keeper, then led him onto the deck where the men were herded into stout iron cages. Marine guards stood like sentinels at each end of the deck. Jack pulled a kerchief from his coat pocket and tied it about his nose and face in a futile attempt to prevent the stench from reaching his nostrils. The reek of human filth added to the already fetid, rank air trapped within the wooden walls of the old ship of the line.

Jack had seen enough. Smelt enough. Witnessed enough.

He turned and returned the way he had come. He reached the dockside and lowered the kerchief to breathe deeply the air that swept up the river from the North Sea. He filled his lungs repeatedly and watched as an unknown ship, with two rows of gun-ports, slipped downriver, its topsails filling. Jack watched the men on the raised quarterdeck. An officer with gold epaulets scrutinized the waters ahead. Jack wondered where the warship was bound and, as he wondered, his mind went on its own voyage.

Where it led surprised him.

Chapter 1
The Lawyer

True patriots all, for be it understood,
We left our country for our country's good.
—A convict couplet

Jack expected the worst of reactions.

The news he had just delivered to his father, Henry Vizzard Esq., Attorney at Law, could scarcely have caused greater anguish.

He had known for some weeks now that this meeting would be necessary, but he had postposed any confrontation until the events of the previous day had forced him to this partial confession. He had told his father enough to make it clear that he must leave, although he had withheld the real reason why. He didn't dare speak of the dreadful thing he had done, for as an officer of the court his father would then be faced with a dreadful dilemma.

How could he confess to murder?

Admitting that he had obtained a commission in the Corps of Marines was grave enough. That was the reason for his father's anger.

He must keep silent about the murder. For the remainder of his life, whatever became of him. A dark secret to take to his grave.

The elder Vizzard's eyes were dilated with anger. Jack feared that his father might suffer some physical harm additional to the emotional distress, given the redness that suffused his face, the hue of well-boiled beetroot.

'You have done what, sir? I will not have it, by God! Damn it. I will not, Jack. One son to the king is enough; I will not lose another!'

Henry Vizzard paused, breathing heavily, struggling with emotion as he glowered at his favourite child.

'How you could ever hope to persuade me of the sense of the course you have set upon?! By the Blessed Christ, boy, have I striven to see you educated, to make of you an advocate worthy of Blackstone himself, only to see you engage in such folly? For you only to, to... waste your life in such a manner? Become a damned soldier? By all that is holy, what has possessed you?'

The large, beamed room seemed smaller to Jack, much smaller than it had appeared to him in his childhood, or in his youth. He studied the blackened ships' timbers forming the beams above his father's head, seeking words to explain, but he knew that inspiration was not to be found in this dark room, a temple of his father's profession.

The walls, once neatly painted white, had yellowed over the years, from the smoke of the log fire and the pipes habitually smoked by the local men of business and farmers alike, and all about seemed confusion. Books of many sizes were stacked on the floor and on a table next to Henry's large oak desk, which was littered with papers. The heavy velvet curtains, inhibiting the sunlight, were faded after hanging languidly for more than a score of years, adding to the gloomy atmosphere of the room.

So many hours had he spent here when he was younger, watching his father at work, listening to his pronouncements on his fellow man, on the perfidious nature of the clients from whom he had acquired his wealth, in this thriving town on the southern edge of the Cotswold Hills.

Outside he could hear the sounds of the market: traders calling to the townsfolk; the hawkers and peddlers advertising their wares, exhorting custom; and the shouted voices of excited children. There were horses, sheep, geese and ducks in cages, farmers and their dogs, all competing to be the loudest creatures in town this morning. The farmers were more intent on catching up with news and gossip, before getting down to trading.

It seemed to Jack that the real business of the day would continue with no acknowledgement of the agony in his own heart, nor of the misery he felt at this meeting with his father. He wished he were back at the tavern that he used when at home from Oxford or London, almost any other place than standing here, in his father's chambers.

He watched the tall, but now slightly bent, figure of his father pacing in front of the large, mullioned bow window overlooking the Market Square. Henry pulled a large, bright green silk handkerchief from his breeches pocket, turned quickly away and blew his nose softly, looking out through the window on the activity below.

'I would that I... could have your blessing, Father; although perhaps I seek that in vain. However, your understanding is something I did hope for... do humbly ask from you.'

Jack loved his father and wished he could have avoided this meeting, but he knew that he could not have callously left for Portsmouth without telling him, as his older brother had done only two years before. That memory was uppermost in his mind, as it surely was in Henry's. He shifted weight from one foot to another. *What has become of George?* he wondered, not for the first time.

Henry Vizzard stared through the window, not seeing the activity below. He knew himself to be a formidable man and a respected resident of the town; loved, respected, but perhaps no longer held in such fear or awe by his children as when they were young. He had been so very distressed when his elder son, George, had left the family home, 'like a thief in the night', to seek his fame or fortune in the Navy, with no word of him since. Henry had made enquiries, but none of his efforts had succeeded in discovering any trace of the wild youth who had carried Henry's dream of a dynasty of lawyers with him.

His dream had then passed down to his second son, Jack, the dark-haired young man before him now—the image of his mother, Henry had always thought, she who had died giving birth to him twenty-two years before. Where had those years gone?

The boy... No, that was an error. The boy had become a man. His son was tall: six feet and one inch at last measurement. The dark hair, curling upwards at the collar, so much like Caroline's, framed a face like her face, but stronger, and coloured by the sun. The eyes, a hybrid green and bright blue —so very like hers!—shone now with a threat of welling tears. Henry felt Caroline had passed those eyes to him, at the very moment of her death, as the boy entered the world. Those broad shoulders he'd got from his father; those lobeless ears and that jaw declared him to be a Vizzard, and his son.

Henry stared at the worn Wilton carpet and remembered when his wife had chosen it, so many years before. *I should perhaps replace it*, he thought absently.

Henry was a wealthy man, although he lived modestly. His advice and opinions were sought by many of the mill owners and merchants in the five valleys of Stroud, and they paid well for his services.

He had not started out as a rich man. Indeed, the large manor house in Woodchester, in which the three children, George, Charlotte, and Jack, had grown up, had been bought with Caroline's money. However, in the years since, he had become shrewd with his personal investments. The fees he'd earned had provided for the education of his sons, particularly Jack, who had a quick and imaginative mind.

For all his bluster, Henry was possessed of a strongly developed sense of humanity, a concern for the plight of the folk of the villages who laboured on the farms and in the mills that Henry leased, bought and sold, or raised mortgages on, or assigned, or any of the other matters required of him by the merchants and men of business in the towns of Stroud, Gloucester and Bristol. He had gained the respect, not only of the men of property, but also of the common folk. Often he would take on work without thought of reward, or fees. He donated large sums to the church, and to the village school.

Jack had inherited the impulse of generosity, Henry mused. Perhaps his mad decision was a misguided expression of chivalry.

The boy was known to all as Jack; always had been, since his days in the nursery. His mother, God rest her precious soul, with almost her dying breath had named him John after her favoured brother, but it was always 'Jack'.

Henry's breathing had slowed, and the flush had faded from his face. His eyes caught the figure of a well-dressed gentleman stepping down from a carriage that had pulled to a halt below his chambers. He casually raised his hand, acknowledging a greeting. The new clock on the far side of the market square chimed the hour. His client, prompt as ever.

He turned away from the window, facing his son, and his eyes steadied on Jack's proud, determined face, returning his hard look.

"Tis that romantic and impulsive streak of your dear mother's to blame for this,' muttered Henry. 'Georgie had it, too.' He sighed audibly. 'At least that is not a problem I have to contend with in Charlotte.'

Henry debated within himself what to say next. He gazed at the face that stared back at him with something of the defiance he used to see in his wife's eyes, on those rare occasions they'd found a point to argue. Henry had attempted to be master in his house, but Caroline had been the real authority; he'd always understood that.

'What that sister of yours will make of this decision of yours I shudder to think. I am at quite a loss to understand it myself. Why, Jack, why? It is because of Mary, is it not?' Henry knew it had to be so. He was as distressed as his son at the verdict. *Damn the judge. Damn him to hell.*

Chapter 2

Guilty

Mister Justice Oswald Paul had been in no quandary about the verdict or the sentence to pronounce. The girl was patently guilty. He would waste no more time on the troublesome case, or on the bloody-minded, impertinent young lawyer she had defending her.

'Mary George, you have been found guilty of a most despicable crime. It has availed you nought.' His cold eyes flickered around the courtroom. 'It is the order of the court that you will be transported across the seas to New Holland for a term of seven years. Take the prisoner down.'

Mary sank to her knees and sobbed. The gaolers gave her no opportunity to even look at Jack, pulling her brutally from the courtroom. She heard his voice, distant, as through a fog. His words faded in her ears as she descended the stone steps, concave from centuries of use, leading to the depths of Gloucester Gaol, to the horrors that awaited her there, all hope gone. She was lost, and knew now the real meaning of despair. Total, pitiless, chilling and thought-numbing despair. To be transported for seven years. It might as well have been a life sentence. It would destroy her. She could not hope to survive.

Sobs racked her weakened body, and her crying echoed along the murky, damp, stained, stone walls. She tugged at the gaolers pulling her onwards to a cell, her struggles useless against the strength of two men.

The dozen or more shadowy forms within the cell did not look at her as she was thrown amongst them. The heavy wooden door was closed and locked. Mary slumped on the cold, damp floor and wept.

What would her dear father think of her now? How happy her father had been when first he had learned that Jack Vizzard was showing an interest in her! How had it come to this?

Mary had been a bright girl from the start. In her short life, she had learned that she could better herself by hard work and education, especially education. She had been schooled, oh yes; she had learned to read and write well enough. She had been determined that she would not end up working in the mills or on the farms. She had seen how her brothers, David and Richard, had aged from the hard labour demanded in the wool mills.

Her mother had said that Mary had ideas above her station. Perhaps her mother had been right. But her father had wanted more for his bright daughter, and so he'd encouraged and aided her studies.

Mary had enjoyed her schooldays. The schoolhouse was a small building of a single room, with a few rows of simple desks, each with its own inkwell. Only children from the village were permitted to attend, at a cost of a penny each week. Father always paid the penny each Monday morning and spoke to her teacher every week. 'Just to make sure I'm getting value for my money,' he would say. Mary knew it was to enquire as to her progress, so he could help with any difficulty. Father knew and understood the value of an educated mind.

Their home was a small cottage in South Street that Father had improved through his own labour, adding a lean-to kitchen at the rear, laying flagstones, replacing the broken or fallen roof-tiles, building a wall upstairs so that Mary could have a room separate from her brothers.

Mother had been pretty, but that had been long ago. Villagers said Mary was as pretty as her mother had been. The same fine features, the same thick hair, they said. Now her mother was worn down by the burden of bringing three children into the world. Mother never talked much, always fussing over her sons, as though she had no daughter. Mary had helped with the animals, milking the cows and collecting eggs. But Mother had to do any killing of a chicken. That was not something Mary would do. 'Too squeamish,' mother had said, and in that she was right.

Jack Vizzard had taken Mary's heart the first time she had met him properly, *that* evening at the vicarage. He had called to meet Giles, his friend from boyhood. Mary had bobbed a small curtsy, head down, eyes lowered, as was proper—he so obviously a gentleman, she a mere housekeeper's assistant, and on probation at that.

She had spent those first weeks at the vicarage learning her duties from Mistress Clutterbuck, the housekeeper, avoiding the vicar, who often appeared to be 'in his cups', as Eliza Clutterbuck would say.

'Please, don't be shy,' Jack Vizzard had said gently. 'I cannot see your face if it is staring at my boots! May I ask your name?'

Her hair hung down, a soft copper shroud with natural waves, framing a small face, with high cheekbones. Her smooth skin, unmarked by any blemish, glowed with health. Above those cheeks, large and bright eyes of hazel, with minute flecks of the palest green, looked on the world with interest and intelligence. Her mouth, wide and with full lips, opened, revealing straight, clean teeth.

'Mary, sir, Mary George... sir.'

'Well, Mary George, I am John Vizzard, but my friends do know me as Jack; and I would have you know me as a friend, Mary. You will be my friend, will you not?' He had spoken gently, smiling, sensing her nervousness, wanting her to feel at ease.

She had blushed; she always did when addressed by a man, and this one was so obviously and carefully taking in her appearance. She was struck by his directness and bold manner, and by his piercing blue eyes. She found his gaze unnerving, and she fled for the sanctuary of the kitchen, Jack's soft laughter pursuing her.

She had closed the door to the kitchen, her heart sounding loud in her ears, and busied herself in the larder.

She heard light steps on the stairs as Giles Mountjoy descended. His voice carried clearly enough that she heard every word of the conversation that ensured.

'What is this, Jack? Has she spurned you so soon?'

'Where, pray, did that vision of loveliness spring from?' Jack replied.

'The lovely Mary?' Giles answered offhandedly. 'Yes, she is a bit of a beauty, is she not? Great Uncle Richard was obliged to find an assistant housekeeper after old Clutterbuck fell and broke her wrist. It's been, oh, more than a month since she arrived, and the old place is the better for her coming, I don't mind saying.'

Mary had blushed even harder at these words.

'I am loath to move from here, but I am obliged now to find a place of my own. Do not glower so, my friend, I am not straying! Quite the opposite! Louise and I are to be married next July, and that is why I shall be departing, and why I wished to see you. You will assist me at the ceremony, will you not? Say you will, Jack, for I can think of no better man to be at my side on that day!'

Mary had bitten her lip. Alarming as the young man's presence was, he was also company for his uncle, the vicar. She felt an uneasy dread at the prospect of his remove. But now she listened for Jack's reply.

'Of course I shall! It will be my honour to do so. My heartiest congratulations to you! Well done, Giles—hah!... This is excellent! Indeed, this calls for a celebration. Come, I hear The Ram calling, and a bottle of something special to drink, I fancy. You can give me all your news, and I must also tell you something of mine.'

The two young men had departed, and Mary had returned her attention to the crockery, but her thoughts followed the young man who had addressed her so warmly.

CHAPTER 3

FRIENDSHIP

Jack also recalled that evening. It had been drizzling, a fine, misty fall of rain, entirely typical of the season. He and Giles had walked briskly to The Ram. A small roadside tavern at the lower end of the village, adjacent to The Old London Road, it was popular with villagers and travelers alike. The thatch was worn in places, but still waterproof. The ridge, recently reformed, displayed a pair of peacocks, skillfully fashioned from local reed harvested from nearby Sharpness, the trademark of the local master thatcher, Will Peacock. Tendrils of reddened vine leaves covered most of the walls.

A chimney, the mellow brickwork spalled and flaking, the mortar in need of re-pointing, poked through the centre of the roof. Wisps of wood-smoke wrapped around the wrought iron weather vane fitted to the top: a long-horned ram, cleverly made by the village blacksmith when the inn had been his property, some years ago.

Bill Brice had bought the inn on leaving the Navy, and had turned his hand to brewing. He called his beer 'Old Spot', after the local species of pig. The Ram had a large room used by villagers on a Saturday evening, where they would stand and drink cider and home-brewed ale until Bill threw them out, either when they became too drunk to stand, or the coins in their pockets had all passed to him. Bill was not a man to give credit to mill workers.

A smaller room, which Bill called 'the gunroom' and kept in a more comfortable state, was for the use of more 'genteel' customers. A large blue ensign decorated one wall, and a miscellany of naval artifacts gathered dust on shelves and sills around the room.

The mellow, golden sandstone walls, extracted centuries before from the local Cotswold Hills, displayed the staining from smoke of many years. Traces of straw on the flagstones forming the floor gave evidence of the farmhands who had been drinking earlier. A thin layer of tobacco smoke hung beneath the beamed ceiling, swirling each time the door opened and allowed the cool, damp autumn air to swoop in. A pair of local wool merchants talking quietly in a corner nodded their heads towards Jack and Giles in silent acknowledgement as they entered.

'Good evenin', young sirs, and what'll be your pleasure, Master Jack, Master Giles?' Bill called to them. 'We're not seein' so much of you lads now's you're all grown up an' gennelmen an' all'—his eyes moved quickly from one to the other—'what wi' you, Master Giles, takin' up wiv Lord Ducie's daughter, and you, Master Jack, off to London in all your finery!' Brice stood, legs apart, as though still on a rolling deck, a beer-stained cloth over his left arm and his mouth in a wide grin.

'Off to the cellars with you, Bricey!' Jack waved him away. 'You won't catch us sniffing around your cider press this time.' Jack laughed. 'Old Bill' had caught them once, when they were still quite young boys, helping themselves to his cider. He had sent them home with a cuffing to the sides of their heads. 'Tonight we are celebrating an engagement and have need of something finer than that cow's piss you pass off as cider.'

Jack and Giles sat by the window overlooking the lane. The first of the mill workers had started drifting home, coat collars turned up against the drizzle, caps pulled low over tired eyes. A few, those with coins in their pockets, entered the inn. Others, most of them, glanced wistfully at the inviting warmth inside, then continued on to the cottages scattered about the hills surrounding the village.

Brice snorted, but replied readily, 'I have just the thing for you lads—a bottle of the best port to be had in Bristol.' He limped away to retrieve the bottle—his left leg was never free of pain—chuckling as he walked. *Two fine lads*, he thought, *the best in the valley*. He was as proud of them as if they were his flesh and blood. The pleasure on his face was real enough.

Giles leaned forward. 'Louise has made me the happiest of men, Jack. To think she has accepted me, *and* his lordship has given the match his blessing!' Giles leaned back in the chair, a broad smile on his face. 'I have never wished for more, and I still wonder at my good fortune, I don't mind telling you.' He looked for signs of doubt in his friend's face, but saw none and was relieved.

"Tis wonderful news, Giles, and I am glad for you, very glad for you both, and that's the truth. Perhaps I, too, should now look a little harder for a mate. Possibly even the lovely Mary—or is she just for a hay barn on a summer evening, hmm?' Jack was teasing, and Giles well knew it.

'Hah, now that's a thought, Jack. No, I do not believe so. She is a good lass... the only daughter of Marling's overseer, by the way. Educated, I understand. Her only known friend is Mistress Wallace, the old schoolteacher. Talk is that she has ambition, that one. Village gossip has it that she wishes to become a governess, but the truth is that no one really knows her. Keeps her own company, mostly. Do you know the family? A brace of boys as well; they work with the old man. She's pretty as you like, but she doesn't take to a certain Captain in the South Gloucester Yeomanry!'

Jack knew his friend well enough. He guessed that Giles had tried and failed with this girl. He had succeeded with many of the girls in the district. If this one had resisted Giles' advances, she was worth taking an interest in. He found himself thinking about her: a vision in his mind of a tall, copper-haired young woman, with high cheeks, a wide and full mouth, and those large, innocent eyes that for a moment had met his own, and struck something within him. He was about to ask a question of Giles when Brice returned with a dark blue bottle and two glasses.

'There you be, boys, a drop of fine stuff, an' no mistake. Here's health to you both, but if you'll excuse me, I must get back to my work.' He placed the bottle on the worn oak table, then passed the glasses to eager hands. He made an odd clucking noise with his tongue and winked at them both before returning to the other room.

The evening passed, the two men enjoying each other's company. Oil lamps were lit and Brice placed a flickering candle on their table, casting oversized shadows that danced on the walls. Giles became exuberant and told tales of murderers, highwaymen and villains of various description. Jack knew that the formerly peaceful valleys of Gloucestershire were no longer as they had been in his childhood. The flourishing wool mills of the Five Valleys of Stroud were attracting some undesirable people, men and women, and crime in the area had become a problem.

Magistrates had charged Giles' company of yeomanry with the task of seeking out the more notorious, dangerous and active criminals. A gang of footpads and a highwayman, known as Galloping Dick Fergusson, had been working the Bath Road between Chippenham and Bristol, and reportedly along the Cheltenham Road. Giles had spent most of the summer months looking for Fergusson, with never so much as a glimpse of his coat-tails.

'The gaols are overflowing, Jack. There is plenty of work for you here, my lad, and several good causes for that liberal mind of yours. I do not begin to comprehend the law, that is your domain, but it seems to me that one may be hanged for sneezing in a public place, if it happens to be Shrove Tuesday!' Adopting a more serious tone, he asked, 'Are you to join your father in his practice, or is it back to London for you?'

The glass in Jack's hand halted on its way to his lips. 'Father has asked me to join the practice. It is his dearest wish, you know that.' Jack hesitated; he knew Giles would be aghast to learn the truth, that he intended to take a commission instead.

'But that is simply excellent, and another reason to celebrate!' Giles eagerly interrupted, happy that Jack had decided to return.

'Ah, but that is not all the news I have to tell this evening. The remainder may give you less cause to celebrate. The true reason I am home is to bid farewell to my father and sister, for I am to take the King's Commission and become a marine. You must, I implore you, Giles, say nothing of this for the moment. I beg you. I have yet to finalise my plans and affairs, and cannot speak of this to my family.' Jack observed the reaction his news had on his friend. Seeing Giles open-mouthed, he continued quickly, 'My heart is no longer with the law, Giles; it brings me but little satisfaction. There is too much injustice, and I cannot continue, in all conscience. The judiciary create more mischief every day. There is need of great reform, but I fear it will take years, and I have not the stomach to enforce unjust laws. My father will not understand, and it will be a hard business for him, I know; but my mind is now resolved. It is the deck of a man o' war and foreign adventure for me—that's what calls, Giles.' He rocked back in his chair.

'But why not the Navy, Jack? Your brother...' Giles' voice tailed away, knowing that subject was a raw point with the Vizzards.

'Ah, yes, brother George. I miss him right enough, and I pray we may meet again. It is strange and saddening that we have had no word at all.'

'You are a good shot, and strong, as you will need to be, Jack, for it's a hard course you seem set on. When will you go?' Giles' face was sombre and his voice low.

'I had planned to take my commission and join the Portsmouth Division in two or three months. However, your news has caused me to re-think. I will be at your wedding, have no fear.'

Jack explained how he had met an officer of the Corps in London earlier in the year, and how he had become convinced that the future for him lay in foreign service. He wanted to see something of the world, learn of different peoples, explore other territories, and increase his knowledge of science and nature. He had learned from his time in the yeomanry with Giles that he could command men, and he had learned weaponry under the tutelage of Major Stonehouse, one of his father's friends, from a young age.

'There must be something in the blood of the Vizzards that sets us wandering. I know that in my heart I cannot settle to the life of a provincial lawyer. There is so much to discover about the world, and there is adventure to be had! I believe George must have felt that way too. There it is then, my news. Still—what of you? Are you to continue with soldiering?'

Giles hesitated. He had always enjoyed being a soldier, but he was ambitious for property, status and wealth. His father had been a timber merchant in Gloucester, but had died leaving only a small inheritance and many debts. Giles slowly shook his head from side to side.

'No, Jack. I will be resigning my commission and will assist his lordship, my father-in-law to be, to manage his estate. He has that place near Chipping Sodbury. I have had enough of chasing villains over the Cotswolds through all weathers and sleeping rough. Time to settle to a comfortable life and enjoy my sweet Louise, to raise a family in time. I am a very lucky man, and I do know it.'

Their conversation was interrupted as Brice returned to the table, another bottle of port in one hand, and a glass in the other. 'It appears you gents are more concerned with nat- terin' like a pair of old fish wives than drinkin' this fine port, so drink up now, and mebbe I can join in your reminiscin'?'

The old sailor was still tanned, the corners of his eyes wrinkled, and his squint remained from years of peering at distant horizons.

'Sit you down, Bill, and have a glass, by all means,' offered Jack. 'We have decided our futures, and as an old friend you must tell us the news. So what have you to say?'

Bill pulled over a chair, sat, and filled all three glasses. The young men took hearty swallows, but Brice drank slowly and spoke between sips. 'Well, lads, 'tis hard to make a livin' from The Ram these days.   Hard everywhere, I reckon. Farmers are a' strugglin'; even old Caldwell next door has left us, and the fields just left to rot. Many of the boys have gone for the big towns, and those what is left are mostly thievin' scoundrels! Master Giles knows that full well, he bein' out at all hours tryin' to catch 'em. The old hands spend a few pence on me cider and ale, but trade ain't what it was, and that's no mistake.   I be hard pressed to keep the old house goin', in truth.'

Jack grunted. 'You're a scoundrel, Bricey. What of this business with Henry Wills in Bristol? That must be bringing in a pretty penny. I hear he's doing well with his tobacco, and most of the village knows you helped him with some of that prize money of yours! Then there is that inn on Welsh Back—

folk say you are a sleeping partner and are seen there in the company of... Well, I will speak no more of that.'

Both knew that Brice was a shrewd old bird, and not the man to squander his money. Although no one really knew how much he had legitimately received from the Admiralty, Jack was certain that a lot more had come his way 'under the canvas', as Brice was fond of saying. He had sailed as a bosun of Admiral Lord Hood, and seen much action.

'Now you keep quiet about that, Master Jack.' The florid, weather-beaten face grinned back at him. 'Your father put me in touch with Mister Wills, aye, and a few other gennel-men, too. It's been a profitable arrangement, and doubtless helped you on your way, I don't mind sayin'. Still, I am right pleased that you boys've turned out as well as you 'ave. I've had to keep my eye on you boys over the years, an' there's tales I could be tellin' if I had a mind to!'

'In that case, we had better finish this bottle and settle up with you, before your tongue runs away with you,' was Giles' response. 'It is time we were away from here and off to our beds while we can still walk.' He laughed and rose to his feet, a little unsteadily. 'Come, Jack, I'll take part of the journey with you and make sure you get home safely!

Chapter 4

Gloucester

Jack had grown up in the five valleys of Stroud, learning something of living on the land. With his elder brother, he'd gained skill in riding and hunting. He'd played cricket, swam and fished in the Severn, rode horses, shot game-birds and rabbits. He'd become more proficient with firearms than his brother and had greater skill with a sword.

After the grammar school in Gloucester, he'd gone up to Oxford, to Oriel, his father's old college. He enjoyed his time there. He studied diligently, unlike many of the students of the day, and investigated the taverns of the city. Was it the majesty of law, or the logic of the subject? Did he relish the verbal, intellectual combat? Was it something more subliminal? In his heart he knew the answer. He was there for his father. History he enjoyed. He was competent in mathematics, although it did not captivate him. The sciences he had grown to appreciate and value. Literature was his love.

Jack was still unsure of his future after taking his degree. Often he stayed with a college friend with access to rooms in

Middle Temple. He dined in, as was required of his intended profession, but increasingly became drawn to other pastimes. His interest in politics, his quick wits and ready, natural charm attracted the attention of more established members of society, and instead of returning to Gloucestershire, he found amusement in some of the grand houses in London.

It was at a ball, and by a mutual friend, that he was introduced to Cecelia. She was the daughter of General John Mostyn, the colonel of the 1st King's Dragoon Guards, and she had pursued him with vigour. It had been a strange affair, because she was the wife of one of her father's officers. The major had been wonderfully ignorant of the matter.

During a dinner in Cadogan Square, he found himself seated directly opposite an officer, a Captain of Marines, dressed in a scarlet coat. The man was tall, broad of shoulder and patently strong, and Jack found him a fascinating individual. A scar crossed his forehead, just above the eyebrows. His hair was short, wiry, and greying. Jack listened to the man, realising that here was one of the few to have survived the slaughter of Bunker Hill.

'I was a mere sergeant then,' the captain was saying. 'I was commissioned in the field that day, one of the first to be so honoured, as it were, but then nearly all our officers fell in those attacks.' His immediate neighbour, a young woman of plain visage, eager to impress, smiled encouragement.

Jack questioned him. 'Surely, though, sir, it is necessary to purchase one's commission? Does it not take a good deal of capital to take up in your regiment?'

'Not in the Corps', he answered. 'In the marines gold will not buy a man a captaincy, but courage and merit will.' His chest swelled perceptibly. 'You should try it, young man.'

This was spoken almost too intensely, thought Jack.

Still, the suggestion set his mind working. *Why should I not?* Military service in foreign lands, the chance of adventure, and the opportunity to distinguish himself? A sailor he did not wish to be, but a soldier of the sea, well, that was a very different consideration altogether. The conversation turned to other topics. Later, Jack attempted to engage the officer in further discussion, but by then the man was too focused on entertaining the adjacent young lady to indulge him.

During the following weeks, Jack spent a good deal of time thinking about such a life. On an impulse, he took a coach ride to Chatham just to observe the marines who were in barracks there. He watched the officers in the Kings Arms and spoke to two of them during dinner. He observed, with other townsfolk, a field drill held outside the town. He became convinced that the life they had was a good one, and that it would suit him well. On his return to London, he took a carriage to the Admiralty and arranged an interview with a senior officer. Assured that he was suitable for a commission, he promptly visited a new tailor's shop, Plater and Co. of Cheapside, and ordered additional clothes, including uniform coats, breeches, shirts, regimental small clothes, and a cleverly crafted trunk for his various possessions. Hessian boots he ordered from Gilbert's of Old Bond Street. Other equipment, he was informed, could be obtained once his commission had been confirmed and he reported to barracks for duty.

In the interim, Cecilia continued to amuse.

*****

'Jack, there you are, my boy,' his father greeted him at breakfast a few days later. 'Now, what are you about? Have you any business in Gloucester?'

'As chance has it, I do, Father. I am due to call on Sir Robert tomorrow.'

Sir Robert was the former colonel of the 28th Foot and had taught the young men of the yeomanry something of military tactics. Jack had taken more interest in the lessons than his friend Giles.

'I am appearing for an unfortunate woman accused of stealing from Mister Day, and it may be instructive for you to assist. The information laid comes from a most disreputable source and you may enjoy the opportunity to sharpen your skills in examining the witness.' Henry had not seen his son at work since he had been called to the bar and wished to see Jack appear before the Assize at Gloucester. 'We should make a formidable team, methinks. I have the brief right here for you to read.'

Jack swallowed the cheese he was eating, and drank some of the expensive coffee he enjoyed at home. 'Father, it is rather difficult for me...' he started to say.

'Nonsense, it's a capital idea!' Henry interrupted, clearly excited at the prospect. 'Willoughby is for the Crown, awful man, simply dreadful advocate, and it will do your career no harm to cross swords with him. Judge Marshall has the assize—good judge, that man—and I will be dining in his rooms tomorrow evening. Send a messenger to Sir Robert and see him another day.'

Henry looked at his son across the breakfast table, with an earnest expression that inhibited any refusal. Further protest was futile, Jack could see.

'What facts are alleged? And who is this disreputable source? How do you intend to persuade the court of her innocence?' Jack asked, resigned to his fate of spending a day in court.

'That's the spirit, my boy.' Having received the response he desired, Henry Vizzard launched into a detailed account of the circumstances that had resulted in the unfortunate lady, a valued worker at Day's Mill in Nailsworth, finding herself thrown into Gloucester gaol. Now, after many months' delay, she was finally to make an appearance in the dock.

Jack listened attentively while studying the brief his father's clerk had carefully penned in an extremely neat, copperplate style. Seeing the Crown had a flawed case, he realised this was one young girl whom he could assist.

Jack was all too aware that the Assize and Quarter Session courts were committing folk to long terms of imprisonment for even minor crimes because lawlessness was rife in the cities and increasing in the country. The gaols were crowded and there was much concern, frequently expressed in the newspapers, over the growing criminal population. The war in America had closed the main repository for transportation of 'the criminal class', a motley assortment that included thieves, bandits, forgers, and even those convicted of manslaughter, to be sure, but also those who had the misfortune to be homeless or in debt. The prison ships, hulks that Lord North had commissioned to this purpose a dozen years ago, were growing in number, with a thousand convicts sent to them every year. William Wilberforce, the parliamentary member for Kingston upon Hull, had pressed for reform of the prisons. Jack had heard him speak on the subject, had even met him last year.

Henry came to the end of his explanation and interrupted his thoughts. 'So, what do you think, lad? Can we do something for the girl?

Jack put down the brief and smiled across to his father. He leaned back in the chair, lacing his hands together behind his head. 'Yes, Father. I believe we can.'

*****

The judge's lodgings were in the grounds of Gloucester Cathedral, a short walk from King's School, where Jack had first encountered Latin, grammar, and mathematics, and where he had walked around the old cloisters, gazing at their intricate stone filigree, and looked down at the old stone benches, which still showed the scratchings of students from earlier centuries. Gerald of Wales was reputed to have studied there.

Jack 's father wished to have time alone with the judge, so to occupy himself he entered the Church of Saint Peter. The cathedral housed the tombs of Robert Curthose, Duke of Normandy and the eldest son of the Conqueror, and that of Edward II, murdered in a brutal fashion at nearby Berkeley Castle. Jack walked along the nave, gazing upwards in awe at the Arcadian columns, each seven feet wide at the base, reaching over thirty feet in height. He stopped before the great East Window, commemorating the Battle of Crecy, marvelling at the scale, colour and magnificence of the craftsmanship.

The ringing of 'Great Peter', the largest Bourdon bell in England, announced evensong and reminded Jack that time had passed, so he left the building through the West Door and strode across College Green to the judge's lodgings. He was to join his father and the judge for supper.

'Never saw Willoughby so bested, young Vizzard, I must say, sound arguments, and a commendable final speech. Thought I would have to send the woman down, until you illuminated the flaw in the prosecution's case. Even he had to admit that the missing items had not been discovered in her room; he simply relied on opportunity, alleged motive, and the reputation of the accuser. And that would have been enough, I am sorry to say, without evidence to the contrary. But tell me, if you would: how'd you know that she was at The Ram that night, and how did you persuade that old sailor to give evidence on her behalf?'

'There you are, William!' Henry Vizzard had been beaming all evening. 'I told you the boy was a natural advocate.' Pride was visible on his face as he grinned at his younger son. 'Sharp as a pin, and I don't care who knows it!'

Judge Marshall was helping himself to a large portion of well-roasted lamb as he looked hard into Jack's eyes, ignoring Henry's outburst.

'Your Honor, I knew the date she was alleged to have committed the crime, the 21st of December last year, was an evening that she could not have been at Mister Day's house, stealing silver. I happened to know that she spent the evening, and indeed the night, in the company of a young gentleman who was staying at the inn.' Jack paused and sipped at his wine.

'Mister Day discovered the loss of the silver, which had been in use earlier in the evening, shortly before retiring for the night at about midnight. The sailor, Brice, could honestly say that from early evening the woman in question was in his sight, eager to bestow her charms on a travelling gentleman—a young man rendered memorable by being somewhat over-generous with wine and with the money in his purse. I could not ask him to name the gentleman; he would have been, ah, unwilling, reluctant to do so, and I am frankly delighted that our opponent did not pursue that matter.' Again he paused, hesitating, then forged ahead to add, 'For that person, I am sorry to say, was myself!'

His father spluttered into his glass. 'By God, it was you! Yes, yes—now I recall. You arrived the following morning, and your sister was much put out at the time, because she had expected you home for your birthday. I assumed that you had stayed overnight in Oxford. Didn't you say something of the sort?'

Marshall thought it politic to interrupt. 'Your father tells me that you intend to leave London and join his practice.' He raised a forkful of lamb to his mouth, his clear eyes shining in amusement.

Jack took a large swallow of hock but just smiled. 'So he proposes, my Lord,' he answered in as non-committal a manner as he could manage.

'Excellent. Fine lawyer, your father. Should do very well to have another Vizzard on this circuit. Might just see a few more innocents escape the gaols, what?'

Marshall was liberal, a Whig, and had been known to shake his head when sending a man to the gaol for poaching to feed a hungry family. On the other hand, he ordered the hanging of hardened murderers or highwaymen without a second of remorse.

'A toast, then, to Mister Vizzard, Gloucester's newest advocate. May all his cases have happy outcomes, but perhaps without his personal and close interest!' The old judge chuckled and raised his glass. 'I see a good future ahead of you, young man. Who knows? Perhaps in time there will be a Vizzard on the bench, hmm?'

'That would be an honor beyond my desserts.' Jack thought, with increasing discomfort, of his commission.

'We shall see, Jack. We shall see.' Henry could see only his dream of a son following his path and finding fame in the only noble profession.

CHAPTER 5

A KITCHEN TALE

Mary balanced precariously on a short wooden ladder, as she pulled apples from the tree. Windfall apples littered the damp grass around the tree; she would gather those later for making apple pie. Right now she was expected to bring the best apples to the kitchen so they could be served as an accompaniment to the next meal. The best fruit hung on branches tantalisingly just beyond her reach. Standing on ladders made her anxious.

Concentrating on the task, she did not notice Jack slip through the orchard gate.

Her mind was only partly on apples and the pie that Mistress Clutterbuck wanted her to bake later. Breathing in the cool, clear air of morning, she was thinking of the lawyer's son whom she had met, the one who had caused her to flee in embarrassment. A more handsome man she had never met. There were some lads in Stroud who tried to court her, but none that she took seriously. They seemed frivolous, disrespectful, and, to her way of seeing, unattractive.

She smiled inwardly as she called to mind the encounter. She was not always so shy, but there was something about John Vizzard that confused her mind. Handsome, certainly he was that, but a curious and indefinable energy had also passed from him to her at that first meeting.

She hummed a tune that reflected the lightness of her mood. The basket was more than half full; she mounted the next rung of the ladder and pulled two more apples, dropping them into the basket, then started to reach for another. Humming and looking upwards, she neither saw nor heard Jack's approach.

'Now that's a pretty sight,' Jack called up, stepping under the branches of the apple tree.

The basket slid from Mary's hand, the ladder slipped sideways off the trunk of the tree and, with a scream, she fell backwards, landing on Jack, so that they both fell in a tangle of limbs onto the damp grass and half-rotten apples.

'Oh, see what you've done! All the apples spilt and my dress muddied!' Mary exclaimed.

Jack was laughing and unable to answer for a moment. 'But it was worth it, by God. That tree is one I know well from my youth, and it never bore such treasure then as it did today.' He grinned at her blushes. 'Here, Mary, let me help you up, and we'll gather these apples that I caused you to spill.'

Mary gathered herself. 'Now, Master Vizzard, what are you about this morning? If it's the vicar you want, he has already left for church, although the condition he is in will make for an entertaining sermon, I'm thinking, and Master Giles is still snoring in his bed.' She rubbed her left wrist and wriggled her fingers, still blushing in embarrassment. She found the nerve to look directly into those blue eyes.

'I have given you permission to call me Jack, and, no, it's not the vicar but you I have come to see.'

Jack's gaze was on the loveliest face he had ever seen. None of the society ladies he had met in London compared with the girl in front of him. He looked with unabashed admiration at her cascading copper hair and those large hazel eyes, at her face with skin as soft as cream. With an effort, he turned his attention from her face and took her left hand in his and examined her wrist with elaborate care.

'I see no sign of serious injury here, but if you wish I will find a physician to attend to it. I am truly sorry I startled you; I should have announced my presence. Please, I beg forgiveness for my foolishness.'

She smiled now, her earlier shyness waning as she returned his gaze.

'There is no need for a doctor,' she said. 'I thought to gather some apples for the table, as apples are sovereign for... clearing the mind'—she didn't want to say 'alleviating drunkenness'—'but I am also tasked by Mistress Clutterbuck, who is away this morning, to bake a fruit pie for the vicar's supper.' She continued, to counter the awkwardness she felt, 'Perhaps you would like to help me?'

'I have no skill with pastry, Mary, but the least I can do is peel the apples for you, certainly.' It sounded a little strange to his ears to use her name; not wrong, but almost intimate. 'Would that be a help?'

She regarded him wide-eyed for a moment. 'I suppose it might,' she said, not at all certain that it would be.

They gathered up apples, then walked towards the vicarage kitchen, an odd and novel sensation passing between them that each felt. Jack wanted to know about this girl, for she captivated him like no other. He had thought of little else for the last few days. He studied the vicarage, as though seeing it for the first time. A black cat crept along the garden wall, eyes wide, viewing them warily. It stopped, stared in the direction of the couple, then, with a sudden spring, dropped out of sight on the far side.

The awkwardness Jack felt was unnerving, and he sensed that she wished he would speak. Now that he was close to her, he found light, easy, conversation difficult.

'Mary, do you ride?' he blurted out. 'I wondered if you did and might accompany me this afternoon. We could take my father's horses up on the common; there are wonderful views over the Severn from Selsley, and it is a fine day for a ride.'

She stopped and hesitated before answering. Her eyes met his and she coloured again. 'I know the common well. My father and I walk there sometimes. I would like that very much, although my skill with a horse is doubtless comparable to yours as a pastry cook.' She smiled at the jest and was pleased to see, from the broad smile, that he was amused.

'Then it is agreed. I shall bring the horses around after luncheon, if that scoundrel the Reverend Barnwood will release you.'

'Oh that will be no bother. He will be full of wine by lunch and asleep for much of the day. Besides, Sunday afternoon is my time off.'

They continued towards the house, and he felt more able to talk. The kitchen aroma was of fresh-baked bread, rising from several loaves cooling on the oak bench by the oven. On a long table bowls, a spoon, a paring knife, a slicing knife, and a lemon were arrayed. Mary had been busy, he realized. Removing his coat, he rolled back the cuffs of his shirt and set to work.

In the scullery, trimming and peeling the windfall apples, he found himself asking more and more questions. It was in his nature to be inquisitive, but he took pleasure in listening to this girl. He was enchanted by her modulated west-country voice and her laugh when he made some silly remark. She was only eighteen years old, he discovered from initial questions, but had a maturity and confidence he had not detected at first. She talked easily of her family and her childhood. He learned, too, that she loved reading and had learned to write, a skill of which she was particularly proud. The more she talked, the more he could observe her, and he liked what he saw.

Mary was slender of waist but full-figured, and her face radiated health and pure joy of life. She was clothed simply in a blue dress of coarse wool, tied at the waist with an embroidered belt, which emphasised her figure. She was taller than most girls, although not as tall as he, and her hair, long and shining, had been cared for in a fashion that was uncommon amongst the village girls. She had a curious mannerism that he found bemusing: a habit of raising a solitary eyebrow.

Her figure was classically proportioned, and he mildly scolded himself for imagining her naked. This was not some wench that he could take to his bed and forget, nor some predatory society lady of the kind that had given him some amusement in London recently. Mary was different, he realised, virginal and unexplored; and not for the first time he questioned his thinking.

As she talked, Mary stole glances at this man, who in a matter of a few minutes had managed to learn more of her life than she had willingly offered to any other, and wondered why she could do so. He was certainly handsome. His hair, although dark, was not quite black, she realized. The white shirt he wore—he had removed the apple-stained coat—was tight across broad shoulders and powerful upper arms. His eyes, with a brightness that appeared when he smiled, were rarely off her, and she knew he was attracted to her. Why, she could not understand.

Father described her as beautiful, but that was merely a doting father's natural partiality. Now for the first time in her short life, a man, a true gentleman, was taking a close interest in her. It was an alien sensation, and her developing emotions were in disarray. *How do I treat this? Am I to take his interest seriously? Or is he merely seeking a diversion for the short time he has at home?*

She busied herself with the fruit, slicing the apples after he peeled and cleaned the windfalls. She set the slices in a bowl, drizzled them with the juice of a squeezed lemon, sprinkled them with sugar, and then, carefully, with three dashes of the precious cinnamon spice. A wonderful, warm aroma filled the kitchen as she did so. Then she handed Jack some logs from a basket, indicating with her head that he should place them in the large cast iron oven.

'The pie is needed for this evening, so says Mistress Clutterbuck, and I best be getting on with the pastry.' She held his eyes, almost a moment too long, but he grasped her meaning.

'I have to go, too. Father is expecting me for luncheon, and it would not do to keep him waiting.' He brought her hand to his lips, brushing her fingers gently. 'Until this afternoon, then.' He picked up his hat and coat, and left quickly through the kitchen door, striding out into the orchard.

She thought she heard him whistling, as he disappeared from her sight. She continued gazing through the window, until the kitchen cat leapt onto the long table to investigate the apples, and Mary had to shoo her away.

CHAPTER 6

A RIDE

Jack rose from his father's table in some haste. 'May I take the horses out this afternoon, Father? I have a mind to ride on the common for an hour or two and blow some cobwebs from my head.'

Before his father could answer, Charlotte looked up sharply. 'And why, pray, should you wish to take both Barley *and* Humbert, dear brother? Who is to accompany you on this excursion, may I ask? You have behaved in a most mysterious manner of late.'

'A fair question, my boy,' Henry added, now taking an interest with an amused expression at seeing his son colour slightly. 'Well, out with it. Can't be Giles, he has a stable full of hunters from which to choose.'

'I see I have a most inquisitional court today.' Jack grinned. 'May I therefore plead for mercy and offer the explanation that I wish to entertain a certain lady of this parish, one Mary George, who now resides at the vicarage as an assistant to Mistress Clutterbuck.'

'I knew it!' his sister exclaimed. 'Meg Dauncey mentioned she had seen you and the George girl conversing in the orchard this morning.' Charlotte did not even attempt to withhold a smirk of triumph from spreading across her face.

Henry was intrigued. 'You mean that daughter of Marling's man, what's his blasted name? Well I never, she is a mere slip of a thing. Wait a minute—at the vicarage, you say? Thought she was to work for James Champion in Dursley, last I heard.' Henry was visibly consulting his knowledge of local postings.

Charlotte, sensing her brother's embarrassment, thought to capitalise on it. 'I have yet to have the pleasure of a *formal introduction*,' she jibed, 'but my informant tells me she is a pretty maid. Is that your opinion, Jack dear?' Jack's features reddened. 'What is the matter, Brother? Cat caught your tongue?'

'It has to be conceded that she has a not unattractive countenance. And the pleasure will be yours, my dear sister, for I intend to invite her to join us for lunch next Sunday,' Jack added on impulse. Turning to his father, he asked, 'With your agreement, Father?'

'By all means, dear boy, if that is your wish.'

The older man's eyes glinted with the thought that some romance was in the offing. His son had never before invited a companion to his table. All too often, the guests at Lampern House were rather dull gentry, or the even more dreary mill owners. The occasional officers from the 28th Foot that Charlotte dared to introduce were, in the main, only marginally more entertaining, and only because they strove to cultivate his approbation. He had once hoped that his daughter might set her cap at young Giles Mountjoy, who was a decent sort, but she had clearly never taken to Jack's friend.

When is she going to be off my hands? Henry wondered. *I must encourage her to accept one of her many admirers.* Of course, there was some question as to what the gentlemen admired: his daughter's charms, or her prospective dowry.

'Yes, Jack,' was what he said aloud. 'We could do with more company here. I shall speak to Neave and make the arrangements.'

'Does she ride, or is that to form part of your tuition?' Charlotte enquired, a little haughtily.

'We shall soon find out. Now, with your leave I will ask Neave to saddle the horses and be on my way.' Jack left them to speculate on his interest in the vicar's new assistant house-keeper and went in search of his father's servant, Neave, who with Mrs Neave looked after the family and their house.

As he rode through the village some ten minutes later, he felt lightness, a sense of recklessness, a rising of his soul. He had Barley on a leading rein and so rode slowly, nodding to a few villagers as he passed along the lanes, unable to restrain the wide grin that spread across his face.

It must be infectious, he thought, as a pair of village women returned his smile, evidently believing that he had directed his good humour at them. He felt more contented with his life than he could remember. The sun was shining, covering the valley with a visible warm haze so that several white-washed cottages on the hills danced in the light. Life, he decided, had suddenly improved immeasurably. He sat straight in the saddle and unbuttoned his waistcoat, whistling to himself and enjoying the sun's rays on his face.

Charlotte could tease all she wished.

Chapter 7

The Escarpment

They climbed slowly along the tracks leading from the village to the edge of the escarpment, which ran for miles along the east side of the Severn Valley. The horses disturbed the sheep grazing on the common, sending them scattering in various directions. A dozen or more red-throated barn swallows dived and soared above their heads, eagerly and efficiently taking the last of the sleepy flies before heading to a warmer climate.

Jack talked of his childhood in the village and of his time at school. Like the sons of the local gentry, he had boarded in Gloucester. Mary asked about his time at university, and strove to understand all that he said of his studies.

To her great delight he described Oxford, the many colleges there, the fellows and the lectures, the intimate evenings spent in quiet debate and discussion, the times drinking in the taverns along Blue Boar Lane and St. Aldates, of boating on the River Isis.

She was entranced by his accounts of the Oxford dinners he was obliged to attend as a student.

'All served on the longest table you have ever seen.' He smiled at the memory. 'Gifted to the university by Good Queen Bess herself, and, legend has it, shaped from a single oak tree cut from Windsor Forest.'

He then described something of his life in London; he did not recount the intimate details, but told of his friends and his work, of the old buildings in the Temple and Lincoln's Inn. She was aghast at the expense of a tenancy in a set of chambers. She listened wide-eyed to his tales of 'devilling' for his master, researching precedents, preparing arguments, and writing opinions on torts, property and trusts.

In turn, she told him of her family, of her brothers and of her father, and how he was always encouraging her to learn more. He was the one who came home with borrowed books, and had paid for her attendance at the village school. However tired he had been, he had never failed to listen to her learning her numbers, letters and words. He would sit by the fire in their small cottage, helping her sound out and understand new words.

The horses munched on grass as they talked, their long tails swishing from side to side.

After talk, Jack led the horses to another part of the escarpment, further to the south, and challenged her to a fast ride past the many tumuli that dotted the landscape, the burial mounds of the ancients who had lived on the high ground five thousand years before.

Jack pulled up at the peak overlooking the Severn Vale, the broad, sleepy river a thousand feet below. The beech woods along the escarpment provided a rustling backdrop.

The leaves would be falling soon with the first frosts of autumn, but now they danced in a light breeze as the sun started its descent over the Forest of Dean on the far side of the water

Mary pushed the hair from her face, aglow after their canter across the common. Jack gazed with admiration at her, feeling more contented than he had for many months.

He pointed out the small villages of Uley and Frocester, and the curiously shaped Smallpox Hill, where local villagers had taken refuge from the plague centuries before.

Standing upright in the stirrups, he looked at her and said, 'You astound me, Mary. Most obviously you can ride, and ride well at that!' Jack was breathless as he dismounted, and not only with the exertion of keeping Humbert, his father's favoured hunter, on track. He walked toward a wall where the ground fell away. Mary had kept up with him and rode with a natural ability. The knowledge pleased him. He was enthralled by her beauty, captivated by her energy, her patent joy in life. He delighted in her company.

'As well as a London lawyer?' She was equally breathless.

It had taken all her concentration to ride Barley, who had wanted to move ahead of the older, larger horse. She had been alarmed when he'd suggested this afternoon's excursion, for although she had lived among horses all her life, and loved them, her background had never permitted her to own a courser. She had learned to ride on horses owned by Dick Caldwell, the farmer her father was friendly with. Exhilaration sparkled in her eyes.

Mary joined Jack by the low stone wall that guarded the precipice of the escarpment above the great river that ran meandering through the flat farmlands in the wide valley below. A pair of geese sailed noisily overhead, squawking to each other, engaged in some esoteric conversation of their own, heading towards the marshes at Slimbridge a dozen miles south on the River Severn.

'Look at that, Jack, is it not beautiful?'

The late afternoon sun was slowly dying as it completed its declivity with transient pools of colour, deep oranges, reds and purples, all spreading across the western sky. A dense mist was filling the valley below, the trees across the river seeming like galleon sails on a silken sea. The warmth of the afternoon was dying with the sunset and the air was becoming cooler.

'It is—but there is something more beautiful for me to look upon.'

His voice dropped as he held her hand, and he felt his voice quiver slightly. He moved a little closer to her, seeking a response, some confirmation, an acceptance.

Mary's heart beat a little faster. 'Please, don't speak more... I am confused enough.'

She looked up at him and a sense of desire, of longing, came on her, such as she had not experienced before. *How can this be? What is happening to me?* she wondered. She directed her eyes to the valley below. A silence grew between them. Jack broke it.

'You sense it too, then? I wondered if it was only I. I barely know you and yet... perhaps I do.'

He cursed to himself for his hastiness, his lack of subtlety, his impulsiveness. This girl attracted him as no other had. He could not explain it as simple lust. This feeling was complex, unfamiliar and exotic. He felt intoxicated and had to swallow hard before he felt able to continue.

'I came here often as a boy and still do when I need peace and time for myself. Whenever I do, it feels as though I am the only person alive. Today, though, Mary, today I feel more alive than ever before. That can only be because of you. I felt it the moment I first saw you.'

He looked away, eyes dropping as though looking at the sheep scattered along the fields far below.

She hesitated, not knowing how to answer, trying to make reason of her emotions.

'Jack—this is not right, my dear. My father... works in a mill, whereas yours is a man of position and wealth. We are from different worlds. In truth, nought can come of this.'

This thought had already entered his mind.

'Ah, but all men are created equal in the eyes of God, Mary. The Americans have declared it so, echoing the words of Francis Bacon, and that is also my opinion. You must not think it should be otherwise.'

He continued talking, his mind going back to his days at Oxford and to the teachings of the jurists he had studied there. All the time his eyes were seeking hers, his hands holding hers. She listened intently, knowing that he was knowledgeable, a philosophical man, with empathy and compassion for the labours that most men had to face daily to put bread in the mouths of their children.

He believed, as did other enlightened men, that prisons should not merely be places of confinement and punishment, but places where inmates received the means and encouragement to reform.

She knew that Jack Vizzard was regarded by many as a gentle man with a sharp brain, given perhaps to romantic notions and impulsive ways. His own father had been discussing him with Mister Marling some days ago and had repeated the conversation to her. She sighed inwardly and shivered visibly.

'What is it, Mary? Are you cold? Yes, you must be. Come, it draws late and I have talked enough.'

'No, wait. For a while longer. I love to hear you talk so. I could listen to you all day. It is even better than reading! Do you know, that is in part how I come to be working for the vicar. He has many books in his library, some quite rare he tells me, and I hope to improve my position with his help.'

Her eyes flickered, as though challenging him in some way. *Only with an education*, she thought, *can I hope to improve myself, become more than a servant to others. To find some purpose to my life.* Secretly she harboured a desire to teach, hoping to find employment as a private governess. For that, she had to have access to books, more than her dear father could ever hope to provide.

'But, Mary, you must feel at liberty to borrow all you wish from our house! Most of our books are treatises on law and casebooks, to be sure, but Father has a large collection of other works, as do I. We are not lacking in books!'

He knew the family library was well stocked, reading being one of the interests he had inherited from his father. Indeed, Charlotte also had a passion for books and was writing a romance herself; she had been doing so for many months at great expenditure in paper, quills and ink, but so far she had not permitted any eyes but her own to see the manuscript.

He was delighted that Mary loved to read. It was something he could help her with, and an excuse, if one were needed, to spend more time with her.

'In fact, if you would care to join us for luncheon next Sunday, you could browse at your leisure and select some books to borrow.' He watched as an array of emotions played over her face.

'I... That is to say, do you think I would be welcome at your home?'

'It is all arranged, dear girl. Father has agreed and is expecting you; and Charlotte, my sister, cannot wait to meet you. I do hope you will say yes.'

He regarded her anxiously, fearful that she might be too frightened to accept, dismayed at the prospect of dining at the Big House, as Lampern was commonly known in the village.

She reached a decision.

'Jack, dear, if the vicar has no other duties for me, I should be pleased to come.'

Inwardly she had doubts, knowing that some would consider her impertinent, and looking above her station. She wondered too, how his family might receive her. And she would have to borrow some pretty dress to wear.

His sister, she was aware, was one of the most sought after young ladies in the district, and regarded as an arbiter of taste and fashion, regularly attending soirees and balls in Cheltenham and Bath and the large houses of the area.

If she could find a pretty dress, and prepare her hair, she should look presentable. Mother would help, but would fret and fuss about the reason for the invitation. *Dear God*, she thought, *what have I agreed to?*

'Good, that is settled then. I will collect you at twelve. No —I have a better thought.' *Again an impulse*, he thought. 'May I suggest that I accompany you to church? My friends,

Giles and Louise, are betrothed and are to attend and perhaps they might join us for lunch as well.'

The presence of Giles and his fiancée might divert his sister's attention a little, he thought. She would want to impress Louise, being eager to secure an invitation to their wedding, which promised to be a grand affair.

'Oh, well... I am not sure.'

Mary attended the parish church every Sunday, but recently her attendance had lapsed as her duties at the vicarage increased. She considered with some anxiety the prospect of taking a place in the pew reserved for the Vizzard family, positioned immediately beneath the pulpit, with the Reverend Barnwood's drink-sodden face leering down at her. She could say nothing of her fears about that man, however. He was a respected personage in the community and was on very friendly terms with the dean of Gloucester Cathedral.

'That... may be possible,' she finished meekly with a lack of conviction, and with a smile that did not entirely reach her eyes.

Even as he suggested it, the thought struck Jack that he was being rash again. To escort Mary to church was to excite gossip. Tongues would wag; he knew that. She was the daughter of an overseer, employed at the vicarage, and he the favoured son of a respected and wealthy lawyer. His father might be prepared to accept Mary as a guest in his house, but to see her on Jack's arm and sitting in the family pew was another matter. And Charlotte would have more than a few words to say on the matter. What would his mother have thought?

To the devil with them, he decided.

CHAPTER 8

THE ADVICE

The following morning Jack rode up to the common alone and exercised Humbert for several hours, riding north among the gentle limestone hills, his mind full of thoughts, before directing Humbert towards the estate of a family friend, one Sir Robert.

Jack had always turned to him in times of uncertainty. The old soldier was reliable and discreet, an avuncular figure. Sir Robert had watched Jack and his brother as they turned from boys to men, taught them something of military ways, and in the process had become a close friend to both.

The old Elizabethan house with its twisted chimneys stood welcoming in the morning sun, the driveway fresh with new stone chippings from the quarry. A muster of peacocks strutted on the neatly cut lawn at the front of the great house. Jack rode to the large oak doors.

'Is the general expecting you, sir?' a young servant, whom Jack did not recognise, enquired politely as he took the reins of Jack's horse.

'Probably not, in fact. I was to see him last week and sent my apologies. Vizzard is the name, John Vizzard,' he answered in response to the unspoken inquiry.

He was taken to a large drawing room and invited to wait. He paced slowly about the room, studying the artifacts of a distinguished soldier's career. Near the conclusion of the American war, Sir Robert had commanded a brigade, which included the Second Battalion of Marines.

The door opened behind Jack and a strong bass voice sounded loud to his ears.

'Home at last, young Jack! How is it with you? Come, come, take a chair. Not too early for a glass, is it?' Robert Pigot's whiskered face beamed in welcome as he moved to a large mahogany chiffonier and deftly poured from a flat-bottomed decanter. Holding the glass out toward Jack, he added, 'Madeira. Quite a good one, actually.'

Jack grinned, accepting the glass, and raised it in salute to the old general, who looked as fit as he had when commanding the 28th in America.

'I am well, Sir Robert, thank you.' He settled back in a leather winged-chair and sipped at the wine. 'I felt bound to apologise in person for failing to see you last week. Father insisted on hauling me to a trial.'

'Indeed, indeed. Saw your father on Friday and he told me about it. He looks well. Obviously delighted to have you back under his wing. So, my boy, how may I be of service this time? What have you done that requires my advice? You only visit when some disaster threatens your equanimity, hah!' The smile was wide across the soldier's wrinkled face.

'I admit the truth of what you say. This is indeed a matter that I would rather remain... confidential, if you please, Sir Robert.'

With no further prompting, Jack outlined his plans. He told the older man his feelings and shared his thoughts with a directness and ease that was not possible with his father. Then he described, haltingly, how he had visited the gaols at Tyburn and, since coming home, Gloucester. He knew that the stench of those places would live with him; he had seen the utter despair on the faces of men, women and children, thrown together with no distinction for their crimes. Boys confined with homosexual rapists, factory workers with murderers, prostitutes with housemaids, all of them cast together in one mass that bred only further degradation and inhumanity. He wished for a better system of justice and criminal discipline; one that promoted health instead of disease and contagion; one where the prevention of crime was allied to individual reform.

An hour passed as Jack explained his change of heart, how he felt unable to continue with the practice of law, of his meeting with the marine captain in London, of his investigations in Chatham, his meeting at The Admiralty, his waiting for confirmation of his commission. The complete plan unfolded as the general listened carefully.

'I understand your concerns, Jack. I will say this: the military will suit you, my boy. I always saw in you the potential to be a soldier, and a good one. Let me see what I can do to hasten matters along. I know one or two influential people— some who have not forgotten my own service. But there is a another concern, is there not? I see it in your face. Let me hazard a guess. You are worried about your father's reaction!'

'Indeed, that is so. Since George left, my father seems to have aged, and I know his expectations of me, Sir Robert. He has always demanded... this sounds churlish and ungrateful, but he demands excellence, and with George gone he will... has already made clear that I am to join his practice.' Jack extended his hands in a gesture of regret. 'It is his dearest wish, and here am I set upon a course that will deny him that. He will be wounded.'

'Ah, yes. I doubt that I can help you there. Not your confessor, after all, but I will keep an eye on him. Fine man, your father, not military, but a good man nonetheless.'

Jack left feeling that he had an ally.

Over the next few days, Jack found himself visiting the vicarage daily. He watched Mary gathering vegetables from the garden that Eliza Clutterbuck and her grandson tended so carefully. He talked to her over the dry-stone wall in the orchard. He persuaded her to walk up to the common one evening and they talked until late. They rode several times during the week that followed: over Selsley Common, to Rodborough, once as far as Gloucester. He showed her the cathedral, with its exquisite cloisters. They walked around King's School, where he had started his education, and they talked and talked, sharing childhood experiences, learning more of each other, and, as they came more together, they fell deeper, deeper in love.

One evening, when Barnwood was in Gloucester, Jack was able to spend time in the vicarage, under the watchful eye of Eliza Clutterbuck. He read to Mary and she to him, from books borrowed from the library at the vicarage. He found warmth, comfort, and simple pleasure in her company.

She listened to him, enjoying his resonant, modulated voice, entranced by his reading. From time to time, she asked him to explain a word she did not know. He did so happily, not in a patronising or superior way, but with obvious pleasure in teaching. He delighted in her obvious joy of books, and her quiet laughter at his occasional witticisms.

The cheese and bread that Eliza Clutterbuck placed on the table went largely untouched as they read and talked to each other, quite oblivious of the housekeeper. Eliza dozed in a chair until Jack finally, reluctantly, left the vicarage. He walked home with her face before him and she filled his dreams that night, as she was to do for many more.

The following day, Sunday, he collected her early, meeting almost clandestinely at the orchard wall. They walked slowly through the fields adjoining the village, until they came to the stream that wandered carelessly around the undulating pastures. They sat on the bank of the Ewelme, the brook that bubbled through the meadows, watching the cows flick their tails, chasing the flies. He removed his boots and stood in the clear gurgling water.

'My oath, but this is a beautiful morning, Mary.'

She had borrowed her mother's best calico dress and sown a green hem to it, and she wore a wide-rimmed straw bonnet, fastened with a ribbon of the same green. Her mother had said, with more tenderness than was common with her, that it matched her eyes.

The sun was now well above The Bury, a rounded hill rising a thousand feet and overlooking the village, and was melting the mist that still drifted among the hedges. Some sparrows were busy nearby, and a boy whistled to his dog as he walked along the lane on the far side of the hedge.

She threw a large round pebble into the stream, and the splash touched his face.

'None of that, if you please, m'lady, else I will have to duck you under, and that would ruin your pretty dress!'

Mary laughed, knowing that he had no intention of any such thing.

'Why, sir, I could not resist the temptation! You look far too smug standing there. Is it not cold?

'Now that you mention it, yes, it is. Help me out of here if you would; I best get my boots on so we can make our way to church. Father would not thank me for arriving late.'

Mary picked up a fallen branch and held it toward him. Jack eased himself back to the riverbank, and sat back against the stump of a beech tree. He dried his feet with some grass and brittle leaves. He pulled on his boots, stood and straightened his breeches, and looked across at her smiling features, the sun adding sheen to her hair and causing her to incline her head.

'God's teeth, Mary, but you are beautiful.'

His mouth straightened and he grasped her shoulders, gently pulling her toward him. He kissed her lips, with no great passion; gently, but with increasing pressure, half expecting a rebuke, or resistance. None came; he was surprised that she returned his kiss, hesitantly at first, but with growing strength and a hint of innocent desire. Her hands took hold of his head, until they separated, to take a long breath. He shook his coat and picked up his hat. Mary looked down at her chest, as if that would be enough to silence the beating of her heart that he must surely hear. He took her hand and led her back to the lane.

'I have very much wanted to do that for a great many days now.' He glanced sideways at her, noting her slightly reddened cheeks, feeling the barely discernible tremor of her fingers. She did not answer immediately, and he thought, *Perhaps I have offended her*. No, surely not, he judged.

'That was lovely, Jack; truly lovely, but please, I beg you, not again, not yet, my dear. I cannot, would not, do more.'

He faced her. 'I should apologise, say I am sorry, but by God, I am not!' He was beaming, his face illuminated. 'If I have offended you I am sorry, but I confess I do not regret it, not a jot!'

She fluffed the skirts of her dress, and said, 'Dear Jack. I am not offended, but perhaps I am troubled. You and your brother have, may I say, a certain reputation. Now, sir, but me no buts, if you please, dear man. It is true and you do know it. It is also true that I am drawn to you, that must be obvious, but I have no desire to become another Vizzard conquest. Our friendship... means all to me. But I must be cautious. You do understand that, do you not?

He did. 'My sweet, sweet Mary. Yes, I do sense that our romance has progressed rapidly, but that is only because it must be right. That is my conclusion.' He took her hand and gave it a gentle squeeze. She smiled, and her features relaxed.

'Please be patient with me. I had no thought that we should ever... well, you understand my meaning, I think.'

He would be patient. He had to be, for now there was much for him to think on.

CHAPTER 9

THE SERMON

Barnwood's eyes were rarely far from Mary, who edged closer to Jack seeking the reassurance of his shoulder. The vicar's hands were white as he gripped the edge of the pulpit, its elaborate front intricately carved from local beech wood, heavy with the sheen of decades of waxing. A shaft of sunlight coloured by the stained-glass window paid for by Henry Vizzard, struck Barnwood's face so that his eyes were narrowed against the light, adding to an impression of menace that Jack sensed in the man. A worm of concern about this vicar crawled into his brain. He stared coldly at him, forcing the man to look at him and avert his eyes from Mary.

The vicar had quickly read the banns for Giles and Louise, as though he had no ecclesiastical interest in the matter, and he was now addressing his congregation on the evils that were plaguing the county. He urged that villains be brought to justice and be incarcerated in gaols. Thieves and murderers were to be shown no mercy, for 'honest citizens' continued to have their homes violated and 'decent folk' could not safely travel and be about 'their lawful business'.

As he spoke, the pitch of his voice rising and falling, small spots of spittle gathered in the corner of his thin mouth. He urged that 'violators of women' be hunted down and receive the full consequences of their 'hideous depravity'. He made a plea that 'the Lord's innocent children' be protected from the horrors of drink-sodden parents.

Henry was nodding agreement, but Jack thought the sermon lacked any real sense of humanity or understanding. Trite rhetoric and vain piety, he thought, of the kind he had heard before.

Jack had been saddened to hear, weeks after taking his place in college, of the death of the previous vicar, Benjamin Coaley. Vicar Coaley had baptised all the Vizzard children, and had been a much-loved leader of the parish. Jack stared coolly at Barnwood with no emotion showing on his face, conscious of Mary next to him, and a hundred pairs of eyes on his back. He touched her hand and felt her move.

The man is a fool, or worse, he thought to himself. *What does he know of the despair of a man who cannot put food on the table for his family, who can do nothing to aid a sick child, who cannot find employment?* Jack had seen naked hardship with his own eyes; his family wanted for nothing, and yet thousands were hungry. The farms struggled to produce crops each year as the labourers left the villages in search of higher wages in the cities of Birmingham, Bristol and London. A wool brusher in any of the ten mills in the valley could earn twice the wages of a farm labourer, more if he became a mule spinner or wool sorter. But it was also true that a move to the city meant a man had to pay more for lodgings and meals. So what, Jack wondered, did this vicar do to truly alleviate suffering, to aid his flock? He studied the man in the pulpit, and saw him as a repulsive creature.

Jack Vizzard did not countenance violence to innocents and had little sympathy for a proven murderer, but for the hundreds of unfortunates cast into the gaols that were already overcrowded, riddled with disease, with all hope removed and dignity gone, he could and did feel compassion. These men and women were frequently convicted for little more than seeking food for their children and themselves. They resorted to all manner of crimes just to keep fed and clothed. He had seen the beggars on the streets, many of them old or maimed soldiers or sailors, and had read John Howard's study *The State of The Prisons of England and Wales*.

His reflections were interrupted when he realised that his father was getting to his feet.

'A sound sermon, Jack, and we should think on it over lunch.'

Mary was smiling at Jack. 'A penny for your thoughts?' she asked. 'I sense that you were not in full accord with the vicar.' *Neither am I*, she thought to herself. *The man is a hypocrite.*

'Ah, Mary, were he to spend just five minutes in Gloucester gaol he might moderate his rhetoric somewhat. I suspect that Barnwood long ago forgot any true Christian beliefs he may have once held, and perhaps now serves a different master.'

Instinctively he felt an aversion to the man. Irrational, perhaps, but real enough.

Following the short drive through tree-lined lanes, the carriage drew up at the entrance to Lampern House, where Neave was waiting to assist them.

'Lunch will be ready presently, sir,' he announced to Henry.

'And ready we are for it, too.' Henry Vizzard looked forward to his Sunday lunch, and today it was roasted lamb, one of his favourite dishes.

'Come along, Miss George. We shall have a sherry before we dine, and you and I can become better acquainted,' he said, offering his arm.

'Yes, indeed,' Charlotte agreed.

She had been discreetly observing the striking young woman that her brother was so obviously captivated by. It appeared to Charlotte's eye that the attraction was mutual. Taller than Charlotte, and with darker hair, the girl carried herself with poise unexpected in one from such a humble background. The dress was plain and of poor quality, but the girl wearing it was undeniably beautiful.

'You must tell us all of your family and home. Your father is employed by Marling, is he not? That must be interesting. We know the Marling family well, do we not, Father?'

'I have had some business with him over the years and have met Fred George on occasion. A good man, if I may say, Mary. Exceedingly well thought of by his employer.'

Henry spoke honestly, having talked with Mary's father concerning the purchase of a new boiler and other machinery for installation in the factory, for which Henry had negotiated a substantial capital loan.

'Thank you for saying so, sir.' Mary was pleased that her father was regarded so, for she loved him dearly.

'Please, my dear girl, you must call me Henry. I have no knighthood from His Majesty!'

Henry chuckled at his own joke. He had learned recently that such an honour might well come his way, and was not displeased at the possibility. Caroline would have been proud, he thought. She would have enjoyed becoming Lady Caroline Vizzard. His late father-in-law would have also been content at last. All a very long time ago. He shrugged off the ghosts that crept into his mind.

'Now, let's find that sherry!' Henry came back to the present and escorted Mary up the stone steps and into the house. With a glance behind, he said, 'Captain Mountjoy will be with us shortly, Neave. We left him in conversation with that scoundrel Brice, but show him in as soon as he arrives.'

Neave knew Brice well. The master did not know the half of it, he thought. That sherry and the fine French brandy that he drank with Brice was 'imported' right enough, but often from contacts of Bill's in Cornwall, not always the merchants in Bristol. But Neave kept his thoughts to himself and just smiled benignly and nodded.

The hall was light but cool as they entered and Mary shuddered slightly as she walked into Jack's home for the first time. She noticed a sweeping staircase to the right as Henry led her through a pair of doors that led into a lambent drawing room opposite. The fine furniture positioned carefully on a polished wooden floor looked valuable and well cared for. The room was comfortable and ordered. A small pillar of books lay in a neat pile on the floor by a pair of worn leather armchairs.

The sunlight caught a portrait in oils on the wall of a beautiful young woman. Mary stared at it for some moments; Jack's mother, she concluded. A dark-haired young woman, with curls hanging loosely about her oval face, and bright, cornflower blue eyes whose gaze crossed the room to penetrate into her heart, challenging, perhaps questioning, and yet in a way radiating warmth.

She caught Jack gazing in her direction, a warm smile across his face and realised in that moment that this woman exercised an influence over her son still. Hers was the feminine version of Jack's own. His mother's portrait showed a slender, graceful neck supporting a simple gold chain, on which hung a single stone of blue, drawing attention to the beautiful, intelligent eyes. As Mary moved further into the room, it seemed to her that those eyes watched her, the smile offering her welcome, reassurance and confidence.

A lurcher hound dozed by the fire that crackled in the grate beneath the imposing fireplace of local stone. The dog raised a disinterested eye and yawned as they entered, then stretched and, rising from the rug, waddled with some difficulty towards them.

Henry patted the dog on the back of the head and played gently with his ears. As he made for the decanter and glasses the dog followed.

'A very old dog now is Ralph. The last of my hounds, and I shall have no more. One becomes too fond of the creatures.' Henry looked at his children. 'Your dear mother always loved dogs, too.'

Again, he remembered Caroline, his wife of only eight years. She had left him birthing his youngest child, the young man who now kept stealing glances at this pretty servant girl.

He had never remarried and missed her every day. He looked at the portrait, as he had done countless times, never tiring of its image. It had been painted in Bath, during one of Henry and Caroline's visits to the spa city. He recalled the week spent there before her last confinement. The solemn moment passed quickly as he poured the contents of the decanter into four fine glasses.

'A toast now, I think: to the Vizzards, and their newest friend, Mary George.'

Henry raised his glass with a broad smile. *Would she have approved of this young woman?* he mused. *Most probably*, he decided. She had admired beauty, and Mary was a beautiful girl.

Mary's cheeks coloured as she raised the delicate crystal glass to her lips, the alcohol unfamiliar to her taste. She looked to Jack, his glass raised in silent endorsement.

'To Mary, who will always be welcome in this house,' was his eventual response, his voice a little lower than normal, his eyes lingering on her a moment too long, a look noticed by both Henry and Charlotte, who exchanged a glance. Charlotte commenced to talk of the local hunt, intended as a prelude to asking Mary about her riding out with Jack, on which one of her friends had passed comment earlier at the church. She felt slightly annoyed when she was interrupted by the opening of the door and Neave appeared.

'Lady Louise Ducie and Captain Mountjoy, sir,' he announced as Giles and his fiancée entered the room behind him.

'Here we are at last, Henry. Hope we have not kept you waiting, but Brice collared me at the gate. Could not get away from the man. Charlotte, delighted to see you again. May I present Lady Louise Ducie, my fiancée. Mister Henry Vizzard, his daughter Charlotte, Mistress Mary George, and, not least, my close friend Jack, whom you will know already.'

Charlotte stepped forward quickly. 'Oh, I am so very pleased to meet you at last, Lady Louise. Giles is one of our dearest friends, and we are so excited at the news that you are to be wed. Come over to the window and please tell me something of your plans.'

Charlotte gently ushered her new friend towards the window seat, chattering like a schoolgirl. 'Come, Mary, you must join us.' Charlotte was used to taking charge. Louise glanced over her shoulder, but could see that the men were more concerned with the decanter than talk of weddings. She declined the sherry that Neave placed on a small silver tray and proffered to her.

Mary looked at Louise silently. She was certainly a beauty, if perhaps a quiet girl. She saw that Louise was petite, with shining blue eyes and hair that was the colour of corn after the harvest. Her face carried an innocent but aristocratic expression, and she wore an exquisitely finished velvet dress, the value of which must surely exceed her father's earnings for an entire year.

Louise listened to Charlotte with only one ear, more interested in the attractive young woman who was trying, without success, to observe without it being obvious that she was doing so.

She turned towards Mary and, regarding her with just a hint of bemusement, asked, 'I believe you are employed by Reverend Barnwood, are you not?'

'Yes, m'Lady,' was all Mary could say, not at all used to being addressed by the daughter of an earl, albeit the youngest of his many daughters.

'Well, now, you must tell me of your circumstances, how you come to be lunching with us today. You are—how shall I say?—a good friend of Jack's, is that right?' Louise Ducie spoke clearly, quietly and without obvious mischief.

It appeared to Mary that Charlotte was a little envious of this deliberate change in the conversation, of the interest Louise now showed in a girl most would not expect to see as a guest at Lampern House. She also thought she detected an amused look in the eyes of this beautiful young woman, who sat with such poise and elegance.

Feeling that there was no guile or impishness in the question, Mary talked, hesitantly at first, then at some length, of her meetings with Jack, forgetting for the moment that her audience included his sister. By the time she paused, she realised that she must surely have given away something of her true feelings for the man she had known such a short time, and who now stood with his back to her, talking to his father and closest friend by the fire.

How could she be so stupid, she thought. To have given herself away so easily, so readily, and to a complete stranger at that. And yet, at the same time it seemed so natural to do so.

She answered other questions, about her family, her home and such, all the while feeling comfortable with Louise, less so with Charlotte, whose questions were, it seemed to her, more barbed and insidious. She countered with a polite question of her own, enquiring as to the location of the wedding, and was answered with equal courtesy.

Louise appeared satisfied. She rose, smoothing her dress.

'Mister Vizzard,' she began, quickly correcting herself, 'Henry, I for one am ready for luncheon. Do you think we might see if your cook is able to satisfy us?'

With that announcement she approached Jack, and leaning towards him she spoke quietly, 'She is quite captivating, Jack dear. Take care, do, for I sense she is much taken with you.'

Jack inclined his head towards her, but before he could ask for her meaning, she floated away towards his father, offering her arm, intent on avoiding his enquiry.

'Giles, you may sit next to me at lunch,' Charlotte commanded and, taking his hand, followed Lady Louise through the open doors to the comfortable dining room, leaving her brother looking enquiringly at Mary.

'Please don't look so anxious,' he whispered. 'You have naught to fear.'

'But I have, and I think we both know it.' Biting her lower lip, she threaded her arm through his as they followed.

Chapter 10

A Sunday Lunch

Sunday lunch with his family was always a pleasure for Henry, the more so today because of Jack's presence, and the fact that his younger son was so obviously happy in the company of Fred George's daughter.

Henry sat at the end of the long dining table, with Jack to his right, and Mary opposite him. The table was a simple yet elegant piece of furniture by George Hepplewhite, and greatly prized by Henry. Today it was dressed with crisp white linen, a gift from a client, the owner of Egypt Mill in Nailsworth. Shield-backed dining chairs stood evenly spaced, and good quality silverware, sufficient for six diners, adorned the surface, although the table would comfortably accommodate a dozen. Crystal glasses, two for each place, were shining in the bright sunlight that darted into the room, as passing clouds allowed.

Family portraits hung on the walls, including a large one of Henry, obviously painted when he was a young man. Mary stole surreptitious glances at a pair of smaller ones, hanging between two large windows. The two brothers, she realised, painted when both were quite young. She studied the picture of George, and saw a striking likeness to Jack. The same thick, dark and wavy hair, cut shorter; a strong, pronounced jaw-line, and the eyes, staring back at her, with the confident look she had grown accustomed to seeing in Jack's eyes.

Jack kept up a diverting conversation, but Henry noted that his son stole a great many glances at Mary. *The boy is smitten*, he thought, *quite smitten. Now the village will have some more gossip regarding us Vizzards.* He sighed silently.

'Giles, and Louise, your health', he said raising a glass of Champagne. 'I imagine you are both growing in anxiety now that you are betrothed and the banns have been read.'

Giles answered the toast. 'I speak for myself, Henry, but yes, I am anxious that my dear Louise will find me a worthy husband.' He smiled towards his fiancée, who returned his look with genuine affection.

'Then, Giles... take this thought, if you will, from one who speaks from personal knowledge,' Henry replied. 'Marriage may have many pains, but I assure you that celibacy has few pleasures!'

While Jack and Giles laughed loudly, Charlotte frowned in disapproval, and Louise showed the faintest blush.

'Oh, very good, Henry. Very amusing,' Giles chuckled.

'Alas, my dear boy, I cannot claim that observation as an original thought, for it belongs to Samuel Johnson, whose works I am reading.'

He had spoken for some minutes about the account of mental illness in the book, which had caught his interest, when, almost absently, he realised Charlotte, seated next to her brother, was probing and making Mary nervous. The main course of roast lamb now having been consumed, Mary had dropped her knife.

Jack flashed his courtroom stare at his sister.

'Mary, you simply must have some treacle tart,' Henry proclaimed. 'Neave makes a splendid pastry! Neave!'

His shout brought his housekeeper bustling in from the kitchen. He always addressed both by their surname, having long ago forgotten their Christian names. 'We'll take some of that damned tart you were gabbling on about earlier, please.' He smiled kindly at his housekeeper, who merely raised a single eyebrow as a reproof.

Jack looked with some gratitude at his father, understanding his motive.

'Oh, absolutely, Mary. Why, 'tis almost edible!' Jack joked, easing the atmosphere further. 'And I had nothing whatever to do with it.'

A tap on his foot told him to make no more mention of apples or pies or pastry, not at this table. He pushed his plate aside, wiping his lips on a napkin, to cover his smile.

'I am sure it will be a pleasure, Mister Vizzard,' was Mary's contribution, directed now toward Henry. 'I have an appetite today'.

'Now, then, my dear, if you are to spend more time in my house, you must learn to call me Henry—unless I meet you in court, of course!' He laughed loudly at his own wit, rapidly clearing his throat, realising, just in time, the poor taste of his humour. Fortunately, it passed unnoticed and the meal continued in a convivial atmosphere.

Following lunch, leaving his father to converse with Giles and Louise, Jack showed Mary the grounds of Lampern House; they were not extensive, but of sufficient size for Henry's taste. He was no amateur gardener, but

Edward Neave and his wife tended a kitchen garden with a well-stocked vegetable patch.

Behind a high beech hedge there was a paddock and stables, with an outhouse for storage, and beyond that the land rose steeply up to the wooded escarpment and an undulating common above.

He showed her the library and they spent some time examining the shelves, which lined three of the walls, extending from the floor to a point just below the plastered ceiling. A portable ladder, used to give access to the highest shelves, was in the corner by the large French windows that led out to the gardens, and to an ornamental pool and fountain. The fountain had not flowed for many years, although Henry fully intended to have that restored.

Neave served them both coffee, a drink that Mary had never previously tasted, and she declared it delicious. She walked along the shelves and found, with Jack's help, three books, including *Robinson Crusoe* by Daniel Defoe, and some poetry by Alexander Pope. He tied them together with some red ribbon used to secure written opinions, taken from his father's study, immediately adjacent to the library.

'It is a beautiful house, Jack. You and your family must be very happy to live here.'

He placed his cup on a small table and looked at her fondly. 'Yes, it is a fine property, and father will never leave it. He tells of a family story that the Vizzards owned a larger estate centuries ago, somewhere near Oxford, but which we lost after the Civil War. It belonged to an ancestor, father tells me, a supporter of the king during that time. Obviously he backed the wrong horse, else we would truly be lords of the manor!'

'Oh, and do you know what happened to it? The estate, I mean.'

'Both father and I have every intention of discovering more of the history; however, neither of us have conducted any investigation. It could take years of research, and in truth neither of us really knows where we should start. I suspect it is mere legend passed to us from grandfather—and he was half mad!'

'Then you must, Jack. I could never ignore such a legend. Think of the story that must lie hidden in the dusty records of... Well, I am not sure where the records would be, but you must try at least.' She loved to read of mysteries and romantic tales of chivalry.

'Little is known to us. If grandfather spoke the truth, we do not know our ancestor's name or what became of him— likely as not he was beheaded, poor man.'

'How awful, and how romantic—dying for the king.'

'Well I would disagree with that. I see nothing romantic in losing one's head for the misfortune of supporting the 'wrong' side in a conflict. You forget also, Mary, that the particular king in question was a tyrant, who believed not in the laws of man but in the divine rule of kings.'

'How, then, does our present king differ from Charles?'

'Now you ask a question which begs an involved answer, my dear. He has lost us the American colonies, and filled the government with mediocre men of no talent or ability, servile creatures that were his to control. He will never control Pitt in the same way. I also venture to suggest that our king is very possibly mad. I would never make a politician, Mary. Be quite certain of that!'

'Would that be such a bad thing, Jack dear? I believe you would make an excellent politician—you actually care about people—the poor, the hungry, the homeless. Eliza tells of your generosity to some of the beggars of Gloucester. You cannot deny that.'

'It is little enough, I fear. The problems that face us now, Mary, must be addressed now. We should provide for education, for health, and reform the law and the atrocious prisons we have. There is so much that must be done, and I doubt I have the patience for it.' He smiled at the intensity of his words. 'Here ends the sermon for today!'

'It is your impatience I fancy that would be your success, Jack. Young men always want to seek change, do they not? Perhaps you should consider it. Jack Vizzard, Member of Parliament for Gloucester. I think I like that.'

He grunted, but did not answer further. He took her instead on a tour of the house, and she looked with wide eyes at the spacious rooms; the drawing and dining rooms she had seen, but the kitchen she wondered at. There was so much space, a large range at one end, with a baker's oven to one side. Cupboards everywhere and a large and very heavy table in the centre of the room, above which were suspended the largest collection of copper and iron pans and pots she had ever seen gathered in one place.

They stopped to thank the housekeepers for an enjoyable lunch, and took some tea outside, sitting on a worn bench by the fading rose garden, talking for a while, reluctant to let the afternoon come to an end.

But end it had to and Jack, with a lack of enthusiasm, escorted Mary back to the vicarage. They walked slowly along the deep narrow lane from Lampern House, down the hill towards the church and vicarage. The village was quiet that afternoon, most villagers at home tending to their chores. They were silent for some of the way, each with their thoughts, conscious of a novel sensation that passed between them. A dog ran into the lane, making them both start, before disappearing through a hedge. Then they laughed together, releasing the tensions of the lunch, still a little nervous in each other's company.

The hedges were already shedding foliage, exposing the twisted, silvery limbs of the beech that made up so much of the woods in this part of Gloucestershire. Mountainous white clouds billowed towards the sky, interspersed with darker clouds nearer the earth. The air felt warm and moist, promising rain later. Even the sparrows seemed more nervous than usual, twittering amongst the cows grazing lazily in the adjacent field. Jack knew little of cows, never having worked with them, but he had once helped in the milking sheds as a boy. He had also helped at shearing time, and had been reasonably adept with the shears. Mary would not be interested in such things, though, surely? He glanced sidelong at her, pondering her mood. She appeared relaxed, a soft, more self-assured expression about her eyes.

Passing Richard Caldwell's farm, where a flock of Ryeland sheep ran uncertainly in mobs, he offered, 'When I was younger, I used to shear those sheep... When I say, "those sheep", I mean... not those same sheep, of course. You understand my meaning, Mary?' He was struggling for once and she was instantly amused at his confusion.

'I understand you perfectly, my dear. That is so very sweet. I mean, to imagine you straddling sheep, and sweating as you clip the wool from their backs. I have seen it done by others and 'tis hard work for a city man! I find it difficult to see you other than with your nose buried deep in a book on trusts, or tort, or something equally dull!' She sought to tease him again, but he was not to rise as a fish to her bait this time.

'Father was anxious that Georgie and I learn something of nature, I suspect, and of the benefit of honest toil, that we would better understand the labour that other men are obliged to undertake to make a living. I believe it was beneficial, although I thought otherwise at the time. You are quite correct, of course; it is by far the most demanding labour I've ever done. Georgie hated it.'

She knew the village gossip concerning the elder Vizzard boy, although she had not known him. Her mother had spoken of it, had cautioned her not to raise the subject with the younger brother. 'Do not talk of him, my child. He ran away to sea, probably to escape a vengeful husband, if you ask me, but the brother will not wish to hear you speak of him.' Her mother had been unusually evasive and emphatic, she thought. She ignored the warning.

'You are very fond of your brother.' The subject was broached and she almost regretted doing so, for fear that she might open a wound. She was relieved to see that Jack did not appear offended.

'We were inseparable as boys and I miss him greatly. I often wonder what has become of him.' He paused, his mind flashing back in an instant to that summer two years before. 'The hurt was immense at the time, because he never confided in me, when we used to share everything. I did not understand.' He sighed. 'I reasoned much later that he probably wished to avoid disturbing my studies. I was preparing for my final examinations and he left before the long vacation. It took me a long time to forgive him, but I believe I have since. My dear, must we talk of such matters? It can be of little interest to you.'

So he did still hurt, then, she decided. Usually brothers fought like cat and dog, but clearly the Vizzard boys were different. How alike, or truly different, were these two men, she asked herself. Then she asked him the same question.

'Father thinks we are "peas from the same pod", but we differed. George was the leader in all things, in our games, in our learning—he never went to Oxford, though, much to father's ire, but in all else where he led, I tended to follow. It usually landed me in one scrape or another!' He laughed, not in amusement, but ironically. 'By God, Georgie, where are you now when I need your counsel most!'

'"Georgie"?' she asked.

'Yes, he was always Georgie. As in the nursery rhyme: "Georgie Porgy kissed the girls and made them cry." He kissed a good many girls! Father would never call him that, but Charlotte tells that mother used to sing that rhyme to him at bed-time.'

Now here was another wound to open. With less fear, she asked of his mother.

'You never knew her, did you, Jack?'

He stopped, looked at her, and decided that she deserved an answer. He walked to a gate leading to a field and sat on the bank at the side of the lane, gently taking her hand and pulling her down beside him.

'No, Mary. She died birthing me, and I know that something inside father died that day. I often catch him looking at her portrait. You may have noted it yourself this morning. It is a fine portrait.' He looked up at the sky, collecting his thoughts.

'I stare at her myself for what seems like hours whenever I am home, wondering about her, what kind of person she was. Beautiful, that much is clear from her picture, but what was she truly like? How did she speak and sound? What thoughts did she have? How did she move? Often I ask these questions of myself. Perhaps that is one of the reasons I miss Georgie. He has some memory of her. Charlotte loved her, everyone did. I never had the opportunity, and I used to blame myself for causing her death. Now I know that death comes to many women in childbirth, but as a child.... Neave came to us as my wet nurse and stayed with us ever since. We are very close, she and I. Why, she still gives me the largest portions at dinner!' He laughed again.

'I think', Mary said, holding his hand more firmly, 'that she must have been one of the most beautiful ladies in the county. I did see her portrait, and could not help but notice the likeness. You follow her looks more than Charlotte, I feel. Your sister has your father in her bones.'

'And in much else, I fancy!'

A warm breeze ruffled the grass and he plucked a blade from the bank, absently chewing on it, before continuing.

'Charlotte and I are very different. She has father's temperament—if not his discretion. Please, do not misunderstand me, I love her dearly, but she can be such a basket of trouble! That is one of the questions that I ponder on sometimes. Was my mother like her? Father said that she was an 'impulsive romantic' and that both his sons have inherited that trait, but not so Charlotte. I sometimes think that Charlotte has no romance in her soul whatever. She is so very independent. Why else has she not found a man to take her off father's hands before now? She is not ugly and has charm of a kind, but seems unable to find the 'man of her dreams', as she puts it.'

Mary loosened the sash from her dress. Looking at her feet she said, 'And you, Jack, do you have romance in your soul?'

His face turned to hers now, and he spoke softly. 'Need you ask me that, Mary? Before returning home I would have answered your question differently, but now, yes, I believe I do.'

His eyes looked deeply into hers, and he understood that she knew the answer to the question already.

As did he.

CHAPTER II

THE YOUTH

The youth shivered in the kitchen. His hair, matted and soaking, stuck to his scalp, his face shining with moisture. The morning rain was running off his muddy clothes, forming dirty puddles on the cold flagstone floor, and the blanket that Ed Neave had placed around his shoulders did little to stop his teeth knocking. He had run as fast as he knew how until he had reached the 'Big House' and found the door at the rear that obviously led to the kitchen.

Because no lights were showing, he had waited until he had seen a lamp flicker illuminating the kitchen and heard the sounds of the kitchen fire being stoked and re-fuelled, and pans clanking. Then he had knocked, quite loudly, waiting, it seemed to him, a very long time before the door opened and a surprised Neave let him inside.

'What is all this about, young Tom? You look afeared for your life, boy.'

He sat the boy down on a stool by the fire, pouring him a small tankard of beer from a large stone bottle.

The boy told his tale quickly, in nervous, broken sentences, eager to complete his mission.

'It's true, sir. Mistress Mary said I was to tell Mister Vizzard to come at once. At once, she says. The charley... he came in the night and they've taken 'er away, sir.'

The charley was the village night watchman charged by the parish with keeping the peace and catching any thieves. Neave, listening to this strange tale, struggled to comprehend, but there was no denying the boy was in earnest. Why should the vicar's housekeeper be arrested and taken away in the middle of the night? It had only been a fortnight since the young lady had dined at Lampern House, and she and Master Jack had both been so happy.

'They two have fallen for each other, that be plain,' his wife Maddy had told him later that same day, after the lunch. She had started to speak of wedding plans that she would have to make. There was no doubt in her mind of that, and it had become a topic of some gossip in the village. Ed conceded that to those who knew them both it seemed they had become inseparable. His wife fretted over the younger son as though he were her own child, which in many ways he was.

'Now then, my lad, where be she taken to?' He looked at the boy kindly. He knew him to be Eliza Clutterbuck's grandson, Tom, and not a bad boy. 'Tell me all you know, and quickly, now. Before I raise Master Jack I shall need to know all.' He placed his hand on the boy's shoulder.

'Please, sir, I don't knows no more 'an that, sir. My nan says to tell you there was a great hullabaloo during the night and to fetch Master Jack straightaway, sir. I don't know nothing more, sir.' Tom had a fair idea of what had gone on but was not about to say so. Best to play ignorant of grownup ways, he decided.

'Give the lad some breakfast, love,' Neave said to his wife, loading the fire with fresh logs of seasoned wood. 'I had best go and wake the young master. What he will make of all this the good Lord only will know.'

He lit another candle and, placing it carefully in a pewter holder, started for Jack's room at the rear of the house. He was very ill at ease. *Folk ain't taken off in the middle of the night with no reason*, he thought, *and certainly not the likes of young Mary George. This is an ill wind and no good will come of it, that's for certain.* He climbed the stairs with a sense of foreboding. Once before he had had to raise the master in the middle of the night. That was when George had left to go to sea, leaving Lampern with no farewell to Mister Vizzard. He shuddered at the memory.

The heavy oak door of Jack's room creaked as he entered, but only the sound of deep breathing reached his ears. His candle threw dancing shadows across the room, and cast a huge silhouette behind him. He crossed to the large bed, using the candle to light the wick of the oil lamp on the table beside it, and firmly placed a hand on Jack's shoulder. The young master stirred as he gently shook him.

'Wake up please, Master Jack, wake up. There's trouble and you be wanted.'

Jack was awake. 'What is it? Who is that? Oh, it is you, Neave. What do you want? My God, it is not yet light.' Through the window that Jack always left ajar, with the curtains drawn back, stars still sparkled between clouds that drifted slowly across the face of a half-moon. He rose sleepily onto one elbow.

'There's a boy downstairs, sir, with urgent news that you must hear for yourself. I'll fetch a cloak for you, but you best be getting dressed for you must go quickly, I'm thinking.'

The urgency in Neave's voice struck Jack and he was up, pulling on a pair of black breeches and a woollen shirt from his trunk. Grabbing a leather jerkin, he was off after Neave's candle, his mind already in turmoil.

'What's happened, Neave? Have we been robbed?' Neave was moving quickly down the stairs with Jack close behind. He led him to the scullery where Tom Clutterbuck was chewing on a piece of bread and cheese, with a small tankard of light beer in front of him.

'Here's Master Jack, Tom. Now you tells him wot you just told me.'

Tom Clutterbuck stood up, swallowed hard and looked at the tall figure of Jack with rabbit's eyes.

'Sir, it's like I told Mister Neave, sir. Nan tells me to tell you there's been a commotion at the vicarage and the charley's taken Mistress Mary to the lock-up, sir. That's all I know, sir... and my nan says for you to come quick, sir.'

Jack needed no second telling. Running for the door he called to Neave, 'Hurry and help me saddle, Neave!' He stopped and looked down at his feet, realising his boots were missing.

'Leave it to me, sir. Here's your cloak. I will saddle up Barley while you find your boots. Will you want me to come with you, sir?'

'No! Just get him ready as quick as you can. This cannot wait, man!'

His boots were in the boot-room, adjacent to the scullery. With half a dozen rapid steps, he located them. Pulling them on, he returned and studied the youth. He picked up a loose piece of cheese from the platter in front of Tom and looked at him, a quizzical expression on his face. The boy blinked and stopped eating. Jack decided the boy had spoken the truth, that he knew nothing more. Pouring some milk into a cup from the pitcher on the table, he drained it in a single swallow. The sound of Barley's hooves moving skittishly from the stable galvanised him into action. He fastened the cloak about his chest and strode quickly outside.

Jack's imagination was running as fast as his legs were. The village charley was an Old Bragg from the 28th Foot and had fought with Wolfe at Quebec. Jack remembered how the old man had kept him enthralled as a boy with the story, often re-told, of how the regiment had been in the van of the ascent of the Heights of Abraham, before the battle, and how he had seen Wolfe fall. The youngest general in the army, he had said. What in God's name was he doing with Mary?

The lane was awash with water as Jack took his horse at a fast canter to the village and the vicarage. He had not ridden so fast since that first day on the common when they had watched the sun slide down over the Forest of Dean and the Severn.

The lamps were alight in in the windows of the vicarage as he slowed to a stop at the door, and Eliza Clutterbuck limped out at the sound of hooves on the drive. Jack saw tears on her cheeks and jumped down, running as soon as his feet touched the ground.

'Where is she?' he demanded. 'What happened here tonight? Tell me now!'

'Oh, sir, she be taken to the lock-up in Stroud. The vicar says he caught her stealing some books, sir. Says he found them in her room, sir. He was mighty drunk, Master Jack. Been drinkin' hard all evenin', he was, and Lord he was howlin' and shoutin' and throwin' things about,' Eliza Clutterbuck sobbed.

Jack was no longer listening, but already mounting and pulling Barley round so hard the animal cried with the pain of the bit. He galloped down to the Bath Road, almost causing the animal to fall.

'Come on, my friend, we must cover the road quickly.'

He urged the horse on, turning north into the driving rain that lanced into his face. The black sky was already lightening to grey to his right as he rode on, his mind racing with fear and foreboding. Even as he galloped, his mind reflected on the boy. Thinking of his young face, he now realised that there had been something unsaid, some signal, a subtle warning perhaps. Now he understood what had happened tonight. Anger arose in him, welling up in his throat so that he roared aloud, the wind of his ride pulling the sound from his open mouth. Hooves splashed water as Jack drove the animal harder, galloping through the growing rain, spattering mud. His muscles tightened and he leaned further forward, knees clenching the horse's back more tightly, cold rain lancing his face, his eyes, his neck.

He passed through another village, noticed a pair of weavers walking slowly across the green. They stared as he galloped by, but he did not care. His brain rapidly measured the time already elapsed since she had been taken, praying that he would reach Stroud quickly.

He saw the gloomy outline of Dudbridge Mill approach on his left as he dug harder with his heels. A fallen tree blocked his path and he hauled the animal over it, and then the image turned over as his body flew over the head of Barley and his back hit the ground, expelling the air from his lungs.

There was only darkness.

Chapter 12

A Crime

In the carriage, Mary shook with cold and fear and growing anger. Her feet, she realised, were tightly bound with a cord, and her left wrist strapped by a leather belt to the hand of the thief-taker Barnwood had handed her over to in Stroud. He had stayed behind, seeking the magistrate, giving harsh instructions to Dick Cahill to stop for nothing, and to see she was taken to Gloucester gaol as fast as could be managed.

Her head hurt and a large purple mark had appeared on her cheek where Barnwood's fist had hit her. A dribble of drying blood remained on her chin and there was a sharp pain in her left side, which caused her to wince with every movement. Her right eye was closed and swollen and pain pierced her head. She felt so very cold. Her only hope was that Eliza had been able to get a message to Jack. She needed him now. He had become the most important person in her life, and she ached to see him. *Pray God he comes soon*, she thought.

The carriage crawled up Painswick Hill, sliding sidelong in the mud as the horses strained against the driving rain, nostrils flared and hooves scrabbling for footholds. The thief-taker leaned out to shout at the coachman, some obscenity that Mary only half heard. It was getting light now and she could see the face of her escort. He had a clean scar running down the right side of his face, starting where his eye should have been. The man grinned at her, enjoying every feature of her dishevelled and bruised body. She looked away, feeling nausea rise in her throat. The journey seemed to be but the present part of some dreadful continuing nightmare.

The evening before had passed in much the usual routine. She had served dinner as normal to the vicar and his guest. His guest had been Mister Philp, owner of the butcher's shop in the next village. They had both been drinking quite hard, before and during the meal, and afterwards had played cards.

Mary had been in the kitchen with Eliza Clutterbuck, sewing a new shirt from some material given to her by her mother. She was making it for Jack, although she had worried that it would be of inferior quality to those he usually wore.

Eliza had retired to bed at about 10 o'clock, just after Mary had taken another bottle of Madeira in to the vicar and his friend. Both men had been loud and red-eyed, the vicar gazing at Mary with ill-concealed lasciviousness. She had hurried from the room.

She put the sewing aside and started reading a book borrowed from Jack's father. It was an absorbing tale of nonsense by someone she had not heard of, Jonathan Swift, and the story of a land of very small people. She became entranced by the story and oblivious to the laughing voices of her employer and his guest.

Shortly before the long-case clock in the hall chimed midnight, she climbed wearily up the stairs to her small, uncarpeted attic room, undressed quickly, changed into a heavy cotton nightgown and blew out the candle. As she settled into her bed, she was aware of voices on the drive at the front of the house and the sound of a horse walking out into the lane. She drifted away into a confused dream in which Jack appeared as Gulliver and she as the Emperor.

But then Jack's face mutated, the thick dark hair replaced by thin and grey wisps over a balding pate, his youthful, smiling face now old and blotched; it was grotesque, twisted, leering, with enlarged watery eyes and smelled of alcohol.

The face of the dream spoke to her: 'Now, my precious Mary, 'tis time to reward your benefactor for all his kindness to you.'

The voice and the face were real. She suddenly felt very afraid. He was leaning over her, his breath short and fast. She tried to rise but her shoulders were held down, the coarse woollen blanket thrown over her head and hands fumbled with her nightgown. She struggled but the blanket entangled her like a fish in a net. He fell onto her and she screamed, her voice muffled in the folds of the blanket. Hands pulled at her gown, a knee forced her legs apart. His fingers found her intimate place, and quickly he thrust himself, his hardness probing and pushing. Writhing and wriggling against his weight failed and earned her a sharp slap on her hip. She gagged, her tongue filling her mouth, the revulsion bringing bile to her throat, and she vomited into the blanket. The thrusting pierced her, she sobbed, terror constricting her vocal chords.

He shuddered and coughed, a rasping spluttering drunken cough, as his organ exploded within her, and she seized a half chance to free herself. Struggling now like a cornered animal, she kicked with her knee, catching his loins and leaving him gasping with intense pain. They fell together onto the floor and her hand felt for some other means with which to defend herself, finding the night pail. It was in her hand and she swung it—the heavy porcelain struck the side of his face, the contents splashed them both. He roared with pain and then she too felt pain as his fist hit her hard in the face. She clawed at his face, reaching for his eyes. Another pain in her side as his fist struck her ribs. He struggled to his feet, clutching the side of his face.

'You whore,' he spat at her, 'you filthy whore. My head is broken!'

She pulled at his ankles and he fell back. It had to end, and she clambered up, grasping the chair as a stab of pain, like a knife in her ribs, made her stop. Then she saw the door and ran, ignoring the pain. A scream of abuse followed her and the pail clattered against the wall as he followed.

Eliza Clutterbuck's bedroom door was ajar, and she stood, open mouthed, with an oil lamp in her left hand. Mary noticed this as she cried, 'Help me, please, help! He's mad, he's mad!'

He was behind her, screaming at Eliza, and she fled down the darkened stairs. She reached the door, but he was on her before she could withdraw the bolts. He pulled at her hair, spinning her round, and slapped her hard across the face. She kicked at him and fingernails scratched at his face. He let go, howling with rage. The door to the scullery was open and she ran. Clutterbuck was calling to someone and Mary screamed again for help: 'Jack, please get Jack, please!' She was sobbing now and again he reached her. Some plates were on the table and she threw one at him, others scattering to the floor, adding to the noise.

'Harlot... whore, you daughter of Satan,' he hissed at her. 'I will have you.' His hands reached her and she clawed at his face once more, but his hands grasped her wrists and stopped her. There was mist in her eyes and salt that stung. His fist hit her again and she fell, her head striking the cold, stone floor.

When she awoke, there were voices. She did not recognize them and could not understand the words. A woman was crying somewhere and she realized it was Eliza Clutterbuck. A voice said something about feet and she felt a cord tighten about her ankles. There was the sound of iron scraping on stone and her hands were pulled tightly together. Her brain started to work and she thought it best not to move. The crying continued.

Rough hands lifted her and carried her on the shoulder of the strange voice. 'Leave her to me, Vicar. I knows wots to do,' the coarse voice said.

Then she was out in the cold, wet night and dropped into a carriage. The force pushed the air from her lungs, and pain destroyed resistance. She could smell a horse and heard its hooves. The iron-rimmed wheels moved and it was out in the lane, another horse following behind. She fell into a dark pit of silence, free of pain.

First Fleet

*****

Jack was aching in every bone and wet through. He looked hard as blackened beams came slowly into focus.

'He's coming to.' A voice he recognized. 'Jack, lad, it is I, Giles. You were thrown from your horse and we thought you were gone. Can you hear me?'

His eyes swam as tears covered his pupils; he saw clouds. 'Yes. My God, where am I?' he murmured, his head and sight slowly clearing the pain and mist. He sat up and saw that he was in a small, dimly lit room, a weaver's cottage, with a frightened old man looking at him. Doctor Steele was there beside him.

'You seem to have nothing broken, young man, as far as I can tell, but you have given us all quite a fright, I can tell you.'

'Mary... I was on my way to Mary. What time is it?' He fumbled in his jerkin for his fob watch but could not find it.

'Nearly noon, old chap,' Giles spoke softly. 'She is gone to Gloucester and your father is away to talk to the magistrate. He is very concerned and I am to send word as soon as ever I can as to your condition.' He turned to speak to a trooper at the door. 'Martin, go now—find Mister Vizzard, and report that he is well and we will follow shortly.'

'I must be gone. She is in trouble, Giles.'

'We know all, Jack. Neave was very troubled and woke your father. He questioned young Tom quite severely, scared the poor lad out of his wits, and then sent Neave to find me. We found you on the road and brought you in here.'

'Then I must go to her. She will have need of me now.' Jack moved from the rough horsehair mattress that he was lying on. He hurt but could walk. He sat for several moments, gathering strength. 'Come with me, please, Giles. I fancy I will have need of your help.' He accepted the flask proffered and drank fully, the spirit burning in his throat. He coughed.

With a mumbled word of thanks to the weaver and his wife he left the cottage and mounted the horse that Neave had ridden; the two set off for Gloucester. Jack was deeply troubled. There was business to settle with the vicar but that would have to wait until he had heard Mary's story. Of her innocence, he was in no doubt. What had happened that night he suspected, but of Mary's perilous situation he was already certain. The gaol at Gloucester was not a place a gentle person could view with anything but fear. And Mary was a gentle person. Sweet Jesus, what had gone wrong? Jack kicked his heels and pushed the horse harder. His back and head ached.

Giles copied him, understanding his friend's need for greater speed, but keeping an eye on him just the same. He had talked to Clutterbuck and had wondered how to tell Jack of what he had learned. He decided that it would be best to hear Mary's account, but then he would have to stay close to Jack. His friend would like as not take a whip to his uncle and that would cause more problems than it would solve. If all he had heard was true, he would do the same, he thought.

Jack and Giles arrived at Gloucester some hours later, entering the city through the South Gate, horses spattered with mud and tired after the hard ride. They rode to the castle by the Severn, and entered the gaol. Leaving their horses with a stable-boy, they quickly made for the keeper, finding him in the castle tower, his corpulent form bent over a worn table, checking a list by the light of two oil lamps. 'I be mighty sorry, gents, but I 'as me orders. The prisoner is bein' seen by a lawyer now and I can't go lettin' any more folk in.' The man was proving to be obstructive. He had dealt with several 'toffs' before and was not a man easily swayed from his duty by pleas or threats.

'For God's sake, man, the lawyer is my father and the prisoner is my friend—how many times must I say it?' Jack was losing patience fast and Giles interrupted, his authority taking charge. 'Leave this to me, old chap.'

Jack moved aside, breathing hard to control his anger, and did not see the transaction between Giles and the guard, who very quickly, with a practised hand, pocketed some silver coins.

Giles led the way down the worn stone steps that were damp and cold. They heard voices and entered a small room on the left side of a tenebrous corridor.

'Oh, Jack, Jack!' Mary could say no more but rushed to him and buried her head in his chest, sobbing, her fragile control evaporating at the sight of him. He held her tightly, making reassuring sounds that he felt to be inadequate. He guided her back to the chair, his arm about her shoulder, as his father rose and placed a gentle hand on his son's arm, taking him aside.

'It is a bad business, my boy, very bad indeed, and will require all my skill to obtain her release, if indeed that be possible. Giles, would you please stay a moment with Mary? Jack and I have to talk to the keeper.' Henry gave Giles a knowing look and escorted Jack from the room to the comparative privacy of the corridor.

'The vicar tried to force himself on her, my boy. It is as simple or as complicated as that. He will give some story that she stole some of his books, but the reality is that he tried to rape her, and she fought him.' Henry held his son's shoulders, could feel him shaking, saw the fire in his eyes, as his anger flared. 'I can scarce believe it, but I am in no doubt but that Mary speaks the truth.' He held his son's eyes, willing him to take control of his anger. 'You must be strong, for her sake, Jack. She is hurt—not badly,' he added quickly, 'and very frightened. She fears she will not be believed and that the vicar, a man of the Church, will be preferred to a servant girl.' He looked back over his shoulder. 'I have called for a physician to examine her. Her eye will need some attention and I suspect a rib is broken.'

Jack brought himself under control and said with feeling, 'I will have the bastard's black heart, father. I swear it.' Jack resolved that moment that he would deal with the reverend Barnwood and answer to God himself if need be. First, however, he must see to Mary.

They returned to the small room where Giles and a guard were glaring at each other in silent animosity. Mary sat on the chair, her head resting in her hands, tears still on her bruised face. He went to her and crouched before her.

'Father has spoken to the magistrate and we will see that this business is dealt with speedily so we can bring you home. Is there anything you need now?' Jack's voice trembled but he displayed more confidence than he felt.

'Oh, my sweet Jack, I am lost, can you not see? He will have me rot here, I know. You must help me, please.' She implored him, her eyes begging him to take her with him. She held him very tight; he kissed her and turned away, before she could see his pain.

Chapter 13
The Trial

'If it please your Lordship, I will call Elizabeth Clutter-buck.' Jack looked to the dock and smiled to give Mary some encouragement, but saw that she was in despair.

Henry had used all the influence at his disposal to bring Mary's trial to court as quickly as possible, but still two months had passed. The trial was not going well. Given earlier in the day, Barnwood's evidence was avidly accepted by this judge, Mister Justice Paul, without demur. It had become quite plain to Jack that the judge, newly appointed to the western circuit, was biased. The prosecutor had been allowed more latitude than any counsel should. Henry had challenged several matters during the vicar's examination in chief, and each time his protests had been dismissed.

His father had cross-examined Barnwood, although Jack had pressed him to allow him to have that particular pleasure. Henry was equally adamant that to do so would not be in Mary's interests. Jack was too closely involved, he said, and would not remain calm or dispassionate. He would incur the court's displeasure, he said.

With reluctance, Jack admitted the wisdom of his father's words. As Barnwood coldly but confidently gave his version of the incident, suitably embellished with some fiction of his own, Jack had angrily shot to his feet to accuse the clergyman of perjury, immediately incurring a severe reprimand from the judge and warned that he would be barred from the court in the event of any further outburst. It had not helped Mary's case, and the knowledge of that caused him a good deal of anxiety.

He was on safer ground with an examination in chief of a defense witness. The clergyman was plausible, a credible witness and Henry made no ground in discrediting his account. Even the scratches on the man's face had been explained away to the judge's satisfaction.

Elizabeth Clutterbuck hobbled into the court, looking old and very troubled. She had aged considerably in the two months since the night her employer had raped Mary. Her grandson, Tom, held her arm as she climbed the steps to the dock, glancing towards Jack, who avoided any recognition. Murmuring in the public gallery grew with anticipation, until silenced by the hammering of the judge's gavel. Beneath his full-bottomed wig, he glowered with anger at the gallery.

Several villagers had found places on the benches, but it was mostly townspeople with a morbid interest in the prospect of a capital punishment who occupied the forward positions, leaning over the rail, the better to hear the proceedings.

Jack leaned forward, hands spread on the bench, and dealt as quickly as he could with the preliminaries, moving to the matter of the assault itself more slowly and with some care, as Clutterbuck's face wore an anxious frown.

'Now, Mistress Clutterbuck, please tell his lordship what it was that first alerted you to the assault that was taking place in...' The question went unfinished as the prosecutor interrupted.

'My Lord, I hesitate to interrupt the proceedings, but I really must protest most strongly at my learned friend's terminology.'

Charles Willoughby was not such a fool as to let that pass without objection and Mister Justice Paul was pleased to have the chance to take this cocky young man down a peg.

'Quite right, Mister Willoughby, quite right, sir. This is the last time I will tolerate your insolence, Mister Vizzard. When you have a little more experience, you will understand that I do not permit unprofessional behaviour from members of the bar. You are aware of the rules of evidence, are you not? Any further disrespect, sir, and I will have you leave my court.'

This judge was determined to see the girl in the dock convicted. Jack could almost smell the bigotry emanating from the bench. He seethed silently.

Justice Oswald Paul glared back at him, then turned his gaze on the girl in the dock. He could see the type of girl she was. Quite obviously a temptress, a provocative type, he thought. No humility was apparent in that face, no remorse, no contrition but only false tears. A damned actress.

The reverend Barnwood was a known friend of the Dean, and the Dean of Gloucester, Josiah Tucker, was a man of influence, not only in the county, but also at court. He was acquainted with the Chancellor, Lord Loughborough. Oswald

Paul had ambition and was not inclined to offend such a personage. He looked at Mary, his eyes narrowing. *The girl is obviously guilty, and what is this young upstart doing wasting my time with this case?* he wondered. *There can be no defense to such obvious crime.*

Biting his tongue, Jack continued. 'As it may please your Lordship. Your lordship is correct, and I am in error, as your Lordship often is,' he said, the sarcasm passing unnoticed, except by his father, who smiled at the floor.

Turning to the witness, Jack resumed the examination. 'Please tell the court what it was that first alerted you to some disturbance, Mistress Clutterbuck.'

'Well, sir, it's as the reverend says, sir. I hears this big commotion, see, and when I comes out of me room there's Mary George screamin' and yellin' like a thing possessed.' Her eyes blinked in rapid succession. 'I ain't never seen 'er like that afore, sir. But I can't says what happened.' Eliza looked at her feet.

'I will leave for the moment the question of how you come to know Mister Barnwood's evidence; he is of course your employer.' He paused briefly. 'But the books that the defendant is accused of stealing, you are aware that they do not belong to your employer?' Jack wanted to shout at her. He controlled himself with difficulty.

'As I says, sir, I don't know nothin' about no books. The vicar, sir... well, he has a heap of books in the library, an' I always been most careful with 'em, sir. I dunno know what books he got. I can't read, y'see.' Eliza Clutterbuck fiddled with her hands, looking nervously at Barnwood and back to Jack.

'Her case, the defendant's case, Mistress Clutterbuck, is that she borrowed those books, not from *Mister* Barnwood but from a friend. You know that much at least, do you not?' Jack was not going to dignify his enemy by using his clerical title. And Barnwood was his enemy, as assuredly as if he had a drawn sword or a musket in his hand.

'As I says, sir, I knows nothin' about any books.'

She had told you the week before she had borrowed some books, I believe. Do you not recall?'

No, sir. I know nothing about any books.'

He looked coldly, disbelievingly at the old lady, suspicion rising in his brain. 'Mistress Clutterbuck, your employer had been drinking heavily that evening, had he not?'

'Well, sir, the reverend likes a drop of wine with 'is dinner, but he weren't drunk, far as I knows.'

Jack stared hard at Barnwood across the courtroom. The bastard has bribed her, he thought. That, or he has threatened the old woman. She is lying for him. The man avoided his look and Jack felt his anger rise in his chest again. He looked at a sheet of paper in the brief, breathing steadily to retain control. He decided to change his questioning.

'You left your room because you heard some commotion, a disturbance of some kind? Is that correct?

'Yes, sir.'

'The defendant was running from her room along the hall, in some distress, would you agree?

'Well, like I said, she was howlin' a good deal.'

'Did you not hear Mistress George call on you to help, saying, "Help, please help, he's mad, he's mad", and Barnwood calling her a "whore, a daughter of Satan"? You did hear that, did you not? Have in mind your solemn oath to tell the truth now.'

'She was cryin' and shouting somethin', sir, but I didn't hear what. She might 'ave sworn at 'im, sir.' Eliza Clutterbuck was now looking very frightened, and there were mutterings from the public gallery with a shout of 'Shame on you, Eliza Clutterbuck!'

Barnwood looked towards Jack, a thinly disguised smile of triumph on his lips.

The judge struck the bench with his gavel. 'Silence! I will have silence in my court! You may continue, Mister Vizzard, if you feel the effort worthy of it.'

Jack ignored the jibe and turned to the witness.

'Mistress Clutterbuck, I must press you on this. Did you not believe that Mistress George was in distress and in need of your help? For what did you think she needed you at that hour? To help with some baking?'

There was some laughter in the public gallery that Jack had not intended.

'I have heard enough, Mister Vizzard,' the judge interrupted. 'Now you are browbeating your own witness, and I will not permit this comedic questioning any longer. You will sit down, sir... sit down, and Mister Willoughby may cross-examine if he chooses, although I doubt that to be necessary. Mister Willoughby?' The judge leaned back in his chair, with an imperious countenance.

'But my Lord, I must insist.'

'You will insist on nothing, Mister Vizzard. Sit down, sir. I will not hear from you again.'

His face flushed with growing anger, Jack sat, throwing the brief at his father in petulance.

'Be silent, my boy. You cannot help her in this court.' His father cautioned him, a troubled look on his face.

The prosecutor, Charles Willoughby, rose to his feet slowly, hands resting on his hips, a shallow, insincere and patronising smile on his face, as he turned to the witness.

'My dear Mistress Clutterbuck, in essence your evidence to my lord's court is that you were aware of some commotion, you heard the defendant shouting and swearing obscenities at the vicar, throwing something and your employer trying to restrain the defendant, but know nothing of the books that she had in her room...'

Jack jumped to his feet. 'My Lord, I must strongly call upon your Lordship to admonish my learned friend for his last remark. He implies...'

'Sit down, Mister Vizzard. I will decide who and when to admonish, and if I hear from you again, I will hold you in contempt. Now be seated, sir, at once!'

Jack remained standing and glared at the judge belligerently. His brain goaded him to swear at this judge, to shout at the arrogant old man in red gown and full wig, to denounce his partiality, to declare to the room the innocence of the prisoner. Instead, he turned and, without bowing, strode from the court, throwing his wig down, his gown trailing in his wake. The judge's command to return he ignored. Faces turned to him, but he saw them through a blur of fury. The heavy door slammed loudly behind him. He needed to breathe clean fresh air and think.

Turning a corner, he found himself in Westgate and the cold hit him like a hammer. Carts and carriages passed by, and flurries of snow, churned by a cold easterly wind, swirled about his head. Townspeople, busy with their own lives, walked by hurriedly, heads down, intent on their business, unfeeling, uncaring.

Jack stood looking down towards the River Severn lying beyond the Cathedral, grey and murky in the dying sun of a cold winter's day. He wondered at the insupportable scene he had just witnessed, of which he had been a part, and knew, understood, that he could not continue. The majestic equality of the law! *Hah*, he thought, *what justice is it that permits this? People crushed by law have no hope but from power, and if the law is their enemy, they will become enemies to the law.* Now he saw with his own eyes, had been an integral part. *Well, no more. I have made the right decision.*

He walked briskly into the snow, his head low and his heart lower. His shoulders pushed townspeople aside, oblivious and heedless of their oaths and curses. He ducked into the courtyard of the New Inn. Pulling open the door he summoned the innkeeper, and took a seat in a gloomy corner, feeling miserable, and stared into the glow of the fire burning slowly in the grate. An hour or more passed by; a glass of mulled wine stood on the table, still unfinished.

'Well, my friend,'—Giles was at his shoulder, breathless from his search of the town—'tell me, how do you intend to help her from here?' He sat heavily in front of his friend, his expression a mix of relief and concern. Concern because of the anger that burned in Jack's eyes, like the coals of a fire.

'The bastard, Giles. The bishop is in that bastard's pocket. You heard him. I was never to be permitted to defend her. He means to send her down, or worse—you must see that. What can I do for her now?' Jack was in torment. 'Barnwood has bribed the housekeeper, or threatened her. She perjured herself today, Giles. There can be little doubt of it.'

'You can go back and fight. 'Tis not like you to give up on a fight. Here, take a mouthful.' Jack shook his head. 'Christ on the Cross, it is damned cold.' Giles produced a small silver flask from beneath his cloak and drank fully, feeling the fire of the spirit as it travelled into his stomach. His ears were so cold he felt they would break if he rubbed them.

Jack first sipped on his wine, then he drained the glass. Taking the flask from his friend he took a mouthful. The brandy made his head reel.

'I will kill him for this, Giles. I swear I will. Did you see his smug, corrupt, rotten face? It is he that should be in the dock, not her. Not Mary.'

'Come back with me. Let us see what may be done. Mary has given evidence, and I believe did well. She was very brave.' Giles omitted to volunteer the opinion that she would have performed better had Jack been present to provide some support. 'Regrettably, the prosecutor simply dismissed her account as a "lurid fiction of fancy by a young servant"!' Giles looked despondent, embarrassed. 'I am ashamed that a relative of mine... He—your father is addressing the jury. Perhaps he can sway them.' Giles tried vainly to offer his friend some hope.

'Oh, Christ, Giles, she is gone. He has won. His bloody lordship will see to that.'

CHAPTER 14
THE MURDER

Giles lost sight of Jack on the Stroud road. He thought he saw a solitary horseman heading up to Painswick Beacon, but could not even be sure that it was a rider. It might have been a mere shadow; he was not at all sure that it was Jack. He took that path, but although he searched the area until it was nearly dark, he could find no trace of Jack. The air was cooling and he decided to ride on to Woodchester in the hope of finding him there. Turning his horse, he rode south towards Stroud.

The breeze was rising, more apparent on this, the highest point of Gloucestershire, and Jack pulled his tricorn hat down more tightly on his head as he watched his friend from the security of the dense copse. *Not tonight, old friend,* he thought. *You will not see me tonight, nor, I suspect, for a very long time, for I have urgent business of which you cannot be part—must not be a part.*

He waited another five minutes and left the beacon, taking the path along the higher ground through Pitchcombe. *I have little need to return home tonight, but perhaps I must collect some clothes, personal papers, and some books. And I should see father.* A shiver rippled along his spine at the thought of that conversation. *Then I must be gone because she is lost to me now. Yesterday is lost, and what of the morrow?* He had failed and could do no more for her. Now he must try to forget that which could never be, and move on, take up his new life and forget. Except for one thing. He would ensure that Barnwood never ruined another life.

He rode quietly across the fields towards the village and tied his horse to a tree in the meadow, disturbing the sheep there, walking the rest of the way to the rear of the vicarage and the orchard, keeping close to the hedges, bare now in the cold of autumn. He heard the rumble of carriage wheels and a horse clattering to a halt by the front porch, and the sound of Barnwood talking. His voice was loud, thick and slurred, and Jack could not make out his words. Then he realized that he was talking to Eliza Clutterbuck.

He climbed the apple tree at the rear of the orchard, smiling wryly at the memory of that tree. He settled as comfortably as he could in the bare branches, pulling his cloak closely about him, and prepared to wait. He chewed silently on an apple, suddenly feeling hunger. An hour passed, and he observed Eliza in the kitchen, preparing an early supper, no doubt for Barnwood. His limbs started to ache and he carefully and very slowly stretched his legs, then his arms. As the moon climbed higher, it threw a silver sheet across the wet roof, offering him light to observe. He again heard the sound of the carriage moving out from the vicarage and, for a few moments, panic hit him. Was Barnwood leaving?

As he wondered what he should do, his quarry appeared, briefly, in the kitchen. Jack did not move, and slowed his breathing, although he knew he was sufficiently distant to escape detection. He could not see Eliza, and reasoned that she must have left for some purpose unknown. That must have been her leaving in the carriage, he decided. *Good. No obstacles or witnesses, then*, he thought.

He continued to wait until all the rooms, bar one, had darkened. An owl hooted from the old barn, adjacent to the vicarage. The wind ruffled the trees, and tossed the leaves, spiralling them into the night sky. Smoke whirled about the chimneystack, and he watched the smoke until it slowly dissipated. He thought about Mary, and what had become of her because of the animal inside the old house.

Once again, he pulled the half hunter from his waistcoat pocket and gleaned that it was not yet midnight. Candles still burned in one room, above and to the left of the kitchen. He saw the silhouette of his prey against the curtained window and without a sound he dropped from the tree. Crouching low by the wall, he moved quickly and silently to the house.

The window to the scullery was just ajar, propped open with a bar, and with a good deal of effort Jack forced his way through it.

A cat lay curled on the floor by the still-warm hearth as he crept past, its luminescent green eyes following Jack's stealthy progress through the kitchen. In the hall he paused, hairs on his neck rising, as he thought he detected another's presence. He held back his breath for several moments, motionless, his ears straining. Dismissing his fears, he moved as silently as the cat up the stairs until he was in the hallway on the first floor. He stood still, listening.

The flicker of candlelight shone beneath a door further along the corridor, facing the rear of the vicarage. He moved quietly but deliberately until he was outside Barnwood's room. The door moved under a gentle push, and he saw a candle spluttering in its holder. A large holdall was by the bed and he realized that he was almost too late. The vicar was packing.

As Jack moved into the room he saw that Barnwood was on his bed, his back to the door, with papers, clothes and small purses spread about him. The vicar's face became pale and his eyes widened as he half turned at the sound of a footfall. 'You!'

It was the last word he uttered. Jack strode quickly to the bed, one hand tight on the cleric's throat to silence any sound, pushing him down as he turned the pillow over onto his bulging eyes. He knelt on the man's chest and held him firmly for a very long time. A low gurgling noise slipped from his mouth, bubbles forming between his lips, as Jack's hand increased its pressure. The struggles were strong at first but slowly subsided, then ceased altogether, and Jack gradually released the pressure until he was certain.

Removing the pillow, his breath heavy with exertion, he stared at his enemy, stared into those bloodshot, bulging, evil red eyes. He closed them with his thumb, returned the pillow to its place and picked up some of the papers. He opened the bag and saw some books; they were his books. Thinking for a moment, he decided to leave them.

He breathed out slowly, feeling sick but empty. He did not regret his actions. The man had lost the right to live and preach to people. He had raped for the last time. His evidence, the flagrant perjury, had condemned Mary to effectively a life sentence of banishment, even death. His rape of Mary had been his own death sentence. Jack had decided that, had made the decision that night, during his wild ride to Stroud.

He placed the bedcover over the corpse, and placed the bag on the floor beside the bed. Glancing through the assortment of papers, he paused at one. Reading it quickly, he placed it in his coat pocket. The remainder he put in the bag, closing the strap. He looked around, then, with a sudden movement, he blew out the candle and walked from the room, silently closing the door.

Reaching the bottom of the stairs, he was suddenly aware of the form of someone else. His neck again bristled in alarm, and he reached for his pistol.

'Have yous done for 'im, sir?' Tom Clutterbuck was standing in the shadow of the stairs.

'Bloody hell, lad, you startled me.' Jack's heart was pounding such that he was sure it could be heard.

'Well, have yous, then?' the boy repeated.

'He died in his sleep, Tom. You believe that, don't you?' Jack was not used to lying, but he was even less used to committing murder, he thought.

The boy sniffed with derision, his disbelief plain. 'I don't care, sir. He was a bad 'un, right enough, wicked through an' through, sir. I was sleeping when I heard yous coming through the scullery. Wot yous goin' to do now, though?' The boy was calmer than Jack felt.

'I must go away. There is nothing for me here now. I will go far away. Tonight, tomorrow morning at the latest.' He had made that decision already, but now it was imperative. *Murderer*, he thought. *Sweet Jesus. Now there is a witness.*

'Then I must come wiv you. I can help, sir.'

Jack dismissed the suggestion immediately. 'There is no question of that, lad. Where I am going will be hard, and not for the faint-hearted. Thank you for your offer, but you never saw me here, is that understood?'

'Oh, I understands, all right, but yous be wrong, sir. I can he_p. I can't stay here, not now. Takes me with you sir, please,' Tom pleaded earnestly.

He thought a moment more. If the boy were questioned, as he must be, would he keep his mouth closed? Eventually he would talk. *I could not kill him, not even in anger.* A murderer he was, but never a butcher of innocents. Perhaps the lad could be useful. At least he would be unable to answer awkward questions. He was the only witness, or at least the only one with knowledge that could convict Jack of murder.

'Meet me on the Bath Road at Nailsworth at nine o'clock; bring a horse, but not Barnwood's. If you are not there, I shall not wait.'

'Thank yous, sir, thank you. You'll not regret it, I swear.'

Jack left the vicarage by the kitchen door, and walked Humbert through the fields to Lampern House. The house was quiet, asleep, as he heard the clock in the hall chime the hour. Closing the door to his room, he lit a candle and searched his wardrobe for suitable, necessary clothes. A par-ce_ of books he placed in a bag; some personal papers he wrapped in a canvas case. The box in the wardrobe held cash, and he emptied that into another leather bag.

Glancing about the room, he collected a straightedge razor and lathering brush, a hairbrush, comb and a small pair of scissors. He paused at the door to his father's room. Guilt stabbed at his heart. He carried the candle downstairs, and hesitated in the dining room. He added some items from the sideboard then moved through to the kitchen.

From a strongbox, he collected his sword, regularly cleaned and sharpened by Neave. Quickly placing a loaf, some cheese and a bottle of port wine into his holdall, he squatted down and patted Ralph gently on the head. The dog rolled onto his back. 'Take care, old friend. I will miss you.' He whispered croakily, and left by the rear door. He did not look back.

*****

Bill Brice was asleep in a chair by the inglenook, when he heard a staccato of taps on the window. Ever alert to un-common sounds, he was instantly awake. Grasping the pistol he usually kept below the bar, he moved to the side of the window at the rear of the inn. Waiting, he heard it again. No mistake, he thought. Peering through a gap in the faded cur-tain, he was astonished to see Jack's stern face. Moving to the door, he quickly unbolted it.

'Do you know what time it is?' He spoke gruffly, while reaching for a lantern.

Moving quickly, Jack stepped inside and waved his hand.

'Please do not light that, my friend. I have great need of your help this night.' Brice closed and bolted the door.

'Now what's all this about, then?' he asked. Jack's face glowed by the embers in the fire. Brice could see instantly that his young friend was in some trouble.

'Bill, I need a bed for the night, where I have not been seen. Do you understand? I cannot return to Lampern, and will be away early in the morning. You must ask no questions of me, for I cannot offer any explanation to you.'

Brice looked hard at him for a long time. His inclination was to ask a question. Several questions. He elected not to.

'I have guests in the house tonight. You can sleep in the log shed. 'Tis dry, and you'll not freeze in there. I never saw you tonight. Do you need anything?'

'Thank you, old friend. I will not forget this. No, I have everything I need now.'

Brice led him to the shed and closed the door behind him. He returned to his chair by the fire, but further sleep eluded him.

He stared at the embers for a very long time.

*****

Jack's father was in his rooms early. Jack had known he would be, because it was market day in town and the Town Council was meeting in the George Inn later that morning. Henry Vizzard was a member of that council and had a number of matters to discuss.

'Sit down, my boy, what's to do?'

Jack struggled with his thoughts and decided that he could only come straight to the point. 'I have to leave, Father. I have taken the King's Commission and I leave this morning. I am here to say farewell. I am truly sorry, but I must go. I am so sorry.'

Henry listened to these words with disbelief. His face reddened and he exploded. 'You have done what, sir? I'll not have it, by God. Damn it, I will not, Jack. One son to the king is enough; I will not lose another!'

Chapter 15
Departure

The boy was waiting by the old signpost at the crossroads on the Bath Road at Nailsworth when Jack arrived at a quarter past nine o'clock. Tom was holding the reins of a young horse that looked too large for him. A small sack was by his feet, containing all he possessed in the world. His eyes were red, tears having left tracks on his face. People passing by took no notice. He was just another street urchin, the responsibility of no one. His clothes, though old, were clean and tidy. A leather waistcoat covered a plain white shirt, tucked into darkly stained pigskin breeches, and a long, black woollen overcoat hung loosely from his narrow shoulders. His fair hair—usually untidy because of a double crown—was brushed, but was also in need of trimming, with a widow's peak curling down his forehead into his eyes.

His young face registered his relief and broke into a broad grin at Jack's approach. 'Mornin', Mister Vizzard, sir. I am ready, as you can see. Thought you might 'ave changed your mind and taken a diff'rent road.'

Tom was fourteen years old, rising fifteen, and had been raised and cared for by his grandmother, Eliza Clutterbuck, his own mother having died when he was only five years old. He had never known a father.

'Well, young 'un, I see that indeed you are, and do you know where we are bound? Jack had told him nothing of his plans last night. He searched for doubt in the boy's face and saw none.

'No, sir, but I knows it will be an adventure, and there is nuffin' to keep me in the valleys now. I knows I can trust you, sir, and that you'll teach me things.'

'We are going to sea, Tom. I am to become an officer, a Marine officer, and we are away this morning to Portsmouth. You will be my servant and will join the Corps as a drummer. I know they are looking to recruit young lads. We will see the world, Tom, and it will be a very long time before we see Stroud again.'

'I knew it 'ad to be somethin' like it, after what happened. Where is Portsmouth, sir, and how long will it take us to get there?'

'It is in the county of Hampshire, Tom. On the south coast. It is an important naval port, probably the biggest in England. The Marines are there, and also in Plymouth, and in Chatham. Have you heard of those places, Tom?

The boy shook his head. 'No, sir. I been to Stroud, and Gloucester too, but never been to Bristol, and that's a big place far away from 'ere.'

'Well, Portsmouth is much further than that. We have a long journey, my lad. I reckon on four or five days, perhaps longer.'

Tom pondered that for a moment, before speaking again. 'What will become of Mistress Mary, sir, if I may ask?'

'Ah now, Tom, I really do not wish to talk of her, for she is lost to me for sure. I have nothing to offer her now, even if she were free. We must be going, so follow me.'

He looked about, almost furtively, but trying hard to appear a carefree gentleman at leisure. His thoughts turned to his father, and the tearful parting, the trembling figure that sagged in his chair. He felt wretched and anguished. Outwardly, he showed calm and confidence.

They rode on through the day, with Jack mostly silent, until they approached Bath in the evening, there finding rooms at a tavern on the Warminster road. They attracted scant attention from the publican, the inn being a popular resting place with travellers, and there were several that night. A foppish young naval officer attempted to engage Jack in conversation, but abandoned the effort when he proved taciturn. He did not sleep well, even after a satisfying meal of roasted pork, batter pudding, cabbage and potatoes, washed down with several tankards of ale, all consumed with the hunger of a man who has spent the day in the saddle, with no more sustenance than fresh air and dark thoughts.

Tom proved to be an agreeable companion. He kept up an almost continuous flow of stories, some concerning people Jack knew, keeping him amused and diverted. He was mature for his years and the more he talked, the more confident he became. Once he almost spoke about Barnwood, and then became quiet before changing tack, speaking instead of experiences more pleasant.

The boy had worked at the vicarage, helping his grandmother, and at Dick Caldwell's farm. He'd tended the vegetable garden, and knew how to milk cows. However, he had no prospect of learning a trade. There was no one to pay for an education, or apprenticeship, or to place him in work in the mills, not that he wanted any of those things. He would have run away with a travelling fair rather than work in such places. Tom enjoyed the outdoors, had learned how to sleep rough and catch rabbits, to ride horses, and to fish and shoot.

At the inn he had taken care of the horses without prompting, and when Jack retired for the night he was surprised to find that his bedding had been carefully arranged and his riding boots cleaned, his cloak brushed clear of mud, and a jug of water placed by his bed. Tom slept on a worn mat, covered by a blanket, by the side of Jack's bed, listening to the incoherent murmurings from Jack's troubled sleep, before he, too, fell asleep, dreaming of becoming a soldier.

He woke Jack at dawn, shaking him gently. 'Mister Jack, sir, it is time to be up. I have some breakfast for you.'

Jack sat up, rubbing the sleep from his eyes and stretching, as Tom handed him a plate of toasted bread and cheese, and from somewhere the boy had found a tankard of cider.

'The ostler is about and I've had him ready the horses. I reckoned that you would want to be on the road afore long.'

'Thank you, Tom', Jack said and swung his long legs out of bed, yawning and stretching. 'You are indeed proving useful, and, yes, I do want to be gone. We have another long ride ahead.'

Jack nibbled at the bread and cheese and shaved quickly, pausing only to drink the cider, which was cold and good. He looked at his face in the small mirror. Blue eyes, cold as the sea, looked back. *The face of a murderer*, he thought. *Best get used to it, Vizzard; you will see that each time you shave, and be reminded of your own ruthlessness every day.* It was a revelation to him, that he was capable of such a callous, savage act. He cleaned the razor and packed it away in his bag. The room having been paid for the previous evening, they left as soon as Jack had completed his preparations.

The air was cool and clear as they left Bath behind, with the first light frost painting white the grass and the hedges along the road.

They rode steadily, pausing every hour or so to rest the horses. Tom kept up his animated chatter, seemingly content to receive only the odd grunt or acknowledgement from Jack, who was preoccupied with his own thoughts.

Barnwood's body would have been discovered and surely the finger of suspicion would have fallen on him. Only Giles would have known his intentions—why else would he have followed him? That was something he regretted. But to take him into his confidence would have been foolish. He resolved to write to him, to explain his abrupt departure. They would question him for sure, but Giles would give nothing away, would he?

He felt he was safe enough for the present, but would be happier when he reported at Portsmouth barracks—and happier still to be outward bound on a frigate. He was not due there for another month but judged they would accept him nonetheless. He had considered using an alias, but his commission from the Admiralty prevented that.

They had to stop at Midsomer Norton because the boy's horse had lost a shoe. They lunched at an inn while a farrier replaced it.

'Mister Jack, sir,' Tom said when the landlord had served them some cold tongue, bread and ale, 'I am very pleased you took me with you, sir.'

Jack was a little taken aback by the comment. 'You may not be so happy once we are in the service, lad. It will be a hard life for you. Tell me, Tom, why did you want to leave the village?'

Tom sighed, having explained this already when on the road. 'I should've stayed, I knows. Nan will be having a terrible time of it, but what could I do there? We have no farm and wiv no dad to help me I would be in the poor house, or in the mill. That's not fer me. Once you did what you did, sir, I knew you would have to go, and I thought you and me could help each other. I might have done the same, sir, 'cos Barnwood, well, he was a right bad 'un, sir. I ain't told you all, but I knows fings about 'im.' Tom squinted against the rising sun. 'He used to go after the girls in the other villages—I used to foller him, like.' Tom looked sideways, seeking to gauge Jack's mood.

'What do you mean?' Jack knew what the boy was saying, but some compulsion made him ask the question.

'He used to sneak off with some of the girls in the mill at Dudbridge, and he was in Stroud and Gloucester a lot, too, sir. He never wore his proper clothes, though, sort of disguised hisself as a gent of business, if you like. I saw what he did wiv 'em. He used 'em wickedly, then he would beat 'em, sir, if you take my meanin'.'

Tom made no mention of what he had hoped to gain from this knowledge. He had vaguely thought that he might get some benefit from following the vicar, perhaps some money, but he would have had to be clever, the vicar being an educated man and everything. He would have had to prove what he knew, otherwise who would believe him?

Jack thought about the boy's words. He had not trusted the vicar, but neither had he suspected the truth. It made him feel a little better, not much, and offered some small justification for his terrible deed.

'I think it best, Tom, that we do not talk about these matters again. I will help you all that I can, but speak no more of this, eh?'

The farrier had done his work and, the bill paid, the two set off again, following the road south and east towards the coast and Portsmouth. Each night Tom would repeat his work of taking care of the horses and cleaning Jack's cloak, boots and breeches, before settling down to sleep. Each morning he woke him with a modest meal. Smoked fish, or a bowl of bran and warm milk, or toasted bread, whatever Tom could arrange from the kitchen.

As they rode, they passed the occasional traveller, or mail-coach, and would pull off the track to give it room as it rattled by, horses sweating and the coachman trumpeting a warning as the iron-rimmed wheels clattered, throwing up dust and stones.

They reached Portsdown Hill on the fifth day, by now very weary. With the aid of a new telescope, Jack could see Portsmouth dockyard with its forest of masts. It burst upon him, dazzling his sight, firing his imagination, and he halted to wonder at his future.

'Good heavens, Tom, will you take a look!' His heart seemed to fill.

Full before them lay the broad bosom of the ocean, covered with ships, the Channel Fleet, with more than thirty sail of the line. Stately three-decked warships lay in the harbour, a couple of frigates, too, small boats, like water beetles, crawling slowly between them and the shore. Sloops, brigs, schooners, and cutters, extended all along the vast anchorage of Spithead, reaching almost to St. Helens where the light squadron, ready for sail, lay at single anchor with sails unfurled.

Over to the right was Southampton Water, running along the banks of Hampshire and beyond, to the New Forest. At the extremity of his vision he believed he could see the Needles rocks and the Isle of Wight, the garden of England, glowing in pastoral beauty, with its hills and vales, its woods, its sparkling villages and spires and the town of Ryde rising Venus-like from the sea.

Within weeks, he thought, *I must be on one of those ships, bound where? What lies ahead, fortune and adventure, or disgrace and death?* They rode on through the peninsula, along London Road, through the villages of Hilsea and Fratton, then past Portchester Castle and the garrison of Portsmouth, with its regular lines and fortifications, its bridges and draw-bridges, scarps and counter-scarps, bastions and basins, curtains, dykes and glacis, eventually finding St Nicolas Street and Fourhouse Barracks.

The barracks was bustling with activity. There were men everywhere, all oblivious to the dusty man and ragged-looking boy on two dishevelled horses. A squad of new men were at drill under the orders of a corporal, doing his best to instil some order into their movements.

Jack stopped a sergeant and asked for some direction. The man glanced at him, and with a grunt that could have been an oath, pointed at a building to his right. Jack dismounted.

'Wait for me here,' he instructed Tom and took out a leather pouch from his bag.

A young marine private was standing guard at the door and stood smartly to attention at Jack's arrival. 'I am to report to a Major Ross,' Jack said.

'He's in there... sir,' the young soldier answered, quickly realising that he was dealing with a gentleman. 'But he is busy this morning,' he added with a note of caution.

Jack smiled and walked through the door, into a small, dim room, lit by a solitary window set high in the brick wall, which was white-washed. It smelt musty. A pair of tables, on which piles of paper were stacked in untidy columns, faced each other.

The man sitting at one of them did not look up at Jack's entrance. 'Second Lieutenant John Vizzard reporting, Major Ross.' Jack felt unsure of himself. He was not yet in uniform and his commission was dated as recently as Wednesday 1st August 1786. He had not used his rank before.

Ross's head came up slowly and he pushed to one side the sheaf of papers he had been studying. 'Are you, now, boy?'

Jack bristled inwardly. This was a term to which he was not accustomed. He did not welcome it.

Major Robert Ross was a man of about 45 years, with a sallow, anaemic expression and dark, cold eyes. His smile was thin and unconvincing. He was dressed in full uniform coat, his epaulettes of faded gold appearing heavy on his shoulders. His face, veined and waxy, offered no hint of welcome.

'Your first lesson then, laddie, is to understand that I am to be your commanding officer, and you will at all times address me as "sir".'

Jack stiffened and knew instinctively that this officer and he were not destined to enjoy an amicable relationship.

'Yes, sir,' he said simply.

Ross was a Scot and a man who had seen hard service in Canada and America. He had been present at the siege of Louisburg and at the capture of Quebec. He'd already been a captain at the time of Bunker Hill in June 1775. A censorious, self-important man, he was without humour.

Ross looked Jack up and down. 'I have received orders about you. An Oxford man,' Ross sneered derisively. 'The classics and jurisprudence, too.'

'Yes, sir,' Jack added quickly.

'I have no time for varsity men, Vizzard. Parsimonious, blood-sucking, self-serving parasites, all,' Ross growled. 'You are to be attached to... er... the 55th Company. You will see the Q. M. and draw what uniforms and equipment ye lack, and I suggest you do so quickly, boy. Next time I see you, I wish to see you properly attired, Mister Vizzard, and in some semblance of a king's officer and not some Piccadilly Dandy! Lieutenant Long is my adjutant; he will be your senior, but he has not yet reported for duty. I suggest you find Sergeant Packer and he will see to your needs.'

He glared at Jack and continued. 'Now, as to training, I will see you drill tomorrow and then I will see all officers, with companies, on Friday for musketry. If you satisfy my adjutant as to your fitness, I'll be surprised. Thank you, Mister Vizzard.' The last remark was clearly a dismissal as Ross turned his attention back to his papers.

'May I raise a matter, sir?' Jack waited until Ross raised his head. 'I have with me a servant, a boy of some fifteen years, who wishes to serve with me. I thought perhaps that would be possible?'

'Bit young for the service... Very well, find a recruiting sergeant and have him sworn in, if you must.' Ross returned to his lists.

The meeting over, Jack turned on his heel and walked out. He looked at the dark, cloudy sky and thought that there might be a storm brewing.

Sergeant Joseph Packer was outside, talking to the sentry, when Jack left Ross's office.

'Good morning, sir. Mister Vizzard, I understand?' The sergeant's head was level with Jack's shoulder, his eyes studying Jack obtrusively, causing a moment of discomfort.

'Indeed it is, Sergeant, and you are?' Jack looked at the smartly dressed marine wearing three broad stripes on his arms.

'Joseph Packer. I am appointed your sergeant, sir.' Seeing Jack's look of surprise, he went on. 'I found out about you from your servant, sir. Lieutenant Long mentioned also how we was to have a new officer next month.'

Jack offered a bland reply, explaining only that his personal affairs had permitted him to join the division earlier than expected.

Joseph Packer smiled, taking in the charm that this new officer used so readily, making the assumption that he had bidden farewell to a lady and was anxious to make a new life, away from the women of London society. He had seen that before.

'Firstly, sir, I will escort you around the barracks, just so you can get familiar with things—you will need to know your way around the barracks, sir. Then I'll show you to your quarters. My corporal is taking care of your servant. We need some youngsters in the corps. He will be in uniform afore you see him again.' The man grinned.

Sergeant Packer explained that the marine barracks had been converted from the King's Cooperage nearly twenty years before, with one of the principal reasons being to keep the daily roll call parades separate from the civilian population of the town.

Avoids trouble with the good citizens of the town, and keeps the men out of the taverns,' was his simple explanation.

He showed Jack some of the barrack rooms; there were forty-five of them, each accommodating twelve men, sharing six beds. Two large lockers were provided in each room for the men's personal kit. The rooms were neat and ordered, as though the builders had just finished work.

Jack learned that he was to share with another subaltern one of eight rooms set aside for officers, and thus save the expense of lodging in the town. He was surprised to note that his bags were already in his room, obviously taken there during his meeting with Major Ross.

His quarters differed little from the barrack rooms, save that there were only two beds and the space between them was separated by a pair of desks, placed back to back. Two marble washstands with plain white china bowls and pitchers stood beneath the window. A locker would accommodate his uniforms and clothing, while an empty trunk, obviously the property of a former occupant, rested at the foot of the bed. The name of the owner, painted in a crude stencil, had been thinly over-painted with his own name and rank. Seeing it before him, in thick letters, gave him a curious sensation of position, of some status that he had not felt before.

'I took the liberty of having your things brought here, sir, while you were busy with Major Ross. Not as grand as you may 'ave been used to, I daresay, but as good as you will have anywhere in the corps, beggin' your pardon, sir.'

He recalled the cramped room at Oriel, filled with books and damp clothes, also shared with other men, and considered this room palatial.

'It will do me very well, Sergeant, very well indeed.'

On returning to the quadrangle, Packer escorted him along a colonnade running along three sides of the barracks, used for the men to be drawn up for review in wet weather. The quartermaster had his stores over the main gate, and Jack signed for two uniform coats, belts, two hats, field kit and some additional personal equipment not purchased in London following his interview at The Admiralty. He had purchased a sword and a pair of pistols, but had brought with him his own musket, an expensive weapon from one of the new manufactories in Birmingham.

Packer then took him to the officers' mess, where he was promptly charged a guinea as an entry fee.

'It will cost you ten shillings a week to mess here, sir!' Packer grinned broadly. 'I'll wager the grub is better in the sergeants' mess, an' all, sir.'

Jack warmed to this man, and returned the smile. 'Then perhaps I should seek an invitation to your mess, Sergeant!'

'That would not be the thing, sir. They call that 'un-officer-like' behaviour, and you wouldn't want to be accused of that, now would you, sir? Leastwise, not just as you are recently joined in the Corps, sir.'

'Indeed not, Sergeant—that would not do at all,' he replied, returning a friendly smile. Some of the anxiety he had felt on arriving at the barracks seemed to fall away.

He felt that he now had a new home.

Chapter 16
Training

The sergeant, more used to training recruits in the multiple tasks involved in preparing a musket for firing, worked Jack hard, exhorting him to load and fire ever more quickly.

'Very good, Mister Vizzard, very good, sir. That is fast shooting. A bit more work and you will get it to three balls a minute, and that's as fast as any man in the garrison, an' faster than most!' He did not mention that Jack's shooting was by far the most accurate he had seen from any officer in many years.

'Thank you for that, Mister Packer. I have had little reason to practice lately, but I think that is enough for the day. How is young Tom faring? Do you think he will do?'

'Well enough, sir, well enough. He seems a good lad. Had one or two scrapes with some of the old hands, mind, but 'e'll come through right enough. Seems to think a lot of you, so I 'ear.' There had been some speculation in the mess the previous night about the new officer, but Packer had decided to reserve opinion on the man until he knew more.

Joe Packer was from a village near Colchester, in Essex, and had joined the Corps at Chatham. He was a fit, strong man, now some thirty years of age. Twelve years of service in the Corps had made him hard. He was stocky, of medium height and with a back as straight as the ramrod slung beneath his musket. White breeches, always spotlessly clean, just touched his black bootees, which were always shining. White, pipe-clayed cross belts shone against the red of his uniform coat, taut over his large chest. He kept his hair cut unfashionably short, down to the very scalp of his large, rounded head. Brown eyes stared unblinkingly when he was angered. He had a deep, throaty laugh when amused, and often his mouth formed a bemused half grin, which some officers found disconcerting and impertinent. The face surrounding that mouth was deep brown, stained by the sun, as he had come back from India less than six months before and, with much haste, had been returned to barracks to help train new recruits. He was tough, had survived any number of fights, many in the king's service and some for his own reasons, and had long ago earned the respect of his men.

He regarded Mister Vizzard with a critical eye. He had met very few officers that he liked. He respected some, but like?—no. Most were toffs or drunkards. Some he had known had guts and courage aplenty, and others were plain cowards. He had shot one in India, for running from a fight and leaving the men. Put a ball through his brain from ten paces. Bone and brains had spattered over a young private, who was unable to speak for many days. Then he was fighting for his very life, with bayonet, and the butt of his musket, his bare knuckles and boots, too bloody and exhausted to care. After that fight, no officer spoke against him. He grimaced at the memory. Bastard had upset the lads before he ran.

This one, though—well, he was different. At least he was not as imperious as some of the buggers; treated the men as men and not vermin or scum. That bastard Ross, for example, he wouldn't approve; too bleedin' arrogant and self-minded. Packer had no love for Major Ross. The man had had guts once, but now, well, he was just a bully, ordering floggings for even petty offences. Looking at the new officer he thought, *Those two will cross swords ere long, I shouldn't wonder.*

'You received any orders yet, sir?' Ordinarily Joe Packer would not have had the temerity to ask an officer that, but he felt comfortable with this one, 'familiar' Ross would call it.

'Not as yet, Sergeant. Why the interest?' Jack had been at Portsmouth for a fortnight and so far had received no indication as to what duty might be given to the company.

As a sergeant, Packer could be detached with a small squad to a sloop or smaller frigate, and he did not desire that, never liked being under the orders of snobbish naval officers.

Packer lowered his voice. 'I do 'ear tell that we might be off on a long cruise afore Christmas, sir, but nobody's saying nothin'. Mister Long's been asked to 'elp with a gang tomorrer. They need more men for some ships, they say. Now, that be a bit strange to my thinkin'. 'Tisn't like we 'ave a war to fight.'

That was true. Jack had heard mention in the mess of an important expedition being organized by the Admiralty, for which a large contingent of marines was to be required. He had heard nothing but the most vague suggestions about such an expedition. Some officers speculated on the possibility of an expedition to the West Indies, others to The Cape. A few thought that a detachment was to go to India. He thought that an interesting possibility.

'I will be sure to let you know, Mister Packer, just as soon as Major Ross takes me into his confidence.' His sardonic smile was not lost on the hardened soldier before him. Jack handed the musket back to the sergeant, silently pleased with his showing in front of this experienced man.

He returned to the mess feeling hungry. It was a large room, with high ceilings painted in a stark whitewash. Portraits of naval officers, former colonels and nearly forgotten sea battles decorated the walls. Card tables covered in green baize formed a neat row along one side, with a collection of chairs at one end, gathered around a long, well polished mahogany table. A fire smoked lazily in the hearth, sending small trails of grey smoke into the room, and an orderly disappeared through a door leading to a kitchen. Only one other officer was there, one that he did not recognise. The fair-haired young man sat at a bureau by a window, writing slowly, frequently consulting some large book by his side.

Jack looked around for a servant; finding none, he made his way to a table and poured himself a glass of Madeira from a decanter. The young officer had not noticed him enter, so intent on his work was he, so he called across to him, 'Would you care to join me in a glass before lunch?' At that the man's head came up in acknowledgement and he looked at Jack.

No, thanks, I don't drink, actually.' He smiled, apologetically almost.

Jack walked across to the table at which the other officer was working. He thought he had better introduce himself. Extending his hand, he said, 'Vizzard, Jack Vizzard.'

'Dawes, William Dawes,' the young lieutenant answered, standing up and accepting the hand. 'Delighted to meet you, I am sure. Were you the chap with the musket?'

Jack nodded as he swallowed the wine.

'I assumed so. You have powder burns on your face.'

At that he laughed nervously, almost a girlish laugh, and Jack broke into laughter, too. 'Yes, Sergeant Packer was putting me through some drill. Major Ross feels that I should improve my eye, although he has yet to see me use the damn thing.'

'He is useful with a sword, I am told, but not so clever with fire-arms, it is said.' Jack's new companion returned to his chair. 'Whereas I am hopeless with either.'

Again, a slight giggle, but Jack, strangely, was drawn to the lieutenant. They were of similar age, although Dawes appeared of slighter build. He imagined him to be about 24 or 25 years of age, perhaps a year or two his senior. He had a studious expression and Jack saw that the papers on the table contained many mathematical calculations, notes, sketches and neatly drawn diagrams. A large book on astronomy was next to them.

Dawes noted the glance and looked at the papers on the table. 'My passion is mathematics.' He shrugged. 'It is the basis of all science.' He smiled, and Jack shook his head.

'Mine was law, and it is the basis of all mischief.'

Dawes laughed again and asked, 'Which company?'

'The 55th, and yours?'

'The 32nd, but I am to join the 11th, according to orders.'

'Ah, so you have some orders.' Jack was immediately curious.

'Yes. I am to join Captain Phillip's expedition to colonize Botany Bay. You have heard of this, have you not?'

Indeed he had not. He had heard of Botany Bay, having read James Cook's accounts of his voyages, but he had not heard of plans to form a colony there. Now he understood, his interest aroused. The broadsheet papers had been calling on the government to do something about the growing prison population, and the hulks off Portsmouth and in the Medway were adding daily to their populations. The newspapers were calling it a scandal, which it was.

He had been out to one of these prison ships with John Long, a second lieutenant, only last week, delivering some wretched convicts received from Tyburn gaol. He had not liked what he had seen, and his thoughts had gone to Mary, his anguish reawakened.

It had put him in a black mood for days and again he had been troubled with renewed guilt. He had thought of Gloucester and when he might return there, knowing only that he was probably now wanted in that county, in connection with the murder of a man of the church. Probably he could never return there.

What he desired now, and as soon as possible, was an assignment to a ship, bound for the Americas, India or the Caribbean, and the chance of action and honour, and to forget his past. The expedition needed soldiers, and marines would form the garrison for the new colony. He knew that this was an opportunity for him, there had to be the prospect of adventure in the south seas, and the chance to distinguish himself. He had to join that expedition. The notion of novel experiences, of lands unseen and people unknown struck a chord within him.

Dawes talked of little else during lunch. He explained how he was to work as military surveyor and engineer in the new colony. He talked of astronomy and how he was to map the stars of the Southern Hemisphere, of the observatory that he would one day build, and of the native people there he wished to study. Dawes had the support of the Astronomer Royal.

Jack found himself listening to this quietly spoken, slightly pious young man, who showed such passion for his subject. This was no warrior, but a scholar in a uniform, he decided.

He learned from him that the Navy was to escort a number of ships of convicts to Botany Bay and that the marines would form their guards. Dawes did not know the strength of the guard but Jack thought a sizeable force would be required, particularly to deal with the native Indians, and to explore the hinterland of the country.

This was a task that he would relish, and he resolved to see Major Ross that evening and seek permission to join the expedition.

CHAPTER 17

GARRISON

'Tell me, Giles, please, I beg of you, tell me what he is about.'

Giles was as distressed as Henry. He knew only that Jack had obtained a marine's commission from the Admiralty, but as to the division or ship to which he might have been assigned he knew nothing. He thought that if he admitted to what he knew, Jack would be traced, brought back, probably under arrest, to face an ignominious trial and suffer sentence of death. He decided, for better or worse, to keep his own counsel.

'I am very sorry, Henry, but he never took me into his confidence. I can only imagine he has fled to the continent, or perhaps in truth he has joined the Navy. It looks bad for him, does it not?'

'It does, Giles, it does. I cannot help thinking that Jack knows something of this awful business. It seems to me a remarkable coincidence that Barnwood should pass on in his sleep on the very day that Jack leaves us. He wanted him dead, you know, Giles. He really had hate in his heart. I truly fear the worst. I cannot believe that he, too, has gone.'

Henry's tremulous voice betrayed the emotion he was feeling; his shoulders sagged and tears formed in the corners of his eyes. He blew his nose loudly, to cover his face. Giles was lost for words to comfort him.

They were sitting in the drawing room at Lampern House. They had eaten a simple supper of cold meat pie, bread and cheese, Henry eating with little appetite. Giles and Henry had again talked of the time that Eliza Clutterbuck had found Barnwood dead in his room. She had not found him until nearly mid-day, thinking it strange that he had not risen to visit the mill, as he often did. Giles learned later that young Tom Clutterbuck was missing but had not thought there was any connection between the two.

He worried for his friend. Although Doctor Steele had not suggested any foul play, Giles could not help feeling that Jack was in some way implicated, had perpetrated an awful deed. He also knew of his friend's threat. His thoughts went to the night he'd tried to follow Jack, still puzzled and offended that Jack had evaded him.

The kindly doctor had also let slip that Barnwood had contracted a disease, some unpronounceable Latin term, but what Giles would term 'a dose'.

He thought Jack would have headed south and probably to Plymouth, or possibly to London and from there, to Chatham. He resolved to travel to Plymouth to seek out his friend, but gave no voice to his thoughts.

'I rather suspect that he has gone in search of his brother, they were so close,' he said quietly.

Then I will pray that they find each other,' Henry whispered.

Giles had seen the coldness in Jack's face when he had left the court. He was now certain that his friend had been involved in the demise of the cleric in some way. He would have to see Mary, to see if Jack had said anything to her before leaving.

The curious thing was the disappearance of young Tom. His grandmother had reported that his meagre possessions had gone—and suddenly he understood. They had left together. The boy was a younger version of Jack; he was quick-witted, spirited and always in one scrape or another. He was just the kind of lad to be tempted, and lured, by tales of adventure and fighting the king's enemies. *That is it*, he thought. *By God, yes!*

Henry sat quietly for a long time, his eyes fixed on the portrait on the wall. Giles could offer no comfort to this caring, generous, but now senescent man, and thought he looked his age today. He rose from the armchair, putting a reassuring hand on the older man's shoulder, then left him to his melancholy thoughts.

*****

The mess was near full that evening. Jack attired himself in dress uniform, as required by daily orders since dinner was a formal affair in honour of Colonel Wilde who was retiring. Groups of officers stood in animated conversation. The scarlet of the Corps dominated, with the occasional dark blue of naval coats.

A mess servant served him a glass of sherry wine. He wondered idly if it was from Harvey's warehouse in Bristol.

Taking a sip, he gazed around the room and saw Major Ross by the fireplace, talking to Lieutenant Dawes, and strode across to join them.

'Good evening, sir. I wondered if I might please have a moment of your time?'

'What is it, Vizzard?' The intrusion irritated Ross; his eyes were unfriendly.

Dawes made an excuse and headed for another group of officers.

'My orders, sir. I have yet to receive any, and now understand that you might be commanding a certain expedition. I believe I would be interested in volunteering, sir.'

'The damned sergeants've been talking out of turn again, have they? Big mistake, this, Vizzard; didn't want the commission, don't mind telling you that. It is doomed to failure. The Corps will do their duty, of course, the best men for the task and I will prove it, but the venture is foolhardy and will fail, for the purpose is flawed. Have no part in it, laddie—nursemaid to the dregs of society! Marines to provide escort duty, to guard thieves, cutpurses, cheats, liars and murderers? I tell you, forget the whole business.'

Ross was belligerent at the best of times, and his present demeanour showed his contempt for his current orders. He did want promotion, however, substantive promotion; that is why he had in fact sought the commission. He had immense pride in his Corps, knew the men he commanded were superior to the scum of the army. 'Colonel Robert Ross' would sound more impressive, his own independent command. Every officer ached for that, and he had need of the pay. Lieutenant Governor of a new colony, that would impress, too. His was an extended family, with constant demands on his resources. But this was not his idea of an honourable commission, despite the prospect of substantive promotion on return to England, dispensing with a brevet rank. He took a large mouthful of wine, emptying the glass, and waved to a mess servant.

'No, sir, with respect, this is important to me,' Jack replied. 'I would consider it a personal honour to have your support to join this expedition. I am confident that I could be of service.' Jack had no patron in the Corps and Ross, as garrison commander, was likely to be a man of influence.

There was surely to be some action and the chance of distinction. The voyage would be an adventure itself, he thought. No ships had travelled so far, not since the days of James Cook. He did not know Ross was to be commissioned lieutenant-governor of the new colony.

'Your enthusiasm, at least, does you some credit, Vizzard. I will consider your application and let you know when I have done so. However, you would be well advised to think again. There will be honour for the Corps only in this, none for mere subalterns. Now, excuse me, but I have to speak to the colonel.'

Jack was considering Ross's words as another officer caught his arm and interrupted his thinking.

'Now, Jack, what are you about, hmm? Didn't have you marked as a toady to the major!' He grinned at Jack's reproachful expression. 'Sergeant Packer tells me that you might accompany me on the morrow for a little press duty. What do you say?'

John Long was a second lieutenant in the 55th Company. An experienced officer, Long had already impressed Jack with his capabilities as an organizer. He had been surprised to learn that he had instructions to assist the Navy in recruiting more hands and had agreed to take a section of men to assist a young midshipman in seeking some able seamen.

'Of course, be delighted to help,' he replied.

'I propose to visit The Duke of Clarence with young Ferguson, catch 'em early, afore the buggers are out of their beds, what!'

'In that case we had better not be drunk ourselves, John.'

'Good. I've given orders to that boy of yours to call you at five o'clock, and we'll meet the Navy there at a quarter to six. Should have some sport, heh?'

Jack felt a moment of anxiety. *Still,* he thought, *why not? It may be a problem for the Navy, but we are part of the Admiralty, part of the Navy, so such duty is to be expected.*

They enjoyed a good dinner of roast beef and guinea fowl, followed with a plum pudding and a custard sauce. Poker-faced mess servants served the wine generously. Jack was looking at the regiment's crest, displayed on the wall above the fireplace. A laurel wreath and the Admiralty fouled anchor. Beneath the wreath and anchor, the regiment's motto: *'Per mare per terram.'* By sea and by land. He knew that the Corps had first used that following Bunker Hill, during the war in America. He felt proud to belong.

Several places away, on the opposite side of the long table, Major Ross was discoursing to anyone prepared to listen on his experiences at Bunker Hill. Jack tried to listen, but was too distant to hear it all.

'Bloody disaster, 'twas. Shameful, if ye ask me. Never should have attacked at all, least not against tha' bloody hill. Breeds Hill it were, not Bunker Hill, but nae bugger would listen. Clinton was right, and I was right, but my lads were ripped to pieces by them bloody rebels.' He rambled on, becoming more incoherent with every glass that emptied swiftly as he talked.

'Lost over a thousand men that afternoon, one thousand bloody corpses. Grenadiers and light infantry, of course, but they murdered my marines.' He was flushed with wine, and enjoyed the attention of a small audience of younger officers. 'I told they damned popinjays to land my marines to the north side of the neck, then we could 'ave taken the buggers from the rear, but nay, bloody Navy landed us at the bloody tip, and so we had tae march in ranks up the bloody hill, like the Duke o' York's toy soldiers!' Ross looked grim as he recounted his story.

'Three times we attacked, each time a slaughter. I was one of the first into their redoubt, o' course. 'Bayonet the Yankee bastards!' I yelled—and we did. Needed some leadership, and that's why I was given credit by General Howe. Poor bastards did nae have a chance once we were in among 'em. Run out of powder and ball, ye see. Fought like tigers with anything they could—rocks, sticks and rifle butts. But we had 'em, got 'em runnin' all the way back to Cambridge.' He stretched back in his chair, waiting for favourable comment on his story.

About him faces showed a mixture of expressions; some looked on in awe, others with embarrassment. Jack, sitting several places away, could hear little of the major's words, but thought he was drinking too much, and was too showy, simply seeking attention for his own part in the action.

After the loyal toast, a naval commander, seated on the other side of the table, asked if he was the same Captain Ross involved in the surrender of *Ardent,* a frigate captured just off Plymouth in '79.

The question was barbed with menace and those officers closest recognised it as such. They fell silent as Ross crimsoned with obvious restrained anger.

'I was present, sir, on that occasion, yes!' he snapped curtly.

'Her captain was court-martialled for that, Major Ross. The Navy was dishonoured that day.' The young officer spoke with a dangerous softness, his eyes levelled calmly at Major Ross.

Ross coloured further, troubled by the direction of the conversation. 'Indeed, sir? It appeared to me that in view of the raw crew of the ship, fresh out of port, and the overwhelming size of the French squadron, the captain had no alternative but to strike his colours.'

'There were rumours at the time, as I recall, that it was not the captain that ordered the colours be struck, but a marine officer,' the young commander continued.

Ross spluttered, 'What the devil are you suggesting, sir?'

The commander was now intent on attacking Ross, and oblivious to the consequences. 'I am suggesting, sir, that you, or an officer acting under your command, ordered the colours be struck, thereby bringing dishonour on the Navy, sir!'

'That's a lie and a slur, sir. I demand you retract immediately or I will hear from your seconds.' Ross was on his feet, his eyes bulging in their sockets.

'With the greatest of pleasure, Major Ross, with the greatest of pleasure.'

The entire room fell silent, watching with expectation the confrontation between the two men.

Colonel Daniel Wilde rose and signalled the two officers to sit. 'Gentlemen, gentlemen, please, enough of this nonsense. I will not have this. No officer of the Corps will indulge himself in duelling, whatever the provocation,' he said pointedly, glancing at the young commander. 'As I understand it, this matter was dealt with at court martial and Major Ross was not required to answer any charge.' The room was silently watching the drama.

The naval officer was not to be silenced so quickly or easily. 'That is as may be, Colonel, but it is well known to those on board the *Ardent* what the truth of the matter was. I do not speak lightly.'

'Sir, in the heat of battle many things may be said or done that later, in the calm of the day, may be regretted. However, I cannot have two senior officers behaving in this fashion in my mess. May I suggest you withdraw the imputation and Major Ross will withdraw his demand for the opportunity to draw his sword.' Colonel Wilde waited, allowing the passions to subside in both men.

The silence hung in the room like a sea fog. Ross was breathing hard, his face reddened, and the young man in blue uniform stood poised, ready to move quickly if need be.

Jack watched Ross carefully as the commander, with patent reluctance, and hesitation, muttered a curt, unconvincing retraction. Ross relaxed slightly, and similarly withdrew his words, but then suddenly kicked his chair away, swung on his heel and marched from the room.

A loud murmuring filled the room as Ross left.

Jack, sitting next to John Long, let out his breath slowly. 'Well, what in God's name was all that?'

John Long leaned toward him. 'Back in '79 Ross was a captain serving in the frigate *Ardent*. A French squadron seized her just after she left Plymouth. It was commonly told at the time that the *Ardent*'s commander mistakenly thought he was joining an English squadron. He hauled down his colours very quickly, but at his court martial her captain claimed that the colours were struck on the orders of an officer of marines. Ross was the only such officer on deck at the time, so it is believed, but he was never charged.'

Long pushed his fingers through his hair and leaned back, gently rocking his chair.

'The thing is, neither did he request a court martial, which many thought he should have done, to defend his honour. It was an ugly business, and none benefited from it. It was years ago and I wonder why that blue-coat brought it up.'

The naval officer was making a further apology to Colonel Wilde and preparing to leave.

'Come, Jack, let's take the air—I need a cigar after that.' Long pushed back his chair.

They were leaning against a wall overlooking the parade ground talking of tomorrow's duty when the sound of raised voices halted the conversation. They ran towards the stables and on turning the corner found Ross and the naval officer confronting each other, Ross with sword in hand.

'You stay out of this, it is not your concern,' Ross commanded them. 'Come on then, sailor boy, let's settle this matter here and now.' He pointed his sword at the young man.

'No, Major, I gave my word to your colonel that I would seek no duel with you over this affair. That is my honour.'

'And what of mine, you bastard? You impugned mine, you little shit.'

The commander stood his ground, but still did not withdraw his sword.

Jack felt compelled to intervene. 'Sir, this is foolish.'

Long added his voice, pleading with his commanding officer. 'Vizzard is right, sir. Put away your sword, please.'

'I will not be insulted by this whippersnapper of a sailor boy. He befouled my good name in front of the mess, and for that he deserves to die.'

'Not by your hand, Ross. You do not have the guts for it. It was your cowardice that dishonoured the Navy; you should have stood trial that day... not my brother! Do you know what became of him after the court martial? He was discredited, never given a command again, and hanged himself from the foretop of his ship! It destroyed our father.'

Ross made to lower his sword, putting the young man off his guard, then lunged at him, the blade missing as the young man swiftly and neatly side-stepped, his cloak whipping open.

Jack dived at Ross as the blade rose again. He pulled him aside and the big man fell.

'Get him away from here, now!' he shouted to Lieutenant Long.

The lieutenant grabbed the commander firmly by the arm and took him inside, looking for help.

'You little shit, Vizzard. He was mine! He should be dead but for you.' Ross struggled to get to his feet. 'You hit me, you young bastard, and that's a court-martial affair.'

'Sir, I probably saved your life. He is younger than you, and his hand was on a pistol in his boat-cloak. He was not going to fence with you. He meant to blow your brains out.'

Ross got to his feet. He looked at Jack with cold, doubtful eyes, collected his sword and staggered drunkenly away without another word.

Chapter 18

Gloucester Gaol

The rat was crawling over the dying child's body when Mary awoke. She thought she was awake. There had been so many dreams of late; she struggled to distinguish them from reality. The sight of the rats was so common to her now. The stench was there again, too, bringing bile to her throat, as it never failed to do. It was worse on first awakening. The human faeces in each corner, the closely packed, befouled bodies, and no real ventilation save for a pair of barred windows, high in the wall, which merely let in the cold.

She picked up a pewter plate and threw it at the rodent, missing it, regretting the action immediately, but it gave her some small satisfaction. The clatter of the plate on the straw-covered floor woke some other women, who growled abuse at her. She thought of Jack, as she did every day, cursing him for leaving her in this living hell. She feared for her very sanity, wondered how she could possibly endure it. Henry had visited, and dear Giles once with Louise. Only once. Louise had clutched a fine lace handkerchief to her nose, had retched violently and fled. How long ago was it? A week? Two weeks? She had no sense of time in this place, only pain and melancholia.

Henry had submitted a Petition for Clemency but had heard nothing. She did not believe he ever would. He had looked older, much older than on that day at Lampern, when they had all been so happy.

She knew now Jack had run away. Betrayed her, abandoned her. Giles had told her. The news had devastated her. Before, she had nurtured some small hope of reprieve, allowed hope of support to grow. Now—well, now she had only the anticipation of years in a prison. Not even a prison where her family could visit, but one on the other side of the world. It might have been the moon.

Mary knew, too, of Giles' correspondence. He had written several letters, and was even intending to go to Plymouth, certain that he would find Jack there. She realized also that Jack would not be back, never would come and rescue her from the nightmare that had become her daily existence. He had abandoned her, betrayed her, and that she could not understand. She felt deeply wounded, a pain so constant, never absent from her mind. Mary glanced towards the dark corner where another woman was earning some extra food with one of the gaolers. 'Rutting' she called it, but now she was with child, and what future did that child have, if it survived?

Mary had fought off many men who had promised to be good to her, to help and protect her. Some of the other women openly laughed at her, calling her names, but she felt degraded enough, hardened and surprised at her ability to assert herself, to defend what she thought of as her 'honour'. A wry, self-mocking expression was on her face. *Where is honour now?* she wondered. Even her own beloved father she had sent away yesterday—was it only yesterday?—because it grieved him too much to see her, and distressed her greatly.

A key turned in the lock and the small, studded oak door opened. The gaoler brought in some thin potato soup. She was one of the first to reach it and took her share eagerly. Her father had brought her some cold mutton yesterday, with some bread, but she had shared that with Elizabeth.

Crawling back under the high window she pulled out a small book, one that Henry had left her. She had begun to read when the gaoler returned, this time followed by Giles. She saw immediately that he had nothing to tell her, and her spirit fell as quickly as it had risen on seeing him.

'I am sorry, Mary. I have no news of him. The Admiralty has not answered my correspondence. I returned from Plymouth last night, but there is no record of him there. I felt sure that he was to go there to become a marine. I know only that he was to take the King's Commission.' He noted her confusion. 'Jack has become an officer, Mary. I fear he will be overseas before I can find him.'

Giles looked at her crestfallen features. How thin she was, her cheeks without colour and her hair become matted and lank. His spirit was low at the sight of her.

'Henry assures me that some word will come from court very soon. You must not give up hope,' he added vainly.

'Hope? What hope do I have here, Giles? Tell me. Any day they may come to take me away, send me away from my home, my family... And what then?'

His head lowered and he felt a lump rise in his throat. 'Mary, I am sure he has not forsaken you. He has left because he felt he must.' Giles glanced around, taking in the squalor of the place, and lowered his voice to a whisper. 'What you have not been told, could not be told, is that... Barnwood is dead.' He paused, seeing her shocked expression. 'Yes, he died the night Jack left. Doctor Steele says it was of natural causes, but the man was diseased, infected.' Her quizzical look caused him to hurry on.

'Some loose tongues have already been wagging and linking Jack's name with the death. They believe he smothered him. Do you see, Mary? Do you understand? If that is the truth, and it may be possible, if hard to comprehend, then he will believe himself a fugitive.'

Mary swallowed, slowly taking in the enormity of the news. She looked about but no one was paying any attention.

'My God,' she whispered. 'Oh my God, so he believes himself to be a fugitive, and a murderer?'

Giles nodded. 'He may have used an alias and be presenting himself as something and someone very different. Young Tom is likely as not with him, because he is missing also, but I doubt that he had any part in the business. I also have this suspicion that Jack has gone in search of his brother.'

She shook her head, muttering, 'My poor Jack. Oh, God, my poor dear Jack.' Over and over again she repeated his name.

Giles gave her a small packet of food, embraced her quickly and left her to her tears, feeling more wretched than he could bear.

*****

Early the next morning, Tom shook Jack from troubled sleep. He quickly shaved and dressed, and met Lieutenant Long by the stables. It was not yet light and a thick sea mist enveloped Southsea, creating shadowy, ghost-like shapes. It was cold, and breath formed small clouds before men's faces. The short, frozen grass crunched beneath their feet.

They left their horses by a copse of trees on the common and made their way with stealth and in silence to the Duke of Clarence, an alehouse known to be a haunt of seamen from the Company.

A young midshipman, little more than sixteen, was already at the doorway, with half a dozen desperate looking seamen.

'Is that you, Ferguson?' John Long whispered.

'Aye, sir,' the young, thin voice answered.

'This is Mister Vizzard. He will be assisting this morning. Are your men ready?'

'As ready as ever, sir. They know their duty and are keen to enlist some ship-mates.' He smiled bravely, although this was the first press duty that he had commanded.

Long smiled at Jack. 'I served with his father on *Surprise* some years ago,' he explained.

'How do we get in?' Jack asked.

'With a key, of course!' answered the midshipman, producing the very thing with a boyish flourish. 'The innkeeper makes a profit from this business as well as the Navy.' He grinned.

The door opened with a barely audible squeal and the young officer led the way in, opening a ship's signalling lamp as he did so. His men followed, ahead of the marine officers.

Several sailors were asleep on the floor and on trestles, the remains of last night's carousing lying about them. Empty bottles lay on the floor. A woman stirred, stretching and freeing herself from the embrace of a large black man; her mouth was clamped closed by the hand of one of Ferguson's men.

'Right, you lot,' shouted the midshipman, 'you are now members of the crew of His Majesty's ship *Sirius*. Wake them up, please, Mister Brooks!'

The bosun of *Sirius* was more than willing to comply—he needed more top-men if he was to keep Captain Hunter happy. He set about with a starter and his boot, getting nearly a dozen men out of their drunken stupor.

Jack moved around the side of the warrant officer to help. He did not notice a man in the shadows until a glint of steel caught his eye. He turned and the blade missed, chipping the edge of a table. He recoiled and felt for his sword as the man lunged at him again. He tripped over a stool and realized that the man could reach him. He rolled quickly to his left, struggling to get to his feet.

There was loud shouting—a blur of red and John Long was standing in front of him, the sailor clubbed to the floor by the lieutenant's musket.

'Sweet Jesus, but that was damned close. My thanks to you, John. I thought I was gone then.' He breathed hard, as the adrenaline coursed through his shaking body.

'I am perhaps more used to this work than you, Jack. Some will always resist. It is to be expected that most will come willingly once caught, but there is often one who is willing to fight.'

'Come along, my boys,' Ferguson said to the seamen. 'You are now with the crew of *Sirius*, Captain John Hunter commanding, and no finer ship in the Navy.' He laughed. 'Take them away Mister Brooks, and we'll have them sworn in by the first lieutenant.'

The officers stood aside as the sailors staggered out with an escort of marines and Brooks' own men.

Jack looked at the man who had so nearly killed him. The man was oblivious and resigned now to his fate, his eyes showing no emotion, as one of the sailors from *Sirius* pushed him roughly to the door.

They took breakfast at the inn before returning to the barracks. Tom was never far from Jack, his face showing some signs of fear. He had filled out in the last month and looked taller.

'Are you all right, Mister Jack... er, sir?' he enquired when they were back in the barracks. 'Only there's talk as how you've fallen foul of Major Ross.'

'Don't you be worrying about me, young Tom. How are you getting along?' Jack saw the boy daily, but conversation between them was usually limited.

'Fine, er, sir, I'm just fine. The lads 'ave got me workin' on the drums, and Sergeant Packer 'as been drillin' me with a musket. I fired one the other day, and me ears still buzz a bit, but it's all right, this soldierin'.'

'Good. Packer seems like a good man. Be straight with him and he will look after you.'

'It were a bit of a worry this mornin', Mister Vizzard. I thought you were a goner, I did.'

Jack looked at the boy and felt compassion for the lad. 'There will be more scrapes before long, Tom. We must be better prepared next time, yes?'

He patted Tom's shoulder and sent him away, in order to dress for dinner. Today was the 28th of October, Foundation Day, and a very important day for any marine officer. It was the anniversary of the founding of the regiment in 1664, during the Second Dutch War. Its official name was the Duke of York and Albany's Maritime Regiment of Foot and known as the 'Admiral's Regiment', but all knew it as the Corps of Marines.

After a cold wash, Jack donned a clean pair of breeches and a plain white shirt, over which he wore his best uniform, a scarlet coat with white cassimere turnbacks and skirts. He proudly wore a single bullion epaulette with a plain fringe on his left shoulder. Finally, satisfied that his attire was correct, he placed his hat under his arm and joined his brother officers in the mess.

*****

There was a large number of visitors to the mess that evening. Several naval officers were present, none of whom Jack knew. He did not see Major Ross, but a mess servant told him that Ross was in meeting with an important naval officer, who would be guest of honour and would be joining them shortly. As senior officer in barracks, Ross would be at the head of table, he learned.

John Long joined him, accompanied by a large, broad-shouldered man, over six feet tall, with an open friendly expression and gold-coloured, curly hair. Jack noted his fine forehead and alert eyes, and was immediately impressed with his scholarly, authoritative appearance.

'Jack, I have the pleasure of introducing Captain David Collins. David, this is our most recent addition to the regiment, Jack Vizzard. I feel you will have much in common.'

'A pleasure to meet you, sir.' Jack offered his hand. It was accepted in a firm, friendly grip.

'The pleasure is mine, sir. For reasons which will come clear later this evening, I am destined to get to know you well.' The captain of Marines' expression was enigmatic, and, not_ng Jack's puzzled expression, he continued, 'I can say no more at present, but, believe me, we will certainly become better acquainted!'

Over a glass of wine, Jack learned that this striking officer came from Exeter. His father was a distinguished soldier, Ma_or-General Arthur Collins. He had been commissioned a second lieutenant in 1771, had been directly involved in the rescue of the king's sister, Queen Matilda of Denmark, had fought at Bunker Hill with Ross and had seen service at Halifax. Nova Scotia. Collins was telling him about his wife, Maria, at which point Major Ross entered the room. A naval captain, short in stature and of plain visage, with a long nose and quick, friendly eyes, accompanied him.

'That is Captain Arthur Phillip,' said Captain Collins. 'Now you will learn more, young Vizzard.'

Ross made his way to the head of the table and paused to allow the hum of speculative conversation to fade.

'Gentlemen, gentlemen. Before we take our seats to celebrate Foundation Day, I have an announcement to make. Certain officers have now been selected for special service but have been required to keep silent as to their orders. I am today authorized to confirm our division will form part of the new garrison to be detached to Botany Bay in New South Wales, there to assist in establishing a new colony in that territory.' Ross allowed a few moments for the effect of his words to be fully appreciated, then continued.

'I have the pleasure to present our guest of honour this evening, Captain Arthur Phillip, recently commissioned as commodore of the fleet and to be the first Governor of New South Wales.'

CHAPTER 19
EMBARKATION

Jack had expected to sail within days of receiving orders confirming his appointment to the garrison. However, the days became weeks and then months, with seemingly little progress being made to ready the fleet for sea. He drilled with other officers and his own section of marines. A field day in January was his first experience of exercising with a large body of men. It was foolishly and poorly managed, in his opinion. Major Ross became intent on re-enacting the battle in which he had made a reputation for himself. Lines of marines, slowly marching uphill in close order, to attack a defended hill. Ross reprimanded him for deploying his men far to the left, widely dispersed in skirmishing order, the better to move to a flanking position.

He spent evenings reading, thinking and writing notes about military tactics. His mind worked on the best means to defend a position, how to assault the same location, how to find and use ground to protect his men, where and how to place artillery and troops, how to keep men supplied and fit. He studied and read and wrote late into the night.

Jack saw no more of Captain Phillip; the new governor spent his time in London, preparing and meeting officials at the Admiralty and the Treasury, and ministers of Pitt's government, pleading with and cajoling all he met, to hasten the fleet's departure, and to ensure that the expedition was properly supplied and equipped. Jack expected almost daily to be discovered, taken and arrested, to be shamed before the Corps, and placed under guard to stand trial for murder. He grew increasingly restless and uneasy.

Once, when assisting Captain Collins in the adjutant's room, he recognized the handwriting and seal on a letter addressed simply to the commanding officer. It was from his father, and he slipped it quickly and discreetly into his tunic. Intending to read it later when alone, he forgot all about it.

As had been predicted, he and David Collins worked closely together. Collins had received a commission as Judge Advocate of the new colony and Jack found that increasingly he was called on to assist with drafting correspondence dealing with the supplies and the convicts selected for transportation to the new settlement.

Collins was a good officer, and a competent administrator. He tried hard to select men with skills thought to be of use in the colony. He tried to point out, in some instances, that certain convict's sentences would expire during the voyage, or shortly after arrival. He attempted to reject others who were too old, unskilled or considered beyond redemption, but often his advice, sound as it was, was ignored or rejected. London would frequently send new lists of transportees, requiring additions to the supplies and causing confusion and frustration.

Late one afternoon, having completed yet more lists, Collins announced, 'At last, Jack. Finally, we have orders to board ship. It is time to collect your things, for we are to quit Albion's shores at last.'

'"From Albion's shores, to the last southern isle, Prosperity extend, and Nature smile!"' Jack pronounced with a laugh. 'Forgive me, sir, what I intended to say was 'Not before time!' he continued with a sense of relief. He had waited long and grown impatient to be gone.

'Poetry? From my Classics scholar? I fear your skills will be wasted, Mister Vizzard. Our gallant major has no need of poetry and will not thank you for it!'

'Quite so, sir. I noted it from some recent pamphlet and it has stuck in my mind, as I thought it apposite to our venture. However, I will heed your advice and resist inflicting it upon Major Ross. With your leave, sir, I will see to my equipment.'

He found Tom in the barracks receiving musketry instruction at the hands of an older marine. He gave the boy the news and left him to make ready his equipment and effects.

Many of the officers and men at the barracks were to be part of the garrison, most having volunteered for the duty. None really knew where they were going. The officers had expectation of grants of land or, alternatively, promotion on completion of the commission. For the private soldier there was little to provide comfort.

Abraham Hands was one such marine in Jack's company. An experienced soldier, he was thirty years old, with near fifteen of those spent in the service.

'Mister Vizzard, sir, where is this 'ere Botany Bay we're goin' to?' he asked the next morning.

'It's a bloody long way away, Hands, a very long way, on the other side of the world. You worried about it, are you?' His men singled out Jack as an approachable officer who was sympathetic to their needs.

'Me, sir? Nah. I ain't got nobody but meself to worry about. Just curious, like, about the place.'

'Well, we really do not know much about it. Captain Cook, who found it during his first voyage to the Pacific, has described it in his journal but none have been there since, that I know of. You can read about it if you wish, I have a copy of his account.'

'Me, sir? God bless you, I can't read nor write, sir. I knows how to load an' fire my musket and kill rebels. That's all I needs to know, really.' Abraham Hands was a simple soldier but, generally sober, he kept clear of trouble and was well regarded.

'Look here, when we are aboard I will get the men together and give you a talk about Botany Bay and our voyage there, how would that be?'

'The lads would like that, sir, or some of them would, anyhows.'

Abraham Hands stiffened as Major Ross approached. 'Right, sir, thank you, sir,' he said crisply, giving the two officers one of his smarter salutes, and marched off.

Jack could see that Ross was looking at a paper as he walked. It crossed his mind to continue on his way to his quarters, but the expression on the major's face made that impossible.

'Vizzard, a word, if you will.' Ross was not smiling, and he was anything but friendly.

'Yes, sir?'

'It seems that you are to be favoured, young man. You are to accompany us on *Sirius,* the flagship. What do you make of that, heh?'

'I shall be most honoured, sir.' He would have preferred not to share a ship with Ross.

'Be damned if I think so. Should have you put aboard one of the transports where you could use your charm on the felons. Ensure you do your duty, Vizzard, for I shall be watching you. Report on board 24th February. These are your orders.' He thrust a sheet of paper at Jack and strode away in the direction of the officers' mess, obviously intent on giving further orders to other officers.

Jack read his orders. His appointment was as an assistant to the Judge Advocate of the new settlement for a term of three years. So, indeed, he would be working for Captain Collins. It was a position of some responsibility, but not a fighting job. He would be a uniformed clerk. A clerk to an officer appointed to deal with legal matters, but who had no legal training or education. He smiled to himself at the irony. We shall see what adventure there is to be had there, he thought to himself. The colony would have need for men with spirit and ability, he felt sure of it.

CHAPTER 20

SIRIUS

The morning of the 24th dawned cold but clear, a thin sun causing the grass to sparkle when Jack presented himself at the assembly point as ordered. He saw Tom in the ranks of the soldiers detailed to the flagship and half-smiled. He would speak to him later and see him settled.

The battalion's baggage was on carts behind the men and Major Ross took them out of the barracks for the short march to The Hard where boats would take them out to *Sirius* and the rest of the fleet, to be their new home for the long voyage to New South Wales.

In the cold morning, Jack's breath formed small balloons of mist as he marched behind Ross, who at least had the comfort of a horse. Jack took a last look at the barracks, wondering when he would see this place again. They marched across the common towards the port, with lightness in the pace of the men, anticipation amongst the ranks and, for Jack, a soaring sense of an adventure beginning. The new beginning that he had longed for. He felt enormous relief. He had escaped, without the feared arrest, and, God willing, would be free of the risk of humiliation and prosecution. He would not have to defend himself for his very life before an English judge.

Several men waved at ladies walking along the common, heedless of the cold stares from the men-folk of the town. This was no flag-waving farewell from the populace, however; Britain was not sending its men off to war, but disposing of some of its criminals, the unwanted, unskilled, disruptive members of its society. It was a thankless adventure and received appropriate inattention from the few bystanders who silently watched them march past.

On arrival at The Hard, they found Midshipman Ferguson was waiting with ship's barges and a crew of sailors to ferry the marines on board the *Sirius*. More boats were waiting to ferry the soldiers out to the transports, either the *Lady Penrhyn* or the *Scarborough*.

'Good morning, sir.' James Ferguson addressed Ross with a polite smile and eyes steady. He was a confident young man, and not in the least put off by the scowl Ross was wearing. *Father is Lieutenant Governor of Greenwich Hospital and I already have five years' sea-going experience, and a major of marines is not that intimidating*, he thought. Another year and he would have the sea time required to pass for lieutenant. Then he was firmly on the ladder reaching up for command. Not that there would be the prospect of a promotion board on this commission, he knew. There were only two captains in the expedition and precious little chance of sitting his examination until the colony was established, with a full complement of officers.

'Are you ready to get us out there?' Ross pointed to the flagship. He was anxious to be going.

'Aye aye, sir. Ready as ever.'

'Then let's be about our business, Mister Ferguson.'

The marines trooped onto the barges and the midshipman and the mates pulled away smartly out into the harbour, facing a long pull to the Motherbank.

Jack grinned as Ferguson gave him a wink. Major Ross was looking intently at *Sirius* as she rose and fell on the gentle swell, the growing sun dancing across the waters.

As the senior officer of the detachment, Ross was the last to scramble aboard.

Lieutenant Philip King greeted him. 'Welcome aboard, Major Ross. Philip King, sir. I am the second lieutenant, sir. Mister Bradley, the first, is below with the captain. Delighted to have you and your men with us at last.'

King was a Cornishman, born in Launceston, and an officer with already some eighteen years' experience. 'Ferguson will show you to your quarters, sir.'

Ross muttered an acknowledgement and made for the companionway.

Jack, following behind, looked at Lieutenant King. 'Good morning. Vizzard, Jack Vizzard. She seems a fine ship, sir,' he said, looking around him.

'Only a sixth rate now, Mister Vizzard. She's five hundred and forty tonnes. She used to be the *Berwick*, an armed store-ship with the Company on the East Indies trade. We will have to see how she sails in deep water, but she is pretty enough, I'll grant you that. She's a short, beamy tub of a thing, and the yard has done well to increase her cargo qualities. We need that, Mister Vizzard, for I have rarely seen so much loaded aboard one of His Majesty's ships!'

'She looks big enough to me,' Jack replied. 'But then, this is my first ship.'

'In that case you had better follow me and I will show you around.' King was a cheerful, kindly man of about thirty years, and of a benevolent nature. Small, pale blue eyes were set in a somewhat rounded but fresh, tanned and handsome face. He wore his hair short and his uniform hung loosely on his shoulders. He moved slowly, stooping between the decks, as he pointed out the various parts of the ship.

Jack followed, trying to take in all that the lieutenant described, and looked in wonder at the strange new wooden world of which he was to become a small part.

He was struck immediately by the cramped space allotted to the crew, the lack of light below deck, and the odours that reached out to him. His face wrinkled.

'She can take one hundred and eighty souls, Mister Vizzard, but I doubt we will have that many, even with all your redcoats!' King smiled. 'Apart from myself there are two lieutenants, and we should have nine "young gentlemen" or midshipmen. With luck we will have a full complement of seamen, about eighty or ninety of 'em, and all the warrant officers.'

King ducked as he passed along the deck. 'Now, to our guns. Major Ross will detail some of your lads to work at least two of them. We have no heavy artillery on *Sirius*—sixteen 6-pounder carriage guns, six 18-pounder carronades and twenty-four small swivels. You will note those about the deck as we go.' King halted to direct a sailor. 'Steady with those carbines, Buddle, or Mister Vizzard here will be after your hide!' Turning to Jack, he continued, 'They are your small-arms; should have two hundred short muskets and a dozen sergeant's carbines. We are to receive two field pieces as your shore artillery, but when and where, I have yet to be informed.'

King moved to follow the sailor down into the hold; the stench of the bilges reached Jack's nostrils, and he put his hand to his face.

'You will get used to it,' his guide smilingly informed him, noting his reaction. 'She has had much work done for this voyage, Vizzard. As a lobster-back you will not observe it, but I am informed that the Admiralty has expended nigh on seven thousand pounds on this ship.'

A young boy ran past him, followed by one of his own lads. In the gloom, he did not recognize Tom Clutterbuck, who caught him a glancing blow as he ran.

'What the devil!' Jack shouted.

'Sorry, Mister Jack—I mean, 'sir'!' Tom called back, as he scampered after his new friend and made for the companionway leading to the lower deck.

'One of your boys, I take it?' Lieutenant King enquired.

'Yes, I brought him into the service with me. He has only his grandmother and she is not well. Otherwise, he is an orphan. I find him useful.' Jack had no desire to elaborate further.

King decided against a tour of the hold and instead led Jack along the gun deck, pointing out the ship's armaments and explaining that in the event of action Jack's station would be on the fore-deck, with his marines, directing musket fire against the enemy.

'We are not at war, but we may cross with pirates, and your chief duty on this expedition is to guard the prisoners, but it is as well to know these things,' he continued.

They worked their way aft, and King showed him a screened area on the port side that was to be his berth.

'No cabins for subalterns on this ship, Vizzard,' he remarked, seeing Jack's expression. 'Only the captain, the first lieutenant and the governor have that particular comfort. And your own commander.' His teeth showed in the dim light.

'Then I must make the best of it.' Jack grinned in response.

Around them seamen were carrying stores below to the hold and cursing with each breath. They lowered their eyes as they passed the two officers, for fear of attracting unwelcome attention.

Lieutenant King stopped a seaman on his way up the companionway, and instructed him to erect a screen at the aft end of the deck and to collect Jack's trunk. He ducked below a beam towards the stern and turned to ask, 'Do you have a cot, or will you take a hammock, Vizzard? Your space will hardly allow a cot, I fear.'

'I hear a hammock is a greater comfort at sea. That will soon be proved, I hope?'

Jack was eager for news of the fleet's departure.

'We will learn soon enough,' King said. 'Now, if you will excuse me, I must see to my other duties. I will see you at dinner in the ward-room.' King went below to supervise the men in the hold and Jack decided to see to his own quarters and equipment.

A sailor was busy fixing lengths of sailcloth to the beams on the starboard side of the deck as Jack approached. A young midshipman was standing in the shadow of an oil lamp, watching the work.

'Morning, sir,' he said. 'Waterhouse, sir, Oliver Waterhouse, at your service. Mister King instructed me to assist you. My station is on the weather deck, forrard. With your marines, sir.'

The youth was about sixteen, stocky and broad-shouldered, with hair the colour of coal, and dark eyes that seemed to smoulder with restrained emotion. He had already some four years of sea service. He was also hoping to pass examination for lieutenant at the end of the voyage.

'Let me show you how to stow your hammock, sir.' Waterhouse rolled a blanket in the stiff canvas, deftly rolling it tight and binding it with cords. 'It must be able to pass through this hoop when you are finished, sir. Mister King usually instructs me to check the men's hammocks with it.' He passed a wooden hoop over the end of the roll, pulling it along the length of the hammock.

'There, a perfect fit, if I do say so myself.' The boy seemed pleased with his work. 'Now I must show you where to stow it when we are called to quarters, though I fancy we will see little action on this cruise.' Waterhouse looked rueful.

Jack smiled. 'Do you not think we will see any action, then?'

'An unlikely prospect in my opinion, sir. My father wanted me to accompany Captain Phillip on this expedition, but I was hoping for the Mediterranean this time. The ladies are so —how shall I say?—well, accommodating, in Spain and Naples.' The boy led the way to the quarterdeck, carrying the rolled hammock over his shoulder, dropping it neatly into the nettings just above the entrance to the captain's cabin below the poop.

'There, now you have it. May I show you to your station now, sir?' The midshipman did not wait for an answer, but led Jack along the larboard deck towards the bow, where some of his company were already drilling under the watchful eye of Sergeant Packer.

A young marine was handling a boarding pike, and coming under a good deal of abuse from Packer's sarcasm.

'You stupid pillock, Bates! Carry it properly, or it'll be up your arse, an' I ain't larfin', boy!'

The marine quickly shouldered the pike, his face colouring as the others about him stifled their own laughter at the sight of their officer.

'Afternoon, sir.' Packer stood straight, facing Jack. 'Just thought I'd get the lads working with these things, get them familiar with the ship, like. Any word yet, sir?' Everyone was now keyed up and wanting to get to sea as soon as possible.

'Governor Phillip has yet to take me into his confidence, Packer, but, rest assured, I will ensure that you are the first to know, the minute he does.'

Private Bates quickly turned his laugh into a cough and Jack climbed onto the foremast ratlines to look at the constant stream of small craft ferrying supplies and people to a variety of ships anchored in the harbour and at the Motherbank.

In the quiet times his mind would take him to Gloucestershire and to the life he had left there. He was guilty, he knew, of a capital crime. He had also deserted a girl. A lovely, sweet-natured and innocent girl. The knowledge caused him endless sorrow and distress. He felt ashamed, but knew that once she had been convicted and he had resolved on revenge, there could have been no future for them. He had risked all but had run away, and the thought haunted him. In his bag was a letter written weeks ago now, but never sent. Perhaps now was the time to do so, he thought. *They cannot reach me at sea.*

'I am to show you the foretop, sir.' Waterhouse broke into his privacy, instantly dispelling the ghosts that haunted his inner mind. 'You will be expected to be familiar with it, sir.' Oliver Waterhouse started quickly up the ratlines, not waiting to see if Jack followed, although he did, with a great deal more caution than his young guide.

He reached the lubber's hole some minutes later, struggled to pull himself through and felt very uneasy as he looked at the deck seventy feet below.

'This is where some of your men will be positioned in action, sir.'

Jack thought there was barely room for the two of them, and no protection from the elements or from enemy fire.

'How many are to be placed here, would you say?' he asked.

'It would be common for two or three, even four of your best shots to be posted here, sir,' the youngster replied. 'But you had better speak to the captain about that.'

Oliver Waterhouse was enjoying this, as always. Most marines hated the fighting tops, preferring the security of the deck. This officer was no different, he thought.

'The ship is one hundred and ten feet in length overall, and thirty-two feet in the beam, sir.' Waterhouse grinned. 'Where we are now is seventy feet and seven inches above the deck, sir. Thought you would wish to know these things, sir. I have to. Captain Hunter will most likely question me on the morrow.'

'Where are you from, lad?' Jack thought to divert his attention from the swaying of the mast. *Seventy feet and seven inches.* He held tight to the mast.

'Rochester, sir, but I have been at sea for nigh on five years now. I shall not return home until I have my commission as lieutenant.' He looked at Jack with a determined expression on his young face.

'Well, with your leave, I shall now return to the deck. Perhaps you will kindly demonstrate the descent first.'

The midshipman nimbly swung out over the platform and, as agile as a monkey, disappeared down the ratlines. Jack followed, holding his breath as he hung suspended for a time, and slowly made his way down, greeted by the cheers of his men.

'That showed the Navy, sir,' volunteered Packer, who now made to follow Jack's example and lead a section of marines up to the foretop.

Jack watched them crawl up the ratlines for a few moments, again wondering how it would be if they were ever called on to defend the ship from an enemy. How he might behave, really. Would he be able to fight hand to hand, with cannon fire about him? A cold shudder passed through his body. He was no coward, at least he did not think so, but some of the tales he had heard, particularly from some of the old sweats in the company, made him swallow hard.

The ship's bell rang eight times, signalling the end of the afternoon watch, and he went below to the wardroom for supper.

There was only one other officer present, a surgeon, busy writing up a journal. The man seemed disinterested in engaging in conversation, so Jack ate some cold meat and cheese, then left and went to inspect his men before the drummer beat 'To Quarters' and they were dispersed about the ship.

Packer was familiar with the drill and had the men ready. Jack looked them over in the thin light that came through the half-open gun ports. Packer had done well, he decided. He explained that before the bosun's mates piped 'Down Hammocks', he would speak to them about the voyage and the little he knew about the coast on the other side of the world that was their destination.

The drummer arrived and he was amused to see young Tom standing at the foot of the companionway, a proud grin stretched across his face, as he beat out a ragged roll on the cumbersome drum hanging from his shoulders.

'Be careful with that, young un,' Packer said kindly. 'That there drum was with Major Ross at Bunker Hill, an' he won't thank 'ee if it be broken.'

Quickly, the marines were swallowed up, as scores of sailors rushed by to their positions, bare feet drumming on the deck, and Jack made his way rapidly up to the weather deck and took up his position by the foremast.

'You will have to move faster than that, Mister Vizzard, if ever we find ourselves up against an enemy,' a rasping Scots voice from the quarterdeck called at him. Ross was not simply trying to impress the captain, but, thought Jack, making a show of his authority, and perhaps attempting to belittle him.

'Very well, sir,' Jack called back. 'I hope to have the opportunity to improve, sir!' he shouted, hiding a smile, noticed only by the observant Packer.

'Thee'll have to watch thyself with Mister Ross, sir. He be a bit of a stickler for drill.'

'Packer, you are an insolent bugger. Pay attention to your own duty and deal with Bates. He has yet to load his musket, man.'

'Ain't you 'eard, sir? Our powder and ball ain't been loaded yet, sir. Muskets and carbines are aboard, but the quartermaster says the ordnance cart's gone missin'.'

He had not been aware of this. He wondered if Ross knew, and decided he would say nothing, but would speak to the quartermaster at the first opportunity. *Hell and damnation*, he thought, *that spells trouble for the quartermaster*.

'Get him to go through the drill anyway,' he snapped, annoyed at himself for his ignorance.

He took the time to look at the captain. He had yet to be introduced to John Hunter, but had some knowledge of the man from his conversations with Midshipman Waterhouse and the ship's officers, Bradley and King. The captain was motionless on the quarterdeck, hands firmly behind his back, his eyes slowly traversing the ship before him, the other vessels at anchor, the sky above and the sea all around.

Hunter was an officer of good reputation as a sound and skilled seaman and navigator. He was not yet fifty and had a plain, open expression, with eyes constantly searching his ship, his rather thin mouth rarely smiling, but he was well respected by all who knew him as a competent and resourceful officer with over thirty years' sea experience.

As Jack watched him now, Hunter walked across his deck, his eyes taking in all the detail of the ship that he was now to command. Arthur Phillip was the commodore, but Jack realised that Captain Hunter would effectively command the ship, and navigate it around the globe to Botany Bay. Phillip would relinquish command when he officially assumed the post of governor on stepping ashore at Botany Bay.

He appeared satisfied with what he saw and spoke to a bo-sun's mate at his side. The order 'Down Hammocks' whistled loudly along the deck, and the ship again transformed itself into a colony of ants, as each man on deck headed to collect his hammock and make ready for the coming night.

Jack followed the first lieutenant as he made his way down to the gun-deck on his rounds, inspecting the sailor's messes. He reached the marines' mess by the aft bulkhead to see that already they were filling tankards with ale and lighting long-stemmed pipes, filling the low space with a blue-grey haze.

Sergeant Packer offered a tankard to Jack as he perched himself on one of the six-pounder carriage guns that had been assigned to his men. He took a long swallow of the beer and grinned at the expectant faces in front of him.

'Not as good as Gloucester ale, lads, but it will do.' He was pleased to see that a few of the men laughed. He looked at their expectant faces, eager for news.

'The place that we are going to is on the far side of the world,' he started. 'Botany Bay is in New Holland, which is in the Great South Sea. It will take us many months to get there, and when we do we have to mind a lot of criminals.' He continued, 'You are thinking that this is not a duty that will bring you fortune or glory, and in that you are probably right.' He paused to judge the mood and decided that his men were in agreement with him. 'But it will be an adventure, have my word on it! You will see things that no others have seen.'

He spoke about the discoveries that Joseph Banks and Dr Daniel Solander had made during the remarkable voyage of the *Endeavour* with James Cook. He talked of the coasts and islands of the South Seas that Cook had charted with such exceptional skill and care. He spoke of the peoples they had met. He talked of the lessons learned about caring for the health of sailors. He spoke of the astronomical studies carried out by Charles Green during that same voyage.

As he talked, he sensed most men listening more carefully. A few, clearly disinterested, drifted away in the gloom to find other entertainment, but his own men stayed and listened with appreciation as Vizzard spoke of strange animals, of blue skies and seas, and a land of dense forests and white sandy beaches.

At last, he finished and drained the tankard, which Joe Packer had discreetly re-filled several times that evening. His head felt loose on his shoulders, and his eyes reddened from the tobacco smoke that filled the deck. Satisfied he had retained the attention of several of the men under his control, he felt they, and he, had become closer.

Swaying gently in his hammock, he lay awake a very long time, listening to the night breeze in the rigging and to the gentle slap of the sea against the wooden wall of *Sirius*.

CHAPTER 21

CONVICT

Mary already felt sick. She had endured rough treatment for months, but now she felt utterly humiliated and desperate.

The petition Henry Vizzard had submitted to His Majesty was still unanswered. It would remain so, she was certain of it. Henry visited her each week, for which she was grateful, as if it maintained some connection, however tenuous, with Jack. He left her food and brought with him a book or two, a change of clothes—and surreptitiously gave the gaoler coins to ease her situation, but Mary knew nothing of that.

When she told her parents she was to be sent to Portsmouth to join the fleet assembled to transport a thousand souls to Botany Bay, they wept pitifully. It was cruelty itself to see how her father had aged during her term in gaol. He visited her frequently, making the long journey to Gloucester, always tearful at the parting. Her brothers came also, offering words of comfort and supplies of food, which she shared with a few other prisoners. Now she was to go and never see them again. Her heart was shattered.

The news of the actual date of her departure, though expected, was nevertheless a shock. With less than two days to prepare, her emotions were in turmoil, her despair found new depths. The final farewell to her family tore souls apart. The last vision of her father, broken, his sobs echoing, fought for attention as the convicts were pulled and pushed away from their beloveds.

She journeyed in an open cart from Gloucester with a man, Edward Pugh, and two women, Elizabeth Parker and Betty Mason. It rained several times during the journey and she was cold and weak. Some folk jeered at the cart as it passed by. Once, a kindly innkeeper thrust a flagon of ale and some stale bread into the cart, as they were left outside while the gaolers had supper in the warmth inside the tavern.

There were two babes with them, Annie and Thomas. The women sheltered them as best they could, feeding them what little they had to offer. Mary helped; she at least had money and food given by Giles and Henry—it had been a tearful parting with both.

The turnkey at Portsmouth signed for them, separated them from their male companion, and told them they were to board a transport, the *Lady Penrhyn*; then, with obvious relief, he hastily put them on a lighter taking stores out to that ship.

There was a rising swell as they cleared the harbour, and grey, rain-filled clouds scudded low over the huddle of ships at the Motherbank, bringing a drizzle that penetrated everything. Mary shivered, her teeth chattered uncontrollably and she felt nausea rise in her at the sight of the ship that was to carry her away from home.

She looked up at the stern of a warship as the lighter passed by it. The name *Sirius* was picked out in gold lettering eight inches high below the stern cabin. She half wondered who or what *Sirius* was. Jack would know, she thought, wrapping a piece of canvas sailcloth closer to her body and over her head against the rain that had now started to fall.

Above her, a solitary marine officer leaned over the stern rail, eyes absently taking in the activity about the ships at anchor, only briefly glancing at the small craft passing by, carrying another handful of convicts to one of the transports. He shrugged as a gust threatened to remove his hat, and Lieutenant Jack Vizzard turned away to his duties.

Minutes later the small craft hooked onto the side of the ship and a coarse voice bellowed at her to move quickly. She fell as the sea rose and missed the tumblehome, almost falling into the cold, grey-green sea.

The turnkey struck her back with a cane and she painfully climbed the side, pulling on a greasy rope hanging from the ship's side. A dirty, calloused hand pulled her roughly up onto the deck as a grimy face looked down at her.

'Welcome aboard, my lovely. Welcome to your new gaol.' The sailor grinned, revealing a toothless mouth, the legacy of scurvy, and Mary turned away as the man pulled Elizabeth onto the deck, with the same greeting. A bosun's mate shouted at her, telling her to follow him below. She turned at the companionway, hesitating to descend the near-vertical steps, and slowly lowered herself down.

There was light, at least, but the putrescent smell that struck her was overwhelming—worse, far worse than she had encountered in Gloucester gaol—and she vomited, falling to her knees as the spasm tied her belly in knots.

'You'll get used to it—they all do, in time.' The mate was concerned only with the mess on the deck. 'Fetch a bucket and clean it up, and be quick about it.'

Elizabeth helped her to her feet and looked around for the bucket. She saw a leather pail and quickly poured water over the mess; taking a mop, she swept the puke up into the pail and threw it out through an open gun-port.

'Move along smartly, now. This way.' The mate beckoned to the lower deck, now converted into cells.

Rough hands pushed them along the deck past a pair of inquisitive young marines standing guard, and into a cage made of stout timbers fitted with iron bars. They sat on a wooden bench set into the side of the ship. A dozen other occupants looked at them without interest and then resumed the murmured conversation their arrival had interrupted. Mary closed her eyes and put her hands to her face to smother the tears that had again started to smear the grime on her face. Her sobs moved her friend to speak.

'Don't you fret now, my pet.' Elizabeth Parker put a comforting hand on her arm. 'We'll be all right, now.'

Mary opened her swollen eyes and a half smile appeared on her face. 'Thanks, Lizzie. I don't think I could have borne all this without you.' She pulled her legs up and hugged her knees.

'We stick together and we'll be fine, I promise you. Now let's get us comfy, and try and get some sleep. You look quite done in. My little Annie needs a feed first, though.'

The baby strapped to her chest had been quiet for the last hour but now started to cry from hunger, until Lizzie managed to start her sucking at her emaciated breast.

Mary unrolled a blanket, lay down on the boards and was soon asleep, too exhausted to care or do more.

Lizzie Parker stretched out on the floor of the cage and closed her eyes, too, but did not sleep at first. She lay there listening to the sounds of the ship that was to be her next prison for many a long month. Her mind went back to her own home at Nibley, nestling under the Cotswold escarpment at Wootton-Under-Edge. She was not bitter. She had done wrong and had accepted her punishment with grace.

Mayhap this Botany Bay will offer a better life for my child than the desperate poverty in which I have grown up— and for me. I worry for my brothers and sister, probably now on the mercy of the parish. How will they manage without me to care for them, feed them?

She had listened with some envy to Mary's tale and was truly sorry for the lost life that Mary had so nearly had. But she had to survive. The rest of her life was now. The future was less certain than ever, and more than ever she had to use her wits just to survive. Mary turned and moaned in her pain and Lizzie Parker fell asleep.

The bell on the quarterdeck rang and the mate bellowed along the deck, 'Mess captains to the galley, on the double now!'

A number of women, trusted by the naval agent, were unshackled and they rose quickly to their feet, heading to the galley for the evening meal.

Because the ship was still in port, dinner was more than simple potato or pease soup. There were some lumps of quite good pork, and boiled rice, too. Eager hands grabbed hunks of fresh coarse-grained bread on wooden platters placed on the floor. Those too slow, or more distant from them, received none.

Lizzie Parker sat on the end of the bench and gently shook Mary awake, as a boy of about sixteen or seventeen years came into their cage and placed the wooden tubs on the floor. Some of the women made to fill their bowls, pushing aside some of those who were older or less quick.

''Ere, wait a mo'!' Lizzie shouted. 'If we're to get through this we gotta be better 'n animals.'

'What's your game, then, luv?' a London voice rasped back at her from the gloom.

Lizzie sought out the owner of the voice and calmly rephrased her thought. 'I'm just thinkin' that we've a long way to go an' we must be fair to all. Make sure that all gets a fair share, like. No use us fighting over a bucket o' stew.' There was a muttering of agreement. 'We must pull together, try and 'elp, 'cos they buggers up there won't,' she said, pointing her thumb upwards.

'That's right,' said the boy. 'We got to be fair to all.'

'Give the nippers theirs first, then we share out the rest equal, like.' Lizzie moved to the tubs on the floor and picked up a ladle.

'Right, then, ladies, let's have the kids' bowls, an' the rest of you stand back.'

No one tried to challenge her authority and she deftly started to pour the steaming stew into the small bowls that each convict carried with their meagre possessions.

Mary sat upright, stretching as much as she could in the cramped space, and waited until Lizzie placed a bowl in her lap.

'There you are, then, Mary. The best meal we've had since Gloucester.'

And it was. Mary spooned the food into her mouth, enjoying the hot, greasy meal, and feeling the warmth of it spread through her aching bones. Within a few minutes she wiped the bowl clean with a piece of bread, and if she was not satiated it was indeed the finest food she had eaten in months. The journey to Portsmouth in the open cart during the freezing, wet winter had all but exhausted her.

The boy returned with some wooden tankards of beer that the captain had released for the prisoners and Mary drank that too. She started to feel stronger than she had for a very long time.

'Thank you, Lizzie. I feel much better. I might have missed out if you hadn't taken charge.'

'Don't you fret, girl. You helped us in Gloucester, and on the way down country,' she said, looking at her child, 'and wore yourself out doin' so. As I said, we've got to look out for each other, otherwise what's going to 'appen to us?'

They talked for a while, mostly about Gloucester, the time spent in gaol and the journey to Portsmouth, but also about their fear of the voyage ahead of them. Lizzie talked of her hopes for her baby, whom she adored.

Mary still ached, but now she felt revived. She started to concern herself with her appearance, and wondered when—indeed, if—she could wash herself. It had been so long since she had done so. She wished now for a bath of hot water, and a piece of soap. The sailors seemed rough and crude, but not overtly cruel, and she began to believe she was safer than she had been for months.

Somewhere a bell rang, and she heard a voice call out an order. The marine guards outside the cage extinguished the lanterns, and the entire deck was cast into darkness. She listened to the groans from the ship's timbers and the water gurgling past the hull, inches from her head.

As the cages fell silent, and with the lanterns turned off, noises from the forward part of the ship intruded and shadows began to appear from the foc's'le. Women stirred as the men sought out partners for the night, even for the entire voyage. Terms were quickly discussed and agreed in whispered, murmured tones; sometimes a bottle of gin sufficed, for others a few coins clinked, signifying agreement. Having paired off, the shadows moved quietly forrard and into the darker corners.

From the gloom, a large shape appeared in front of Mary.

'Are you all right now, my pretty?' The man was the sailor who had hauled Mary aboard earlier. She looked at him coldly.

'Come, now, you could do worse on this ship, and I can protect you.' In the gloom of the 'tween decks the man, although he spoke gently, looked more menacing than he had when she'd first encountered him, his eyes glowing and sweat beads running down his face. His open mouth, below a bulbous nose, smelled strongly of rum, and belied his promise of protection.

'I have no need of your protection—and no desire for your hammock. Leave me alone,' Mary said, her rasping voice a warning.

'Now don't be takin' on so. It's a bloody long way to Botany Bay and 'tween here and there you will have need of a man.'

'If I do, then be sure it will not be you. I say again, go and leave me be!' She spoke more sharply this time. Still he did not move. He opened his mouth and lifted a hand, but stopped as a blade touched the back of his neck.

'You heard the lady—now piss off before this knife tickles your neck a little closer.' Lizzie was capable of using the knife; she knew that. The sailor was not prepared to take a chance, and raised his arms in submission.

'All right, all right, then, no harm meant. I'll leave you both. There's more fish in this sea, and there's another sweeter catch to be havin' elsewhere, I'm thinkin'.'

The man stole away into the shadows, searching for company that was more pliant, and Lizzie put away the knife.

'As I said, we got to look after each other, 'cause these bastards won't.'

Mary started to tremble and shake. Tears welled in her red-rimmed eyes and Lizzie knew that she was remembering the night of the attack at the vicarage, so long ago now it might have been in another world, as indeed it was.

She put her arms around Mary and rocked her as she did her own child. They slept uneasily that night, huddled closer together, entwined as lovers might, listening to the sounds of rutting in the shadows and of babies crying as their mothers bought protection and, perhaps, some extra food, anything to make their misery more tolerable.

Chapter 22
Ordnance

The following morning Jack woke to the unfamiliar sound of the ship's bell as it clanged above his head. He shaved uncomfortably in cold water before a mirror the size of a saucer before dressing, finding it difficult to do so while his small rectangle of deck rolled and yawed beneath his feet. *This will require some practice*, he judged, spreading his feet.

The flap of his canvas cabin parted and Tom entered. 'Mornin', Mister Vizzard, sir. Sorry I'm late, sir. Mister Ross says you are to report to his cabin at once, sir. He seems very out of sorts, if I might say.'

'What? Oh, very well, I will come at once, Tom. Thank you.'

Irritated by the early summons, he finished dressing. *Perhaps he wants me to count the stores again, or some such nonsense. Breakfast will have to wait*, he decided. *Hell and damnation.*

He made his way to the wardroom, offering a greeting to the officers off watch, and knocked on Ross's cabin door. As commander of the marine detachment Ross had the luxury of his own small cabin, although he felt aggrieved at that, believing he had an entitlement to one of the two cabins below the upper deck. Captain Phillip had denied him that, explaining that the stern cabins were properly allocated as *Sirius* had two naval captains to accommodate, and they outranked a major of Marines.

'Enter!' That grating voice again. Jack adjusted his tunic and, crouching between the beams, entered. Major Ross was unshaven and had a fresh pot of coffee steaming on the small table next to his bed. His eyes were ruddy, and his breath smelled of alcohol. He held a crumpled sheet of paper in his left hand.

'Vizzard, morning to you.' Manners? Jack was surprised. 'I have a duty for you. It seems that our stores are deficient.' He looked embarrassed. 'The Q.M. tells me that the stores of ball and armourer's tools for our muskets have not come aboard. How we are supposed to guard a fleet of scum without our ordnance defeats me. You will have to go ashore and find it. I want our munitions on board before supper; is that clear? Another thing... nobody is to know about this.'

'Yes, sir, I understand.' He did not understand. The supplies of muskets and ammunition had come down from Woolwich weeks ago; he had personally seen them into the stores at barracks. He knew that muskets and carbines had been loaded onto wagons and taken to the dockyard, for he had witnessed that with his own eyes. 'I will go at once, sir.'

'See that you do, Vizzard, and find my ammunition, or there will be hell to pay.'

Jack took two men with him, including Sergeant Packer. He was in a black mood by the time he reached the yard commissioner's office.

Jack, as a newly commissioned marine, was not familiar with the administration of His Majesty's naval dockyards. He reported first to the controller's office, who sent him on a goose-chase to the surveyor's office, where he was sent away by a very angry retired naval captain, before finally reaching the yard commissioner's rooms.

'No, young man, I cannot help you. I know nothing of your missing ordnance. I suggest you take it up with the storekeeper.' Samuel Farmer was not an unkind man. He had reached his position through years of hard work, and taken the post of yard commissioner when it had become clear that he was not to be offered flag rank. Having now been passed over for promotion to that coveted rank twice, he resented the fact that he would have to mark time until seniority delivered the prize. Portly and florid, he filled the chair behind his untidy desk. He was used to dealing with demanding young officers.

'But, sir, our ordnance should have been aboard yesterday. I know it is here as I saw to the delivery myself. With respect, it is your responsibility.' Jack was at risk of a firm rebuke and knew it.

Farmer took a long breath, and with patience born of long experience said, 'Lieutenant Vizzard, I will excuse your impertinence this once, because of your undoubted inexperience and ignorance of the Navy. I take my orders from the Navy Board, and you must take your ammunition from the Ordnance Board, for which, thank heaven, I am not responsible.

You must see the storekeeper. I wish you *bonne chance.* Good day to you, sir!'

Nothing Jack could say would sway this officer. He saluted and turned quickly to hide his face. 'Come along, Packer. We are clearly wasting time here.'

They strode down Long Row, past the rope-maker's sheds, until they reached the ordnance stores. Crates of all kinds were stacked everywhere, barrels of powder of differing sizes and quality, sacks of fuses and garlands of ball for every calibre of gun in use in the Navy. Jack stared in awe at the volume of munitions held in the storeroom. He found an office at the other end of the building. A thin-faced man of middle years appeared to be the senior, with two younger men working from high stools in a corner.

The clerk, with a large pile of paper on his desk, was busy scratching notes on a list. Jack tried a cheery greeting, and when that was ignored his tone hardened.

'I am looking for the Marines' ordnance for *Sirius*. It should have been brought aboard yesterday. Where is it?' Jack waited for a response.

Eventually the man looked up. His eyes noted the fresh single epaulette and looked back at his papers, all in a single, slow movement. 'I am very busy, come back later.'

'I will not. You will please find my supplies now or give me an explanation as to why they have not been loaded. I would prefer the former.' His patience was now evaporating.

'I have half a dozen vessels to deal with. You may wait or return later as you please.' The man returned to his list.

The sword rasped as it swiftly flew from its scabbard, and the point hovered over the pile of papers as Jack leaned forward and whispered, 'You will deal with my request now or your damned lists will be given to my sergeant to clean your arse with!'

The clerk put down his quill and stood up. 'I am accustomed to dealing with gentlemen and will not be threatened in this way!' he spluttered, his pomposity quavering in the face of Jack's sword point.

'I can always find alternative means, even as a gentleman.'

The clerk looked at the cold eyes that Jack showed and decided that his cooperation was justified on this occasion. He called an assistant over and whispered to him. The man ran off down the warehouse as though the devil was after him.

Jack sheathed his sword as Joe Packer showed his broken teeth in a wide grin. 'There'll be the devil to pay, sir, when that little weasel reports you.'

'Then he can take his complaint to Major Ross. I am not much concerned.'

Jack pulled a silver flask from inside his boat cloak and took a swallow. He offered it to Packer who shook his head.

'I will take a drink with you later, if I may, sir, when this business is done.'

The clerk's assistant returned and whispered a lengthy explanation to his superior.

'It seems, Lieutenant, that an error has occurred. Your ordnance has been—how shall I say?—misplaced. Ned here believes it may have been sent to the *Albany* by mistake. I will cause enquiries to be made and send word. What ship did you say?'

'The *Sirius,* Captain John Hunter. Major Robert Ross commands the marines.'

'Then I will see your supplies are with you by Monday forenoon, sir.' Obeisance now played across the clerk's face;

his hands clasped together at his chest. He smiled and gave the smallest nod of the head.

Vizzard ignored the shallow compliment and, satisfied he had done his duty, turned smartly away. They made their way back to the ship's jolly boat.

It was Saturday 12th May 1787.

*****

As Jack approached the flagship, he could see a stream of seamen scurrying along the weather deck and a flurry of signal flags hauled up to the mizzen top. Looking about him, he could see similar activity amongst the other ships assembled at the Motherbank.

'Somethin's a happenin', Mister Vizzard. Buggered if I knows what all those signals mean, though.' Packer was perplexed, and Jack equally so; he immediately resolved to spend time with the signals midshipman and master the Navy's signalling system.

'Whatever it is, we had best get aboard quickly. Smartly now, you men!' he shouted to the crew of the lighter ferrying them from the harbour into the swell of Spithead.

'Looks as though you'll be leaving us, then, sir,' the ferryman said, spitting overboard.

'What are you saying, man?' Jack snapped.

'The flagship's makin' ready for sea, sir. I reckon you be off with the tide first thing in the mornin', if you ask me.'

Jack swore. The ferryman started in alarm.

Sergeant Joseph Packer pulled his hat down over his eyes and exhaled slowly through teeth gritted tight, understanding coming to him only a moment or two after the same realisation had struck Jack.

'Hold off, mister ferryman. I need to go to the *Albany*. Where is she moored?'

'Ah, now, sir, I can't be doing that. You see, she sailed this mornin', sir. She been waitin' for a good easterly for a couple o' days now.'

Jack's shoulders sagged. There was nothing for it, then, but to report to Ross and inform him that the ammunition for the marines' muskets was on another ship; that the marine guard, on the first fleet of convicts to Botany Bay was without the ammunition needed to do its duty. In the event of any attack on the fleet, or rebellion by the convicts, the marines would be unable to defend themselves. He did not relish giving Major Ross the news.

The ferryman took them back to the *Sirius* and Jack and his men climbed the nettings up the ship's tumblehome. Lieutenant King had the watch and greeted Jack with good humour.

'Welcome back, redcoat, and what are you so glum about? Looks as though you lost a guinea and found a shilling!'

'Sorry, sir, but I can't discuss it at present. I must see Major Ross. What's all the bustle about?'

'Have you not heard? The commodore wanted to weigh anchor but some of the crew on the transports refused to sail. Some have been aboard for nearly seven months without a shilling of pay, and, I dare say, want a last run ashore. Your lord and master is over yonder, aboard the *Prince of Wales*, with Captain Hunter, seeking a settlement to their demands.'

'So, we are to go at last?' Jack asked.

'It surely appears so. The ship is ready for sea and the commodore anxious to be away.' King looked up at the furled topsails. 'The wind has veered a point. If it holds we shall be off on the next tide.'

'Not before time, sir. I shall go below. Perhaps you would be so kind as to send word when Major Ross returns?'

'Most certainly I will, though I expect you will hear his arrival! Are you in difficulty, Vizzard?' King asked, his voice low.

'Please do not press me on this, sir. You will hear more of it later, I have no doubt.' Jack went below and took a coffee while he waited and mentally composed his report to Ross. He did not have to wait long before he heard voices on the deck above, one of which was the unmistakable, coarse, stentorian voice of the major. The summons to report to him arrived within minutes.

'Mister Vizzard, your report, if you please,' Ross demanded immediately he entered the wardroom.

Taking a deep breath, Jack related the events of the day, concluding with the information that the division's musket supplies were now down channel on board a ship bound for Antigua.

Ross exploded with venom. 'You clump-headed fool, Vizzard! Laddie, I have just quelled a near mutiny on the poxxed transport astern, with no better armament than a handful of muskets, one packet of ball for each man, some bayonets and you tell me... you tell me I have no more supplies! It's a bloody disgrace and I hold you responsible for this incompetence!'

Jack protested. 'Sir, with respect, this was incompetence on the part of the Ordnance Board. They delivered our ordnance to the wrong vessel. I have spoken to the clerk and obtained his assurance that our supplies will be loaded on Monday morning.'

'That is simply not good enough, boy! In case you have nae heard, we sail on the morning tide. What do you suggest I tell the commodore, hey? "Sorry, sir, but please ask the scum convicts not to take the ship for a day or so, because I cannot defend it!" Is that what I should do, Vizzard?' Ross paced the width of the wardroom in his agitation, spilling red wine from the glass in his hand.

Jack tried to be helpful. 'But surely, sir, we cannot sail until we have our ammunition. Captain Phillip must delay his departure.'

'You're a bloody, incapable fool, Vizzard. I gave you an order and you failed. You will take watch and watch for a week, and reflect on your duties, you young pup!'

Jack opened his mouth and quickly closed it again, realising that further protest would only bring further punishment.

'Will that be all, sir?' he said instead.

'Aye, damn right it is, boy. And you can report to my Q.M., Mister Furzer, at the end of each watch. I hold him responsible for this inefficiency as well.'

Jack's face coloured at the insult, unjustified as it was, turned on his heel, and went up to the quarterdeck to breathe some fresh air.

Lieutenant William Dawes was talking to the midshipman of the watch, but came across when he saw Jack on deck gripping the side rail.

'Well, my lad, I see from your expression that you have had your meeting with our fearless commander. What ails you?'

'The bloody man has put me on watch and watch for a week. Look, Will, you must know this. We have no musket ammunition, nor cartridge paper, nor tools to make any ball. It has all been loaded onto the wrong bloody ship. Ross holds me responsible, because he sent me to find it. The man is exasperating. I'll not do it.'

Lieutenant Dawes considered this situation. He knew that his young friend was distressed, but he had to do his duty.

'Jack, listen to me. You must or he will make life decidedly unpleasant. 'Tis only for a week and then he will have forgotten.'

'For God's sake, Will, the crew must know nothing of this. The consequences could prove very awkward, to say the least.' Jack paced towards the stern.

'Just make sure that you comply with his orders or it will be the worse for you, my friend.'

The midshipman started to take an interest in the conversation between the two marine officers and made to join them. However, a voice from the cabin door behind the wheel made him stop.

'Mister Brewer, see that the watch below has a good night's sleep. I shall be weighing at first light.' Captain John Hunter strode casually onto the deck, his experienced eyes quickly taking in the readiness of his ship.

From Leith near Edinburgh, he had been at sea since he was seventeen and was now nearly fifty. He put a finger to his hat to acknowledge the marines, and then started on his rounds of the ship.

Jack watched him walking forward, noting the state of the rigging and then making his way to the foc's'le, before disappearing down the companionway to the 'tween deck.

Jack bade his friend goodnight, made his way to inspect the guard at the marine walk between the foremast and bowsprit, and prepared for what he suspected would be a sleepless night.

CHAPTER 23

A MUSTER

Captain Hunter was back on deck shortly before the watch changed. He addressed the first lieutenant. 'Mister Bradley, the wind is in the southeast, I believe.'

'Aye, sir. It has shifted half a point and seems steady.' Bradley stood still, anticipating the next order.

'Then I think we should weigh and be gone. Please prepare the ship.'

Bradley sniffed dismissively. *The ship is as prepared as she always should be*, he thought, but decided against any comment. The entire crew had been waiting for this moment. From the wardroom to the lowliest boy aboard, all were ready, waiting. The word had passed the instant Hunter had donned his hat to go on deck.

Instead, Bradley checked his watch and nodded at the boatswain, Tom Brooks, who rang for the change of watch, and immediately blew on his pipe the order for 'All Hands', passing the word loudly. Pleased, his mates quickly echoed the order along the ship. He expected nothing less; the crew were trained and expectant.

Arthur Phillip appeared on deck shortly after and stood next to Captain Hunter.

'I have waited a long time for this day, John.'

'Yes indeed, sir,' Hunter agreed. 'It has been long enough coming.'

'Is my signal to the fleet ready?'

John Hunter looked at Midshipman Waterhouse, who was tying off the last of the signal flags onto a halyard. 'Hoist it, if you please, Mister Waterhouse.' He smiled as the young officer hauled on the signal halyard, deftly breaking out the general signal to weigh anchor.

The only ship to acknowledge was the flagship's tender, *HMS Supply,* an armed Thames trader of 175 tons, commanded by an old friend of Phillip's, Lieutenant Henry Ball. He had the 'Acknowledge' signal tied on in readiness.

'At least Ball is awake this morning, John.'

Arthur Phillip smiled at his second captain. He looked up at the mizzen top, feeling pride in the broad, swallow-tailed pennant flapping there. Its presence was an act of minor protest by Arthur Phillip. Commanding two of His Majesty's warships, with transports and supply ships, he had requested the right to fly a commodore's pennant. Lord Sydney had denied the request, a decision that irked him. This commission must surely mean he would eventually advance to flag rank and, after years as a half-pay captain, that was a matter for rejoicing. *But one day*, he thought, *one day I will fly a rear admiral's ensign.*

'He has pestered me daily for the last two weeks. I believe he is more anxious than you or I to be gone.' Hunter could not prevent a wry grin.

'He is a good officer, and will be kept busy on this voyage, I fancy.'

Phillip was a slightly built, dark-complexioned man of below medium height, quick in manner, self-controlled and courageous. The task assigned to him was to make a settlement in a wilderness on the far side of the globe, with a host of mostly broken men and women. He had the determination that enables men to achieve under the most arduous of conditions. Like many men of his profession, he had a strong sense of duty, allied to a belief in the humane treatment of all in his charge. It was these qualities that would be tested to the limit if this venture were to be a success, and Phillip was resolute: he would make a success of this commission.

They watched in the growing light as the other vessels of the fleet acquired spectral form and slowly made ready to sail, although none had acknowledged the order.

Sirius' crew was aloft on the yards, unfurling the topsails of the fore and main masts, as a gentle breeze slowly filled the sails. The deck-men and landsmen started the capstan that dragged the anchor slowly from the muddy seabed of Spithead.

'Signal *Prince of Wales* to hurry, please, John; she seems reluctant to join us.' Captain Arthur Phillip scanned the sea quickly through, checking on the transports and store-ships that constituted his command. He snapped the brass telescope closed.

Hunter gave an order to the midshipman who picked up a trumpet and shouted across to the transport, receiving a raised hand in acknowledgement from someone unseen on her deck.

'*Prince of Wales* has acknowledged, sir.'

'Very good,' the captain answered, returning to watch his crew completing the work aloft.

'Take her to sea, Mister Bradley, and call me before we clear the Needles. I shall take breakfast now.' With a last look at Portsmouth, he went aft to his cabin. As his cabin door closed Jack came on deck, having had only two hours' sleep. He yawned and stretched like a cat, rubbing his bloodshot eyes.

'D'ye find this tedious work, Mister Vizzard? Many tides will ebb and flow afore you see Old Pompey again.' Bradley smiled as the marine shook the sleep from his head.

'Not at all, sir. I have been looking forward to this time for many months.' Jack was also gazing at the ships in Portsmouth harbour, and looked aft to the lumbering transports taking ragged station astern of the flagship. The grey waters of Spithead coalesced with the rain clouds that hung low over the premier naval base of England.

'*There is a tide in the affairs of men, which taken at the flood, leads on to fortune; on such a full sea are we now afloat, and we must take the current when it serves, or lose our ventures.*' Jack smiled wryly. 'Shakespeare's Julius Caesar, sir'

'I believe I recall it. I wonder if our voyage will lead us on to fortune. Take a good look, Jack. It will be a long time before either of us see Albion's shores again.'

'I am in no hurry, sir. England will wait for me. Unlike the wretched people we are taking with us. They may never see England again. How do they feel this morning?'

Bradley was watching the receding harbor, too. 'That is my town, Jack. I grew up there. So many expeditions and explorations have had their starting point here. Do you feel a sense of history-making, Jack?'

'In a way I do. My father is the one for history, but not the history of exploration or adventure, sir. History of the country and parliament would keep him occupied. Alas, it was not for me.'

'I feel the same, Jack. For me it was mathematics and the sciences, but we become like our fathers, it is said.' Bradley was thinking of his father, master of mathematics at the Naval Academy, who had encouraged him to go to sea some fifteen years before, when he was still only thirteen years of age. 'Many times have I watched from an outward-bound ship and seen that harbour slip astern.'

'It is my first time, but I understand your meaning.' Jack felt a stirring in his chest and thought again of his home and family. Not for the first time, he wondered if he was doing right. He kept his eyes on the wake of the ship, not daring to look at Lieutenant Bradley, for fear of revealing the emotion in his eyes.

The breeze increased by a knot and Hunter called for more sail on the mizzen.

Jack shuddered and went below to report as the fleet took untidy station astern of *Sirius*. The transports formed a ragged line with *Supply,* under full sail, speeding along like a racehorse. By 10 o'clock the fleet had cleared the Isle of Wight and started the run down the Channel. One of the transports, the *Charlotte,* was already falling astern and Hunter ordered *Supply* to chivvy her master to make more sail.

Immediately astern of the flagship, the *Prince of Wales* wallowed in her wake. Blunt-nosed and round-bodied, she, like the other transports, rolled in even a moderate sea.

It took three days to sail down the Channel, collecting an escort, the frigate *Hyaena,* en route. Ten days after leaving Portsmouth the commodore ordered the fleet hove to, some ten miles to the west of the Scilly Isles. He sent his first dispatch back to Plymouth with the *Hyaena* and ordered removal of the leg irons securing all the convicts, excepting those under recent punishment. Continued restraint in fetters seemed to him a quite ludicrous situation, although Major Ross opposed the decision most vocally, fearing an increased risk of convicts attempting to take one of the transports and make an escape from British jurisdiction, perhaps to America.

Many now experienced seasickness, although the weather remained fine and moderate. Except those prisoners under punishment for some shipboard misdemeanour, most were allowed to exercise on deck, making avid use of the privilege. The decks resembled a laundry, with under-garments drying from makeshift lines.

From the deck of *Lady Penrhyn* Mary and Lizzie looked across to *Sirius,* and the red-coated marines exercising on the foredeck and in the rigging. Lizzie waved toward them, but none noticed her. Both found the motion of the ship unsettling, and staggered and lurched uncontrollably; they decided to return below after only a short time.

Jack, too, was on deck working with his men on musket drill and swordsmanship. Cirrus clouds laced the sky high above the fleet like the drifts of snow formed against the dry stone walls of a Cotswold winter, with columns of grey cumulus building in the west, heralding a storm. The force of the Atlantic was now making its first show, and Captain Hunter ordered some reduced sail.

'That will do for this morning, Sergeant Packer. Have the lads report to the armourer and get a sharp edge put on those blades. Then they can get to their dinner.'

He had enjoyed the weapons training session. One or two of the men handled themselves well. Others lacked basic knowledge and technique with a pike, thrusting the weapon with no sense of purpose or direction. Swordsmanship was completely absent, and many of the marines had never used a sword, had never so much as fixed a bayonet to a musket. He intended that they should have more practice, and instruction.

'Right, sir. Shall I take your sword as well, sir?' Packer had been impressed with Jack's skill with the weapon.

Before he could answer, a private ran up, stood smartly at attention, and said, 'Beg pardon, sir, but Mister Dawes would be obliged for your attendance in his cabin, sir.' The soldier added, leaning toward Jack in a conspiratorial manner, 'He's had a bit of a set to with the major, sir.'

Packer looked sharply at the private. 'Mind your tongue, Jones!'

The good humour that Jack had enjoyed dissipated immediately on receiving the summons, instinct telling him that there was bad news awaiting him.

'Very well,' he replied. He made his way to the stern, dropping down the companionway to the wardroom.

William Dawes was at the small bureau in his cabin, studying some papers, when Jack entered. His normally cheerful countenance was disturbed. He looked miserable.

'Jack, there's a discrepancy in the convict musters. Damned surgeons cannot seem to add up. Commodore Phillip wishes it investigated, and our esteemed commander has directed that you and I inspect all the transports and clarify the true position. Apparently you and I are 'the scholars' of the battalion and should be capable of such a task!'

'I see, and when are we to do this, William?'

'Immediately, old chap.'

Jack laughed. 'That's preposterous, Will. Has he not seen the sea that is running? The fleet is already becoming scattered over the ocean. They are not about to escape. Surely this can wait until we reach Tenerife?'

Lieutenant Dawes sighed. 'That is precisely what I advised Major Ross. Unfortunately, and perhaps inevitably, he disagreed with me. I share your opinion entirely, but we are required to go on board each vessel and personally make a fresh muster.'

'The man's mad! This is insanity! There is no rhyme or logic to this, Will, none at all!'

'I advise you against telling him so, Jack. He is quite adamant that the records be accurate. The truth is that his own muster has been questioned... challenged, perhaps, by the commodore, and he is blaming the surgeon, accusing him of incompetence. It was all very heated.'

Dawes had not enjoyed the discussion with Major Ross. He resented the order to undertake such a task. He already had responsibility for the timekeepers and other instruments made available to the expedition by the Astronomer Royal, as well as others from the Board of Longitude.

Dawes explained how the exercise was to be undertaken. They were to take two boats and each be assisted by a midshipman. The transports were each to be visited, the convicts inspected and counted individually.

The two lieutenants reported to the master who shook his head in disapproval.

He looked at the sky in the west. 'If ye ask me, it's a fool's venture. The sea's rising, and the wind keeps shiftin'.'

Thank you, Mister Morton. We may be marines, but we can see for ourselves.'

Dawes was anxious. Jack was anxious too, but not so anxious that he would give voice to his fears.

The boats were lowered with difficulty. Oliver Waterhouse commanded one, Jack taking a place beside him at the tiller. A growing swell caused the boats to rise and fall against the ship's side. Boarding called for careful judgement by each man. Sailors cursed. Lieutenant Dawes took his place in the boat commanded by Midshipman Ferguson.

The sea now rose and fell with the swell, the boats pushed up and down like corks. The sailors were exhausted by the time they reached the first of the transports. Jack consumed more than half an hour in inspecting the human cargo on board the first of his allotted ships. The master was astounded to see a marine officer clamber aboard his vessel, and made his thoughts on the matter plain, grumbling and cursing.

Three hours later, Jack was soaked through and shivering with cold as he slowly boarded the last of his three ships, the *Lady Penrhyn*. The master, William Sever, took him to his cabin and shoved a large tankard in Jack's hand.

'Get that inside thee, man—ye look about done in.'

'Thank you, Captain. I am in sore need.' Jack felt the neat rum slowly exploring his veins and sat gratefully, his body still heaving from the pounding of the sea on the ship's long-boat.

'There's some cold tongue and pork on the table yonder.' Sever pointed, and added, 'P'raps some bread, if you have a mind.' Jack rose to reach for a plate, suddenly feeling in need of food. He was trembling a little from the exertion, the cold and a strong feeling of anxiety. He attacked the meat garnished with some mustard and pickled cabbage with enthusiasm. He gulped more rum, coughing a little as he did so.

'This be madness, Mister Vizzard. To put men in a boat in this sea, 'tis asking for trouble.' Captain Sever spoke with genuine concern. 'My return to the commodore be accurate. There be no need to count 'em again. I ain't lost any yet, not like the *Scarborough,* I unnerstand.' The master sat down heavily opposite Jack, and poured a small measure of rum and water. 'Your other redcoats are below at their game of cards. They have approved my return also.'

'I am in no doubt, Captain, but I have my orders.' He consulted a small notebook. 'I am to inspect and count the convicts you have on board. According to the return you have 101 women and only one boy in the cages?'

'That's right. As I says, not one of them dead yet, though plenty are as sick as dogs, and we ain't seen bad weather!' He laughed. 'I reck'n the gov'ment wanted a breedin' stock for the new colony! Leastways, that ain't my worry. I'll take the old lady on to China when I hand this cargo over to you redcoats, and make a handsome profit from the tea I shall bring back. Me an' old Billy Biscuit are the owners of the *Lady P.* As like as not, you will have eaten old Billy's sea biscuits. Tough as boots, like Billy himself!' He laughed again, louder this time.

The master's words rang true. Jack had heard that the Admiralty had chartered a ship to transport a large number of women for that very purpose. She was to sail for Botany Bay with a second fleet of convicts the following year, and some of the transports and store-ships were to return by way of China, laden with tea.

'I had better see the ones you have and get back to the flagship. The light will be fading soon.'

A master's mate, holding a lantern in front of him, took him below. The deck was dark, with all lights out, because of the rising seas.

He walked slowly along the side of the cages, counting heads. It needed a sharp eye to detect, among the huddled mass of humanity within the cages, the form of any one individual. The lantern held by the mate shed a cold, pale light in which tired, soulless eyes blinked in silent, resentful confusion. They sat or lay together in their patched, ragged clothes, colourless, almost shapeless forms, from which gaunt and withered limbs protruded. He stared into the cages, again trying to identify bodies and count heads, halting when Lizzie Parker called out, grinning, 'You lookin' for a good time, then, sir?'

Jack stared into the cage, ignoring her, counted the sleeping bodies, and made a note in his book. He observed a mix of expressions on the faces that stared back at him: apathy, fear, intoxication and, on some, undisguised hatred.

'Any babies in here?' he asked.

'Only two so far, luv, but if you can spare a few minutes we can try an' make anuvver.' Lizzie giggled at Jack's discomfort.

'Hold your tongue, woman, or you will meet the cat!' he said sharply, and counting once more the featureless shapes in the cage, passed on, again making entries in his notebook. He felt nausea rising in his throat, the odours of the bilge below invading his nostrils. He now regretted the large measure of rum he had consumed, and left the prison deck quickly.

'Who was that?' Mary asked sleepily, the sharp words waking her from uncomfortable sleep, and a fragmented dream, inevitably of Jack.

'Only some bleedin' officer makin' sure we still alive, or p'raps checking to see 'ow many 'ave died.' Lizzie pulled a bottle of rum from beneath her skirt, taken as her fee from a member of the crew, and swallowed deeply. 'Quite a good lookin' one, though,' Lizzie murmured, more to herself than to Mary. She lay back against the bulkhead, and pulled her baby closer to her chest, cooing gently to her.

Jack introduced himself to the other marines on board, explaining briefly the purpose of his visit. He had not met Captain James Campbell or his subalterns before the fleet's departure, and did not feel immediately welcome in the cramped quarters occupied by the marines of *Lady P*, as her master described her. Campbell was another Scot, on good terms with Major Ross, and met Jack with a cool reception. Jack declined a polite invitation to make a foursome for the card game in progress, and bid all a good night and safe voyage, promising to join their company once the fleet was safely at anchor in Tenerife.

On deck, Jack grabbed a lubber's line that the crew had rigged out earlier when the prisoners had been on deck to take some exercise. He breathed in a deep lungful of air to clear the foul taste in his mouth and reported to Captain Sever that the muster was complete and correct.

He looked at the sea and sky and was troubled to see that the waves were higher, the sky darker and angrier, white foam springing from the wave-tops. There was the sound of thunder to the west, and the unmistakable show of lightning in the clouds. The wind was blowing harder.

He found that he had to raise his voice to be heard. 'Mister Waterhouse, we had best get back to the flag-ship while we still have light!'

'The crew are ready, sir, but I suggest we wait 'til the morning. This looks bad, sir.' The midshipman was not unhappy at the prospect of a night away from his own ship. 'May I suggest we stay aboard for the night, sir? I suspect a bit of a blow will be on us before we can return,' he added with his usual understatement.

'No, Oliver, we must get back aboard. I have no desire to spend a night aboard a convict transport, and Commodore Philip needs our report. Come on, let's get the men busy.'

'If you say so, sir, but I would encourage caution. This is a wild sea, and can only worsen, I feel.' The midshipman thought he knew more of the sea than any officer of marines.

Once more, the crew lowered the ship's boat to the turbulent sea, with two men aboard to hold it steady, the rest using a cargo net to negotiate the tumblehome. Jack was the last to go, pausing to judge his moment, as the small boat tossed on the sea, rising and falling a dozen feet. He dropped as it rose, landing awkwardly and heavily on a stocky seaman.

'You all right, sir?' the man growled.

'Yes, thank you, Eldridge. Push off now—quickly.'

Waterhouse shouted, 'Pritchard and Smith, get that sail up, and let's get away! Flagship is about three or four cables distant, sir. Sit tight.'

The wind started to howl as the midshipman pulled on the tiller.

'Any sign of Lieutenant Dawes, Oliver?' Jack shouted back.

'Not sure, sir, but I thought I just saw him abeam of the *Scarborough*.' Midshipman Waterhouse half rose from the thwart to obtain a better view. 'Yes... there he is, sir!'

They cleared the lee of the transport and the wind hit them, heeling the small boat over to her starboard gunwales. Cold, dirty grey water drenched their already chilled bodies.

Waterhouse corrected swiftly, making his tack when the boat was in a trough, and steadying the craft on a course to run down onto the *Sirius*.

Vizzard could see the other boat now, as it rose on a wave. Dawes was slightly ahead of them, off to leeward, but his boat had taken water and was sitting low. As Jack looked, he could see several men baling frantically. They appeared to be on a course away from *Sirius*, and Jack was puzzled.

Dawes was waving his hat trying to shout something, his voice whipped away on the wailing wind. For a few moments he was lost from sight as Jack's boat slipped down another trough, then Jack caught sight of it again, as both craft rose together. 'They are in some difficulty, Oliver. Make for them, please! We must see what help we can give!' Jack instructed.

'Sir, I believe they are making for the *Alexander*. They may be unable to make it to the flagship!'

They were closer now, about half a cable or less apart. Dawes started to stand, again waving a hand in the general direction of the transport, the largest in the fleet, when he stumbled and appeared to slip, falling over the side. His boat slewed away as he drifted into a trough and young Ferguson pulled hard on the tiller.

There was no time to think. Jack plunged over the side, even as Oliver Waterhouse cried out to stop him.

The shock of the water hit him with the sharpness of a thousand needles passing through his body as he struck out, his strong arms pulling him along. The salt stung his eyes, but as he rose on another wave, he could see the other boat. He pulled harder, spewing water from the side of his mouth. He swam rapidly, pulling hard with each stroke, trying to gauge the direction. He heard shouts from the boat, but could not understand for a moment. The wind shrieked across the waves, shredding them to spray that obscured all vision. His body rolled with a wave that threatened to push him under. Then it was clear. Dawes was to his left, and he saw the flash of scarlet of the Lieutenant's coat. He pulled again, three or four hard strokes, and his hand hit a body.

Dawes spluttered something incoherent, and struggled to grasp hold of him.

Jack tried to kick; his right arm went around his friend's neck and with his other hand he clamped onto Dawes' flailing arm. He felt himself go underwater; he was sinking. Holding fast to Dawes, he managed to kick one boot free. He kicked again, pulling up. His face felt cold air, and he gulped in gratefully, his lungs burning with pain.

Once again, he was under, unprepared, as if a giant hand was propelling him down. Water was in his mouth and gut. He kicked, more wildly, desperate now for air, lungs seared with heat, and suddenly other hands were holding his collar, and he felt himself hauled aboard the boat, young Ferguson shouting in his ears. He collapsed in the scuppers, coughing, retching and gasping as the air filled his bursting lungs, vomiting the food recently eaten, frothy red bubbles filling his mouth. All around him grew a deepening darkness.

Ferguson shouted encouragement at his crew. 'Pull together, lads! Keep baling! We're going to make it!' He looked down at the marine, and a frown manifested itself on his young face. *We have to make it for his sake*, he thought.

With the level of the water in the boat rising, the crew all but abandoned the oars and used anything to keep afloat.

Sirius had hove to but had difficulty holding position. Seas pounded her sides and men called, shouting encouragement from the nettings. A line was thrown but fell short, and was then thrown again, and again. A seaman caught hold and made it fast. Within a minute or so, they had pulled alongside and the crew scrambled up the tumblehome, pulling themselves up with muscles screaming with pain.

Ferguson could see the climb was beyond Jack. He swiftly looped a line around the marine's chest and under his arms. Suddenly, another marine dropped into the boat. Joe Packer tied another rope around Dawes. Men above hauled them up as Ferguson and Packer steadied their ascent from below.

As the two climbed, supporting their human cargo, the wind roared and the ship's boat hurled itself against the side; it splintered and broke apart, slipping under the waves, consumed by the ever-hungry sea.

CHAPTER 24
HERO OF THE ATLANTIC

George Bouchier Worgan was a kindly, gentle man with an amiable, friendly manner. He had long, pianist's fingers with fingernails that were always immaculate and well trimmed. Music and medicine were the loves of his life. They had mocked him, in a good-natured fashion, for insisting his piano accompany him on the voyage to Botany Bay. It was a Broadwood, a square piano, of a light shallow tone, with the new brass under-damper. It was his most treasured possession and he could never have left it to gather dust at home. Worgan loved it and Captain Phillip, who had agreed to its being stowed in his day cabin, had not regretted it, for Worgan had already entertained the officers to his music. He was particularly fond of the work of George Handel, and often played the largo from Handel's *opera seria, Serse,* one of his favourite pieces, almost forgotten now in London. Worgan loved its buoyancy and originality. He hummed it now as he carefully regarded the marine officer he had watched dive into a wild, storm-blown sea to rescue a friend.

The young man had spent the night retching, bringing up some blood. That had caused Worgan concern. Now, however, he was asleep, albeit a rather fitful and disturbed sleep, punctuated with blasphemous language, and pleas to the Virgin Mary for forgiveness. At least, that was how it sounded to Worgan's ears.

A knock at his cabin door preceded Captain David Collins, who crouched between the beams until offered a seat by the cot.

'How are the patients, Doctor? Will they recover?'

Worgan regarded him sympathetically. Dawes was in his own quarters, in the adjacent cabin. He had swallowed a lot of water, much of which Worgan had been able to expel.

'Your marines are hardy men, Mister Collins. Lieutenant Dawes should have drowned and this young man has a fever, a slight one, but enough to take him from his duties.' He fiddled absently with his waistcoat, and continued, 'However, I may also have a pneumothorax here, Collins.' Noting the officer's puzzled expression, he explained. ''Tis commonly called a collapsed lung. He breathes with difficulty, so I shall need to insert a drain and expel what I suspect is a pocket of air over his left lung.'

The early relief Collins had shown on his face now turned to a more anxious expression. 'I had feared the worst. It was a damned brave thing he did yesterday.'

Worgan agreed. 'I never saw a braver act. Where he found the strength to make that swim, I will never know. Some angel was watching over him, that much must be certain.'

'Please send me word if... when he awakes, Mister Worgan.'

'I am confident of a recovery, Captain, but he will have considerable discomfort for some weeks, I think.' Worgan made a pencilled note on a paper. 'He will not be fully fit for strenuous duty, however.'

The surgeon followed Collins from the cabin and entered the one adjacent.

Dawes, too, was sleeping. Worgan leaned over and listened to the heart. Satisfied, he climbed to the next deck to report to Captain Hunter.

*****

The stench in his nostrils was overpowering. Human excrement and vomit, mixed with coal tar, vinegar and bilge water. A baby was crying and a woman, breathing fumes of brandy, was baring her bosom for his inspection.

He was running—no, that was wrong, he was on his back; cold, salty water was filling his eyes, his mouth, his belly, his lungs. He coughed and retched—again and again, he retched. There was scarlet in his face, blood—no, a coat, a marine's coat. He coughed again, a long gut-wrenching cough, which did not end. The pain seemed to stab directly into his heart. This must be death, he thought.

Worgan wiped the dribble from Jack's mouth and placed a cold, wet cloth across his forehead.

'All right, lad, you will be all right.' He examined the sputum. *At least there is no blood now*, he thought. *By Christ, this one is a fighter. Should have died in the night.*

A low moan crept from Jack's mouth. His head moved to one side and his eyelids flickered and slowly opened and closed.

'I was just thinking of some breakfast. Do you feel ready to eat something?' Worgan said as he watched closely for a reaction. The eyes opened, flickered a few times and steadied, staring at the beams above his head.

'What...?' Another rasping cough, but this time a dry one. 'What happened?' Jack managed to say.

'Ah, well now, young man, it seems that you chose to enjoy an Atlantic swim. You damn nearly drowned and almost took another officer with you. Be hell to pay for it, I shouldn't wonder. The Navy prefers not to lose too many officers in one day, even if they are redcoats!' The surgeon smiled as Vizzard's eyes slowly recognised the sparkle in his and registered the jest.

'No... I mean, what happened to Will... Lieutenant Dawes? Is he alive?'

'With thanks due to you, he is indeed. That was quite a remarkable thing you did. The whole ship is talking about it.'

Jack lay back in the cot and closed his eyes.

'Well, I will let you rest, while I see to my other patients.' Worgan received no reply. He examined the site of the drain in Vizzard's side, grunted in satisfaction and again reported to John Hunter.

*****

Captain Arthur Phillip paced his cabin. He was in a sombre mood. The well-polished mahogany table was littered with papers that he had spent many days poring over studiously.

'I tell you, John, it is abject nonsense. Half the prisoners have no value to a new colony. Most of them are listed here as labourers. What good is that, pray! Where are the carpenters, masons, the brick-makers, the husbandry men, and the fishermen? The bloody fools have given me no skilled artisans, or precious few. I am expected to build a new settlement with no more than the dregs of Newgate.'

Some will be of use, sir. They know they must work to live. You plan to give land grants, do you not? The prospect will surely encourage some to reform, to seek emancipation.' John Hunter had discussed this with his friend before, and although he shared Phillip's vision for the new colony, he had concerns such an incentive would prove of limited value.

Phillip resumed his seat at the desk. 'Aye, in time... but only to those who do prove worthy. I must instigate some detailed enquiry as to their histories, and occupations, though I have no overseers, John. We should make great use of the warrant officers, and we need the marines to supervise the work parties—the sergeants and subalterns, I think. Here, I have prepared some details of those. Will you talk to Ross about these matters? We need his co-operation.'

Arthur Phillip had not had many discussions with his deputy, the lieutenant governor. Major Ross was something of a troublesome martinet, not a man he could warm to, or empathize with. Thus far, he had maintained a civil relationship with the soldier, but not without difficulty. He considered him acerbic, truculent and uncooperative. *I will not cross swords with that man just yet. John is the diplomat, tough when needed, but slow to anger; he will handle the bugger for me.* He smiled across at Hunter.

John Hunter smiled back at his friend. He was a man who saw confrontation as failure.

'Very well, Arthur. I will see him, although he will argue agin' it, for sure.'

'Yes, I have no doubt. I will leave it to you, then.' Arthur Phillip quickly read a note on his desk. 'Now, John, this matter of Lieutenants Vizzard and Dawes. How are they both?'

'Worgan reports that both are well. Dawes should be fit for duty tomorrow, possibly the next day.' Hunter waited for further comment.

'And the... 'Hero of the Atlantic', as I understand the lower deck now refer to him, young Vizzard, how does he fare?'

'Mister Worgan tells me that he had a... something Latin —the man will be in pain for some time.'

'Have them both dine with us tomorrow, would you, please? I think it time I knew these young men a little better. Philip Stephens tells me Dawes is a very competent astronomer and engineer, and Maskelyne, the Astronomer Royal, sponsors him. I should like to discuss my plans for the new town with him. As to Vizzard, I know nothing of him.' Phillip looked enquiringly from across the table.

'By all accounts a competent young man. His commission is only very recent, I believe, so he is very inexperienced. He is an Oxford scholar I am told, so must be educated, I suppose. His prompt and courageous—but, if I may say, rather foolhardy—action undoubtedly saved Dawes. His men think well of him, it is said. Ross has no high regard for him, so he is probably destined for great and glorious things... if he survives this commission.' Hunter grinned.

'Good, then we will have some stimulating conversation. Ross had better join us, too.' He made a sour face. He thought of that last occasion at the marine's barracks, and the rumour that Ross had challenged another officer. He wondered, not for the first time, why the man had been selected for this task. Evan Nepean was behind it. He had learned they had served together in America, and now that Nepean was the senior official at the Admiralty, he was supporting Ross. Ross was tough, no doubts on that score. A hard, fighting man, but an officer who had not risen as high in the service as he would have wished.

They would all face some hardship, he knew that, but the prisoners under his care would need more than just hard discipline. They would need strong leadership, given in a humane way. They would have the opportunity to redeem themselves in the new land.

By the words of his commission, the King had personally commanded Phillip, and he fully intended to reward hard work and good behaviour with emancipation. He needed officers who shared his aims, who would assist in that object.

In addition to establishing a penal colony, England wanted, needed, a new trading base. There were many Americans, still loyal to the Crown, who would support the venture, and who were anxious to find a new home and develop business. That was the true purpose of the expedition.

'Yes, have Major Ross join us,' he repeated. 'We have some work to do with that man, John, to convince him of what must be done.'

Phillip turned to stare at the wake beneath the sloping windows of the stern cabin, lost in his thoughts. He did not hear Hunter leave as he closed the door quietly behind himself, wishing he could do more to ease his friend's burdens.

Phillip stood there for a very long time, watching the sea stretching back to England.

Chapter 25

Transition

Mary felt better than she had for many months. The master of the *Lady Penrhyn* allowed them to work on deck as the weather improved, and she was eating more and better food than she had ever received in gaol. The colour in her face, extinguished during her captivity in Gloucester, had now been brought back through fresh food and sunshine. She would not describe her state as one of happiness, but she was nonetheless more content, more accepting of her situation. Her melancholia remained, but was not felt as frequently nor as deeply as before. Why, she had even caught herself laughing once or twice.

She and the other women were making shirts. The ship's master had purchased a large quantity of material for his personal business before leaving England and intended that the government stores would buy his stock. It was a common arrangement, and one by which he intended to profit handsomely. Other prisoners grumbled at being used in this way, for private profit, but for Mary it was to be preferred to wasting away in a cramped cage below decks, away from fresh air and the warming sun.

The last ten days she had spent learning cutting and stitching from a girl, Ann Yates, who had worked in Lambeth as a seamstress. Basic skill she had, but under Ann's tutelage she improved, finding the work satisfying. When she was not sewing, she spent her time cleaning. The sailors, and even more so the marines, she discovered, were more concerned with cleanliness than the labourers in her father's mill. That had surprised her.

The fleet was passing through warmer latitudes and she found herself enjoying the work. Other convicts would talk to her; but at times, like now, she could let her mind wander. Inevitably, she found herself thinking of Jack. She sighed audibly at the memory.

'Now, my girl, dreaming again, eh?' Lizzie broke into her daydream.

'I cannot help it, Lizzie. Try as I might, he is ever in my thoughts. He must be suffering because of me.'

Lizzie snorted her disapproval. 'Nonsense, my girl—he left you soon enough, if you ask me. 'Tis you what is the prisoner, not 'im. If he cared for you half as much as you do for 'im, he would have stayed and fought for your liberty.'

Lizzie thought that Mary's 'gentleman' was little more than a charlatan, but would not wish to hurt her friend's feelings with her opinion. She even questioned the fact of his very existence, allowing the possibility that the man was merely a fiction, a device to hide Mary's guilt.

'If you take my advice, you'll forget about 'im,' she continued kindly. "E'll be off to India or the Americas, an', like as not, you'll not see or hear from 'im again.'

She knew that Mary would not, could not, forget about her officer. Mary had told her that he was her first love, that she had fallen helplessly for him and that she could never hold the same feelings for another. *The girl's fallen for him, but 'tis a familiar tale and she'll have to make a life in Botany Bay, same as the rest of us*, she thought. None could expect a knight on a silver charger to provide rescue.

In her memory she recalled her own crime, a house burglary where she had stolen an old coat, valued at six shillings. She had kept quiet at her trial, for she had taken more than that, but the silver cutlery she had hidden before capture. Seven years she was given, and was thankful that a kindly gent had limited the value of the coat, or she could have faced a scaffold. No, Botany Bay could only be a better place, somewhere to build a life, find a good man—that was what she should do. Ned Pugh seemed to like her, and was kindly, but there was not love between them. She shook herself free of her own private dreams and resumed her sewing.

The watch changed and a marine ordered them below. Mary smiled at him. He smiled, too, and she looked closer. He was young, probably about her age. Quite handsome. Uniforms made men look handsome. He appeared sober, too, which was unusual. Many of them were drunk.

'Come along, now. Time to get below. Don't yous be gettin' me in trouble,' he said kindly.

'We won't be doing that, Ned Palmer, don't worry.' Mary gave him one of her brightest smiles.

Ned Palmer melted. His face crimsoned, and he turned to hide his embarrassment.

Mary giggled as Lizzie nudged her and rolled up the material she had been cutting. As she stood she noticed the flagship was signalling and she asked the master's mate what the flags said.

'Dunno yet, luv. Can't make 'em out. Wait a mo'—land! They's seen land to the southwest. That must be Tenerife.' The man became animated. 'Boy, go tell the cap'n: "Land to the Southwest." We should be in Tenerife on the morrow.'

Instantly, the man's excitement infected Mary. A surge of anticipation made her eyes shine. Staring out in the direction indicated, she could see nothing. She knew nothing of Tenerife; the name was meaningless, but the chance of being off the ship gladdened her. She hurried below to tell her friend.

'Mary, luv, don't you be gettin' too excited, now,' Lizzie replied. 'They ain't goin' to let us loose ashore, in case some make a bolt for it, you just see.' Lizzie's words dampened Mary's happiness, but proved prophetic.

Mary spent the next week staring at the port of Santa Cruz at every opportunity, as the fleet obtained fresh provisions. The colour of the harbour and the island struck her as beautiful. She saw boats from the island bringing a variety of goods to the anchored fleet, and a regular flow of boats between the flagship and the transports.

Once a boat hooked onto the *Lady Penrhyn* and an elderly midshipman came aboard to take an inventory of stores and make a list of those on board listed as sick or injured. She watched the marine guards that came with him, and saw they were surly, several of them drunk. They accosted her with lewd suggestions until the sergeant in charge berated them, and she went below to escape. The crew was no better—at least they left her alone in the main, but other women happily traded their bodies for drink or money.

Even Lizzie. At first, Mary had been dismayed when she had discovered the full extent and the frequency of her friend's activities with the crew and the guards. She had found her by chance in the sail-maker's locker with a marine guard. Lizzie had just laughed at her, and carried on, the guard grunting like a pig, as his buttocks rose and fell.

She had run from the scene, Lizzie yelling that he would 'do 'er for a shilling'.

Later, in the cage eating their supper, Lizzie tackled her about it.

'Listen to me, Mary. Don't be so 'igh an' mighty. I've a kid to feed an' the extra cash 'elps. How d'ye think we been gettin' better grub these last weeks? Because of your fair looks an' charmin' ways? No, my sweet, 'tis a bit of the other that keeps the men happy, the gin flowing, and extra rations for you and me.'

Lizzie looked away, focusing on baby Annie as she spooned the broth into her eager mouth.

Mary fell quiet. Not once had she realized the extra and better food she was eating had been earned by such behaviour. She thought of the wine that she drank, in place of the dark beer that upset her so, or the rum she had tasted and disliked. Her own morality she valued highly, from some deep-seated sense of right and wrong, probably the result of her father's words over the more formative years of her young life. *Dear father*, she thought, never able, nor wanting, to stop thinking of him. She sighed deeply and turned to her friend.

'I'm sorry, Lizzie—I didn't think. I should be grateful, and I am, but ...'

Lizzie Parker looked at her.   Selling her favours never caused her a moment of regret.   She had done so before, and frequently, not just to feed her younger brothers and sisters, but because, if she was honest, she enjoyed it.   She also enjoyed the odd bottle of gin or wine she earned from it, and she pulled a bottle from under her mattress.

"Ere, 'ave a drink and forget it.   S'pose I was a bit sharp. In truth it's never bothered me, but I can see 'ow you would be.   I tell you, Mary, we may 'ave a lot worse to do, if we're goin' to make a go of it.   Look 'ere, the way I sees it, we got two choices: we either gets a man to take care of us, or we starve.   Who's goin' to give tuppence for us when we get there?   Answer me that.   Them lot ain't goin' to be givin' free 'andouts.   We're the bottom of the bleedin' pile, an' we got to take every chance we can.   We've been lucky on this ship.   I 'eard they lost another two last night on the *Alexander*.'

Mary knew that Lizzie spoke a good deal of common sense.   They had indeed been lucky on this ship.   So far none had died, although a number were sick, but the fresh food brought on board had been welcome.   Mary settled onto her bench and pulled the thin blanket up to her chin.   She lay there a long time before deep, dreamless sleep removed some of her fears.

*****

Jack Vizzard lowered himself into the boat and looked at the marines in front of him.   More than half of them were showing the excesses of last night, with red eyes and sour expressions, although Joe Packer, for one, looked awake and alert.

224

The midshipman in command of the boat, George Raper, gave an order and the sailors pulled away smartly enough. In truth, he was glad to be off the ship, and the interminable routine. At least he had a job to do.

Overnight the *Alexander* had reported a bolter. One of the convicts had bribed a guard and had made his escape in one of the jolly boats. Ross had ordered him to take a party and bring the escapee back to face punishment. The guard responsible was flogged at first light, on the peremptory order of the major. One of the carpenter's mates had visited the island before and knew of a small isle off the east coast where the man might be in hiding. It was a hard pull for the crew; the sun was rising and growing in strength, the men soon sweating. Jack loosened his neck-cloth and checked his pistol.

'There, sir, just before the point, I can see part of the jolly boat.' Raper had good eyesight. Jack raised a field telescope and saw the stern of the boat, crudely camouflaged with branches of palm trees. The dark sand had been freshly disturbed, reflecting the light.

'Silence in the boat!' Jack spoke harshly as some of his men started growling. 'Sergeant Packer, check weapons. I don't want some clump-head giving warning before we get there.'

Joe Packer set his jaw and scowled at three privates, who promptly lowered their heads.

Raper directed the boat onto the beach and left two of the able seamen to guard it, as Jack led his men to the hidden boat. 'Spread out—he may be armed,' he commanded, wary of stalking even a hunted convict.

A quick inspection revealed that the ship's boat was empty. No provisions were to be found and Jack concluded that the man had sought out somewhere to hide until the fleet had sailed, before making for Santa Cruz, and possibly a merchant ship to America.

The island was small, that much he knew. So small it was not shown on any chart, and was little more than a long spit of black rock and sand, with a small hill on the western side. There was a range of sand dunes, formed of the dark, volcanic sand, through which a few palms and halophyte shrubs reached for the sun and struggled for life.

He led his party toward the hill, reasoning that to be the most logical refuge for an escaping prisoner, Packer following at the rear with the seamen and the midshipman.

He was pleased with this section of men. Packer had trained them well: Corporal Munday, the Welshman, a man with a voice for a song; Abraham Hands, the quiet but competent soldier; George Winwood, the tough Cumbrian; Morty Lynch, the Irishman who enjoyed a drink and a scrap, and who had lost his corporal's stripes because of it. Then there was Tom Bramage, the former tin miner from Cornwall. Jack had watched him load and aim one of the ship's guns as though born to it. The elderly marine, Tom Cornwall, had carried a mortally wounded friend from Bunker Hill and had not put him down until both were back aboard their ship and a surgeon had pronounced his friend dead. They were his men now, and he respected them, had grown to admire their spirit.

It took nearly an hour to reach the hill, the men making hard work of the alternately soft sand and sharp, rocky terrain. They rested at the foot of the hill, and Jack ordered them to take a small drink of water before they commenced the ascent. He had them spread out, in open order, as they climbed. Some thought it strange, preferring to keep closer together.

The marines were sweating hard, the sun nearing its zenith as they approached the summit. He gave a hand signal, pausing the climb, while he used a telescope to view the rocky summit.

Jack felt, rather than heard, the shot. The ball passed his left shoulder as he spotted the smoke from a large rock, just below the summit.

He dropped to one knee to take aim. 'Just to the right of that large rock, Joe!' He shouted to Packer. 'You and Munday move round to the right, divide his fire.'

'I've got 'im, sir.' Packer moved quickly. 'C'mon, Ed, let's 'ave that bugger.'

The muzzle of a musket appeared from the side of the rock and Jack fired. His shot hit the rock, spitting dust and fragments, and the musket disappeared.

'Now, Joe! Move!'

If the man was any good he would take at least half a minute to reload, and by then, they could be on him. He started to race uphill, pulling his sword from its scabbard. Packer and Ed Munday obviously had the same thought; he saw they were running too. His chest hurt, and slowed his run, Packer and Corporal Munday now just ahead of him, twenty or thirty feet to his right.

With a yell, he was at the rock. Swinging the blade down, he realized the man had moved a yard or two to his right. The musket was up to the man's shoulder and his aim was towards Packer. He fired as Jack's foot hit him hard on the side of the head, spinning the musket from his grasp. Jack's sword point stopped at the man's chest, as he lay on his back, his hands outstretched, seeking clemency.

'I could stick you now, you little shit, and be thanked for it,' Jack snarled at the ragged little man before him.

'Please sir, no—I beg you. They'll hang me soon enough anyways,' he whimpered.

Packer appeared at his side, panting hard. 'He hit Ed, sir. I should do him for that.'

'Where is he?' Jack asked.

'Back down the hill, sir.'

'See to him, Joe. I doubt he will be any trouble now.'

Jack went down twenty yards to the marine, who was sitting on a fallen banana tree.

'Don't thee worry 'bout me, sir. The bastard only hit my boot. Took the heel clean off, made me fall, 'e did, sir.' Corporal Munday grinned up at Jack, holding out his damaged boot for inspection. Jack laughed.

Packer trussed the convict's hands behind his back and, with the point of his bayonet at the man's back, started the descent to the beach.

Jack gathered up the knapsack, which the convict, established as Daniel Smart, had used to store some biscuits, stale bread, salted pork and a bottle of wine, and followed. He knew nothing of the man, and was surprised to learn later that he was one of two brothers, convicted in Gloucester of stealing wool.

Packer continued to mutter a variety of curses at the man, who half walked, half fell down the track to the beach.

'Good piece of work, sir,' Midshipman Raper complimented him as they made their way back to the flagship. 'The captain will be well satisfied.'

'I expect the captain wants to discourage similar attempts,' he replied. 'The poor bastard will either hang or have his back-bone exposed, in return for his day of liberty.'

George Raper pondered the marine officer's words. He was an enigma, this man. Any officer would have been more than satisfied at having discharged his duty. Vizzard seemed to regret having done so. He looked towards the small fishing village nearby.

'Are you not pleased to have captured the convict? He could have shot you.' He stared at the subject of his remarks, now cowed in the boat, chin on his chest, sobbing.

Jack levelled his gaze at the young midshipman. 'He could have killed one of my men, yes, and I would have shot him myself, had he done so. However, he has done well to survive the voyage this far. They are dropping like flies on his transport. I sometimes think that we are little better than slavers ourselves, George. I would be tempted to make a run, should I be in his situation. You should see for yourself how they are expected to live on these fine ships.' Jack looked up to see the flagship appear in view as they rounded a headland, the water around them a clear, flat, blue sheet of glass, with the setting sun throwing the ships into sharp silhouette. Yes, he had done his duty, but he felt no pleasure.

*****

As Jack stepped onto the quarterdeck he was surprised to find Major Ross awaiting him arrayed in full uniform, in contrast to the more casual wear of the naval officers on deck.

'What kept you, Vizzard? I expected you back on board this past hour or more!' He spoke with the Scots growl Jack had come to detest. 'Best be quick, man, we are invited to dine with Captain Phillip, although his request for your attendance is a matter of surprise to me.' With that sour comment, he turned away stiffly, not expecting nor inviting any response.

Jack watched his retreating back and turned to Lieutenant William Dawes. 'Will, one day I will hang for that man. He is the most boorish bully. Why he is constantly berating me I do not know.'

'Perhaps he envies your youth, my young friend.' Dawes placed his hand on Jack's shoulder in reassurance. 'Jack, you must watch yourself with him. He has the power of God over us for three years or more. Do your duty and be true to yourself.'

Jack's mouth broke into a smile. 'I do, and I will. But for now, my friend, we must join our superiors below. At least the captain's table may offer better fare for one night. I must confess, I am ready for a good meal this night!'

*****

On the deck, the watch changed. Midshipman John Ferguson checked the log, turned the hourglass and assumed command of the flagship. He imagined himself as captain of a frigate, although *Sirius* was no frigate. He stood with legs apart, hands resting on the rail, and considered that she was every inch the 'eyes of the fleet'.

He looked up at the yards and above them to the unfolding stars, thinking that one day he would have command of such a ship. He should have taken his examination for lieutenant. It was all that he wanted; 'blind ambition' it had been dubbed, but, by Christ, he should exchange the midshipman's jacket for the coat of a lieutenant. But his mother had wanted him home. He had missed the commission to the Mediterranean; his lieutenancy would have been assured there. Forbes had said he was ready. He knew he was ready, at least to stand watch, if not more. He was a reasonable seaman, could navigate—the master had assured him of that—and knew all he could master of gunnery, but still he had to make do with a midshipman's jacket and dirk.

There were voices below; the cabin was only two feet below his feet. There had been laughter earlier, and the seniors had obviously been enjoying themselves, but now the voices were more subdued. He thought he heard that marine, the one the men were talking of as a hero.

Ferguson had never known a marine officer spoken of in the way Vizzard was. Sailors had no time for redcoats. His men, a drunken, unruly mob of soldiers, he thought, almost stood at attention whenever the man appeared on deck. He knew how to lead—it seemed instinctive and natural to him. *And that is what I want too*, he thought.

Ferguson adopted what he thought would be a more austere, commanding expression, and commenced pacing slowly across the deck, imitating the senior officers. At the wheel, the bosun winked at one of his mates, and made the slightest correction to the rudder, keeping to the course noted in the log. Ferguson had failed to notice and omitted to give him any order.

*****

Below Ferguson's feet, the officers were finishing their meal. Lieutenant Bradley passed a large flat-bottomed decanter of port to Captain Phillip, who poured a small quantity into a glass, sliding the decanter across to John Hunter.

Phillip's eye caught that of the young marine at the end of the table.

'Mister Vizzard—we have heard little from you this evening. I prefer to know something of the officers I command, particularly those that distinguish themselves.' Arthur Phillip glanced pointedly in the direction of Lieutenant Dawes. 'You will be aware that the ship's people now regard you as something of... well, shall I say you are now the subject of curiosity, both before and abaft the mast? Please, tell us something of your history, we are most interested.'

The faces around the table turned to look at Jack and he swallowed, embarrassed at the sudden and unwelcome attention.

'I fear, sir, there is little to tell. My father is a lawyer of some note in Gloucestershire. I, too, studied classics at Oxford, but felt that the King's service would provide more— how can I say this?—satisfaction,' he said hesitantly.

'Ah, yes—the Oxford scholar with a sense of duty,' said Arthur Phillip. 'A rare attribute.' He smiled kindly and then probed a little deeper. 'Why would you think that, Mister Vizzard?'

'Sir, it seemed to me that a military career might offer more interesting prospects than those of, say, a country gentleman.' The officers around the table laughed.

'Why, then, not a career as a sea officer, Mister Vizzard? We 'blue-jackets' have a penchant for adventure, do we not?'

Jack stole a glance around the table, and realised that there was unexpected interest in his answer to this question.

'Sir, it occurred to me that a regiment of the line, or the cavalry, would demand too much by way of capital; the Navy, I reasoned, would demand too much of my intellect, and a commission would require many years' service from me—whereas a lieutenancy in the marines is available to any fit man of average education!' Again, there was laughter from the Navy officers present. Major Ross sat stony-faced, although the other officers joined in the laughter.

'Tell me, Mister Vizzard, we are ashore in Tenerife on the morrow, what do you know of these islands, hey?' Captain Phillip continued to smile, for once in a convivial frame of mind.

Jack returned the smile. 'I have never visited them before, sir, but I have read of them; they are thought by some scholars to be "The Garden of the Hesperydes".' He paused as the faces about him acquired expressions of puzzlement. 'One of the labours of Hercules?' he asked of no one in particular. Receiving no reply, he continued.

'The story starts with Atlas. He was condemned by Zeus to support the sky beyond the Columns of Hercules—the Straits of Gibraltar.' The sailors at the table knew of that at least, he thought.

'Atlas had three daughters, the Hesperydes: they were Egle, Eritia and Aretusa. The three lived in the westernmost land of the world, some wonderful islands in the Atlantic Ocean, a Garden of Eden where weather was always mild and where golden apples grew on the trees. The goddess Gea gave those apples as a wedding gift to the king and queen of the gods, Zeus and Hera.' Jack raised the fine glass to his lips and drank. A good number of the officers around the table had studied, but none seemingly had knowledge of mythology, as their facial expressions clearly showed. Gaining courage from their silence, he continued more confidently.

'The Hesperydes cultivated the Garden, but a fierce dragon looked after it; he was called Ladon, and he had a hundred flame-spewing heads. Hercules had to perform twelve very difficult tasks, almost impossible to accomplish, the 'Twelve Labours of Hercules'. You will have heard of them, no doubt. The eleventh of these consisted of stealing the Hesperydes' golden apples.' To his surprise, Jack found he had an audience. The officers were looking at him with genuine interest.

'Hercules found Atlas supporting the sky near the Ocean, in the mountains which today we call Atlas. Since the Hesperydes' dragon knew Atlas, Hercules persuaded Atlas to go to the islands and steal the apples, while he stayed as supporter of the sky in his place. Atlas went to the Garden—into which he could enter since the dragon recognised him—killed the monster, stole the golden apples and returned to the place where Hercules had stayed. Atlas, tired of his task, intended to leave Hercules with the burden upon his shoulders, but Hercules managed to cheat him and fled with the apples.'

Again Jack halted in his story; he took another swallow of the wine and completed his tale.

'However, the tale is not ended. The apples were given to the goddess Athena, who gave them back to the gardeners, the Hesperydes, who are said to watch over them still.' He sat back in his chair, and grinned. 'That is all I really know of these islands, sir.'

'A good tale, Mister Vizzard, and well told. 'Tis a pleasure to add to my knowledge of the classics. However, it is of doubtful benefit to a sailor transporting a fleet of convicts to the other side of the world!' Phillip laughed, joined by the remainder of his guests, with the exception of Ross, who merely scowled at his subordinate.

'Bloody nonsense, if you ask me, sir,' he said, the words slurring, as he drained another glass of port. 'Bloody Greek gods'll be nae help to you when the shot and shell are flyin', boy.' He glowered at Jack.

Captain Phillip snorted derisively. 'Major Ross, we will need a good deal more than raw courage in the new colony. We will need officers with brains, too, by God. People who can think, not just those able to act under the orders of more senior officers.' He smiled, but the point was not lost on Ross, he thought. 'Men who can plan, and design, those who can teach and learn.' He looked at William Dawes. 'We will learn a good deal in the years ahead, will we not Mister Dawes?'

'Indeed, I do hope so, sir.' William Dawes looked towards his friend. 'I am most interested in the night sky of the southern hemisphere. I would hope that some of our navigators will wish to assist me in that matter, sir.' He gazed about him, but none offered any particular comment. 'I understand part of my duty to be in the design of fortifications, and artillery. However, I trust that such skills as I may have might be put to more, shall I say, peaceful ends, sir.' Dawes smiled.

Arthur Phillip was no great scholar, but his father had been a language teacher, from Germany. Phillip himself was sleight of build, with large, penetrating eyes, beneath dark and pronounced eyebrows. His high forehead suggested a deep intelligence and determination. An aquiline nose over-shadowed a small, pinched mouth, which belied a sensitive, compassionate nature.

'Time enough for forts and ramparts, Mister Dawes. We will need a harbour and wharf, farms, a hospital, barracks, houses, streets... In time a park or two, perhaps even a library, and a school,'—he smiled broadly—'most certainly a school. There will be an abundance of children to fill it, I am certain. One only has to consider the births we have had already, and the fleet not yet half the way there!'

He discoursed for some time on his hopes and plans for the new colony, deftly probing other officers for opinions, knowledge and suggestions, his subjects ranging from animal husbandry to horticulture, hospitals and military fortifications. He made clear his view, indeed his requirement, that the indigenous natives of the country were to be treated equitably by officers and men alike, and with justice and humanity.

He spoke of his hopes for emancipation of convicts once their sentences had expired. While talking, he discreetly observed the faces of his officers, and noted with approval that most, if not quite all, indicated agreement.

Major Ross did not express approval, or voice any contrary opinions, but Phillip discerned from the major's expression that he was not to be counted as an ally. He detected support in the faces of Lieutenants Vizzard and Dawes, he thought.

The junior naval officer present, Midshipman Henry Brewer, offered his thanks to Captain Phillip and left the cabin. Jack took his cue and likewise expressed his thanks.

'I thank you, sir, for the hospitality of your table, and the company of similar spirits. I bid you a good night.' He rose from the table.

'Goodnight, our classics scholar, and if I may offer some advice to a young officer: '*Aequam memento rebus in arduis servare mentem*'. Homer, I believe, Mister Vizzard.'

Jack glanced at Ross, who glowered in return, lack of understanding etched on his face. Did Arthur Phillip know of the ill will between them, he wondered.

'I regret to say, no, sir. The Book of Odes: Horace, the Roman poet, sir. If I, too, may make use of my limited Latin: *Quis custodiet ipsos custodes?* Goodnight to you sir, gentlemen.'

Ducking below the door of the cabin, he acknowledged the salute of the marine sentry, and made his way carefully below.

CHAPTER 26
A RITE OF PASSAGE

The wind was light from the northwest. The fleet weighed anchor at five o'clock on the 10th June and left Tenerife for the next port of call, Port Praya, in the Cape Verde Islands. Lieutenant Bradley had the deck as the fleet approached the reef guarding the eastern point of the bay when they reached Port Praya eight days later.

He was troubled. The heat during the last week had been all but unbearable. A number of the transports had reported brawls amongst the sailors. Some seamen had to be sent from the *Friendship* and had been flogged for breaking into the female convicts' cages and removing four of them to their quarters.

However, the present cause of Bradley's troubled mind was not the irksome women of the transports; neither was it the seamen he had seen flogged. He sensed storms in the air. The winds were blowing from all points of the compass, and a swell was rising. He trained his telescope on the reef and then along the straggling fleet of ships.

'Haul the mains, Mister Ferguson. I fancy that we had better stand clear. Please offer my compliments to Lieutenant King and beg him to join me on deck. I am much troubled by these winds.'

The request was made to Phillip King, who appeared very quickly, obviously alert to the movement of the ship. The sounds of men running to trim the sails were heard.

'Sir, you have need of me?'

Bradley passed his telescope. 'Take a look, Phillip. What d'you make of this?'

Although the junior of the two, King was a respected sailor and they were the same age. Having served with King on *Ariadne*, under Arthur Phillip, Bradley had come to trust his friend's judgement, particularly in matters of seamanship.

King glanced quickly up at the masts, noted the scudding clouds, and put the telescope to his right eye. He turned to the signal midshipman. 'Mister Fowell, immediate signal to *Charlotte* and *Lady Penrhyn*, if you will: "Make immediate offing, you are in danger of grounding." I think the signal gun as well, please.' He yelled to the gunner's mate, who was already loading the gun with powder only, 'Wake them up, Mister O'Mara!'

Almost too late, the ships reacted.

He passed the glass back. 'They are too close, William. These winds will cause a catastrophe. The current here is quite contrary, too. We cannot get in here. I must speak with Captain Phillip.'

A few minutes later, he was back on deck. 'We're to stand well clear, my friend, and make for Rio.'

'We need water, Philip. He will have to reduce the ration. Lord, the sun is hot today.' William Bradley pulled a linen handkerchief from his pocket, drawing it about his face to dry the beads of sweat that glistened on his forehead.

The Cornishman in Philip King came to the fore at times such as this. 'Better'n bein' on a lee shore, with a swell likes this be, my beauty!'

Bradley grunted, but smiled at his friend's humour. Some two hours later, clear of the islands, the fleet found a true wind at last. The danger past, the two officers relaxed a little as the watch on deck continued with the routine of the day.

'What news of our impetuous young marine, Will?' King enquired of Bradley.

William Bradley looked up at the sky.

'I fear we are due some storms, Phillip—and not just from the heavens. Mark my word. That young man will bring trouble on his head before we make our land-fall, of that I have no doubt!'

'Aye, he seems a hothead, for sure. To show defiance to our gallant major is to court disaster. He is not a man one would wish to have as an enemy!'

'I hear they had a confrontation in Portsmouth, over the matter of the marines' ammunition. Ross holds the young man responsible. But then he is fond of relinquishing re-sponsibility, I understand...'

Bradley's voice dropped as he saw the subject of their conversation appear at the top of the companionway.

'Good morning to you, Major Ross.' He spoke almost too loudly. 'Have you come to observe real sailors at work, sir?'

Ross flushed at the barely concealed insult. He was not a popular member of the ward-room, never could be as a marine, the more so because he was not considered a 'gentle-man' by these naval dandies, with their gold buttons and buckled shoes and with friends at court and in Parliament. Damn the Navy. Yes, it was their task to transport real soldiers to the place where they were needed, but more than that they were of no importance. Soldiers, not sailors, won battles. Damn them all for their foppery.

He snorted his disdain and strode aft to the rail, staring at the ship's wake for a very long time. Young Mister Vizzard was clever, had gained the respect not only of his men, but also of the senior officers. The bastard had become popular. Too popular by half. Now he had the governor's favour, too; all that Latin—a secret code between 'educated men'. He was a threat to Ross's own position and authority, and that would not do. Something more would have to be done about it. The man should have drowned. Vizzard was now talked of as a hero, damn the upstart. *I am the hero of this detachment; it is I who command them. Major Robert Ross will be lieutenant governor, and should anything happen to mister high and mighty Arthur Phillip, then it is I who will become governor of the colony, and these bastard Navy men had better understand that*, he thought. He stood motionless, his mind working, considering options and plans and hoping for an opportunity.

*****

The air was heavy and still in the cage; even the cockroaches seemed languid, lacking their usual aggression. Mary flicked another off her leg and stamped on it.

She would never get used to this. Whatever Botany Bay held for her, it would surely be better. Insects and pests had become part of her life; initially distressed by them, now she extinguished them habitually, without thought, as though she was oblivious to their very existence. The fleas bit her, and her clothes became home for lice. Her smooth skin was covered with rashes, which itched. She countered their infestation by bathing under a pump whenever the opportunity arose, and she obtained some extract of coal tar from the surgeon, which she used to wash with, and clean the floor and walls of the cage. Mary found that their cage was one of the healthiest in the ship. The heat and airlessness, however, she found suffocating. The women lay around like discarded ragdolls with which a child had grown bored.

The day had passed like all those before. The heat had become oppressive, so much so that she had abandoned her modesty, and, on an impulse, she had made a crude shirt for herself with calico from the captain's stocks, and cut her skirt to just below her knees.

That night a violent storm had thrown the ship about. The crew had been on deck for hours, fighting with the sodden sails and she had been sick, for the first time since coming on board. In the morning, the women were allowed on deck, made to work on the captain's stock of linen and old canvas, making shirts and trousers. The fleet could not be seen from the deck and she heard the captain swearing at his mates, bemoaning the fact. The *Lady Penrhyn* sailed poorly and kept company with the fleet with great difficulty. She was often some miles astern.

The water ration was reduced again, on the orders of the commodore. Women became desperate for water. Some barrels, damaged in the last storm, were condemned. One prisoner, a foul-mouthed prostitute from Stepney, found a brown glass bottle and without thought had taken a large swallow. It was a solution of mercury, and she coughed up blood for two days. The surgeon, Arthur Bowes Smyth, treated her with an emetic to induce vomiting, and she recovered.

Subsequent days saw more storms. The crew set up water catchments, but they became contaminated with seawater. Always the sea was present. Constantly rolling, crashing into the ship. Always wet below. Continuous motion. Never any respite from the sea.

No respite from the men. She had resisted until now, but today she was hungry, and thirsty, so very thirsty, and wanting, wanting a protector, a confidante. She had come to comprehend the wisdom of Lizzie's advice. Jack was gone, but she could weep for him no more.

It was the need for water that had driven her to seek out the young marine, Ned Palmer. She had noticed him before. A shy man, but he liked her; she sensed it. He was quiet, but not submissive. She was sure he was not a drunkard, not like his comrades. He had given her small beer before, and wine. He was kind, of that she was sure. She found him that evening after sunset, by the marine walk at the stem of the ship, just behind the bow. He was alone. *Good*, she thought. He sat facing the bowsprit, idly carving a length of wood, smoking a long-stemmed pipe.

'Ned,' she said, causing him to jump in alarm. 'I have need of water. Desperate, I am. Can you help me, please?' Her voice sounded low in her throat.

He offered his bottle, staring up at her in wonder.

'No. It's water,' he said, seeing her shy away. 'It ain't wine this time.'

It was warm, and tasted of wood, but it was water. She drank fully, spilling some on her chin, the drops glistening in the starlight. She sat down beside him.

'They are beautiful.' Her head back, she stared at the heavens, surveying the myriad of stars.

'The master says that group up ahead be the Southern Cross.' He was pointing over the starboard cathead. 'Brighter than them at home.' He looked wistful.

'Where is home for you, Ned?' She knew nothing of him, but that he had been gentle and kindly.

'Dorset. I comes from a village near Poole. Lytchett Minster, but you would not 'ave 'eard of it, miss. Used to walk there an' look at the ships, then one day I didn't go home.' He turned to look at her. ' I 'ad a sister there, I did. Just like you, she was. But she died, and there was none else for me to worry about, so I went to sea. Did two years on an Indiaman, then I took up soldiering. The grub's better.' He laughed at his speech. He had not spoken so much to the beautiful girl from Gloucester throughout the whole voyage.

She sat closer to him, as the warm night breeze rose, tugging at her hair.

'How d'ye come to be on this slaver, then, Mary?' Using her name, he felt shy again.

'Slaver! Yes, you speak the truth.' Her mouth pinched firmly as she glanced astern.

'The wonder is that so many of us have survived. The cages are foul. The deck is often awash with water, and nothing stays dry for long. There is never quite enough food, our cages are infested with lice and other crawling creatures, the children fall sick and the crew treat us as whores!' Some of her anger spilled out. 'You at least have been considerate.'

She smiled kindly at him. 'I stole some books belonging to my employer. Leastways, I was convicted for the theft of them. The judge was against me from the first.'

Mary paused, wondered if she should tell Ned the truth. She decided she would. 'He tried to rape me, the drunken bastard. He was a bastard right enough, 'scuse my language, but he had violated a lot of women in Stroud and Gloucester.' She raised the bottle to her lips once more, and drank two or three mouthfuls of the tepid water. 'I fought him but got seven years from a judge who had no interest, that or he had been bribed.'

Silence. Neither spoke for several minutes. Watching the sky, listening to the slap, slap of the bow wave beneath them.

'I believe you.' He spoke with sympathy. 'A lot here will plead innocence, but most are thieves and cheats, and hardened cases, too. No rapists that I knows of, though. I 'ear tell as 'ow the guv'nor don't know who done what, nor 'ow long they got. My officer says the papers for all the convicts ain't come wiv us.'

She settled closer to him. He stirred at the sight and closeness of her, the loose fabric of her shirt. The pipe no longer glowed in the darkness. He placed it on the deck. His hand found hers. It did not pull away. *Perhaps she will.* Uncertain, he put his arm about her shoulders. Expectancy rose in him, and his mouth opened to speak.

'Hush, now, Ned. I know you like me. I have seen it in your eyes. My man left me after my trial, and until now I've not... needed another.' She felt a need rising quickly. *Lust, I suppose,* she thought. *God help me, is this right? Oh Jack, where are you when I really need you?* she anguished over her confusion. Her eyes seemed to him to shimmer, reflecting the starlight.

His arm tightened about her. She laid her head into his shoulder and responded by stroking the inside of his duck breeches, and their lips came together in heat. His hands explored her, the thin Indian cotton of her shirt parting with the urgency of his need.

She felt his weight on her as she rolled over, her own hands reaching and squeezing as the desire in both their bodies rose. Hands tugged at her skirt, one of them her own, and her undergarments tore as she pulled him to her, his strength growing as he entered her. Animal instinct had overwhelmed her and she wanted him. Her moistness exploded as he went deeper, and deeper, penetrating her soul, her conscience and her spirit, raising a ghost, an image she had not seen for a long time.

They rolled on the deck, hard and warm beneath their aching, sweating bodies, all care gone for a few moments in the need to satisfy the lust each felt. She surprised herself with the force of her demand for him. As her tongue explored his mouth, her hands gripped him, pulling him deeper in. Her nerve ends screamed, her voice also, as she felt an energy course through her body, rushing like a wind through a forest. A sharp pain. The night exploded as the stars reeled across the sky, and she pulled away from him, guilt pulling her away, panting, her chest heaving, rising and falling like the sea.

Then she wept. She wept for her lost innocence. She wept for the love won and lost. She wept for Jack and her own act of betrayal.

CHAPTER 27
THE MALAY

Vizzard put the glass back in the rack, but continued to gaze with longing at the sharp, flat-topped mountain that dominated the sky above Cape Town. His shirt hung loose on his damp back, yet he remained oblivious to the heat of the sun.

The fleet had been at anchor for over a fortnight and only now were supplies coming on board the transports. He longed to be ashore, to feel solid earth beneath his feet, to walk without rolling as though drunk. He had not been permitted ashore even in Rio de Janeiro. Each request to Major Ross had been refused, adding to his ennui. A month the fleet had remained there and all he could do was stare at the foreign city and all its colour and vibrancy, and vicariously enjoy the pleasures experienced by the other officers. Even Joe Packer had been granted leave ashore, on his return making a gift to Jack of local wines. It was small consolation.

Captain Phillip had kept the officers busy, mostly with maintenance of the ships, and watering and obtaining fresh stores. He had even procured armourer's tools and 10,000 musket balls for the marines, greatly to Jack's amusement.

Seeds, too, he had purchased, and local beef, which was excellent. Other officers had bought a locally distilled spirit; *aguardente* the Brazilians had called it. Jack had shared a bottle with another marine officer, Captain Tench, now deployed on the transport *Charlotte*, and both had found it unpalatable.

He enjoyed the captain's company, finding this senior officer, at least, to be cultured and educated, a man of humour and wit. Tench was fluent in French, a language of which Jack had only rudimentary knowledge, which he wished to improve. He spent many hours with Tench, learning from him, making use of his French grammar and dictionary.

Here now, in Cape Town, friends had returned to *Sirius* extolling the delights, and horrors, of this last contact with civilized society the fleet would have before crossing vast oceans to whatever destiny awaited them. He was restless and fatigued at the same time.

He climbed the fore-mast and sat cross-legged, staring out over the bay of cerulean blue to the curious mountain behind the town, and felt the breeze run through his hair as the ship swayed, once more alone with his private thoughts. Ross hardly spoke to him, issuing his orders through others, relentlessly requiring him to undertake yet more and more meaningless tasks. Finding fault in everything he did. Drill in everything; 'spit and polish' was the way young Tom described it. Endless lists, double checking of supplies, and drilling the men.

The fleet continued to take on provisions, many of the officers hoping to augment their personal supplies. Arthur

Phillip invested in seeds, plants and much-needed livestock. He bargained hard with the obdurate Dutch traders, but also took the opportunity of ensuring the convicts, the 'human cargo' he was responsible for, ate well, with extra supplies of meat, soft bread and fresh fruit and vegetables.

This morning, as Jack had searched his chest for some writing paper, he had found the letter from his father, long forgotten. He pulled it from his pocket and read it once more.

Lampern House
Woodchester, Glos
12th April 1787

My dearest Jack,

I know not when, or indeed if, this letter will reach you, but have this desire to reach out to you. I pray daily for news of you, to little avail. Our parting caused me such unhappiness, such deep sorrow. That much you will have understood. You did have the grace to speak to me before leaving, for that I am grateful, and spared me the wound that your dear brother caused me some years ago. I still have no word of him and wonder at my circumstance, a father with two sons, but neither by my side.

Firstly, let me assure you of a father's love. I struggle each day to understand your decision, and pray that one day you will return safe and well, to Lampern, and to your rightful place with me. Your dear sister joins with me in that sentiment.

Next, I must relate the most unwelcome and dis-tasteful tales that have been circulating since your departure, concerning the demise of our Revd. Barnwood. The suggestion is made by some malicious tongues that you, in some measure, and by unknown means, and for reasons unknown, caused his early and regretted death. Now, my good friend, Doctor Stee

Whatever else it was that his father had written was spoiled by mildew and mould, with the remainder of the letter completely illegible. No amount of peering, including the use of a magnifying glass, had revealed the final contents of the letter. He sighed. Probably there was news of Mary, but whatever his father's words, it was beyond him to decipher. In exasperation, he tore the note into several pieces, and cast them to the breeze now fluttering about the masts and causing the stays to whistle and hum.

A shout from the deck brought him back to the present. The midshipman of the watch called that his presence was required in the captain's cabin. More competently than on the first occasion, he descended the rigging and hurried to find his uniform coat. He fastened the final button as he stood at the door of the main cabin. The marine sentry, sweating in the growing heat of the day, opened the door and stood aside for him.

'There you are, Mister Vizzard. Thank you for being so prompt.'

Arthur Phillip was pacing a small semi-circle about his desk. Major Ross was standing by a table littered with charts and papers, drinking coffee from a china cup. He feigned interest in one document in particular.

'Sir?' Jack asked, wondering why he had been summoned to the commodore.

'Doubtless you are curious as to my summons, young man.' He glanced sideways at Ross, who ignored him. 'The Governor of the Cape, Mynheer Van Graaffe, has been—how shall I put this?—not the most pliant of men to deal with. Hospitable, but inclined to obduracy. I am obliged to pay the most outrageous of prices for... Well, no matter, Vizzard.' Phillip paused in his pacing, and looked directly at Jack, seeking and receiving full attention.

'However, this morning he related to me a tale of some misfortune, and I have offered such assistance as His Majesty's Marines are capable of, to, ah, encourage his further cooperation. Major Ross and I have discussed the matter, and he, that is, we feel that you may be the man needed for the occasion.'

Jack tried, but failed to conceal the look of bewilderment on his face.

Phillip smiled. 'I am not explaining myself at all well.' The commodore continued. 'He tells that a very dangerous man is loose in the town, and it would benefit our expedition if this man could be caught and dealt with expeditiously. He is a Malay, banished here from Batavia for some crime in his own country, and who has been refused permission to return.'

Captain Phillip cleared his throat and drank some water from a glass on his desk.

'The man has been smoking opium and is reputed to be in a frenzied condition. He has already murdered upwards of a dozen men in the town, sorely wounded many more, and fled to Table Mountain, where he has taken refuge. He even attempted to assassinate the governor himself. The authorities here are anxious to secure his confinement.' He looked directly at Jack, his intention clear. 'I could, of course, command you. However...'

'That will not be necessary, sir,' Jack replied. 'I am honoured to have the opportunity to be of service. How am I to be involved, sir?'

'Major Ross wished to have command of the detachment, but I believe a small force only will be most appropriate. A dozen men should suffice, I should think. I leave the selection to your judgment; however, if you could be ashore within, say, the hour? Regrettably, the Dutch governor is unable to spare any of his own troops but is willing to provide a guide.' Commodore Phillip clasped his hands behind his back as he waited for Jack's response.

'Certainly, sir. I have the men well drilled. Major Ross has been most particular about drill, sir.' Jack kept his eyes on Phillip.

'Very well, then. I am content to leave the detail to you, but must caution you: this man is heavily armed and is obviously extremely dangerous. He will not succumb to an arrest and force will be required. You have authority to kill him if you or your men are at risk. However, the governor would doubtless welcome the prospect of applying his own form of justice on the man, should it prove possible for you to take him captive. He has killed a number of prominent citizens in his murderous spree.'

'I understand, sir. He is to be taken, alive if possible; if not, then I am at liberty to ensure his, er, termination. In the circumstances, sir, I would appreciate a written order to that effect, should my actions be subject to any challenge by the Dutch authorities.' Jack was concerned should it be necessary to shoot the man, that the Dutch might be less well disposed to the officer responsible.

'So be it. Bernard will have a note ready before you leave. Lieutenant, just be sure you catch this fellow for me, please. I am relying on your skill.' Arthur Phillip wore a frown and a serious expression.

'If he is to be found, sir, he will be caught. I have the best of the regiment to work with.' Jack glanced once more in the direction of Major Ross, who pointedly ignored him.

'I am certain of it, and have all confidence in you, Mister Vizzard. I know you will not fail, but I wish you good luck. This may be no easy task.'

Taking his leave of the commodore, Jack was ashore within an hour of leaving the cabin. He had with him Sergeant Packer and sixteen good men collected from three of the transports, all trusted marines who were eager for a fight and who could be relied upon.

A short, rather embarrassed young officer of the Dutch East India Company introduced their guide. As soon as Jack had proffered his written order the officer made an excuse, and disappeared into an office of the Dutch company.

'Not many of them Hollanders to be seen this afternoon, sir,' offered Joe Packer, holding a carbine casually in the cradle of his left arm. 'Reckon they are bit scared of this renegade Malay.'

'That is why we have the job, Joe. Make no mistake, this will be hard work. First we have to climb the mountain, and that will be work enough; then we have to catch the bugger!'

Joseph Packer looked up at the Cape Town landmark and whistled. 'That's a hard climb, sir. Best we make a start, although this heat will sap us, and that's no mistake!'

Jack smiled. 'Tell the lads to leave their coats with the boat. Carry only water and ammunition in knapsacks. I do not think we need show our scarlet coats today, Joe.'

The men left their coats with the boats, guarded by a mid-shipman and sailors, who were surprised at the order.

Their guide took them to the summit through the Platteklip Gorge, directly from the town. It was early evening by the time the platoon reached the top. The setting sun was throwing long shadows, and the air was cooler, but the men were sweating and breathing hard, after a climb up the cleft in the mountain, grateful to be without their heavy red coats.

Jack had the men rest for a quarter of an hour, while he found a patch of rocks at the summit. Careful to shield his telescope, he searched the plateau. The mountaintop was at least a mile and a half in length, possibly two, he estimated. *This bastard could be anywhere*, he thought, surveying the craggy surface with care. Minute after long minute his eye slowly and carefully scanned the landscape. He picked out a pair of rock hyrax, on a boulder rising above the fynbos shrubland with which the mountain was covered. He took a drink of water and continued his search. Packer slid silently into position beside him.

'Seen anything, sir?' he asked.

'Nothing, Joe. I begin to think we are here on a goose chase. Wait, though.' He steadied the telescope on a rock and adjusted the glass. In a cluster of rocks, about a thousand yards away, a shadow was in the wrong place. No, not a shadow, but a figure resting in a space between two rocks. For a moment or two Jack was uncertain, and then the faintest movement betrayed the position of their prey.

'There he is, Joe. About a thousand yards to the east.' He passed the glass to Packer. 'That crop of rocks over there. Do you see?'

The sergeant hesitated, studying the terrain carefully. He watched for a while, not seeing anything.

'I don't see nothing, sir. You sure you spotted him?'

'There, just to the right of that rounded rock. He is trying to move position slowly. He must be expecting an attempt to take him, but by now he must be tired and sluggish.'

Jack slid back a yard and rolled onto his back. Packer followed.

'No purpose in a frontal approach, Joe. Three sections of four, I think. You take one to the north. I will approach from the south. Corporal Munday can take the direct line, but this has to be a stealthy move, a crawl through this rough grass. He has a good field of fire from that point. If you can keep concealed, you have a good chance of being on him before he knows you are there. I will engage him from that gully, about a hundred yards to his left and distract him from your approach.'

'Not much cover from that point, sir. Have Ed move along the escarpment; the bugger will be expecting a move from about there. Ed has some good marksmen in his section, and can keep the bastard's head down.'

'Yes, I see. Very well, then. Pass that on to the sections, and have them ready to move in five minutes. I will stay here and keep an eye on him. Oh, and, Joe, one more thing—better post a couple of the lads at the top of the gully, just in case he should slip behind us.'

With those orders, Jack crawled up to a clump of long grass and again put the telescope to his eye. He slowly pulled some long grass over his face, weaving some into his hair. He wished his shirt were other than white. He was conscious that they would stand out as ghosts in the fading light. He rubbed some earth onto his neck and face.

'Got that, you lot?' Packer had explained the tactics and deployment to the detachment in a whispered voice.

'Seems a rum way of going about it to me, Sarge. There's enough of us—why don't we just rush the bastard and be done with it?' a private in Ed Munday's section grumbled.

'Because Mister Vizzard has a different way of doing things, Brannon,' Packer growled back. 'We're marines, boy, not bleedin' ordinary foot sloggers, and our officer thinks differently about things!'

Jack gave a pre-arranged hand signal for an advance and the first section moved off along an old track close to the jagged cliff edge. Packer took his section to the north, wriggling along like an extended snake, and Jack waited until they had moved a hundred yards, then started to crawl to the south of the outcrop of rock in which the fugitive was hiding.

The setting sun was very low over his left shoulder, and there was now very little light left in the dying day. He found a shallow gully and crawled slowly along it. He was in position some ten minutes later and signaled his section to move apart. 'At least five yards, you men,' he whispered.

Again rolling onto his back, he bit on a cartridge, dropped a ball down the barrel, silently rammed it home with a wad and leveled the weapon towards the rocks. He was gratified to note that his marines had followed suit and were ready in firing positions. He noticed that the two men closest to him had emulated him and smeared their faces with dirt, recognizing the purpose. *If Ross could see us now...* He smiled. Marines lying prone on the earth, not standing erect waiting to be shot at; it was contrary to all field practice.

He looked at the shadows again, and judged the other sections would be in position. He gave a soft hoot, akin to the wood pigeons of home, which was answered by Packer over to his right, about three hundred yards away. Then took aim at the gap in the rocks—a sudden movement and he fired, the rest of his section following with an almost simultaneous crackle of fire. His ball blew pieces of rock to dust, and an answering crack told him his quarry was waiting for them. So their approach had not been undetected after all, he thought. White cotton shirts were too visible.

A cry to his left told him that one of his men was hurt, but now Munday's section had opened fire on the position, and smoke was hovering over the field. He fired a second ball, this time simply to keep the man pinned down, but moments later another ball hit the earth in front of his face, sending dust and grit into his eyes. *Sweet Jesus*, he thought, *this man knows his business.*

Now he heard an oath from the cliff edge and guessed that one of Munday's men had been hit. Then a shout and Packer's men were running. He, too, was on his feet, shouting with a mix of fear and a rush of blood pumping through his body. Another ball sang overhead, to his right. Two of Packer's men reached the rocks and there was a clash of steel on steel. Jack reached the rocks, sword drawn, and saw a marine on the ground, with another grappling a dark-skinned man who fought with surprising strength, a long bayonet in his left hand. Jack's boot struck him hard in the back and he sagged. Jack hit him across the temple with the butt of his musket and it was finished.

'Truss him up, Joe, and make them tight. This one has caused enough trouble.'

Two men quickly tied the man's hands behind his back,

anc shackled a short length of chain Packer had brought to his ankles. Jack moved to the motionless marine who had a knife buried deep in his throat from which the blood still slowly seeped, staining the earth around him.

'Davis is dead, Joe.' He sat on a rock and felt the guilt hit him. The man was the first casualty under his command. He felt the responsibility heavily in his chest, as if he had been struck a blow by a prizefighter.

'He was a good 'un, sir. Must have been the first to reach the bastard.' Packer looked at Jack's face and continued, 'Take a tot o' rum, sir; it weren't your fault. Could've cost more if we'd charged in, like.' He passed a stone bottle from his haversack, and Jack took a large swallow of the spirit. He thcught of a cold day in Gloucester with his father and Giles. He felt as low as he had that day.

'I should have got the timing better, given closer support to you.' He rose slowly to his feet. Another man had a wound to his thigh, where a ball had passed through. Packer placed a cartridge wad on it, and bound it with a handkerchief.

'You'll be right as rain in a week, Griffiths. Doubt the surgeon will have to take that one off!' He laughed at the private, who was obviously in pain, and kicked the prisoner. 'Get to your feet, you bastard, and thank whichever god you have that I ain't in charge, or I'd blow your mucking brains out myself, right here and now!'

The Malay pretended not to understand, and was still reeling drunkenly from the blow of Jack's musket. Packer collected two pistols, a pair of muskets and a vicious bayonet. Then he searched the Malay for other weapons—a hidden knife was found in a boot.

Jack turned to the men and said, 'Right, well done, lads.

Good work by all of you, but time to get back to the town and hand this bugger back to the Dutch. Ed, detail some of Davis's mates to bring him back to the ship.'

He drank from his bottle, a long swallow of warm water to quench the thirst that now made his throat dry and tight. His tongue felt twice its usual size.

Gathering his musket, he started the slow descent to the town, made very difficult in the dark of the evening, but a full moon was rising and lit the track down the mountain—the same moon that had illuminated the vicarage that night, so long ago, he thought.

Eventually he found the house and the Dutch officer, now waiting with a small crowd of officials and citizens. The firing had attracted the populace, who had watched the marines' progress as they'd descended Table Mountain.

Feeling very dirty and now more tired than he would've thought possible, he handed the Malay over to the officer. 'This is your murderer. He killed one of my men in the taking of him.' The Dutchman looked confused.

Jack did not wish to explain. He turned and walked to the ships' boats waiting at the jetty and sank onto the sternsheets, his shoulders slumped and his chin on his chest. Within a minute, he was sleeping.

The bosun's mate glanced at Sergeant Packer, who just shook his head and made a sign to move off. The moonlight sparkled across Table Bay, as though a giant hand had cast thousands of minute diamonds across the surface, as the boats returned to *Sirius*.

CHAPTER 28

A BONDING

'He did a damned fine job, Arthur. The governor is extremely satisfied.'

Captain John Hunter was reading a dispatch from the Dutch governor as Arthur Phillip sat on a chair on the quarterdeck.

'He reports that the man was 'immediately executed'—in a barbaric fashion, it seems. He was broken on a wheel and then... beheaded and quartered. Good God! No pretence of a trial, just... off with his head!'

Captain Phillip looked at his friend with a shocked expression. 'Dreadful, simply dreadful. The Dutch were barbaric in the Spice Islands. I had thought such treatment was now beneath them. Better not relate that to young Vizzard. He seems upset as it is.'

'Yes, indeed, he is. Dawes tells me that he is much distressed at the loss of one of his men. There were two wounded as well, I believe.' Hunter had Jack's report of the episode in front of him.

'There really should be no record of this, John.' Phillip

stood and started pacing. 'It would cause the Dutch some small embarrassment if it became known that they had need of the Royal Navy and its marines to maintain order in their precious colony; and we have need of their co-operation, for the present at least. Remember, 'tis but four years since we were at war with Holland. I fancy that we will, one day, seek to displace the Dutch here to protect our own trade, and our routes to India, of course.' Arthur Phillip looked at the brief report that Jack had written that morning.

'Keep it in your personal papers, John, but make no official reference to it; in fact, the incident is closed.'

'Yes, I understand, Arthur. Our young marine deserves some recognition, I think, but in the circumstances, perhaps that plan would be best. Actually, sir, Major Ross takes the position that the incident was entirely routine, and undeserving of mention in any dispatch, as he puts it!'

'So it shall be, but for my own reasons, John, rather than to accommodate our major!'

*****

At last, on 12 November, after a month at the Cape of Good Hope, re-provisioning the fleet was complete. The capstans squealed and the anchors rose once more, as the small armada set off on the final part of its unprecedented odyssey. Arthur Phillip learned from a visiting English vessel of a second fleet of convicts in preparation. He took reassurance from the news.

The seas the fleet encountered as it left Africa were some of the worst the seamen had ever encountered. Great rolling hills of spray-driven, green water with spume at a level with the crosstrees of the ships. First crawling heavily up, and then racing down, ships slipped into the dark, frightening valleys. The wind screamed and roared, as though defying the ships, as if the heavens above had decided that they would not reach their landfall. Tons of dark, cold water dumped solidly on the decks, searching out the gloomy cages below and their despondent inhabitants shivering, often waist deep, in the water that swirled about them. It was relentless; day followed day of dark skies, black tumbling clouds and winds that shrieked and kept the crews at hard labour, fighting the elements. The ships rolled, yawed and pitched so much that many of those locked below were heartily sick.

To Jack it was almost beyond his comprehension. Nothing in his experience could compare to the forces at work on this ocean. He was awed at the skill of the seamen. They turned out from the wet decks below to climb the swinging masts, dwarfed by the seas on either side of the small ship. When the wind eased, and the sun made the decks steam, they had a small respite, only to be assailed again by another storm.

Officers appeared drained, their eyes shot with thin scarlet veins, and their feet constantly wet. Captain Hunter rarely left the quarterdeck at these times, ordering changes to the helmsmen—never less than two—lashed to the wheel, trimming sails, furling them, eyes scanning the seas about him.

Jack stayed below, reading by the light of a lantern when he could. It was permanently dark and wet, and cold, so very cold his teeth chattered until his jaw ached. The odours and poisoned air from the bilges permeated everywhere, contaminating clothes, uniforms, and bedding, turning metal black, and he longed for clean, purifying fresh air and the warming sun on his body. He considered himself fortunate he had not succumbed to sickness, as had some of his men. Bradley told him the fleet was making good progress, with the ships miraculously keeping together.

The days rolled together, like the constantly surging ocean over which they slowly sailed, so he often was confused. Only the ritual of the ship's routine reminded him of the passing hours and days. To occupy some of the time, he scribbled in a journal, recording the monotony. At first, his notes recorded bare facts, gleaned from observation and discussion with the officers, changing to more intimate, personal reflections of the journey and its ultimate purpose. He wrote of his lost love, Mary, and at such times became melancholy.

He wondered, too, how Captain Phillip must feel today. The governor of the new colony had impressed Jack through the little daily contact he had enjoyed with him. Phillip had presented as a very thoughtful, caring man. That had become very evident to Jack as he learned from Dawes, and others, of the strenuous efforts made by the man before the fleet had sailed, and during the voyage.

During any lull in the weather, Jack spent time with the watch-keeping officers. He found their technical discussions of value and learned of the science of navigation and something of the skill of managing a crew, as well as some knowledge of seamanship. As he did so, he thought of his lost brother.

'Jack,' Dawes said quietly, 'I confess I have increasingly wondered about you since the governor's dinner. I have never thanked you properly for, well, you understand me, I believe.'

Jack smiled at Dawes. 'It was an instinctive matter, William. I'm aware that it is spoken of below deck as if I am some kind of hero.' Jack now looked his friend more directly in the eyes. 'I am no such thing, of course. I saw you fall and dived in, without thinking of the consequences. That is the way with me, and has landed me in hot water before!' He grinned, a little embarrassed. 'Although, with you, it was very cold water.'

Dawes was one of a new breed of officers in the Corps. A scientist, with a passion for astronomy, he was tasked with and excited at the prospect of establishing an observatory. The scientific community, in particular the Royal Society, had learned much from earlier voyages of discovery, but much more was to be learned, not only of the lands and peoples of the Pacific, but also of the night skies above.

William Dawes slapped a hand on Jack's shoulder. 'I am your servant for life, Jack, for I am sure no other would have acted thus. I owe you my life, and will never forget that. However, there is an enigma that I must question you on—David Collins has informed me that your time at Oxford was not spent studying classics, but the law. You told me so yourself. Now, I ask, why should a lawyer choose an arduous and uncertain future as a marine? Answer me that, Jack Vizzard!'

Jack coloured slightly. 'I am discovered, then?' He failed to conceal a small note of alarm in his voice.

'Be assured, my friend, your secret is safe. I merely seek to know why you should wish it so.'

'Will, I told the governor the truth. My past is simply that; I have no wish to discuss it, even with you. I am sincere in my desire to serve as a soldier. It is my true vocation. A decent-minded lawyer—and I fear there is an insufficient number of those—aspires to attain justice, not as an abstract concept, but as a reality, to do good for the people. I learned that I could not achieve that. I suppose I was not sufficiently committed. You must promise me to respect my confidence in this. Please?'

Dawes offered his hand as a sign of his willingness to do so, and Jack took it and clasped it firmly.

CHAPTER 29
THE SUPPLY

Thirteen days out from the Cape of Good Hope, Captain Phillip once more summoned Jack to his cabin. A large group of officers was present, including Lieutenants Bradley and King of the Navy, and Captains Shea, Tench, Collins and Campbell of the Marines. The murmurings amongst them ceased as he entered. One or two gave him a friendly glance and a greeting. Ross, standing next to Phillip, could barely conceal his displeasure.

'Sir, you wished me to report.' Just a hint of a question emerged in Jack's tone.

Arthur Phillip looked hard at him, hesitating before speaking.

'Mister Vizzard. Thank you. Yes, indeed, I did. I have had conference with my senior officers, and have reached a decision. I am now resolved that I and the swiftest transports must press ahead, taking with me as many artisans as we have, in order to reach Botany Bay ahead of the majority of the people, and prepare the way. However, I intend to take the *Supply* and make reconnaissance of the land before the fleet arrives. Major Ross will remain with the flagship, but I need capable young marines to accompany me. Lieutenant Bird has none aboard. We are all agreed,'—a swift glance towards Major Ross gave a hint to Jack that in fact not all were in agreement—'that you are the fellow. I shall have need also of Mister Dawes, and will speak with him as soon as he reports. I would be obliged if you would collect your dunnage, and a section of your more sober men, and be ready to transfer with me in an hour.'

Clearly, this was a snub to Ross, who as lieutenant-governor could expect the honour of landing first with Phillip. From the expression on his face, Ross had known nothing of this. He was plainly incensed that part of his command would be landing in advance of his own arrival. Jack could not prevent his eyes from glancing quickly towards the man, who opened his mouth to speak but instantly changed his mind as Phillip raised an eyebrow to silence any protest.

'Aye, aye, sir.' Jack could not prevent the boyish grin that instantly came to his face. He quickly turned on his heel, remembering to duck his head to avoid contact with the beam.

Closing the door of the cabin, he heard voices raised but was too pleased with his orders to care. He slid down the companionway, calling for Sergeant Packer as he did so.

'Packer, you and the five best men of the company in full order to transfer with me to *Supply* within the hour, if you please! Tom, my kit within half an hour. We are off to... Well, do not stand gawping, boy! Let us be busy, quickly now.'

In fact, another four days were to pass before the sea conditions allowed the transfer to be safely undertaken. Jack grew increasingly restless, as a horse might before a race. Ross now ignored the very fact of Jack's existence, but he at least gained the satisfaction of learning that Ross was to continue the voyage on board the *Scarborough*, one of the other transports. He would be free of the man, for a time. He was also delighted to learn that Lieutenants Philip King and William Dawes would also transfer to *Supply*, with the governor.

He found the *Supply* to be very cramped. Her captain, Lieutenant Henry Lidgbird Ball, was an obliging and friendly officer of alert and aristocratic bearing, with a straight, if long, nose and a high forehead. He was some thirty years of age and the *Supply* was his first command. Although she was the smallest in the fleet, Ball was intensely proud of her. The ship's master was David Blackburn, a reluctant appointee to the *Supply*, but a diligent and competent officer. Both men had been shipmates in HMS *Victory*.

Supply was an armed tender of 170 tons and with eight guns, a sixth rate ship, with a total complement of fifty men. It had been thought that she would be a poor vessel for such an undertaking, and sail badly, but in fact Arthur Phillip had been pleased with her performance, due in part to the skill of her master. Jack found her uncomfortable and her constant rolling and pitching after the comparative size of *Sirius* was inclined to disturb him, but he enjoyed the company of the officers. Within a week, he had adapted to the small vessel and grown to share the captain's affection for her.

The days slipped past and Christmas was celebrated in modest style. Early in the new year of 1788, they observed the Aurora Australis, faint and smudged at first, but on the night of the 6th of January the crew were able to observe the phenomenon in full splendour. Initially it appeared as a long, writhing, snake-like ribbon, stretching across the horizon from starboard to larboard, turning into a rippling curtain of ghostly green light, with fingers of pink and red, all waggling furiously. Lieutenant King sketched it, intending to make a watercolour of it when time allowed. Jack stood on deck watching it in wonder for an hour or more before it dissipated itself and vanished from the night.

Two days later he heard the cry that had all had awaited—land had been sighted. He shared the excitement of the rest of the crew, and rushed up to the quarterdeck to see this land they had travelled so long and so far to see. The men starting cheering and laughing, jumping with the joy of land to look at, not mountains of foam-topped seas.

'Van Dieman's Land, Mister Vizzard, not New Holland!' Lieutenant Ball smiled. 'But we shall anchor in Botany Bay soon enough.' Ball was as excited as any man aboard, but his new position constrained him from revealing his feelings—that, and perhaps his natural reserve.

Raising his telescope, Jack surveyed the land just visible off the port bow of *Supply* and allowed himself a glow of satisfaction. It had been a good voyage, far better than any had predicted or expected. The governor would be pleased. After the months of planning, and nearly two hundred and fifty days at sea, they were almost there. He heard movement behind him and sensed William Dawes at his shoulder.

'We have a landfall, Jack?' he asked.

'Aye, Will, that we do. Van Dieman's Land is perhaps twelve miles off. Another week or so will see the fleet in Botany Bay. At least the worst of the weather is behind us now.' It was still blowing hard, with rain driving from the north-west.

Captain Arthur Phillip arrived on deck, just a little short of breath, obviously stirred from his desk by the news. Jack moved to the lee side of the quarterdeck as demanded by custom in the Navy, leaving the two sea officers to observe and converse in some privacy. As word spread, other officers sought space on the now-cramped deck, and Captain David Collins joined them. The marine officers gazed across the expansive sea for some time before Collins finally spoke.

'Our time is nearly on us, then, Jack. Very soon we will be ashore and our real work will begin.'

'I have been wondering about this time since we left Portsmouth. It is a strange feeling to be looking at land that very few men have looked upon before.'

They stood together, gazing at the mountainous country, each wondering about the future.

Chapter 30
Botany Bay

Lieutenant Henry Lidgbird Ball lowered the telescope from his eye, then turned and passed an order to his sailing master, David Blackburn. 'Ease her off, Davy. Prepare to anchor, if you would. Two cables from the north head should do very well, I think.'

His eyes scoured the shore, noted some natives brandishing short spears. He was not encouraged.

'A reception committee awaits us, sir.'

Arthur Phillip shaded his eyes against the white sun, blinking several times to aid his focus.

'Yes, Harry. It is to be expected. We must all of us be mindful that it is we who intrude here. We must show them we intend no harm. I will take a party ashore presently and make contact with them.'

The anchorage secured, at about three in the afternoon sailors lowered the ship's boats, with Governor Phillip, Lieutenants King, Dawes and Vizzard aboard. A party of seamen from *Supply,* accompanied by Jack's men, followed and landed on the north side of the wide bay. The first task was to find a supply of water with which to replenish the fleet's casks. Finding nothing suitable, the party returned to a point opposite the *Supply*.

They encountered a small group of the natives, who shouted at them menacingly, waving their short spears. Arthur Phillip held out a selection of brightly coloured beads, strung on necklaces, ordered one of the sailors to attach them to the canoes they had pulled up onto the sand. The natives showed no interest, but the threatening attitude moderated. By use of crude sign language Phillip indicated the need to find water, which they understood, and by similar sign language they made reply, indicating the other side of the point on which they stood. When they reached the far side, the natives pointed to a fine stream of fresh water draining into the bay.

Governor Phillip again advanced towards the group, alone and unarmed, once more holding out a selection of beads and ribbons. One of the natives appeared desirous of having them and came forward, but not so close as to receive them directly from Phillip's hand. He made sign to place them on the sand. On that being done, the man, completely naked and in obvious fear, was emboldened enough to advance further and pick them up. With more confidence, he came closer still and took possession of other articles offered, including a mirror, with which he was very amused. He danced and shouted excitedly, waving the mirror at his fellows. Arthur Phillip took encouragement from that, and relaxed.

Jack watched very carefully, looking particularly at the Indians to the rear, but, mindful of his orders not to engage closely, remained with his men by the boats, until Phillip decided that sufficient contact had been made for the day and ordered the party to return to the ship.

To Commodore Phillip's surprise, the remainder of the fleet arrived at the anchorage within twenty-four hours of the *Supply* lowering her anchor. Their passage had not been as inhibited or delayed as he had expected.

During the ensuing days, Arthur Phillip made a number of small-scale expeditions, exploring the area and the inlets around the bay. Encounters with the natives continued, some with a show of hostility towards the Englishmen, some with a more affable conclusion.

One evening, in the cabin of *Sirius*, the officers discussed the day's encounter with the indigenous people of New South Wales. To all they were known as Indians.

'They appear a very simple race of Indians to me, sir,' offered Lieutenant King. 'They seem to have dispensed with any form of clothing, and their weapons are crude and rudimentary.' King crossed his arms. 'Their canoes also are of the most elementary design, barely seaworthy, I would hazard.'

'Indeed they are, Mister King, but be very aware of His Majesty's wish to treat these people well, and that is my instruction, too. It will go badly with any man—officer, seaman, marine or convict—who causes any distrust or harm. We will have need of good relations with them, if we are to settle this place.' Phillip drank from his glass, gathering his thoughts. 'However, gentlemen, I am yet to be persuaded that Botany Bay is as it should be. In my candid opinion, it does not accord with Captain Cook's account. I intend that we explore further before any general disembarkation is made.'

There was general agreement with that opinion, it being the consensus that the bay offered poor shelter for the fleet. The brief forays off the beach reinforced that conclusion, the ground in the vicinity being of poor quality and unsuitable for cultivation.

Jack spent time ashore with watering parties, making short-range patrols through the hinterland under the increasingly aggressive supervision of Major Ross, who kept a flow of sarcasm directed at Jack, seeking to undermine the obvious respect the marines had for their young officer. 'Keep your blade sharp, Mister Vizzard. I fancy you will have need of it afore long, laddie,' he goaded Jack.

Jack clenched his teeth, his fists by his sides, breathing hard. Packer had heard the jibe. 'Stay calm, sir, please. He ain't worth it, sir,' he muttered.

A shadow passed across Jack's face. 'Quiet, Joe. Be about your duty.'

He spoke calmly, but he knew that one day there would have to be a reckoning between them.

CHAPTER 31
SYDNEY COVE

The brightness of the light had surprised all aboard *Lady Penrhyn.* The women had often had the opportunity to exercise or work on deck since leaving England, of course, but never before had their English eyes experienced such blinding whiteness, such pellucid skies. The blue ocean sparkled with the light cast down from a sun that appeared larger than any they had seen before. The sand was cleaner, the clouds sharper, and the trees greener, against a sky of the deepest azure blue.

Some days later, after a number of short—and for the most part fruitless and unsatisfactory—excursions in the immediate hinterland, the masters of the transports were ordered to bring their ships to Port Jackson, and although only light breezes blew from the south-south-east, the crews had great difficulty in working out of the bay.

A series of orders fluttered from the flagship: Governor Phillip was in a hurry. He had explored some miles to the north and his party, in three ship's boats, had discovered a most excellent harbour, entered between narrow heads, in which he judged it possible for the transports to anchor in deep water very close to the shore. He had observed also that the land in that area was superior to that examined in the present locality.

Having encountered the ships of La Perouse, the French explorer, at the entrance to Botany Bay, Captain Hunter knew it was time to be gone from this place. He was more than a little anxious to conceal the fleet's intended destination.

The *Prince of Wales* became fouled with the *Friendship*, rending her new mainsail and topmost staysail. The latter lost her jib boom in the collision. By evening, however, the entire fleet had left Botany Bay and was safely at anchor in a small cove within Port Jackson. The tymbals of a hundred thousand greengrocer and double drummer cicadas sang a continuous mating song, almost expunging the other sounds in the cove. A flagpole, erected earlier in the morning, was proudly flying the Union Jack. Officers drank to the health of the royal family, the marines fired several volleys as a salute, and the governor named the place Sydney Cove.

It was Saturday 26th January 1788.

*****

'So, where we off to now, then, Mary? Watcha heard then, luv? Come on, your man must know summat.' Lizzie wiped sweat from her forehead with her sleeve. 'All this coming and going—I dunno what them orfficers think they're about.' Lizzie had no information from her own men, and the frustration she felt had got the better of her. She sat on the deck among a group of women making up shirts and smocks.

Mary closed off another loose thread, plucked at the button she had fixed, placing the finished coarse shirt into a basket in front of her, and stretched out her long brown legs. The hours spent on deck had changed her colouring, and given her face, arms and legs a healthy golden-brown shade.

'I hear the governor has dismissed Botany Bay as a suitable site for us poor wanton women, and proposes to establish a camp further north. How far I know not, but it is said to be more sheltered and with good soil for crops. Lord, how I wish we could get off this ship and be rid of these damned sailors!'

'My man reckons they've given the thumbs down to this place and we'm being sent to China,' another woman volunteered.

'Balls to that notion, Maggie,' retorted Lizzie. 'We must've passed China months back. I reckon they just gonna dump us on some lost island and leave us to rot.' She picked at a piece of rough calico, threading her needle with a deft stroke, and continued, 'Mind you, now, we'll be alright if they leave a few decent marines to look after us, eh, Mary!' She winked and grinned, showing some uneven, chipped and now carious teeth.

Mary looked at her friend. She had grown fond of Ned, and had spent one or two nights on deck with him, and a night in his hammock. They had spoken little during the day, but both understood the nights would sometimes bring them together.

'I only took your advice, Lizzie, just learned for myself that I had to find someone to help me get through this journey and whatever the future has for me.' Imperceptibly, a small sigh escaped and she yawned to cover it, standing and stretching like a cat just risen from sleep.

'Ned's a good man, and better he as a guard than some of the monkeys we've got on board. Now who has the duty for dinner? I'm in need of some home made beef pie and pastry with onions and kidneys and a bucket of gravy.' She laughed and was glad that some of the others did also.

In fact, the women had no dinner that day. The *Lady Penrhyn,* in company with the other transports, was not clear of Botany Bay until 3 o'clock in the afternoon, and reached Port Jackson that evening at about 7 o'clock, fortunately without further incident. The women were not to be put ashore, however, as the landing party were busy preparing a place for settlement.

Each day a party of men would be ashore and, under the supervision of marine guards, were set to work clearing the ground near the run of fresh water at the head of the cove. Saw pits were dug, trees were felled, ground cleared and tents erected. The women observed this activity in frustration.

Lieutenant Dawes worked closely with Governor Phillip at this time. At 26 years of age, William Dawes was designated Officer of Engineers and Artillery. He would have little need of his skill as an artilleryman, but that did not stop him designing bastions for the defence of the new settlement. Major Ross demanded it, arguing a fortress was a priority for the settlement. However, Governor Phillip instructed him to spend no time on such matters. For the present needs of the newly born colony, his skills were used to lay out the essentials of a new town, which Governor Phillip had initially intended to call Albion but had recently decided would be called Sydney, to honour Lord Townshend.

Dawes established the site of the government farm and explored, seeking a site for his observatory. A pious man, he was in truth a mathematician, a savant learned in many things and deeply interested in the sciences and the night sky.

Jack was not so involved with the design of the new settlement, but also spent time ashore with his marines. He cursed them, worked them hard, kept them maintaining their equipment and had them patrolling the area when other companies were standing idly by, drinking openly and talking amongst themselves in mutinous language, bemoaning their lot at standing guard over the dregs of London society. Brother officers, encouraged by Major Ross, began to smirk, and one or two openly mocked Jack. He cared not. This was his first command, and he was determined not to be found wanting in his duty. He chose not to join in the drinking, the gambling with dice or cards, or the petty squabbles that had started amongst some officers.

Corporal Edward Goodall was a reliable marine. Before the fleet had left Portsmouth he had hopes of advancement to sergeant. He was mindful of his duty, kept himself clean and his equipment in good order. He was not one of those men given to heavy drinking or ravaging the women on his transport. He kept his own counsel but felt that Port Jackson was not the place for a good soldier.

In America, he had been lucky. An angel had been on his shoulder that day. When the shot had flown and reduced the front rank of men to bloody rags of red, he had survived. Climbing over the dead and mutilated bodies of his comrades, he had been one of the first to reach the Yankees, even before that Scots bastard, Ross. His bayonet had kept him alive throughout that horror-filled afternoon.

By Jesus, he had earned his shilling that day. Those rebels had fought, he recalled.   Fought like cornered, wounded beasts. The hill had become a charnel house. Ross, his company commander, had immediately made him corporal because there were so few left. Now that bastard had criticised his equipment.   Had called him a slovenly, dirty soldier, merely because his bayonet was blackened. *No fucking wonder*, thought Ned Goodall. *Half my kit is blackened and rotting after that fucking voyage. That bastard Scotsman expects my bayonet to be as clean and shiny as if I was on parade at Chatham.*

Ned had tried to protest, but that had been to no avail. His mistake, he realised later, had been to infuriate his commanding officer further by appealing for transfer to Mister Vizzard's platoon. *He* was an officer to follow.   Not a pompous bastard or a 'spit and polish at all costs' man, either. The suggestion had made the major explode.

'You wee shit of a man!' Ross had shouted. 'Nay, lad, you will nae have that little luxury. I will break ye first. I made ye and I can break ye.'

Ned Goodall left Major Ross's tent a shaken man.   He knew what it would mean to be broken, to be reduced to the ranks again. Not only the lower pay, but also the fact that the marines he had been responsible for would no longer have any respect for him. His life would become hell. They would never obey an order he gave them again. Never again would he feel that he was in control of his fate.

'Mister Vizzard, sir, I done nothing wrong, sir,' he bleated. 'All that I said was I would prefer a transfer to your section, sir. All 'cause me bleeding bayonet wasn't shiny. Begging your pardon, sir, but it been impossible to keep our kit ship-shape and Bristol fashion on the voyage, sir.'

Jack did not know this man. He was not one of his own, but he understood what this was. Packer had mentioned most of the companies had similar complaints. None of the Corps wanted to be here, standing sentinel over mostly London criminals, sent to the far side of the world to form a forgotten garrison, and none wanted to be under Major Ross, who wasted no time in quarrelling with Governor Phillip about the duty his men were now required to perform. Jack had sympathy, not only with the wretched corporal now before him, but, to his surprise, with the 'Mad Major' as Ross had become known in recent weeks.

'I regret I can do nothing to help you, Goodall. You will simply have to manage as best you can.' Jack spoke reluctantly, recognising the man was sincere.

The corporal looked grimly back at him. 'I understand, sir, but, begging pardon, the major and Captain Campbell, well, they been spreading poison around, sir. About the gu-v'nor and Mister Collins, sir.' He looked at his feet. ''Tain't right, sir, an' they say bad things about you and Lieutenant Dawes, too, sir. Reckon you be 'as thick as London thieves,' was what Captain Campbell said, sir. Thought you deserved to know that, sir.'

Jack was surprised. He knew little of James Campbell save that he had been selected from the Plymouth division, and he and Campbell had not socialised at all during the voyage out. *So, another potential enemy*, he thought. *Have to watch him, too.*

'Sorry, Goodall. If the opportunity should arise to effect a transfer, I will see what can be done, but I caution you to keep your thoughts to yourself in future, else you will find a meeting with the Judge Advocate and a court martial for insubordination. Be about your duties, please.'

Many of the men, and at least some of the officers, had given voice to their discontent at the menial tasks and tedious guard duty they were now compelled to perform. Jack quickly realised that he, the other officers, and the governor would have to contend with a serious matter of morale, and perhaps something even more dangerous and sinister.

Chapter 32

Reunion

Some twelve days after the first landing, the governor decreed that the site chosen for the settlement was sufficiently clear to permit the landing of the female convicts. Large tents were erected on the cleared ground to accommodate them. The morning of Wednesday 6th February 1788 dawned grey, and the wind blew strongly from the northwest, bringing squalls and warm rain. Governor Philip decided it was time to bring the women ashore. The ships' masters also wished to offload their cargoes, both human and material, and to continue with their profitable voyages to China; tea and spices were now in demand in London, with prices for the first home likely to be high.

Fresh, clean clothes were issued to the women, and some, including Mary, were observed to be well-groomed and clean. George Worgan, for one, thought some to be most decorative and handsomely attired. The sailors watched them leave, with several carrying infants born at sea, others patently pregnant by the men now watching from the decks.

The disembarkation of the women and their children occupied most of the day. Marines searched each woman before she quit the ship, but such was the haste to disembark them that the search was perfunctory; many concealed objects likely to be of great value ashore. By early evening they were ashore and settling into tents, a lucky few who had come under the protection of certain officials assigned to the basic huts constructed for some of the officers.

Mary George and Lizzie Parker found themselves allotted to a large tent along with a dozen or more other women and their children. It was already oppressively humid, the air still and heavy, and perspiration trickled down faces, making clothes damp and stained. The parrots in the trees squawked incessantly.

Thunder rumbled in the leaden skies overhead, and no sooner had they placed their few belongings on the rough earthen floor than the skies exploded with the most frightening and violent, yet spectacular, storm ever witnessed by many of the colonists, including the officers. The torrential rain quickly turned the camp into a slimy ooze, a mud bath. It continued all evening.

Mary and Lizzie remained huddled together in the darkness as the rain soaked their tent and the waters drained through, rivulets of mud swirling about their feet and legs. Although the tent provided little protection and they were wrapped in sodden blankets, it offered more than was available elsewhere.

The others left them to join the seamen from the transports, who had been allocated a stock of rum and soon were beyond any reason or control. Scenes of drunkenness and debauchery were being enacted throughout the camp.

Women, confined to a stinking vessel for months, thrown into the company of the men with a generous allowance of alcohol available, were very quickly working to find partners who could offer some protection. Some did not care, seeking only to satisfy lust that had been latent. Most of the men were worse, far worse, increasingly drunk, and uncaring as to whom they coupled with, or in what manner, or with regard for the consequences.

A woman from *Lady Penrhyn*, who had been one of the less sociable aboard, was naked with two marines, enjoying copulation with both. Another couple were vying with each other for the attentions of a young man, probably no more than fifteen years old, each seeking to exceed the other in the services offered to the boy. A group of officers looked on and grinned with unrestrained pleasure at the scenes before them. Others were appalled and confounded, powerless to intervene. The governor expressed revulsion but thought it expedient to let the depravity 'run its course.'

'My God, Mary, glad as I am to be on land again, tonight I would rather we were back on that ship. I fear for our very lives with those animals off the *Alexander*.' They listened to the shrieks of laughter without and shuddered. Lizzie had no scruple or pricked conscience from going with a man for money, food, or drink, but now even she was revolted by what she had witnessed outside.

'Sweet Jesus, Lizzie. What is to become of us here? Is nothing to be done about this?'

Mary had grown inured to the harsh life aboard ship, but this complete loss of control and discipline frightened her. She clutched the kitchen knife that she had managed to conceal within her bundle and sat facing the entrance. They ate a meagre supper of cold boiled rice and peas that Lizzie had collected from one of the communal kitchens.

Mary was dozing against a tent pole, neither asleep nor awake. Lizzie shivered and could not sleep. It must have been after midnight, following a particularly severe flash of lightning, when a face, shining with mud and rain, suddenly appeared under the flap of the tent. It was unshaven, and the protruding eyes that belonged to the face were wild with intoxication and lust. Mary tensed, then swiftly darted forward, the blade catching the man on the chin before he could move. He screamed and vanished into the night, howling with pain.

All night the rain fell and eventually the noises in the darkness faded as the convicts, having sated their lust for each other and for drink, slowly fell silent. Neither woman slept as the thunder and lightning continued and the rain fell until dawn.

The following morning found the camp awash with the detritus of the night's riotous behaviour. Many convicts slept where they had fallen, with officers kicking their men awake. Order was restored, albeit slowly, and work parties organised to clear the camp.

By eleven o'clock the governor and his immediate staff were ashore by the flagpole positioned in front of the only two-storey building, the Governor's own house, partly fabricated in England. All the convicts were collected and obliged to sit on the ground, with marine guards forming a protective cordon about them. The governor's commission was read aloud to all by the judge-advocate, Captain David Collins. He spoke loudly and clearly, reciting:

'We, reposing especial trust and confidence in your loyalty, courage and experience in military affairs, do, by these presents, constitute and appoint you to be Governor of our territory called New South Wales, extending from the Northern cape or extremity of the coast called Cape York, in the latitude of 10° 37' south, to the southern extremity of the said territory of New South Wales or South Cape, in the latitude 43° 39' south, and all the country inland and westward as far as the one hundred and thirty-fifth degree of longitude, reckoning from the meridian of Greenwich, including all the islands adjacent in the Pacific Ocean, within the latitude aforesaid of 10° 37' south and 43° 39' south, and of all towns, garrisons, castles forts and all fortifications or other military works, which are now or may be erected hereafter upon this said territory. You are therefore carefully and diligently to discharge the duty of Governor in and over our said territory by doing and performing all and all manner of things thereunto belonging, and we do hereby strictly charge and command all our officers and soldiers who shall be employed within our said territory, and all others whom it may concern, to obey you as our Governor thereof; and you are to observe and follow such orders and directions as you shall receive from us, or any other your superior officer according to the rules and discipline of war, and likewise such orders and directions as we shall send you under our signet or sign manual, or by our High Treasurer or Commissioners of our Treasury, for the time being, or one of our Principal Secretaries of State, in pursuance of the trust we hereby repose in you.

Given at our Court at St James's, the twelfth day of October 1786, in the twenty sixth year of our reign.

FIRST FLEET

By His Majesty's Command.
Sydney.'

Jack Vizzard stood at attention through the recital of the Act establishing the colony, and with more interest than most listened to details of the Court of Judicature, and the punishments with which Governor Phillip was now empowered. Arthur Phillip was now officially endowed by the king with extraordinary, plenipotentiary powers.

Governor Phillip delivered a severe reprimand, cautioning the assembled convicts that repetition of the previous night's behaviour would incur the severest penalties. He harangued the convicts in the severest terms, declaring that he was now convinced that they were the most incorrigible set of rogues and villains he had encountered. He was now compelled, he said, to adopt the sternest measures to induce them to behave properly and decently in the future. The pettiest, most trifling theft was henceforth a capital offence, because the well-being of the entire community was now dependent on good order and industrious labour by all who were fit to work.

Jack did not pay close attention, knowing intuitively the governor's words. His eyes slowly scanned the trees and the convicts in front of him, his hat shielding him from the sun as it climbed higher in the sky. Wisps of smoke from a fire on the far shore held his attention for some moments, but, see-ing nothing of the local Indians, his survey continued amongst the blank, expressionless faces gathered on the earth within the circle of red-coated marines.

Then his head stopped, unable to rotate further. He blinked, and stared, his brain exploding with recognition. She was there, not forty yards from him. Surely, it could not be so. He had to be hallucinating—it must be some cruel trick of light. Was he still asleep? His head hurt. His vision tunnelled rapidly and there was a roaring sound in his ears. He had last seen her in tears, in the cold harshness of Gloucester Assize court. Her hair was shorter, and she was thinner, especially about the face, but, there—she half turned, and he caught more of her image. Incredible as it seemed, she was there. His mind raced. But surely not, for her name was on no list he had seen.

He wanted to break rank and run to her. His left foot came up and he stopped. Still, he stared, wanting, needing to be certain. A woman next to her, a little older and more ragged, nudged her with an elbow, and she turned more toward him.

There! No doubt about it. Mary George had been in the fleet these last eight months, and he had not known it.

A volley fired by a rank of marines echoed about the cove, and there followed three huzzas for the king. The convicts rose to stand, singly and in groups.

'You will be joining us for luncheon, Jack?' The voice in his ear belonged to William Dawes. He realised that he stood alone, detached. His company was being marched away by Sergeant Packer with him wholly unaware of it.

'Have you seen a ghost, my friend? You are as white as a sheet, man.' Dawes' voice trailed away to a soft echo.

Other uniforms appeared around him as a blur. He was walking toward her as though on air, not conscious of the ground.

Now she was only ten feet from him, turning fully to face him, recognition coming to her eyes. Her mouth opened but he heard no sound above the rising beat in his chest.

His arms were about her and she was sobbing, her face wet with tears, and he kissed her, quite oblivious to the stares of others, the catcalls of the women and the whistles of the men next to him.

'Oh, Jack, Jack my own dear heart!' Her voice was broken, and her body shook and trembled, his own barely able to remain upright as his legs turned to water and the anguish and guilt of months burst upon him in a moment of exquisite pain.

'Hush, now,' he said, his voice tremulous, a croak. 'I cannot believe what is happening. You are here.' He dared not speak again. He swallowed and held her tightly, frightened that this image might suddenly disappear.

The ground about them had cleared; still they stood together, neither wishing to break apart and destroy the moment.

His breathing became stable, and he trusted himself to speak. 'We have much to discuss. Come, please.'

He took her hand and led her to his tent, caring nothing for the voices and shapes around him, knowing only that she was by his side again. She sat on the field bed erected under the canvas, and he sat on a low stool, holding both her hands in his.

'Tell me everything. Leave nothing out. I need to know it all,' she said softly, but there was no doubting her resolve. Her grip on his arms was firm, and her eyes drilled into his, those hazel eyes he had seen so many times in his dreams. He would have to tell her his story before she would tell him of the trials she had endured.

He left out nothing, telling her of the events of that night at the vicarage. He was controlled now, and more dispassionate. Thoughts of the trial, the prejudice of the judge, the evil of Mary's accuser and the murder itself, all came together in a steady outpouring of language. He spoke calmly, without interruption, and Mary sat expressionless until he had finished.

She smiled at last, a thin, tired smile, but with real warmth now spreading from her heart and through her body. 'I am very glad that Tom is with us. He is a good boy and will serve you well,' she said, then added, 'Jack, my dearest, but you did a terrible thing.' It was stated almost as a mere observation, not accusingly, nor reproachfully or judgmentally. 'You would not know—how could you?—that he was judged to have died naturally. Doctor Steele would not say he was killed. Giles searched for you. Your father also...' She left unfinished any mention of Henry's grief, knowing it would serve no purpose, would only add to his burdened mind.

'I am a fugitive for nothing, then.' His voice was low, not with bitterness, but with a sense of irony at his circumstances. 'Well, I am in the best of company. Now it must be your turn, my love. How have you fared since I abandoned you?' His eyes reflected the shame he felt within.

This was not a time for recrimination. She was still lightheaded at the joy of their reunion. She spoke of her time since the trial. She told him of the suddenness of her removal from Gloucester Gaol to Portsmouth. She spoke emotionally of the heartbreak when taken from her county, from her family. At that she paused, controlled the rising emotion in her throat. The voyage itself he would understand, but she knew now he had been on *Sirius,* the flagship, not a convict transport.

She described the women and how they had fought and made alliances, how they had worked together to endure the hardship of the cramped, fetid prison cells where the sun never reached, but how they had fared better than when in gaol. She alluded to the means by which the women had gained extra victuals or drink, or simply because of alcohol-induced lust. Of the men, she said little. He would know, would understand. There was time enough for confession, were it necessary.

He looked at her at that point, and his eyes softened. He had learned much during the voyage. Some of his innocence had gone, and his understanding had grown. He understood that she, too, had lost her innocence, but to a greater degree.

He lowered his head, and his voice was quiet. 'I felt desolate that day. A loss of reason took me over, and all I could think of was removing that animal from society; and of revenge, too, for what he had done to you. To us. He violated you, Mary. I could not bear that.' He looked deep into her eyes, reaching to her soul.

'Tom has told of worse things done by him. He was a rapist and hypocrite, deseased and debased. I have no pride in my actions but little regret. Had I thought of it then, I might have pursued that bastard judge. My God, Mary, I never knew such anger, or that I was capable of such things.'

'Hush, my sweet man. It is the past and we must start anew. Perhaps we can do so in this country.'

Mary wanted to believe that, had to believe it, and now, at last, began to feel that she could make a new life. She and Jack were reunited, and she would know happiness again.

She embraced him and Jack sobbed.

Chapter 33
Marriage

Tom Clutterbuck chewed hungrily on his piece of pork, flicking ants from his breeches as he did so. 'This 'ere meat's dry and tough as boots,' he declared, his complaint not directed at any of the three other boys nearby. His teeth pulled at a tough piece that was stubbornly adhering to its parent bone, raising his head when Corporal Munday tapped it with a ramrod.

'Mind you don't let the sergeant hear you, boy, or he'll 'ave you wearing it 'stead o' eatin' it.' The corporal grinned at the lad. *Young Tom is growing up fast*, he thought. *Could be a good soldier, given a bit of time.* He had shown he could shoot, and hunt, but he was a bloody cocky youngster.

Tom half turned and grinned back at the tall soldier. 'Well, it's the bloody truth, an' all, corp. Mister Vizzard didn't warn me 'bout the grub in the army when 'e 'ad me join up!' He thrust another piece of wax-like meat into his mouth, with a spoonful of greasy rice to accompany it.

'Talking of your lord and master, I just seen 'im 'urry into his tent after the parade, with a very 'andsome wench clingin' to him for dear life. One of the wimmin off the *Lady Pen*, I reckon, bleedin' cracker of a wench...'

The words tailed off as Tom's young brain made a connection and his eyes widened and drilled into those of the tall marine. He dropped his platter and started running towards the officers' tents.

'Now what you 'spose he's up to, lads?' The corporal's puzzled look was entirely genuine.

Tom covered the rough ground as though pursued by the devil, reaching Lieutenant Vizzard's tent breathless, his young heart thumping a staccato in his chest. He pulled to a stop, remembering his duty, and shouted at the tent, 'Sir, Mister Vizzard, sir! 'Tis me, Tom, sir. Is it true, sir?' He panted and a moment later the tent flap opened, Jack beaming and looking happier than Tom had ever seen him.

'Aye, lad. You have heard, then? Come in, boy, come in.'

Mary stood slowly, pushing her hair back from her face, and opened her arms as Tom rushed into her embrace. The boy's face buried itself in her shoulder and he felt his eyes fill with the moistness of pure joy, such as he had not felt in a year or more.

'Mistress Mary,' he choked when the air returned to his lungs. Gently she held him away from her and stared into his tear-streaked, grimy face.

'Well, now, look at you. My, but you have filled out. Nearly a man, and a fine soldier, too.' She started laughing. 'I am so very happy to see you again, Tom Clutterbuck.' Her gaze moved toward Jack, then back to the boy. 'Mister Vizzard has told me of the help you have been to him. Yes, I know it all now.' She answered the question unspoken in his eyes.

Mary sent Tom to find a pot of boiling water and prepared to brew some tea. Jack—mysteriously, she thought—'suddenly recalled' an urgent appointment with Major Ross and swept from the tent with a promise to return with no more delay than necessary.

She sat on the large chest, studying the few possessions Jack had scattered about the tent, handling the shaving brush and silver-handled razor. A matching brush and comb lay side by side, engraved with the initials 'JHV'. It struck her that she had not known of any name other than Jack. That omission must be rectified later, she decided.

There was, however, another matter she had to attend to, one equally important if not more so. She had to speak to Ned, had to explain. Understanding he had made assumptions, she would have to hurt him.

Tom escorted her to a work party, clearing ground by the head of the stream. Sensing her need for privacy, Tom stood by while she took Ned Goodall to the shade of a spreading flame tree, and then gently broke his heart.

She and Tom walked back to the officers' tents, without a word passing between them.

*****

Lieutenant Vizzard stormed from Major Ross's, tent his expression showing barely contained rage. His stride took him unintentionally in the direction of Governor Phillip's large prefabricated, temporary home and administrative rooms. He turned and glanced back but Ross had not followed. In frustration, he kicked at a rock, sending it with a splash into a shallow pool of muddy water. He strode into the governor's residence and snapped to attention before Captain David Collins.

'Good afternoon to you, Jack Vizzard. I see you have some cause to add to the interminable list of troubles I have to wrestle with.'

Jack felt deflated. He knew this officer had more problems than any other, save for Arthur Phillip, and instantly recognized that his own needs were as insignificant as a grain of sand on the white beaches he had seen. He hesitated. Collins spoke. 'Jack... I do not have the luxury of time. Please be brief.'

'Sir, I wish to marry,' he blurted, 'and Major Ross has declined to approve. I wish to seek the governor's permission as the senior officer. I believe he has the authority.'

Captain Collins indicated a velvet, button-back chair, and Jack pulled at his coat's turn-backs and sat as requested.

'It is the governor's declared desire that there should be marriages, and as soon as possible, but from amongst the convicts, Jack, not from the garrison officers! Perhaps you had best relate your tale, and I will discuss the request with my master—he is grappling with the commissary returns and will not be disturbed with such a matter this morning.' David Collins leaned back, meshing his fingers together and resting his hands on his chest.

Jack described a succinct and highly edited account of his relationship with Mary, saying nothing of his involvement in her trial or conviction, but ensured Captain Collins understood that a crass, incompetent, and probably corrupt judge had betrayed his oath and performed an injustice on an innocent, gentle person.

Collins listened attentively, his expression not changing until Jack had retold his tale. Then he stood. 'I will raise the matter with His Excellency at the first opportunity. Do not be offended if it is declined, Jack. Our master has enough cause for acrimony with Ross without seeking further trouble.'

Jack thought it significant that Captain Collins omitted to name Ross by his rank. He understood that there was already rancour towards Major Ross. He spoke his thanks quickly and left.

On Sunday 10th February, the Reverend Richard Johnson performed several baptisms and marriages. When those of the several convicts had been disposed of, Mary George married Lieutenant John Howard Vizzard in a simple ceremony, witnessed by Lizzie Parker and Lieutenant William Dawes.

Governor Phillip hosted a modest luncheon for the couple, accompanied by a few officers of the official party. Mary's friend Lizzie was excluded, of course, from the occasion, but that did not trouble her greatly, it being a surprise to her that the governor was morally obliged to accept an officer's wife at his table.

Mary felt more confident in the society of the officers, and the stigma of her convict status, while a matter of obvious curiosity to the officers, was not to cause her any embarrassment. She spoke, when addressed, with courtesy and without the soft Gloucestershire burr that had characterized her speech before. She chose not to initiate any topics of her own, happy to leave the conversation to Jack and his friends.

The meal was frugal and consumed without the jollity that Jack might have wished for, the officials of the new colony now fully apprehending the mammoth task ahead. However, the governor proved a charming host, and William Dawes had arranged a gift of linen and wine to be presented to the bride and groom, which delighted them both. Each acutely felt the absence of their respective parents, especially Mary, who showed her emotion during the ceremony itself, which none present, save Jack, fully understood.

*****

That afternoon, the camp was again wet from the thunderstorms that doused the settlement. Later, the summer evening saw the sun setting over the distant hills, edging them with a soft shade of blue. Jack and Mary Vizzard walked amongst the still dripping eucalypts and sat on the rocky foreshore, gazing at the harbour as a sea mist rolled slowly inland. They spoke of their families and of their hopes for the colony, until the humid evening brought the biting insects, and he took her hand and led her to the canvas field tent that would be their first home.

The cot, at one end, had been set with some petals, placed there by Lizzie, and two candles burned, giving the space a soft glow. Jack lay beside Mary and kissed her again, and again, caressing her hair, her shoulders, and her thighs. She responded to his lovemaking with a gentleness that endeared her to him even more. His hands explored her tenderly, and his lips sought her breasts, as her hand guided him into her. She gave herself completely, utterly and without restraint or inhibition, feeling more love for him than she thought possible, finding a completeness of being she had never before experienced.

CHAPTER 34

INSUBORDINATION AND A DEATH

Major Robert Ross paced before the governor. His mood was sour, and his language reflected that.

'By God, Arthur, my men are getting angry. You deal with them in harsher terms than your damned convicts and they resent it, man! I will have you know, I do, too. Now you want to charge them, put them in your damned court, and reduce them to the level of the vermin we are here to guard! I will nae stand for that! You will release them to my pleasure. I will deal with them in my own way.'

Governor Phillip sighed, but fixed Major Ross with a firm glare, rising slowly and with some pain. Of late, he had increasing pain in his side, years of a salt diet to blame.

'You will address me as "Sir" or "Your Excellency", Major Ross. Reflect on your manners and remember to whom you speak. Yes, by God, I do intend to prosecute them. Most certainly I will. A thief is a thief, sir, even though he wears a red coat, Major Ross.'

Phillip was standing very close to the burly Scotsman, his manner toward this martinet more bellicose than it had been before. Glaring up at the major, he declared, 'All here are to obey my orders: convict, sailor, marine... or officer, and you would be well advised to remember that. It is for the benefit of all, and our marines are not favoured exceptions—far from it. And, yes, I expect to punish offenders from your battalion more severely. If I cannot have discipline from them, how am I to have it from those wretched convicts? For me to do otherwise would be to show favour to your men, simply because they serve the king. No, sir, they will be prosecuted, and they will feel the fullness of my wrath in this matter.'

'Governor, ye leave me nae choice but to report my concerns directly to London. I must have command of my own men, ye can see that, can ye not!'

'Major Ross, you may do as you wish, but I warn you now, I will tolerate no interference with my orders. Your men, as much as the convicts, are subject to *my* authority and to military law. I had hoped for your support—I have a right to it—but I see I was much mistaken.'

The two men stared at each other. Ross was ever at odds with the governor. He resented that Phillip never consulted with him, nor confided his plans or the government's orders for the colony. He resented the lack of stores and the shortage of food and clothing for his detachment. He resented the convicts. He resented the flies, the crawling insects, the fleas, the lice, the heat, the natives, and the very country itself, and wished he had never agreed to the commission. He resented the governor more.

He stormed from Government House in a foul temper.

*****

Lizzie Parker was on her knees, trying to extract dirt from the shirts in the already dirty water. In the last hour, she had managed only five shirts, and the pile of laundry by her side showed no evidence of lessening. She felt nauseous and fatigued. Her head ached, her gaunt, lean body shivered in the heat, and cramps clutched at her stomach.

'Hello, Lizzie, how are you this fine...? What on earth is wrong?' Mary dropped the governor's laundry and knelt beside her friend, grasping her hand.

'Oh, Mary, 'tis you. Thank God. I feel so wretched this morning.'

A spasm of pain slashed through her like knives. Her body shook and she vomited blood in a disconcerting amount, mixed with the sputum. A sudden and involuntary evacuation of her bowel added to her distress.

'Lizzie, oh, Lizzie.' Mary looked about her. 'Help me, help, please!' she shouted, alarmed now, searching desperately for someone to come to her aid. She cradled her friend's head in the crook of her arm, feeling the heat of the fever from her face. A marine came running, followed by Mister Worgan.

'Please help. She is very ill.' Mary dabbed at Lizzie's mouth with one of the governor's shirts, as the marine and George Worgan lifted the limp form of Lizzie Parker and carried her to the crude makeshift hospital that the ships' surgeons had quickly established.

There were several beds, all occupied. People lay on the damp earthen floor, between the beds, most occupied by two or even three people each, creating foulness in the air that the surgeons could not remove.

George Worgan placed Lizzie on a pile of coarse woolen blankets in a darkened corner, and called for an assistant to bring water. He looked at her pallid, waxy face and into her eyes. Opening her mouth, he studied her tongue, and cast a troubled look toward Mary, who was kneeling on the floor beside her friend.

A murmur slipped from Lizzie's mouth, followed by a low groan. Mary leaned closer and heard Lizzie say, in a wheezing, shallow whisper, 'Mary, love, please take care of my baby. You're a good 'un, and I am right glad you found your officer.'

Another spasm caused her to retch, again mucus laced with traces of blood. She coughed. 'D'ya know, girl, there was a time I didn't believe you.' Her voice broke and fell to a whisper. 'Mary... you be sure to 'ave a good life, my girl, you deserve it.'

'Hush now, Lizzie Parker, there is no need for that kind of talk,' Mary tried to reassure her friend. 'You will be fine, you'll see. Mister Worgan will make you better, and you can look after your baby yourself.' Mary's eyes glistened, and she blinked hard several times.

Lizzie slowly shook her head from side to side. 'I know I will not, Mary George, but please don't...'—she coughed again, a deeper, rasping sound that came from her soul— 'don't weep for me, luv. Just care for my little girl.'

George Worgan motioned Mary to one side, as an assistant started to clean Lizzie's face and pass a cup of water to her lips.

'I am very sorry, Mary, but I believe your friend has the bloody flux.' He wiped his forehead with a soiled handkerchief. 'We will do all we can, but...' He left unfinished the obvious statement that he held little hope for any recovery.

Mary shook her head, unable for a moment to form any sound. 'She must get well, Mister Worgan, she must. This cannot be.' Her sobs broke out of her throat, and she clutched at the surgeon for support.

'Hush, child, hush now. I will do all in my power.'

Lizzie Parker died during the night. She was twenty-five years old and had been in the colony only twenty-five days.

CHAPTER 35
THE HUT

With convict help, Jack had a hut built a little removed from some of the others, overlooking the rock-strewn western foreshore of the cove. A screen of eucalypts—a ship's carpenter called them 'maiden's gum' trees—provided shelter from wind and rain, but Jack and Mary could look on the harbour from there, and it was but a short walk to the observatory that Jack had worked with William Dawes to construct.

The observatory, built partly on a rock at Point Maskelyne, was named for its sponsor, the Astronomer Royal, and had an ingenious revolving octagonal roof, using cannon balls as bearings. Removable panels, made of painted canvas on timber frames, allowed Dawes to view all parts of the night sky. He had most carefully installed a treble object, achromatic telescope, made by Peter Dollond of Vine Street, London, and several other instruments.

By the time it was completed, Dawes was delighted with it. He worked during the short, humid nights, and slept during the mornings. A young aboriginal girl had taken residence with him and worked as his servant, teaching him something of the language and customs of her people. Dawes had started to compile a dictionary with her help.

Jack and Mary's hut was admittedly a crude construction, composed mostly of rough sawn timber, with infill of a mix of mud, sticks and dung. The exterior had a coating of pipeclay, to act as waterproofing.

A brick-maker had commenced work some time before, but the bricks were few and of poor quality, as none had yet discovered a source of mortar. Gangs of convict women, employed in gathering seashells, spent days crushing and grinding them to a fine powder, with which, it was thought, a lime mortar might be made, but it was poor material and there was an insufficient quantity for the needs of all.

The hut they had made their home was small, barely ten or twelve feet square. The framework was of she-oak, using the drop-log style of construction, with a floor of only compacted clay, covered with flax and dried grass. Mary loved it.

At one end of the building, an obliging Sergeant Packer and Corporal Goodall had fabricated a low bed, fitted with a palliase of horsehair. Jack had purloined some sheets and blankets, and had fitted some oiled canvas, spread over a latticework of wattle sticks, to serve as windows.

A stone fire was at the other end, smoke passing through a simple flue, made of pipeclay-covered mud, with a simple field kitchen comprising two cooking pots, some wooden bowls and Jack's personal mess kit. A pair of old and dented pewter tankards from Lampern House, used as drinking vessels for the dwindling supply of tea, which now was rationed, hung from a solitary shelf.

A single door, about six feet high and hung with leather hinges, provided the only means of access and egress. Shingles, formed of stripped and dried bark, covered the structure, and largely prevented rain from entering.

The silhouette of his brother, George Vizzard, last seen by Mary in the dining room of Lampern House, hung from a nail; Jack's boots stood like sentinels by the smoking fire, cleansed by Tom of mud, drying for renewed use on the morrow. Wisps of smoke blew back into the room, causing both Mary and Jack to have sore, itching, red eyes.

Jack sat on the three-legged stool, shaping the leg of a new chair, using a borrowed chisel and adze. He was no carpenter and found the work taxing.

'You are in need of a haircut, Mister Vizzard,' remarked Mary. 'Here, let me cut some of those locks away, else you will find yourself charged, and in conflict with the major again.'

Jack smiled despite the growing hunger within him. It had been many weeks since he had eaten any meat other than fish. He did not like fish. He detested the flavour and the smell of it. When not on guard duty he had joined in some hunting and had shown his skill with a musket, but the kangaroos had become less frequently seen, and, as ever, the stock thus acquired went to the government store to feed a growing population. He had shot some large parrots, and thought that when stewed, or roasted, they tasted a little like the pheasant he'd enjoyed in England.

As Mary started work on his lank, thinning hair, he thought of the developing problems faced by the infant colony. He was troubled, by the growing indiscipline, the frequent abuses by the marines, and the increase in thieving by all sections of the small community.

'Mind that blade, my dear, you nearly removed my ear!'

Mary laughed; she cut again, this time more carefully, humming a light tune. The swelling of her abdomen was now evident, and he gently placed the palm of his hand on her belly. She smiled down on him.

'I will boil up some rice and some of that salt beef—I removed as many of the weevils as I could find while you were washing. You must keep your strength up. I fear you work too hard.'

Jack had secured some lighter duty for Mary, to protect her from the labour of gathering and grinding shells; nor was she working in the hospital with the surgeons, where she might contract dysentery, or worse. Now the surgeons had just diagnosed an outbreak of smallpox. Several had died, and the toll grew daily. Sadly, many of the bodies discovered about the settlement were of local tribespeople, and that caused Arthur Phillip great distress and anguish. The governor had kindly agreed to provide Mary with work as assistant to Deborah Brooks, his bosun's wife, as his housekeeper. It was undemanding and clean work, for which Mary was grateful.

'I must do my share, Jack. I will not have it said that because I am now an officer's lady I have become high and mighty. Besides, I am still a convicted felon.'

Jack's shoulders dropped. He had had letters of commendation written to the Home Secretary by his company commander, by the Reverend Johnson, even by Governor Phillip himself, all seeking clemency and a review of Mary's case. They were *en route* to England in the care of the master of the *Lady Penrhyn,* but he knew that it would be a year and a half before even a reply would come. Then, he thought, unless some small miracle took place, it was unlikely that Mary would earn any reprieve. She had years of her sentence to run and would remain a convict, subject to the hard discipline of the colony. He did all he could to protect her and in the main her life was as comfortable, and her position as safe, as he could ensure. He had said nothing of this to Mary, of course.

His own life had become dreary and humdrum beyond his imagination. Endless days of duty supervising work gangs clearing the land and, almost daily, now, sitting as clerk of the court, advising the Attorney General. Captain Collins had, very reluctantly, agreed to keep Jack's true profession from the governor. In return, he leaned heavily on Jack's knowledge.

Jack had pondered on the law as it could be applied in the new colony. He considered the practical aspects of interest. The colony was in a legally unprecedented position; in law, it was a military establishment, subject to military law. The Judge Advocate, David Collins, was responsible for chairing all proceedings. His was the responsibility of advising the tribunal on matters of law; he also acted as prosecutor.

In military courts martial, he could have no say in determining judgement, however. Criminal offences were tried before him under the Mutiny Act and the Articles of War. In such matters, Collins prepared the case, prosecuted, and had a vote in the judgement. It was a difficult position to hold, and Captain Collins was acutely aware of the conflicting interests. He relied on guidance from Jack.

Complicating the difficulties he faced, many of the marine officers objected to sitting as members of a criminal court. Jack understood this, and discreetly assisted the Judge Advocate in the preparation of trials and charges, and the gathering of evidence from witnesses, and advised him on points of law. He studied Order Books and regulations, sometimes late into the night, burning candles that were expensive and which were charged to his allowances.

However, he had no wish to acquire any position of prominence in the colony. Here he was simply a junior officer in an all but forgotten dominion over the seas. He was content with that, for the present.

*****

On Saturday 11 October, the governor felt older than his fifty years. Progress had been slow, far too slow for his design. He toured the settlement, inspecting various works, and was saddened to see that so little had been achieved. Before leaving England, he had advised the sending of preceding ships with artisans on board, to have facilities for the convicts and marine guards in readiness for arrival of the fleet. That advice, too, had been ignored.

The convicts worked reluctantly without directed, knowledgeable supervision, and the lack of experienced supervisors required him to use marines, with much opposition from the officers. He had imposed rationing because of the shortage of supplies. It distressed him that his planning and recommendations had not always received support. He entered his house that evening in a despondent mood.

His steward, the Frenchman Bernard de Maliez, greeted him with a smile. '*Monsieur, bonsoir. Vous semblez épuisé, si je peux dire ainsi.*' He took the governor's hat and said, '*Puis-je suggérer que vous preniez une chaise, et que je vous verse un verre de vin enrichi?*'

'*Vous pouvez, Bernard, vous pouvez. J'ai eu assez des affaires officielles pour un jour.*'

Arthur Phillip's education in languages had been from his father, and in private he often spoke in French with his steward.

He walked through to the room that served as his living quarters, to be greeted by Captain David Collins, at the head of a group of officers. Phillip's face was impassive, but he had expected a deputation.

'Sir,' began Collins, 'we have collected here this evening to offer our sincere appreciation of the close attention you give to your duties, the unflagging optimism that you bring to our small community, and, not least, to wish you the happiest of birthday anniversaries!'

He had all but forgotten. Today was his fiftieth birthday. His normally unruffled expression broke into the broadest of smiles. 'Well, I thank you, David. I am most touched that anyone should remember.' He accepted the proffered glass of Madeira wine. 'Thank you, all, this is quite a surprise.'

He moved further into the room, conversing easily, and welcoming each guest personally. He noted the absence of Major Ross but was delighted to see that several other marine officers were present, including young Vizzard.

Jack raised a glass. 'Good evening, sir, and my warmest congratulations on your birthday.'

'Thank you, Jack. I have spent a disheartening day inspecting the works. We really must find ways of progressing matters—I had hoped to have barracks erected for your men, and better facilities for the sick and hurt.' He studied the young officer.

'Sir, it is not for want of effort by the men. They wish to be in barracks. The convicts, in the main, are poor labourers, and we have no skilled artisans to assist. Much is by trial and error, I regret to say.'

'Indeed so, Vizzard. I have been at pains to impress that point upon my superiors in London but fear it will be some time before we are supplied with all that we need. In the interim, we must do the best we can.' Phillip paused to sip his wine. 'It is the way of things in the king's service, as you will have now come to understand. I am gratified that you have played no small part in this business, Jack. Your enthusiasm is not shared by all in the battalion,' he said pointedly. 'Your commander, for one, believes I expect too much of the troops.'

Jack tried, but failed, to keep the sarcasm from his voice. 'Sir, the major is, perhaps, disappointed at the lack of martial activity. I fancy he expected to be campaigning in the hinterland.'

'Lieutenant Vizzard, I would counsel you to tread carefully. Major Ross is your superior officer, and entitled to your obedience, if possibly not your respect.' The governor's eyes smiled, and his comments lacked conviction; most officers in the camp well knew that he and Major Ross endured a deteriorating and hostile relationship. There was support for Ross, but it was dwindling.

'I am always aware of that, sir, and will continue my efforts, but I fear I am unlikely to ever earn the major's respect.'

The governor looked at him kindly. 'I understand your difficulty, Lieutenant. Try to understand mine. Excuse me, I really think I should talk to your charming wife and rescue her from the attentions of Captain Collins.' His eyes showed a hint of bemusement at Jack's reaction.

The evening became convivial, and Mary found herself enjoying the social occasion more than she would have expected. The wife of another marine officer, Sophia Cresswell, befriended her. They engaged in small talk for much of the evening. Conscious always of her history, the stigma associated with her circumstances, Mary was diffident, wary of revealing too much of herself. Sophia seemed alert to that, not probing, but gently, subtly, enquiring.

Talking readily of matters domestic, of the hardships in building a home in such a hostile environment, Mary gained confidence and began to believe that she had a place here, one of some respectability. That night she slowly wrote a long letter to her father, the first of many that were to follow.

Chapter 36
Work Party

Lieutenant Jack Vizzard was supervising another work party constructing another sawpit. 'Mister Vizzard, sir, we need another shovel here, sir. Mine's blunt as a cow's arse!'

Jack looked at the man, not recognising him. He had been standing for two hours or more, and the pit was still only three feet deep.

'Stand down, and let those idlers get to it.' Jack motioned to two other men, who were on their haunches, to get into the pit.

'But these men are ill, sir, by your leave. They ain't fit for work, sir.'

He looked at the men's haggard faces, their beards matted with vomit, and thought he detected symptoms of scurvy; again he felt the frustration of his duty.

'Very well, report to the surgeon, you two. Leave the shovel. You, get back to work.'

Jack was left with but one man. 'Corporal Jenkins, get some of your men in there. Use the bloody bayonet, if you must, but I want this pit finished.'

The corporal, a surly, rat-faced man, spat from the corner of his mouth, giving Jack a sullen look.

'Not our duty to be digging bleedin' 'oles.'

'Enough of your insolent talk, man. I gave you an order, now get on with it!' Jack snapped. The man moved lethargically into the hole, and with obvious reluctance commenced to dig.

Jack was fast losing his patience today. There were not enough tools, and the ones he had were wearing out fast. He wondered again how this new town was ever to be built, if the men and tools needed were not provided. He felt hopeless.

'Sergeant Scott,' he called to the approaching sergeant, 'take over here and keep the men working. I will be back later to check your progress.' He wanted to be away from the heat, the dusty and tedious work, if only for some minutes.

He strode off towards his hut, noting how his left boot now seemed to be loose. On closer inspection, he saw that the heel was parting from the upper. 'Hell and damnation,' he muttered. *I have no other boots*, he thought. The temperature was falling this afternoon and the night promised to be a cold one. It did nothing to improve his mood. He found the cobbler at work in a crude timber shed behind a pile of shoes and boots.

'I have need of your skill, mister cobbler,' he said affably to the stout old man bent over his work.

Without looking up, the man grunted and pointed to the pile. 'Leave 'em there and I'll do 'em when I can.'

'I had hoped to wait while you did the repair, if it is all the same to you.' Jack waited.

A pair of sunken, blood-shot eyes looked up at him, and the mouth below them broke open, revealing a broken row of carious stumps.

'As it's you, Mister Vizzard, I will, of course. Slip your foot up 'ere and I'll do what I can.'

Jack raised his foot and the cobbler pulled at the boot until it slipped off his leg.

'That will be no difficulty, Mister Vizzard. A couple of tacks and she'll be as right as rain.' With that, he slipped the boot over an iron horn and quickly hammered three short nails into the heel.

Jack pulled out a small purse of coins, but the old man's raised hand stopped him from handing over a coin.

'That's not needed, sir. You helped me out a couple of months past. Don't you recall, now? Besides, what use be coin to me 'ere in this paradise!' The old man broke into a wheeze-laden laugh.

Jack looked more closely, with vague recognition of the face. The cobbler had appeared in court, one of a long list of miscreants, charged with some petty and unsubstantiated offence. Jack had advised the President of the Court that day not to proceed because Major Ross had brought the case with no witnesses to support the charge. Ross had been furious.

He pocketed the purse, instantly recalling that currency had no value in Sydney Town. The only real currency was food or drink, or, for the women, their bodies.

'Well, I thank you for that. A kindness, I am sure.' He took a cup of water from the cobbler's bench and drank it down thirstily. With that, Jack returned to the sawpit to find Sergeant Scott very subdued.

'What's afoot, Scottie?' asked Jack. 'You look dismayed.'

'Sir, nothing amiss, sir. Major Ross wishes to see you immediately, sir.' Scott, with almost parade ground precision, brought his right hand to his head in a salute.

Jack was instantly alert. Sergeant Scott was not one for idle chatter and was thought by all in the detachment to be the model marine. It occurred to Jack that Scott had fallen foul of the major.

He found Ross in his tent at a table made of rough planks stretched over a pair of tea chests.

'Good of you to join me, laddie. I have been waiting for you for...'—Ross glanced at the half-hunter on the table in front of him—'ten minutes now.'

Deciding not to rise to the bait, Jack clenched his jaws more tightly.

'I have made my opinion clear to His Excellency, that my battalion is not here to play overseers to convict labour, Vizzard. Now that is a thing he and I are not in agreement on, but I have my duty. We are directed by Mister bloody high 'n' mighty governor to get the swine working, so work they damn well will.'

Ross coughed, cleared his throat, and continued. 'Yon sawpit of yours, Lieutenant Vizzard, is a disgrace. It should have been finished hours ago, man. I have enough to concern me doing the governor's work for him without having to chase young pups like you. This is but another example of your laziness and inattention to duty. We've lumber coming in and how are we to cut it, do ye think?'

The major was aware of the problems facing the working parties, but had obviously decided to make a point, and to make it against Jack.

He had crossed the governor many times over this business. The damned convicts should have proper overseers to watch and instruct them, not his men, not even useless juniors such as Vizzard.

Jack made an effort to be courteous. 'Sir, begging your pardon, but the major is sensible of the shortage of suitable tools, and these wretches have no will to work.'

'And a poor workman will always blame his tools, eh? No excuses, man. I need that pit ready to work by morning. See to it. And in future, Vizzard, you do not leave your post without the permission of a senior officer. That, boy, is a court martial offence.'

Jack took a step back and half turned to leave.

'Have you forgotten the little ye have learned already, boy?' Ross snapped. 'You are expected to salute a superior officer, even in this Godforsaken land.'

Jack gave a casual salute and turned sharply, leaving the tent with a mind to call Ross out. The man was self-centred and arrogant to an intolerable degree. 'Laziness and inattention'. Jack fumed at the insult.

He walked back to where Sergeant Scott was sitting on a rock, his head lowered. He leaped to his feet on hearing Jack's approach.

'I was not sleeping, sir, just resting my bones.' Scott was a decent man and a good soldier. He was friendly with Sergeant Packer, but Jack had not known him before landing at Port Jackson. He respected the man's experience. Scott had over twenty years' service in the Corps and knew his business well.

'Yes, Sergeant. You know that Major Ross is displeased with us?'

'With respect, sir, that's always the case, sir. 'Tis common knowledge in the camp that he wishes to quit this place. Begging your pardon, sir, but 'tis also well known that he don't like you, sir. Sorry for speaking out of turn, but most of the officers have little time for him. Some say he should go, and good riddance. Said too much again, sorry, sir.'

'I must confess, I didn't think service in the Corps would be quite like this, Sergeant.'

'Well to be fair, sir, this ain't what you might call usual, regular garrison duty. 'Tis far better aboard a man o' war, or in a garrison like Gibraltar, but we must be makin' the best o' things, I reckon. I might even settle here if the gover'ment gives us a decent grant, sir. What about yourself, Mister Vizzard? D'you think you might stay when your time's up?'

He took a flask from inside his tunic, and offered it to Jack, who shook his head. The governor had no authority yet to grant land to marines, but only to convicts earning and deserving emancipation. He chose not to speak of that. Morale amongst the marines was low enough, without that knowledge adding fuel to the growing discontent.

'No, I do not believe so, Scottie. I did have hopes for more adventurous duty than that which we have here; or, as you say, some decent sea time. Or perhaps Africa or India. I doubt I shall stay. Nevertheless, you are right in one thing, and that is that we must make the best of things. That includes finishing this sawpit, so best we get the men moving a bit faster!'

Jack turned aside, pulled a small clay pipe from within his now faded tunic, and broke into a pouch of tobacco given to him when on board *Supply*. He had not smoked before but had recently found it to be a tasteful pastime during quiet times. He pulled at the stem and, taking a small brass tinder-box from his pocket, he pulled his pistol and used the flint-lock to throw a spark into the tinderbox, lighting the tobacco. He closed the tin, the damper extinguishing the tinder. He watched as Sergeant Scott chivvied the gang to make more effort. He thought of Ross and the man's boorish behaviour, and of Scott's thoughts of settling in this country.

Not for some time, he thought. *There is more to see and do.* With Mary yet to be reprieved from her sentence and with a family to think of, he would have to look for some advancement.   That was unlikely to come in this part of the world, or for some time, but it would surely come, one day.

*****

Governor Phillip was very distressed.   He surveyed the farm, concerned to see that vermin and insects had attacked the crops again during the night, and wishing, not for the first time, that he had more men skilled and knowledgeable in husbandry.

Henry Dodd, his personal assistant, was the only man with farming experience, and he had created the first crops at Farm Cove.   Phillip had farmed in Hampshire.   All those years on half-pay and the struggle to live the life of a country gentleman.   It had not been successful.   The house had to be maintained, without the luxury of full staff, and it had been a constant drain on his limited resources.   There had been attendance at various functions, donations to the church, his wife's family... All had conjoined to deplete a modest income.

He had been delighted when selected for the command. At last, not merely a ship, but a small fleet. Prison ships, yes, but his first pennant, and a governorship. If his health lasted, then he could expect to raise his own flag on return to England. But this had become a challenging command. Young Vizzard was right in that. A challenging commission, with credit, approbation, and promotion from the Admiralty at the end of it, was that their lordships' plan for him? Or was he merely another expendable post captain, one to be discarded and sacrificed at their whim when no longer of use? A regular sea-going command is what he had truly desired.

Here at Rose Hill, or Parramatta, as the natives called it, the cabbage had been struggling to flourish and the maize sowed was barely at tilling stage but was already looking withered and gnawed.

As he mentally composed another dispatch to London, Captain Collins, breathing heavily from his rapid ride, arrived by his side, interrupting Phillip's thoughts.

'Your Excellency, I bring dreadful news, sir. Two convicts have been found dead, most cruelly murdered, sir. It is clear that natives are responsible.'

Phillip was momentarily shocked, and for once allowed his emotions to show, albeit briefly, on his countenance. This was news he had long feared. The great care he'd put toward cultivating harmony between the settlement and the natives was now, in an instant, shattered. His immediate fear was for the camp.

Collins anticipated the question.

'The camp is secure, sir. Major Ross has a company stood to with arms, and prepares to make an expedition, sir.'

No, this is not the answer, he thought. Certainly, those responsible must be identified if possible, and made subject to British justice, but Ross was raising, had made ready, a substantial force. That was not the way. A show of force at company strength would be seen as too threatening to these simple savages.

'Very well, David, we will return to the camp. I had feared this day would come and am much saddened by this news.'

There had been one previous murder of a convict, thought by most to have been committed by an aborigine, but Phillip had been reluctant to take action. He had been criticized for that, not least by Major Ross. Not only did the governor's orders require him to cultivate harmony with the indigenous peoples, but also it was in his nature to do so.

He understood that the survival of the small colony depended on peaceful subjugation of the natives, securing their cooperation and bringing them under the protection of the Crown. He was acutely aware of how such incidents could quickly escalate, leading to large-scale military action. That was something he could not risk or manage, or afford.

He started back to Sydney with gloom in his heart.

CHAPTER 37
SURVIVAL

The New Year of 1790 found the nascent colony in a struggle for survival. Stores were running low and rations were reduced further; convicts, marines and officers were ragged shadows. Uniforms once proudly worn hung limp and faded on emaciated bodies. Supplies of equipment were all but exhausted, most of the detachment now being barefooted. Drunkenness and brawling were commonplace. Officers were complacent or heedless, and struggled to maintain any sense of discipline. Theft from government stores and private gardens had again increased. Seeds had rotted in the ground and grain became infested with weevils.

The settlement was facing starvation. Convicts and marines alike endured each day under a cloud of despondency as people sought sustenance by any means possible.

Tragedy had touched the small hut; Mary had miscarried and lost the child, causing both her and Jack great anguish.

Major Ross continued to bully Jack. Any expedition beyond the camp was given to Jack; any additional duty caused by the illness, absence, or lack of will of another officer, was given to him. The duty roster showed the name of Lieutenant Vizzard for night duty far more than any other junior subaltern, this in addition to his work with Captain Collins, and supervising gangs of convict labour. Paperwork completed by Jack was returned by Ross for amendment, or became lost or mislaid, or challenged as inaccurate. Anything, it seemed, that might provoke him, or cause him extra work, or keep him from his hut and his wife.

The governor finally lost patience with Major Ross after yet another confrontation. The major's secretary, Captain Collins, privately expressed sheer hatred for his commanding officer. He suggested to the governor that the major would be more usefully employed in developing Norfolk Island. His particular sense of discipline might be more appropriate to the troublesome convicts that Arthur Phillip had dispatched to that remote island under the direction of Lieutenant Philip King in March 1788, shortly after the fleet had arrived.

Governor Phillip agreed. It would enable him to relieve Lieutenant King and send him onward to England with urgent dispatches. *Sirius* carried Ross and another small party of convicts and marines to Norfolk Island in March. Jack was delighted, and settled to a more relaxed, if arduous existence. Then HMS *Supply* brought the news of tragedy; *Sirius,* the flagship of the fleet, had foundered and sunk on the treacherous southern coast of Norfolk Island. Fortunately, all souls aboard had been saved and the men had rescued much of the additional supplies needed for the small settlement on the island. Phillip was privately devastated. He had now only the busy armed tender, *Supply,* as his link with the world beyond the Heads.

No word had come from England.

First Fleet

*****

The hut leaked during wet weather, although Jack continuously worked to keep it dry. The wind lifted the shingles, and rainwater percolated down the walls, such that in winter they were often damp. He kept a fire burning, to add warmth and to dry the walls. And hunger had come to their home. The rationed food was poor and there was never enough. He very carefully managed the meagre allowances issued, frequently pretending to Mary that he had eaten during the day, to ensure that she had just a little more.

He was sallow of face; Mary fretted, worried that he, too, might be struck down with the flux that was rife in the colony. He likewise worried for her, troubled by her shrinking frame, and bowed shoulders. She still brushed her copper hair each night as they sat by the fire, tarnished as it was by the sun, no longer glowing as it had when first he had seen her.

Never did he allow his duty to falter. The convicts were fewer, death having come for many of them, and work had slowed so that very little progress was to be seen. Men were beaten, women too, and the court sat almost daily, such that Jack became heartily sick of the ritual punishment of lashings to which all seemed almost immune.

Men walked about with leaden feet and soulless eyes, each introverted and consumed with his own thoughts and dreams of release or escape from perpetual hunger. None had a care for any other. None showed compassion. Even amongst the marines there was a lack of camaraderie.

During free time he had taken to joining the watch at the lookout by South Head, waiting for the day a sail should appear, showing that England had not forsaken her most distant outpost. Three marines had the duty of manning the lookout, disturbed by the claims that the land was sacred to the local tribe and haunted by the ghosts of their ancestors. A fire was permanently alight, to ward off those spirits. The weeks and months passed in a laggard way, each day much as the preceding, challenging mind and body to function, to exist, to survive.

This morning Jack and Mary were working in their garden, pulling weeds and grubs from the maize that rose slowly towards the sun. Jack had made a shallow trench around the garden, and dribbled lamp oil and salt along it. He was gratified that those defences had deterred many insects, although not the rats.

Mary had successfully grown some fruits, with the help of the governor. An orange tree, some figs and a lemon tree had flourished, and Mary jealously protected them and harvested them, adding slowly to her store.

'We may be hungry, my dear, but I doubt we shall starve to death,' she said.

He smiled at her, again comforted by her optimism, and finding renewed strength in her.

'I pray daily that the supply ships will bring good news, my love. I know that whatever my part is considered to have been, or not, it is my fervent hope that you will be pardoned and become free of the stigma you bear.'

He sighed and lowered his head, feeling the shame that had followed him halfway around the globe for having fled, leaving behind the woman he loved.

She sat on a log and had him sit with her, taking his hand softly in hers. 'My own dear man. I have forgiven you. Can you not forgive yourself?'

His voice was full of emotion when he answered. 'No, Mary, not yet, at least. *Mea culpa*—'I am guilty'—and cannot be at peace with myself until I have secured your freedom. That, I swear to you, one day I will do.'

He laid his head on her shoulder and she caressed his hair and murmured softly in his ear.

'Dearest Jack. It will come one day. I have faith, and your father will do his best for me; of that I am certain. He came often to Gloucester, after you had gone, as if through me he could find you. He was much saddened, I know, but bade me never to abandon hope for my ultimate liberty. He was a great comfort to me, and to my parents, during those months.'

Without outward sign, she shuddered at the memory of that gaol, grateful that she at least had a home and was free of the shackles that had ulcerated her ankles and scarred her soul.

They sat together for a long time, each taking comfort from the other.

Chapter 38

Second Fleet

As the months passed, the struggling community sank further into an abyss of hunger, deepening despair, and a sense of its isolation. There was no contact with an outside world and even the most robust soul was now convinced that England had abandoned the entire expedition. It was over three years since they had departed from Portsmouth and hope had all but disappeared. Very few now saw any prospect of survival.

Governor Phillip carefully examined the crops, as he did every day. The cabbage plants had once more struggled to flourish; the wheat sown was looking feeble, with black spots appearing on the tillers. *Even the damned wheat has the flux*, he thought. He removed his hat and wiped his forehead with a handkerchief. It was the last thing Margaret had given him, a stock of hand linen, and this was the last of it. He felt very tired and weak.

The colony had received one other ship; it was not the promised store-ship, but the *Juliana*, which arrived on the third day of June, bringing limited food stores and, ironically, more mouths to be fed, another two hundred and thirty-seven. A ship full of women, mostly petty thieves, and London prostitutes, intended to increase the breeding stock of the new colony.

Governor Phillip wondered if he was ever to receive the relief he so desperately needed from his masters. More mouths to feed—Arthur Phillip had been unable to contain his disappointment as he and the entire colony waited for fresh supplies. The news from the world beyond Sydney included a severe blow to the entire population of the colony with the report of the loss of the *Guardian*, the supply ship dispatched to provide their much needed, vital replenishment. She had struck ice and foundered, returning, after many trials, to the Cape, having lost all the stores aboard.

And those stores were critical. *Guardian* had carried all those provisions that Arthur Phillip had requested and waited so long for. Apart from personal property sent to officers by their friends and families, she'd also carried a new stock of animals. Sir Joseph Banks had had the deck fitted out as a garden, with hundreds of new plants, including one hundred and fifty fruit trees. There had been new tools and implements, clothing, blankets, bedding, medicines, sails, and cordage.

Amongst the twenty-five convicts on board her had been farmers and artisans, and seven men chosen to act as supervisors. Lieutenant Edward Riou, who commanded her, with a few brave men, had managed to prevent the ship from sinking and returned her to Cape Town, after nine weeks of exhausting work.

For once, Governor Phillip was lost for a plan. *How to keep this settlement alive?* he wondered. This settlement at Rose Hill was viable, he was convinced of that, but more needed to be done. Other areas must be found and developed; but men were tired, dispirited, and felt abandoned. Men in such condition could do little productive, valuable work, and he could do no more.

In the years since they had left Portsmouth, no fresh supplies had been sent; he had charged England's credit by sending the *Sirius* back to Cape Town for fresh supplies, but she had been lost at Norfolk Island, another blow to the community, and one from which Phillip wondered if they could recover. It had even been necessary to send the fragile brig *Supply* to Batavia to purchase supplies and to charter a ship; but she would not return for some months yet.

He had no means of communicating with the world beyond Sydney. His sense of isolation was, at times, overwhelming.

*****

Jack Vizzard was with a work party by the stream at the head of the small cove when he became aware of shouting amongst the ragged marines by the huts. His curiosity aroused, he left a sergeant to continue directing the work and made his way towards a group of officers, quickening his step as he saw they were visibly excited. They were grasping each other and dancing in circles.

'Vizzard, we are saved, thank God! A ship, by all that's blessed, a ship has been sighted off The Heads!' Captain Watkin Tench was jumping with renewed energy. 'It must be the supply ships, it must. I am going to tell the governor, but

please, make ready a boat. We must welcome whoever it is.'
With that, he started running towards Government House,
his long legs eating up the ground.

Jack looked to the small jetty where a party of seamen
stood gaping along the harbour. He now realized the enormity of the news and started running towards them.

'Mister Harris,' he shouted to the figure he recognized as
one of the midshipmen from *Supply,* his voice now hoarse
with emotion, 'make the launch ready! We're taking the governor to meet our salvation!'

Governor Arthur Phillip came down the muddy street with
Watkin Tench by his side, and was quickly joined by David
Collins, who had been similarly attracted by the general
commotion that was rushing around the village of tents and
huts, as people realized that something very important was
taking place.

Word that a sail was visible beyond The Heads spread
with great speed. People were cheering, sobbing, and outwardly and unashamedly shedding tears of relief and deep
joy.

Jack felt the invigoration of the wind in his face as the
launch tacked up the harbour, the same wind that was bringing salvation to the dying colony. He and Mary had survived.

*****

The second fleet that arrived from England had sailed
with another twelve hundred or so souls, but in such extremely dire conditions that barely two thirds of them had survived.
There had been many, many deaths during its voyage, and
many more died crawling off the ships, or when literally
thrown ashore in Sydney Cove by some of the most callous

masters of merchant vessels afloat. Governor Philip was outraged. The stores landed from its ships, however, saved the settlement.

It also brought news and fresh orders for the beleaguered governor; a replacement force had been formed, called the New South Wales Corps, which was to relieve the marine garrison. Phillip was to charter a Dutch ship to transport most of the marines to England, those not wishing to remain.

Governor Phillip was in a more optimistic mood by September. He had learned by then that HMS *Gorgon* was due to reach the colony soon with more supplies, and would retrieve the crew of *Sirius*, still stranded on Norfolk Island.

He had been thinking of late of erecting a monument or beacon at The Heads, to assist future vessels arriving at the colony, and decided to survey a possible site. Oliver Waterhouse and Captain Collins accompanied him. Having marked out the ground and given preliminary directions, they were returning up the harbour to Sydney Cove when a boat intercepted them. The coxswain of the boat informed the governor that his aboriginal houseguest, Bennelong, who had left his house some time before, was now willing to return to the settlement.

That was welcome news to Arthur Phillip, who had expended a great deal of time and patience in befriending the young man, to learn something of the language and customs of his people, as he was required, and desired, to do.

They found Bennelong with a party of his tribe collected around a whale washed ashore in Collins Cove. Phillip instructed the officers to remain with the boat while he spoke alone with the group. The discussions with the tribesmen were proceeding well, until the governor approached another member of the tribe, with hand extended in friendship. At that, the man, becoming fearful, picked up a spear and launched it, striking the Governor in the right shoulder. The bloody tip of the spear protruded through his upper back.

He attempted to run back to the boat, clasping the spear with both hands, but it caught in the ground. Oliver Waterhouse was nearly struck by another spear, which grazed his right hand when he stopped to help the governor.

Spears started to fly now, one landing at the feet of David Collins. He was greatly alarmed and feared for his very life.

The governor fired a pistol, and some sailors from the boat, alerted to the unfolding drama, ran up and placed themselves between the governor and the Aborigines, enabling the officers to retreat to the beach and the boat.

A withdrawal was accomplished and the party was able to return to Sydney within two hours. The surgeons extracted the spear and treated the wound, fortunately not considered fatal, and within six weeks the governor had recovered. It was a very low point, the very nadir, in the progress of the colony.

*****

Major Robert Ross returned to Sydney in December 1791. He had become increasingly bitter and disillusioned because of his enforced exile to Norfolk Island. Now he longed, with all his being, for release from this place and to return to England.

'They are scum, and I'm nae talking of the convicts, Ralph.' He spoke to Lieutenant Clark, a marine officer who had accompanied him to Norfolk Island.

'Will ye look at my marines, man? They have been ruined

by they scum of officers. Pshh! A sad day for the Corps, truly sad.'

The two were sitting on the veranda of Government House, Ross drinking rum and Clark sipping on some water, observing the work gangs and the few marines in evidence, who were supervising the work of building a new storehouse. Lieutenant Clark was perhaps the only officer of the battalion in whom Ross would confide. His regard was not, however, returned.

'They've turned them into gaolers and drunkards. Bloody Governor Phillip—hah! I tell you, Ralph, the man's a soft liberal, and he'll make naught of this place!'

'I am sure you are correct, sir. For myself, I shall be glad to quit the colony and return to my family. I sorely miss my sweet Alicia. I believe we may have our dunnage taken aboard *Gorgon* on the morrow?' Clark too, was anxious to be gone.

'Aye, lad, we'll be away on Sunday's tide, I believe, and not a day too soon.'

Clark pondered before asking a question.

'Sir, I believe I have performed my duties on this expedition to your satisfaction and did hope that you might favour me with a suitable certificate of service? I am hopeful of being honoured with further promotion on return to England.'

Ross appeared not to have heard the question. 'Mister Vizzard! You disgrace to the Corps, what are you about, laddie?' Ross growled drunkenly.

Jack was approaching the governor's house following a summons from Captain Collins.

'I have business with the governor, sir, if you would kindly let me pass.'

Major Ross was on his feet, swaying unsteadily and obstructing access to the door. Jack was tired. He had been on duty during the night watch and had supervised a work gang since first light. It had been a warm day, with little breeze to cool the warming land.

'The governor's lackey! I shall see that you have no further employment in the service—Oxford boy! Too many scum have evaded punishment and execution because of your interfering mischief-making.'

'Sir, if you please. The governor has requested my presence as soon as convenient. Please stand aside.' Jack spoke firmly, but without malice. He had no wish for a scene on the steps of Government House.

Lieutenant Clark looked on, with growing alarm on his countenance. He was aware that these two men had no love for each other, but he had hoped the intervening months on Norfolk Island would have tempered the major's opinion. All that Clark had heard indicated that Second Lieutenant Vizzard was held in high regard by officers and men alike.

'Sir, if you please,' Jack repeated.

'If you please, sir.' Ross mimicked Jack's mid-English, cultured voice. 'You are a damned dandy, Vizzard, and you should have been finished off by that mad Malay in Cape Town! Ye'll amount to nothing in the Corps as long as I have power to do something about it, laddie. You should resign now and be gone.' Ross was slurring, the rum having loosened his tongue.

'I have always wondered, Major Ross, why it is you despise me so. Why do you wish me dead?'

'A wee bastard like you would never understand that!' Ross swayed unsteadily.

Ralph Clark spoke now. 'Sir! That's court martial language. I caution you to say no more, please.'

'Aye, and you are another damned hypocrite, Clark. Christ knows how I tolerated you on Norfolk! All that flogging of convicts you demanded, all the time banging away with young Mary Branham! What say you to that?'

Clark flushed and looked away.

'Major Ross, you are a mean-minded, boorish man! I shall be happy to see you gone from here. In my opinion, sir, you are not fit to command these men!' Jack was having difficulty controlling his temper now. The man was belligerent at the best of times, and worse, much worse, after a drink.

'Hah. I'll see you pay for that, you young bastard!' Ross rocked unsteadily on his heels.

Clark tried to interrupt. 'Sir, please, that is court martial language, and I beg you to cease.'

'At your pleasure, Mister Ross! At your pleasure.' Jack snarled the words into Ross's face, knowing now that the time had come.

'Aye, and that pretty young wife of yours, so prim and polite and proud to be an officer's lady—just another convict whore, who amused her passage with half the crew!'

The major bent double as Jack's balled fist struck him low in the stomach, the punch thrown with all the power Jack could muster, followed with a blow to the side of Ross' head, which dropped him to his knees.

'Now I have ye, Vizzard,' Ross spluttered, vomit trickling from his mouth. 'That's you for a court martial, and probably a rope's end or firing squad, if I have any say in it, you insubordinate whelp.'

Jack brushed past him and entered the governor's house,

shaking with anger, and reckless as to his actions. He'd stood for a while, composing himself, when Captain Collins appeared.

'There you are, Jack. Good. The governor will see you immediately. Be prepared for some good news, my friend.' He beamed. Looking more closely at Jack, he saw his distress. 'What troubles you, Jack? You shake so.'

He breathed out before answering. 'I regret to say, sir, that I have just left Major Ross outside. He threatened me, I believe to a duel, and I fear I have probably accepted. I also hit the bastard, and it was worth it. He insulted my wife, sir.'

'Oh, no, that will not do. You know the governor's views on dueling. He will not permit that, Jack. Whatever the cause, or provocation, it must be dealt with in some other manner.' Collins sighed. Ross had been a thorn in the side since the beginning of the expedition. It was only days until he was to leave the colony. He would have to remove young Vizzard from the camp, for his own safety, he thought. *He is too good an officer to lose in a duel with that mad Scot.* He made a mental note to speak to the governor immediately after this interview.

'Come with me, Jack. The governor is waiting.'

He walked quickly through to the governor's office, where Arthur Phillip sat at a long desk, as always littered with paper—letters, dispatches, orders to officers, daily returns from the commissary. Jack thought the governor was looking older than when he'd first met him. Phillip pointed to a chair.

'Do sit down, Mister Vizzard. I am truly delighted to see you, especially today, for I have some good news for you.'

Jack sat forward in the chair, as David Collins moved to the desk and handed the governor a large document, written in a careful hand and carrying a heavy wax seal.

'I am glad to be the bearer of this news, Jack. Your father now knows where you are and, more importantly, who it is that is with you. He has not been idle these years.'

Arthur Phillip smiled in an avuncular manner. He had been delighted with Vizzard. A good, conscientious, effective officer, touched by humanity and compassion, who had eased his burdens; that was the essence of one of his many reports on his officers. He passed the packet across the desk.

Jack took the document and immediately noted the large, elaborate signet embedded in the heavy wax seal. He looked across at Arthur Phillip's smiling face. Breaking it open, he rapidly scanned the first few lines, etched in thin, black ink, and his mouth opened. He could not control the trembling of his hands.

'Sir, I know not what to say.' He could feel his throat tighten. Tears rose in his eyes.

'It is an important document, and I for one am delighted to hear of the news it brings. I have a copy here somewhere. I am instructed by their lordships that your father has been pestering the Board and various members of the government. There is also a note from your father, I believe.' He passed over a smaller packet, tied in red string, also sealed with wax.

'May I suggest you go to her now, without delay?' He smiled kindly.

Jack stood and reached out a hand. The governor shook it slowly, his shoulder still stiff and tender from his wound. 'I am indeed most happy for you both, very happy.'

Jack walked from the room in a daze. He did not notice Captain Collins lean forward and speak softly to the governor.

CHAPTER 39

A PARDON AND A DUEL

His walk to their hut was as though on air. There was still tightness in his throat, a stinging of his eyes. *Dear father*, he thought, *you have worked another miracle.* Then he realized that Ralph Clark was on a course to intercept him, some fifty yards short.

'Ralph, I am very sorry, but it will have to wait,' he said as Ralph Clark opened his mouth to speak.

'Regrettably, it cannot, Vizzard. I have to be his second; I have no choice. He demands that you meet him and either apologize or engage in combat with him. He maintains that you have dishonoured him. I am so very sorry.' Lieutenant Clark was very downcast. This was not the way to complete a commission, he thought. *Jack's right, the pig is not fit to command.*

So, it has come to this at last, Jack thought. 'Very well, but I will not apologize, Ralph. The bastard insulted Mary, and that is dishonourable. Tell me where and the hour, and I shall be there. I shall ask Lieutenant Dawes to act for me. Good day to you.'

M. Howard Morgan

He strode off, letter in hand, calling loudly for Mary.

*****

Lampern House
Woodchester,
Glos.
   January 8th, 1791

My dearest Jack,

I have just today received the news for which I have long prayed. Finally, my efforts have borne fruit! I pray that this note finds you soon, and safe, for now I have learned your destination. The papers have some reports of the colony, but insufficient to satisfy my overwhelming curiosity. I pray for a report from you, my beloved son.

I trust you have my earlier letters and now know that you fled from us needlessly; at least you have the assurance that the death of Reverend Barnwood is not associated with your sudden disappearance. I cannot begin to tell you of the magnitude of my relief that our late vicar was judged to have died of some despicable disease, and not by your hand.

However, today's news cannot wait so I hasten to dispatch this note, which is to be carried to the colony by the acquaintance of a former associate of mine. The King has graciously agreed to a Full Pardon. Not, I am delighted to say, a mere conditional pardon, but complete, absolute and irreversible Royal

Pardon. Mary is a free citizen once more. Oh happy day!

Since your departure, I have sought leave to appeal to the King's Bench, and suffice to say that I was al last successful in my endeavour. The justices quashed the conviction, and, faced with that, a Royal Pardon was the inevitable consequence. Judge Paul has been retired from the bench, a fact that will no doubt give you satisfaction.

This letter must leave Lampern within the next half hour in order to catch the mail coach to Bristol, so I will bid you both a fond father's best wishes for a safe and swift return. I add your sister's affection and am

Yours etc.
Henry Vizzard

PS. I am off now to see Frederick George and am confident the bells of St. Giles will ring this evening!

Jack finished reading it aloud, for a second time, necessary because Mary had eyes full of tears, and could not see to read.

'Oh, Jack! What news! I am free and have a full pardon from the king! I cannot believe it! Oh what a Christmas present this is!' She wrapped her arms about him, rocking gently and full of a warmth not felt for a very long time.

'We shall return now, my beloved,' he said softly. 'I shall remain in the Corps, but my service here is done, or very nearly so. We shall find somewhere in Portsmouth, perhaps close to the sea and the common.'

She smiled, nodding, lacking the power of speech, tearful at the wonderful news.

*****

At morning orders, William Dawes took Jack aside. 'Jack, Ralph Clark has spoken to me this morning. I know all and must implore you not to proceed with this. It is utter madness. He demands swords, and names Saturday, tomorrow, at first light, by my observatory.' Dawes looked hard into his friend's face. 'I must speak to the governor—you know this cannot be permitted to proceed.'

'Will, it must proceed; the bad blood between us cannot be resolved by talk. That time is past. I am only pleased that he has chosen swords and not pistols. I have a good chance of defeating him.'

Dawes shook his head. He had not acted as a second before, but was familiar with the French code of honour and the protocols associated with duels. In good conscience, he could not abandon his friend, but felt divided. He also doubted Jack's ability to best the major in swordplay. Whatever faults Ross had, they were not in his ability to fight, and fight hard. He had a fearsome reputation as a fighting marine. The 'Hero of Bunker Hill' was a phrase that had been used in the mess at Portsmouth before.

William Dawes was very troubled and slept not at all that night. He looked at the night sky, staring at the stars, but for once making no additions to his notebook.

*****

Dawn was only ten minutes or so away, and the sun's first rays were already showing on the Pacific horizon as Jack tapped gently at the small wooden door of the observatory, from which the light of a single candle betrayed that William Dawes was awake.

'Good God, Jack, you mean to go through with this, then? Dawes' eyes were bloodshot, and his expression, usually sanguine, was this morning anxious. 'I spoke to Clark last night. We have agreed terms. You will duel with épée, over on the point there. Come, have some coffee.'

Jack sat on a rock as Dawes brought him a soldier's mess tin of hot coffee, enhanced with a double measure of rum, and Jack felt the fire of it as it ran down his gullet.

'The usual rules will apply. You will each draw lots for the ground; both must show your chests before 'the commence,' and naturally use of the left hand is forbidden. Finally, Clark and I have agreed that the duel will be complete on sight of the first wound. This is not to be 'to the death', Jack. Do you understand?'

Jack understood. He had no intention of killing Ross, or of dying, either. He merely wished to defeat Ross, and win the contest by humiliating the man, to prove his ability, as it were. Not to destroy his enemy, but to see him beaten, humbled, vanquished.

But deep in his heart he also understood that this might not be sufficient. Ross was a bully; and bullies had to be defeated—totally and with conviction. He was not as fit as he once had been, but that would be true of Ross also, he reasoned. The man was older, but more experienced. *I wonder if he has fought a duel before*, he thought. *Probably*. He wished he had time to practice.

'Yes, Will. I do understand that. However, I fear he is determined on more. You recall his encounter in Portsmouth, with that commander? He intended to kill that man. Will, should he not comply with your 'code', and I should perish this morn, there are some instructions—some requests, I should perhaps say—that I have left in my case. I would consider it a personal...'

'I will not hear of such things, Jack!' Dawes interrupted him. 'There will be no death at my observatory, Jack, neither yours nor Ross's. This is a matter of honour only, not a killing ground.'

Jack proffered his hand to his friend. Dawes clasped it with both of his.

'Here they are come, Jack. Pray, compose yourself.'

Ross approached, accompanied by Lieutenant Ralph Clark and two other officers also. Lieutenants Long and Furzer had learned of the matter and had insisted on attending, the latter as an observer only; John Long had offered to act as a second to Jack and had conversed with Clark while *en route* to the meeting place. He now took the others aside for a final discourse.

'Gentlemen! This is a matter of honour, to be decided by means of a duel,' Ralph Clark announced. 'Major Ross is gravely offended by the insulting language and violent conduct of Mister Vizzard. No apology has been forthcoming and, at this time, my principal will accept none. Accordingly, by custom the duel will proceed.'

'My principal is offended by the insult to his lady wife given by Major Ross. Such is considered contemptible on the part of an officer of the major's rank, and not the language a gentlemen would ever use,' William Dawes responded. 'Lieutenant Vizzard demands an apology and a full retraction.'

Major Robert Ross was not the man he'd once been. He realized that. The young man in front of him was fitter, and faster. He knew that also. *But*, thought Ross, *I know more of fighting than he will ever know. I have wrung more seawater from my socks than he has sailed on. Bugger the code of honour. I will cut the young bastard down to size this morning.*

'Bugger that, Mister Dawes,' he spat. 'This pompous dandy will see the surgeon, for I intend to have satisfaction today.'

William Dawes looked at his commanding officer with deep disdain. *What kind of officer is this man*, he thought, *to speak thus?*

'Major Ross has selected swords as the weapon of choice; that choice is agreed, and I have selected the épée. Both have been provided by Lieutenant Long, whose weapons they are. We are agreed, gentlemen, as to their dimensions, weight and all characteristics, and pronounce them as suitable for this combat.'

Ross looked at the weapons and grunted.

Jack removed his coat, and, at Dawes' request, opened his shirt to show that he was not wearing any cuirass or other device to ward off a thrust. Ross did the same.

The standing ground having been marked out by Clark and Dawes, the protagonists then faced them and drew lengths of grass to determine initial positions. They turned and faced each other as required by the code d'honneur. Jack's blade of grass was the longer; he took up a position, knowing that the sun would soon rise over his shoulder, pushing its rays through the eucalypts surrounding the clearing, burning off the thin mist that lay indolently among the trees. *It should be full in Ross's face within minutes.*

Clark allowed two feet between the points of their swords. Each then used the left hand to grasp the top of his breeches, thereby removing that arm as a target, and ensuring that the left hand was not used in the combat.

With eyes half closed, Clark spoke the words of command: 'Gentlemen, *en garde!*' Then, after a short pause, '*Allez*', and Ross immediately made an attack. A poorly executed, clumsy and wild attack, but one which surprised the observers. Almost caught, Jack clashed and pushed Ross away, to quickly recover his balance. The major's sword tip circled slowly, searching for an opening. The steel clashed once more as Jack initiated a move, vaulting swiftly to his right, throwing the major off guard momentarily, as his sword arm moved to follow Jack, who too late realized that he was jumping back, now to the other side, and the point of his epée brushed Ross's right hip.

'Stand still and fight me, ye pup!' Ross growled.

'I will fight, Ross, but my way, not yours,' Jack retorted.

Ross came on again, harder this time, and steel scraped against steel, as Jack parried each thrust, swiftly and without effort. He felt calm, his eyes in contact with those cold, dark eyes of Ross.

His balance was very good, the line good, but he wanted Ross closer—the distance was too great. He thanked his father once more, this time for the summers spent with Monsieur Le Brun, the French Maître d'Armes—all those hours in his *salle* in The Haymarket.

He tried a *froissant* and was surprised to see Ross lose his composure. *So, Jack thought, you now know I have trained.*

He advanced, with a second, similar move, but this time Ross was prepared and parried well, following with a lunge. Jack had hoped for this and quickly feigned a retreat, drawing Ross on, and then trapped his sword with a *Prise du Fer*, swiftly completing his tactic with a *Reprise d'Attaque* and a lunge of his own, catching the major high on his right shoulder. Ross grunted, baring his teeth. A small red stain appeared and spread down his shirt.

'Halt!' called Lieutenant Long. 'Gentlemen, the combat is over.' He was smiling. 'Well done, Jack. Handsomely done, very pretty work.'

William Dawes added, 'Indeed it was. Clearly, you have studied under a master!'

Some innate sense made Jack move sideways, just as Ross slashed with his weapon, the air whistling as the blade sliced by his nose. He saw Ross's snarling mouth and he swung with the pommel, striking bone and teeth, scarlet spraying from the man's mouth. The major fell at his feet. He did not move as the point of Jack's weapon touched the back of his neck.

'This is over, Ross! Do you understand that, man? Be grateful I, at least, have honour left and do not choose to do more, for surely you deserve to be run through. Never forget this day, for I never shall.'

Within the shadows of the eucalypts, Governor Phillip and Captain Collins stood still. Collins indicated to Sergeant Packer to lower the musket that was still pointing at the prostrated and defeated commander of His Majesty's Corps of Marines in New South Wales.

Jack Vizzard moved away, leaving Lieutenant Ralph Clark to administer to the fallen major. Collecting his coat from William Dawes, he walked back to the hut.

Back to Mary.

THE END

ABOUT THE AUTHOR

M Howard Morgan is a *nom de plume* of Malcolm Mendey.

Born in Carmarthen in South Wales, he spent his childhood years living in France, Belgium, Gibraltar and Germany.   Following an initial career in civil law, he moved into loss adjusting, acting for and advising underwriters at Lloyd's of London and multi-national insurers. With his family he spent nearly twenty years in New Zealand, has traveled extensively on assignments within the UK and Europe, the Far East, Oceania, and N. America.

An interest in genealogy resulted in the surprising discovery of an ancestor who was a marine with the First Fleet of convicts sent by Britain to Australia in 1788. Always a student of history, the discovery triggered an ever more consuming investigation into the Royal Marines and the history of the Golden Age of Sail and tangentially, the conflicts with Revolutionary and Napoleonic France.

First Fleet is a debut novel. The sequel, *The Glorious First* set in 1794, describes the first major naval engagement between Britain and France in what was the first world war, known in Britain as The Glorious First of June. The third novel finds the two principal characters, Jack Vizzard and Joe Packer, back at sea in 1797. They join the Mediterranean Fleet commanded by Sir John Jervis. The story concludes with the major fleet engagement known as the Battle of Cape St Vincent, in which a young captain Horatio Nelson distinguished himself and won his knighthood.

A qualified boat master, a failed golfer, enthusiast of aviation, consumer of fine wines, real ales, and spirits, the author has absolutely no interest in celery.

He lives in the beautiful Cotswolds in Southwest England with his beautiful wife, affectionately known as SWMBO (credit H Rider Haggard; She Who Must Be Obeyed) and a wonderful Sprollie dog called Molly.

On the Lee Shore

by

Philip K.Allan

Newly promoted to Post Captain, Alexander Clay returns home from the Caribbean to recover from wounds sustained at the Battle of San Felipe. However, he is soon called upon by the Admiralty to take command of the frigate HMS Titan and join the blockade of the French coast. But the HMS Titan will be no easy command with its troubled crew that had launched a successful mutiny against its previous sadistic captain. Once aboard, Clay realizes he must confront the dangers of a fractious crew, rife with corrupt officers and disgruntled mutineers, if he is to have a united force capable of navigating the treacherous reefs of Brittany's notorious lee shore and successfully combating the French determined to break out of the blockade.

PENMORE PRESS
www.penmorepress.com

PIRATE CODE

BY

HELEN HOLLICK

Series:Capt. Jesamiah Acorne & his ship,
Ex-pirate Capt. Jesamiah Acorne is in trouble. Big Trouble!

All he wants is to marry his girl, Tiola Oldstagh, and like contented aboard his ship, Sea Witch. But Tiola's husband refused to grand a divorce unless Jesamiah retrieves some barrels of indigo and smuggle out of the Spanish-held Caribbean island of Hispaniola.
The Governor of Nassau wants Jesamiah to go there too, to help incite a rebellion, and Captain Henry Jennings wants him to find a lost spy. To cap it all, Commodore Vernon of the Royal Navy wants to expand his fleet and craves the Sea Witch of himself .

As Jesamiah's hopes for a quiet life tumble about him, the onset of war with Spain scuppers everyone's plans. Hispaniola is governed by a tyrant who has promised to hand draw and quarter Jesamiah if ever he sets foot there again, while the lovely widow Señora Francesca Escudero would prefer to seduce him.

Intrigue, fights, betrayals, and romantic passion follow Captain Acorne like a ship's wake-not the ingredients for a quiet life and not Jesamiah's idea of the Pirate Code.

PENMORE PRESS
www.penmorepress.com

The Dragon's Breath

by

James Boschert

Talon stared wide-eyed at the devices, awed that they could make such an overwhelming, head-splitting noise. His ears rang and his eyes were burning from the drifting smoke that carried with it an evil stink. "That will show the bastards," Hsü told him with one of his rare smiles. "The General calls his weapons 'the Dragon's breath.' They certainly stink like it."

Talon, an assassin turned knight turned merchant, is restless. Enticed by tales of lucrative trade, he sets sail for the coasts of Africa and India. Traveling with him are his wife and son, eager to share in this new adventure, as well as Reza, his trusted comrade in arms. Treasures beckon at the ports, but Talon and Reza quickly learn that dangers attend every opportunity, and the chance rescue of a Chinese lord named Hsü changes their destination—and their fates.

Hsü introduces Talon to the intricacies of trading in China and the sophisticated wonders of Guangzhou, China's richest city. Here the companions discover wealth beyond their imagining. But Hsü is drawn into a political competition for the position of governor, and his opponents target everyone associated with him, including the foreign merchants he has welcomed into his home. When Hsü is sent on a dangerous mission to deliver the annual Tribute to the Mongols, no one is safe, not even the women and children of the household. As Talon and Reza are drawn into supporting Hsü's bid for power, their fighting skills are put to the test against new weapons and unfamiliar fighting styles. It will take their combined skills to navigate the treacherous waters of intrigue and violence if they hope to return to home.

Belleraphon's Champion

By

John Danielski

Deep within each man, lies the secret knowledge of whether he is a stalwart or a coward.   Three years an unblooded Royal Marine, 1st Lieutenant Thomas Pennywhistle will finally "meet the lion," protecting HMS *Bellerophon* at the Battle of Trafalgar.

Not only will Pennywhistle be responsible for the lives of 72 marines aboard *Bellerophon* but their direction will fall entirely on his shoulders since his fellow Marine officers consist of a boy, a card shark, and a dying consumptive. If he has what it takes to command, it will take everything he's got.

In the course of battle, he will encounter marvels and terrors; from valiant foes to women performing miracles, from the skill of acrobats to the luck of the ship's cat, from a dead man still full of fight to a coward who has none. He and his marines will meet enemy élan will with trained volleys and disciplined bayonets. Most of all, he will meet himself; discovering just how dark his true nature really is.

Europe will be changed forever by Trafalgar, and so will Pennywhistle.

PENMORE PRESS
www.penmorepress.com

Penmore Press
Challenging, Intriguing, Adventurous, Historical and Imaginative

www.penmorepress.com